Lucy Diamond

SUMMER AT SHELL COTTAGE

PAN BOOKS

First published 2015 by Pan Books
an imprint of Pan Macmillan
20 New Wharf Road, London N1 9RR
Associated companies throughout the world
www.panmacmillan.com

ISBN   978-1-4472-5780-6

3 5 7 9 8 6 4

A CIP catalogue record for this book is available from the British Library.

Printed and bound by CPI Group (UK) Ltd, Croydon, CR0 4YY

For reckless women everywhere

Acknowledgements

This book might have my name on the cover but it wouldn't be in your hands today if it wasn't for the help I received from so many fantastic people.

Step forward super-agent Lizzy Kremer for all the advice, support and laughs. You are completely brilliant – please never stop being my agent. High fives to the other stars at David Higham: Harriet, Laura, Alice and Emma. Thank you all for your sterling work on my behalf, it's much appreciated.

The team at Pan Macmillan have done it again, and I feel tremendously lucky to be working with so many clever, creative and talented people. Thanks to Victoria, Natasha, Jez, Anna, Wayne, Stuart, Becky, Jodie, Sam, Jo, Emma, Eloise, Amy, and of course a special thank you to Caroline, who said yes to this book in the first place.

Thanks to Gemma DeLucchi and Clare Mackintosh, who answered my police-related questions with such patience and good humour.

Acknowledgements

Bottoms up to the fabulous Glassboat posse – Rosie, Cally, Jill and Emma – for ace lunches, book-swaps and gossip. Here's to many more!

Three cheers for my parents for so many lovely holidays in Devon back in the day. I thought a lot about Cymorth and Saunton Sands while I was writing this book, and all my happy memories from those times. Love to Phil, Ellie and Fiona too, for the fun we had at Granny and Grandpa Mongredien's house. (No tweetle-beetles were harmed during the writing of this book.)

Thank you to everyone who has taken the time to email or tweet or message me to say they enjoyed the last book. It honestly makes it all worthwhile, especially when I'm stuck or wondering if I should have chosen a more sensible career. Heartfelt thanks to all the book bloggers too, who have been so supportive. It's been great to meet some of you over the last year.

I've saved the best for last . . . Much love and thanks to Martin, Hannah, Tom and Holly. Every author should have a family so excellent. Thank you.

Chapter One

The first time Olivia and Alec Tarrant saw Shell Cottage, back in July 1975, they had been married precisely eight hours and twenty-two minutes, and their honeymoon get-away car had broken down in the wilds of Devon. It had been a long, hot day, beginning with the hectic rush of preparations first thing in the morning: the hairdresser arriving to tong and spray Olivia's hair into blonde ringlets, the careful stepping into her long satin dress ('Mind your feet, Olivia!') with her mum and sisters yanking the bodice ribbons so tight she could hardly breathe. Then had come the hushed, nerve-racking journey in the Bentley, borrowed from a friend of Mr Johnson next door, the sweet summer scent of white roses in the church, and all those familiar smiling faces turning towards her as she walked in with her dad. Vows and kisses, photographs in the churchyard, and then lunch, speeches and dancing in the Regent Hotel. *Mrs Tarrant*, she kept thinking dazedly, as Alec whirled her across the dance floor, his strong hands light on her back. No longer Olivia

Marchant, barely more than a girl with her long hair and upturned nose. Now she was a wife. A woman. Mrs Tarrant.

By rights they should have been speeding on their way to Cornwall and their honeymoon cottage at this moment, the wind in their hair, the promise of their wedding night lying excitingly (and somewhat terrifyingly) ahead. Instead they were stranded in the middle of nowhere, after the car had made a strange choking sound and juddered to an abrupt halt. As she stood by the dusty roadside in her brocade wedding shoes, the long train of her gleaming white dress draped heavily across one arm in an attempt to protect it from dirt, Olivia felt a lump in her throat and thought for a horrible moment she might actually cry. On her wedding day!

Alec was rolling up his shirtsleeves in order to tinker with the engine's innards but came to hook an arm around his new wife's waist when he noticed her anxious expression. 'Hey, don't worry,' he said, giving her a comforting squeeze. He smelled of wine and aftershave and sweat: a husband's smell, she thought distractedly. 'We'll get there. Think of this as an adventure, not a problem.'

Olivia sniffed and tried to smile. An adventure, not a problem: that was Alec all over. Confidence ran through the very marrow of him, leaving no room for doubt or anxiety. Olivia, by contrast, tended to have a list of worries and what-ifs as long as her bridal train.

A bird cheeped in the lush green hedgerow; a small,

cheerful sound against the emptiness of their surroundings. 'We'll take the scenic route,' Alec had decided when they set off from the reception earlier but it was almost seven o'clock in the evening now and they still had miles to go. At this rate, they'd end up bedding down in a field for their first night as man and wife, Olivia thought in dismay. (Please, no. She had packed a cream lacy negligee for the occasion, and could only imagine the grass stains.)

Oh, Olivia! her mum had always sighed. *What* will *we do with you?* If her mum and sisters could see her now, standing at the roadside by the broken-down car, they would exchange knowing looks in that irritating way of theirs. *Oh, Olivia! Why do these things always happen to you? We should have known!*

She was just wondering if it would be very forward of her to take off the too-tight garter she'd borrowed from her cousin when there came the sound of a car approaching. Without hesitating, she stepped into the road and waved frantically. 'Stop!'

'Oh dear, oh dear. What's happened here, then?' A tall, florid-faced man swung himself out of a dark blue Ford Cortina, just like the one from *The Sweeney*, and Olivia almost swooned in relief. His eyes twinkled with amusement as he looked at her in her wedding finery, ringlets collapsing in the heat. 'Can I give you two lovebirds a lift anywhere?'

Thank goodness for unexpected blue Cortinas and the kindness of strangers – in this case, the kindness of Jed

McGarry. He wasn't able to fix the car but he offered them transport and a night at his brother's place if they needed it. 'He's got a B&B not far from here,' he told them. 'And we can send one of the lads over with the toolbox first thing tomorrow. Between us, we'll have you back on the road, all right?'

Alec glanced down at the engine again and then at his watch, clearly weighing up the best option. Olivia didn't hesitate, though. She was not spending her wedding night sleeping in a field, or their broken-down car, and that was that. 'Thank you,' she said quickly. 'That would be lovely.'

Jed McGarry drove for about twenty minutes and then they rounded a bend and were startled by the sight of the headland, and the sea beyond, a muted blue expanse stretching far out to the horizon. The sea! Olivia's spirits lifted immediately and she glanced over at Alec, who was smiling too. He reached across the back seat and took her hand in his, his large square-ended fingers folding around her small white ones. She felt a throb of excitement at his touch, and at the whole unanticipated situation of being jolted around on the slippery vinyl back seat of a stranger's car, heading who knew where with her gorgeous new husband.

Maybe this was what life had in store for her as Alec Tarrant's wife: one surprising adventure after another. The thought was not displeasing. In the eight hours that she'd been Mrs Tarrant, nobody had dared say *Oh, Olivia!* at her in that wearily despairing sort of way. This was definitely progress.

Two minutes later, they were pulling up in front of a generous-sized cottage, painted a soft barley colour, with a thatched roof and a poppy-scarlet front door, above which a scallop shell had been carved into the centre of the stone lintel. Behind the house you could see a flower-filled garden, which looked very much as if it might lead straight onto sand dunes and then a pale, curving beach in the distance.

'Here we go. Shell Cottage,' said Jed. 'Now let's just hope Sam's got room for a couple of newly-weds, eh?'

There were seagulls dipping and wheeling above their heads, the mingled scents of cut hay, sweet peas and a briny sea tang in the air, and a soft breeze that tickled the back of Olivia's hot neck as she made her way out of the car. 'This is lovely,' she whispered to Alec, feeling shy all of a sudden as a man emerged around the side of the house with a wheel-barrow, and raised his eyebrows at the sight of the bride and groom.

Alec took her hand and squeezed. 'What did I tell you? An adventure, not a problem. Stick with me, Mrs Tarrant. We're going to have a lot of fun together.'

Despite Olivia's trepidation, it turned out to be the most perfectly romantic wedding night a bride could wish for. *This is my happy ever after, right here*, Olivia thought as she woke the next morning to the glorious sight of Alec sleeping beside her in the wide oak-framed bed, his hair rumpled, his strong jaw and cheekbones rendering him breath-catchingly hand-some even in slumber. She nestled against him, feeling an uncontainable rush of joy that she would be waking up beside him for the rest of her life, and he stirred, throwing a heavy arm across her and pulling her closer so that she could hear the beating of his heart. 'Good morning, Mrs Tarrant,' he murmured without opening his eyes, and she smiled.

Later that morning, following a hearty breakfast on the small stone sun terrace, Olivia managed to peel her admiring gaze away from her new husband for a few minutes in order to appreciate the beautiful old house in which they were stay-ing. She loved how much character it had, with the beamed ceilings, mullioned windows and sea views, and the way that the ancient claw-foot bath could comfortably fit two. It was the kind of house that was hard to say goodbye to, a house made for happy, romantic times.

Afterwards, they went on to enjoy the rest of their honey-moon in Cornwall but Shell Cottage had cast a spell over them both. The following summer, Olivia and Alec returned there for a week-long holiday, and the summer afterwards too, when their baby daughter Freya was just three months old, and then . . . well, every single summer after that, basic-ally, until the year that Olivia rang the McGarrys to book their usual stay – two adjoining rooms now that they had Freya and Robert – only to be told that unfortunately, the McGarrys were retiring and selling up.

At the time, Alec's second thriller had just hit the bestseller list, and he'd recently received a generous payment from his publishers, having signed a new contract to write three more books. Life was good: the family had moved from a small terraced house in Barnet to a slightly larger one in Tufnell Park where the children had a bedroom each, and Olivia was learning to drive her very own Austin Metro on the wide tree-lined streets. Package holidays abroad were becoming popular and when Olivia broke the news about Shell Cottage to her husband, she half expected him to suggest a trip to the Costa del Sol instead, like some of their neighbours were planning. But Alec was a romantic through and through; he loved Shell Cottage and what it stood for. 'We'll buy it,' he said.

Olivia thought this was one of his whims at first – a silly joke, a crazy impulse. People like them didn't have two homes! Her parents had lived in the same semi-detached house in Buckinghamshire their entire lives and had been perfectly happy. A second home seemed wildly extravagant, way beyond their means.

Alec, though, was deadly serious. What was more, when he made his mind up about something, there was no stopping him. They drove down to Devon the very next day, taking the children out of school, so that he could strike a deal. Just like that, it was done.

Of course, for some years afterwards, they were stretched financially, letting out Shell Cottage to friends and family in order to make ends meet, but it was worth all the hardship and extra work. Olivia and Alec were never happier than when they were driving out of London, the car loaded with suitcases, headed towards Silver Sands Bay for a summer holiday, Christmas, New Year or simply a long weekend.

As their fortunes had grown over the decades, so too had the house. When one of Alec's books was turned into a film, they spent the money on an extension, adding a couple of extra bedrooms upstairs and a larger, more modern kitchen. They decorated throughout in cool off-whites, heaving up the old carpets and waxing the floorboards, hanging the walls with seascapes by local artists. There were huge soft beds for the rooms upstairs, a luxurious bathroom with a drenching monsoon shower and a deep, linger-for-hours bathtub.

It was a special place for them all. Freya and her husband Victor had spent their wedding night in the house fourteen years ago, and now there were the grandchildren, Dexter, Libby and little Ted, who came for a fortnight's holiday each summer and frolicked like sleek, shrieking seal pups in the sea. Robert had brought Harriet and her daughter with him three summers ago and announced at the annual end-of-holiday family barbecue that they were going to get married. And for Alec, who had gone on to write twenty-four other successful novels over the years, the house was his favourite place to come and work in solitude for a few weeks every winter, and then again in early summer, once he'd completed a first draft for the final crucial read-through. A routine had developed where he'd take himself off to Devon in July with his printed-out manuscript, straw hat and a bottle of scotch, to be joined a few weeks later by the rest of the family.

Not this year, though, thought Olivia now, as she trudged slowly downstairs in their silent London home, trying to avoid looking at the framed holiday photographs that hung on the wall. Tears smarted in her eyes as her gaze was inevitably drawn to her favourite picture of all, taken the day after their wedding, of her and Alec, perched on the front wall outside Shell Cottage, arms around each other. You could practically see the happiness crackling about them like a force field, fierce and bright, strong enough to protect them from anything.

Almost anything, anyway. A sob rose in her throat and she walked quickly away, but it was no use, the tears were already falling. Summers would never be the same again.

Chapter Two

Freya Castledine pressed the buzzer on her desk and waited for her next patient, idly scratching an insect bite on her arm. All the summer nasties had presented themselves at the surgery today: three cases of hay fever, a woman with a livid red burn on her leg following a holiday in Turkey (it was always the left calf, always following a moped rental, leg pressed accidentally to the hot exhaust; why didn't these idiots *think*?), a child with a painful-looking infection following a wasp sting, and a man with the most rancid athlete's foot she'd ever seen (and she'd seen a few by now).

Freya supposed she should be grateful that winter was over, along with all of *its* special ailments – pneumonia and bronchitis, hacking coughs and gallons of snot – but summer had lost its allure for her this year. It was overrated as a season, full stop, she thought, an image appearing in her mind of the bikinis still languishing hopefully in her drawer, unworn since she became a mother twelve years ago and promptly piled on three stone. Summer meant prickly heat and horseflies, the agony of breaking in new sandals, the indignity of baring milk-white legs in public, and the sheer palaver of juggling childcare with work through August. Worst, though, was the prospect of a summer holiday without her father this year. She still couldn't believe he wouldn't be there waiting for them at Shell Cottage, that battered old hat on his head, shouts of welcome, a beaming smile.

Her heart ached at the thought. Without fail, the journey down to Devon was always arduous and slow, the children bored and fractious, but there had been this kind of magic about Dad which meant that they'd all be smiling within seconds of their arrival, a new-holiday giddiness awakening inside each of them. For Freya, it didn't take much: a long, deep breath of the soft sea air, one of her dad's legendary Sundowner cocktails, her bare feet touching the warm sand and hearing the sound of the waves . . . The cumulative effect always made her feel the same way: that the world was good. That she'd temporarily sidestepped off life's treadmill into her own private heaven, where time moved like syrup, where days were unhurried and full of fun.

Oh, Dad. It was going to be so subdued at Shell Cottage this year without him there, making them all roar with laughter. However would they manage?

She'd held it together each time she'd been back to her parents' elegant, book-filled Hampstead home, taking charge when Mum floundered, distracting herself with the million and one things that needed doing. But she felt like an over-filled vessel these days, perilously close to bursting and spilling everywhere. As well as losing Dad, she'd had to cope with Victor going into hospital, trying to prop up Mum, keeping her wits about her at work and *still* remembering to send Libby in with cakes for the school summer fair, find Teddy's glasses that he'd lost for the hundredth time and wash Dexter's cricket kit . . . It was no wonder she'd taken to sinking into the sofa with a glass of wine of an evening. Most evenings, to be fair. And who could blame her? The moment she took her first grateful mouthful and savoured its taste was like melting into a warm embrace. It was the only time of day she felt vaguely human.

And yes, okay, so the glass inevitably turned into two glasses, and sometimes a whole bottle. And, admittedly, she no longer looked directly at the GOT A PROBLEM? alcohol awareness poster in the surgery reception these days. And yes, all right, so she *had* nipped out on her lunch break to pick up an emergency gin bottle for later because the thought of an evening stone-cold sober made her feel decidedly twitchy.

So what, though? Big deal! It wasn't as if anybody had noticed anything untoward about her behaviour. She put out the clinking recycling box in darkness, covering the telltale empties with the bag of newspaper and milk cartons so the neighbours wouldn't notice. Similarly, she hid the hollow ache of grief inside and kept up appearances to the rest of the world. For the time being, at least. She couldn't help worrying she was clinging on to sanity by the very tips of her fingers, though. One night, when Victor and the children were in bed, she had actually driven out to the middle of nowhere, pulled over in a layby and just howled like an animal. Like a madwoman.

Broken. That was how she felt. A little broken doll.

In the past, if someone had come into the surgery and said to her, *I'm broken, I'm devastated, I'm drowning in sadness and only ever feel better after a bottle of Merlot*, she'd have put on her professionally concerned face and trotted out the usual suggestions: plenty of exercise and fresh air, talk to friends, eat properly, don't make the mistake of relying on props like alcohol or caffeine to see you through.

What a load of bollocks. She'd never be so patronizing again. Now she would lean over, look them in the eye and say, *I understand. My God, I understand. I've been there myself, way down at the depths like you. The thing is, I have no answers for you, only my own question. When will it end?*

Her door opened just then and she plastered on an expectant smile as an elderly man entered, leaning on a stick and breathing heavily. Despite the sunshine outside, he wore a blazer over his shirt and was scarlet-faced and perspiring as a result. Freya jumped up to help him to a chair. 'Mr Turner,' she said, once he had lowered himself into the seat and mopped his shiny brow with a crumpled white handkerchief. 'How can I help?'

By five o'clock, Freya was flagging. She still had one last patient to see but her mind was flitting ahead to collecting the children from the childminder, arriving home and starting on dinner: pork stir-fry tonight, even though she could already predict that six-year-old Teddy would painstakingly pick out all the sugar-snap peas and leave them in a shiny green heap at the side of his plate, and that Libby, nine years old and toying with vegetarianism, would talk mournfully about the cuteness of pigs. Dexter, aged twelve, would eat a huge plateful at least, but then he was in the midst of a gigantic growth spurt and shovelled in food like coal into a furnace. (One of these days Freya fully expected to come in to see him gnawing on a chair leg, having emptied the entire fridge and pantry.) No, the challenge with Dexter would be whether or not she could extract more than a grunt from him when it came to finding out about his day at school. It could go either way.

Meanwhile, her husband Victor, a detective sergeant, was four days into a two-week public order course in Gravesend, simultaneously learning how to be even more of a heroic figure of authority and forgetting to call home and wish his wife and children goodnight. There was over a week left until he came back, and she had the dismal feeling they would seem like strangers to one another by then.

Anyway. Whatever.

She glanced at her computer screen, saw that her next patient was Ava Taylor, and groaned. Ever since Ava had been born six months ago, her mother Melanie had wheeled her self-importantly into the surgery approximately twice a week, fretting that her daughter had a sniffle, a cough, that she had been glassy-eyed during breakfast, that her breathing sounded 'a bit quiet'.

'You understand,' she'd said conspiratorially more than once, glancing sideways at Freya's framed desk photo: the children balancing atop a huge wonky sandcastle on Silver Sands beach, Teddy brandishing a sword perilously close to Dexter's groin. 'Us mums, we do worry, don't we?'

Melanie was right to worry but not necessarily about her daughter. A mere two days earlier, Richard Taylor, her husband, had shuffled into Freya's consulting room looking shifty and uncomfortable before unzipping his trousers and showing her his painful swollen testicles, then describing the burning pain he felt when peeing and the cloudy, blood-tinged discharge he'd experienced from his small, frightened-looking penis.

Gonorrhoea, Freya briskly told him, before administering an antibiotic injection into his pale, hairy buttock and writing a prescription. A nice festering case of the clap, which he almost certainly hadn't picked up from his wife. It was strange and not entirely pleasant to have insights into marriages all over town. Thank goodness nobody could peer into hers right now.

She drummed her fingers on the desk, waiting for Melanie, and her thoughts turned to the bottle of Hendrick's gin nestling in her bag, along with a rather squashed packet of Cadbury's Mini Rolls (for the school summer fair cake stall – they could like it or jolly well lump it). *Good old mother's ruin – bring it on*, she thought. *Ice cubes, juicy lemon slice, enough tonic splashed in to make it respectable* . . . She glanced down at the bag by her feet. If Melanie didn't hurry up, at this rate she'd be uncapping the bottle and having a swig right now.

Too late. There was a knock at the door and Melanie wheeled in the buggy, the usual expression of certain doom on her face.

'Hello there, Melanie,' Freya said politely. 'What seems to be the problem today?'

Melanie wittered on about baby Ava feeling a bit hot, and just sort of, you know, grouchy and not quite herself, but Freya was struggling to concentrate, imagining instead the distinctive rattle of ice cubes being dropped into a tall glass, the hiss of the tonic bottle opening. You were meant to have cucumber batons with Hendrick's, weren't you? Did they have any cucumber? The salad drawer was woefully empty, she thought, remembering the lonely yellowing spring onion and the bag of dried-looking carrots. Did they even have enough for a stir-fry tonight, come to think of it? Bugger it, they might just have to have a takeaway after all.

Freya jerked back to the moment, aware that Melanie had stopped speaking and was waiting for her opinion. *Snap out of it, Freya. Be professional.*

She ran through some basic checks on her patient: listening to Ava's chest, checking her temperature, and gently sliding a finger into the baby's warm, wet mouth to prise it open and look inside. Ava, perched plumply on her mother's knee, stared at Freya with interest the entire time, sucking curiously on Freya's finger when it appeared in her mouth, her round pink cheeks soft and pillowy to the touch.

'Well,' she said afterwards, returning to her seat, 'I don't think there's anything to worry about. She has a mild fever and her throat looks a bit red, but it's probably just a summer cold.' Ava batted the air with both hands as if playing an invisible piano, then stared down at her fingers, seemingly mystified by their behaviour. 'Give her plenty to drink and a spoonful of Calpol if she seems in discomfort.'

Melanie didn't appear satisfied with this bland piece of advice. No doubt she'd been hoping for a dramatic dash to A&E, sirens wailing. 'But she's having trouble sleeping,' she persisted, pursing her thin pink lips. 'She didn't want *any* of her pear and apple puree at lunchtime and that's her absolute favourite. She really doesn't seem herself.'

'She seems fine to me,' Freya said firmly, approaching the fast-unravelling end of her tether. *Go away, Melanie. I want to drive home and see my children now, to fry chopped onions and pork, with a lovely big gin at my side. I want to sit in my garden with the grass tickling my bare toes and not think about anything for a while.* 'Try not to worry too much. She's a lovely healthy baby, with a bit of a sniffle, that's all. Give it a few days, she'll be right as rain.' *And while you're at it, have a word with that pox-riddled husband of yours and tell him to keep his pants on more often.*

Melanie looked affronted to have her concerns rebuffed as being 'a bit of a sniffle'. Mouth pinched in apparent disagreement, she rose stiffly to her feet and returned Ava to her buggy. 'Thank you, doctor,' she murmured in a martyrish sort of way.

Just at that moment, Freya's phone started trilling and vibrating. Damn! She hadn't realized it was even switched on. She lunged for her bag but kicked it over in her haste and – oh Christ – the neck of the gin bottle slid right out onto the grey carpet. She could almost hear the wail of a klaxon – *Alcoholic alert! Alcoholic alert!* – as she leapt from her chair. Face flaming, she made a desperate scramble for the bag, the phone still chirping away.

'Sorry about that,' she said with a nervous laugh, once she'd switched it off. Melanie's face was impassive as she said goodbye and left, and Freya sank back into her chair afterwards, feeling rattled. Had Melanie seen the gin? Had she noticed Freya's panic? Shit. 'Not your finest hour there, Frey,' she muttered with a sigh. She really bloody needed a drink now.

Chapter Three

Ever since Alec's death, Olivia had been thinking a great deal about her last day with him. Dwelling on it, you could say. Should she have guessed what was to come? Could she have saved him somehow? It had all seemed so ordinary to begin with, that was the problem. Just another beautiful summer's morning, the two of them eating breakfast on the patio of the Edwardian Hampstead house where they'd lived for the last twenty-five years. He was leafing through *The Times*; she was thinking vaguely about how she would begin planting up the Fortescues' garden later that afternoon. Then the phone rang inside the house. 'I'll get it,' Alec grumbled, taking a last munch of his toast and marmalade.

Olivia had carried on sipping her tea and gazing out at the dahlias, which were just springing into vivid splashes of colour: crimson, orange, red. She could hear the distant sound of someone practising scales on a piano and the loud *chack-chack* of a blackbird warning that there was a cat prowling nearby. Then came Alec's voice, gruff and cross through the open door. 'How did you get this number?' he said. He was always grumpy when he slept badly, and the stifling June heat had played havoc with his sleep recently. 'You mustn't ring this number again!'

An overenthusiastic fan, Olivia thought mildly. They tracked him down sometimes. Her knuckles tightened on the teacup as she caught sight of the ravaged leaves of her beautiful carmine lupins. Slugs again. She'd really have to sort out the –

Then there came a crash. A strangled sort of shout. She ran inside to find Alec prone on the hall carpet, the dropped telephone beside him. His face was puce, his eyes bulging and shocked; one hand clutched at his chest. A faint line of dribble leaked from the corner of his mouth, his lips parting as he tried to speak. But no words came, only a great, groaning pant of distress.

After that everything happened very fast, as if time had accelerated around her. Despite the best efforts of the paramedics and then the consultants, Alec slipped into unconsciousness and never came round again. She'd sat next to him as he lay unmoving in the crisp white hospital bed, begging and praying for him to come back to her but instead his soul quietly departed with one last hoarse breath, and he was gone. Sixty-four years old and his life was over.

Her world felt desolate without him, unbearably empty. Alec had always been the gregarious one of the marriage, the sort of man who could stride into a crowded room and charm everyone into becoming his new best friend within minutes. He was witty and charismatic, generous and spontaneous; the most fun and interesting person in any gathering. Now that he had died, Olivia felt like a small tugboat cut adrift on a stormy sea, uncertain where she was heading or if she could even stay afloat. She had counted on at least another ten or twenty years together; they had planned to retire down to Devon before too much longer to 'grow old disgracefully', as he'd put it. But no. One rogue blood clot marauding through her husband's body had put paid to that.

Sometimes she wondered angrily who the pestering fan had been on the phone that day – *How did you get this number? You mustn't ring this number again!* – and whether Alec's subsequent ire had been the last fatal strain on his health. Had the caller felt a twist of guilt, a prick of conscience, when they read of his death in the newspaper? Had it even occurred to them that they might unwittingly have contributed to his demise?

Since that terrible airless June morning three weeks ago, Olivia had functioned on autopilot, the big, quiet house silting up with unwanted flowers, and sympathy cards she couldn't bring herself to read. Maria, their Filipino cleaner, tiptoed around now and then, head bowed as she dusted and polished and occasionally changed the putrefying water in the vases, but Olivia barely noticed her presence. It seemed a minor miracle to survive each long, torturous day without disintegrating, turning into a madwoman, clawing at the ground, screaming at the sky. *Alec is gone, Alec is gone.* She'd never hear his husky laugh again or feel his arms around her; she'd never be warmed by the golden, unswerving spotlight of his devotion. How was it possible to go on?

Over the last fifteen years, Olivia had built up a small boutique garden design service, with two members of staff and their own van. She had always found solace in planting and weeding, but this summer she didn't even want to step outside her back door to water her own garden, let alone venture further to tend the flower beds, lawns and shrubbery of her wealthy clients. What the hell. Let them wither and droop, let them dry to a brown crisp. Without Alec, it all seemed pointless anyway. Everything did.

The children helped out where possible. Although she was a busy GP with three little ones of her own, Freya drove down from her home in Hertfordshire to assist with the practicalities of the funeral, as well as briskly tackling many of the horrible, cold formalities: registering the death, winding up her father's bank accounts, and wading through the reams of correspondence and documents piled up under his desk. Capable and pin-sharp even in the throes of mourning, Freya had always been one for Getting Things Done. It had been a wrench when she returned home, leaving a typed to-do list and renewed silence in her wake.

Robert, too, was supportive and helpful, coming over to deal with the extraordinary number of emails which had piled up in Alec's inbox – a task Olivia herself hadn't been able to stomach. All those polite replies to type, all the condolences to acknowledge, not to mention the myriad work-related conversations that needed untangling.

'How's it going?' she asked, walking into Alec's study one Friday afternoon to see her son frowning at the ageing computer screen. It was still strange to find another person there in her husband's domain, cluttered as it was with book paraphernalia, several crime writer awards and ump-teen souvenirs from his travels.

'Not bad,' he replied, stretching his arms above his head. Robert had the same green eyes and dark hair as his father whereas Freya was like her: fair with pale skin that burned easily in the sun. Tall and rangy, Robert was the athlete of the family, walking at seven months old, and not stopping ever since. Even now, he was wearing a running top with shorts and trainers, as if he'd broken off midway through a marathon to pop round. 'Eleanor's asked, in the nicest possible way, if we think Dad's last book is going to be pub-lishable,' he went on. 'She said they could supply us with a ghostwriter if we felt it was necessary, although that would probably mean moving publication into next year.'

His last book. Olivia's heart seemed to clench. That wretched book had helped kill him, she was sure of it: the stress of trying to meet the tight deadline, the dread of another big American tour and festival appearances looming that autumn. Alec was a professional, always delivering a new novel to his editor in July, with the hardback edition published several months later in time for Christmas. Regular as clockwork the schedule went, only this particular book had got to him for some reason. Her husband didn't often suffer from self-doubt but in the weeks before his death, he had agonized to Olivia privately a number of times that he just wasn't sure about this one. Some days he would go off to the heath for a walk and not return for hours, still with the same distracted light in his eyes. She didn't even know if he had been close to finishing it when he died.

'Right,' she said. 'Leave it with me. Is there anything else?'

'Yes. Marcus – solicitor Marcus – has come back with a few queries. Dad left quite a lot of money to someone called Leo Browne. Do you know him?'

Leo Browne. She turned the name over in her mind, but it didn't ring any bells. Maybe it was an editor he'd worked with in America, or his film agent; she'd never been able to keep track of all Alec's contacts. Her lip trembled as she remembered teasing him about the ridiculous number of Christmas cards he used to receive from friends, fans and colleagues; how he couldn't even recall who half the senders were. They would appear like drifts of snow through the letterbox each morning, an avalanche of festive bonhomie. This Christmas the haul would be decimated, though. She'd sign their cards alone, the white space that bit emptier without his confident black-inked scrawl alongside hers.

She curled her hands into fists, digging her fingernails into her palms. *Come on, Olivia. Keep it together.* She had to stop allowing herself to be felled with sorrow by every tiny memory, every single conversation.

'I don't recognize the name, sorry,' she said, after a deep breath.

'No worries. Oh, and there's an email from Katie, checking we're still set for the summer as usual.' He gazed expectantly at her. 'When were you planning to go?'

Katie was their sort-of housekeeper at Shell Cottage, a cheerful thirty-something woman who lived in Silver Sands village and kept an eye on the place when they weren't staying there. During the summer, she was like their good fairy, popping round to clean and make up the beds while they were out. Had anyone even told Katie about Alec? Olivia had lost track of who knew the terrible news and who didn't.

She leaned against the bookshelves, stuffed in a haphazard fashion with all the foreign editions of Alec's books. The idea of being at Silver Sands without her husband was unbearable. Who would organize the lilo races and the crabbing? Who would man the barbecue and lead the legendary hikes out on Dartmoor? Who would appear on the terrace with a cool drink for her just when she was feeling thirsty, or rub suncream into her fast-pinking shoulders? 'I don't know about the holiday this year,' she mumbled, looking away.

'What? Oh, Mum, no. You're not staying here and moping around all summer. You have to go. Everyone else still wants to.'

'It's just . . . without your dad . . .' She shrugged helplessly. If she went to Shell Cottage alone, she'd only feel tormented by memories of all those summers gone by, their precious wedding night, and most recently, last New Year's Eve, when they'd set off fireworks in the garden, just the two of them, and kissed as if they were teenagers. How he'd loved the sheer extravagance of fireworks, the bright pinwheels of colour exploding in the dark velvety sky.

But Robert's fingers were already flying over the keyboard again. 'Dear Katie, Thank you for your email. We are looking forward to our return to the house,' he read aloud sternly. 'If you could have everything ready as usual for my arrival on the . . .' He broke off and glanced up at the calendar. 'What shall I say, the fourteenth of July? That gives you another week or so to tie up a few more things here.'

Olivia hesitated. She couldn't imagine going into *London* on her own right now, let alone driving all the way to Devon. Robert met her look steadfastly with those green eyes, so like his father's, and her resistance faltered. She'd never been able to refuse Alec anything when he looked at her that way.

'Mum?' Robert prompted. 'You could take Dad's manuscript with you, couldn't you? Read it through if you felt up to it. One last story to enjoy.'

His gaze was unswerving and Olivia found herself nodding in defeat. 'Okay,' she said. *Whatever*, as her grandchildren would say. She could always ring Katie and cancel, she told herself.

'Great,' Robert said, typing again. He clicked on 'Send' with a flourish. 'I think it's the right thing, Mum. The sooner we all try and get back to normal, the better. And a holiday is probably exactly what you need.'

Chapter Four

Sixty feet below ground level, Harriet Tarrant-Price heaved her canvas bags of paperwork and folders up onto one shoulder as she heard the distant rumbling of the train far back in the tunnel. Thank goodness. It was steaming down in Camden Town station today, the tiled walls sweaty with condensation, the platform crammed with tourists and schoolchildren. The sooner she travelled the five stops to East Finchley and could re-emerge into daylight the better.

The train wheezed into the station, as slow and shambling as a recalcitrant teenager, and there was the usual hot crush of human bodies as the crowd forced its way on-board. As luck would have it, there was a seat free in the middle of the carriage and after a swift check-around for desperate pregnant women (no), Harriet hurled herself towards it and collapsed breathlessly onto its dusty surface. A half-read copy of the *Metro* rustled against her as she leaned back and she reached round to pull it out, her gaze falling on the headline. *JUICE YOUR WAY SKINNY!*

Oh, bog off, Harriet thought. That was the thing about summer: you had to avoid so many magazines and newspapers with their annoying 'Beach Body', 'Bikini Diet' nonsense. If it wasn't 'Starve Yourself', it was 'Pluck Out Every Last Hair on Your Bod', or – worse still – 'Exercise Your Way to a Size Minus Two', or whatever women were supposed to aspire to these days. Yeah, yeah. Harriet would not be cowed by such body fascism. Let them juice themselves into oblivion. She'd rather have a plate of pasta and buttery garlic bread, thanks for asking.

The train rumbled off and she turned her attention to the nerve-racking prospect of the party she was due to attend that evening. She still hadn't decided what to wear for starters. What *did* one wear to a gathering of scarily intellectual types who were publishing your husband's brilliant first novel? A dress, definitely, rather than her favourite jeans, which therefore meant getting her legs out, urgent depilation and toenail painting and a toss-up between which pair of smart heels she could bear to stand in the longest. (The short answer: none of them. At each of the last three summer weddings she'd been to, she'd resorted to bare feet after a single glass of Pimms, blisters popping up all over her tender pink toes. And she certainly couldn't stay in the knackered silver Converse she was wearing right now, which had the unfortunate habit of making farting noises when her feet got too hot and sweaty.)

She glanced surreptitiously at the woman opposite her – a Nordic blonde looking cool and elegant in a crisp white dress with bronze Gladiator sandals – and wished that she could look so effortlessly glamorous. Even once would be nice. How did anyone keep a white linen dress clean on the *Tube*, unless they were some kind of goddess with magical powers? Harriet would have sat in pink bubblegum or dropped a leaky biro into her lap by now, or a bird would have pooed on her during playground duty.

If only she looked like white-dress woman, she could stride into the party tonight with supreme confidence. Instead, she was short with an avocado-shaped body and chunky calves that looked weird in a skirt ('Legs like a pit pony,' as Evil Simon had always teased, which still made her feel like punching him, seven years down the line). She had dark brown hair, currently cut in a boring, boyish crop, freckles like spilled demerara sugar and a faint, fuzzy moustache shadowing her top lip, which she absolutely *must* bleach into non-existence before a single person at the cocktail party could see it and snigger. Once a teenage acne sufferer, she still had the habit of putting her hand up to her face when she felt insecure in social situations. She pictured herself at the party: a blushing moustachioed hobbit covering her face amidst the confident, beautiful people – the literati! – and cringed. It was going to be a nightmare. It was going to be such a bloody nightmare!

Her eyes fell back onto the *Metro* and despite her earlier irritation, she found herself reading up about the juice camp in Wales at which the journalist had apparently lost half a stone in a week. Hmm. Maybe there was something in this idea, after all. (Why hadn't she booked herself in to a Welsh juice camp in readiness for this party? Why was she always so ill-prepared?)

Oh, right. Closer reading revealed that it cost over eight hundred pounds for the five-day break, and the campers had endured gruelling six-mile runs and freezing river swims every day. Sod the juice camp, then. If Harriet had a spare eight hundred quid, she'd sooner blow it on a luxury week-end away in Paris with Robert, ta very much. If they really put their minds to it, they could probably shag enough to lose half a stone each anyway, *and* tuck into *steak frites* and a bottle of Cabernet Sauvignon afterwards.

The train suddenly braked, and came to an abrupt halt, and Harriet lurched against the sweating man in a too-tight suit next to her, her elbow squelching into his McDonald's paper bag. 'Sorry,' she mumbled as a weary, please-God-no tension spread through the carriage. Breaking down mid-tunnel was always grim but on a roasting hot day, with barely room to breathe, they'd be melting into puddles within seconds. Besides, she wanted to get home in plenty of time so that she could titivate herself for the party: all that hair-removal and outfit-agonizing would take forever. She would make an effort for Robert's sake, though, to show how thrilled she was at his amazing career turn. No problemo.

Goodness, but she was proud of her husband! Not every person had the courage he'd had, giving up a steady job to follow his dream of writing a novel. Admittedly, he'd hated working as a cycle courier, and yes, okay, so he hadn't really talked it through with her before quitting in a fit of pique one day, but he'd knuckled down and slogged through a first draft in six short months. A first draft that was now, by all accounts, the talk of literary London, no less!

She just had to hope she wouldn't look too out of place tonight; the sole pleb in a sea of glittering brainiacs. Would they be able to tell she hadn't been to university? Would it be obvious she only read two books a year, usually juicy psychological thrillers while on holiday, and that she couldn't name a Booker Prize winner even with a gun to her head? And what if one of the hipsters asked what she thought of her own husband's book? Apparently the publisher had called it 'that rare thing – a comic literary novel', but from the few chapters Harriet had been permitted to read, it was about three male characters arguing about the meaning of life in a way that was actually quite slow and boring. That was probably just her being thick, though. Surely. What did she know about books?

The train started moving again, a slow, dragging shuffle

before finally accelerating into a more thunderous pace. *Just smile and nod to the other guests*, she reminded herself. *Smile and nod, have another cocktail, and if all else fails, talk about how clever Robert is.*

Ahh, East Finchley station. At last! Her cotton blouse sticking to her in the heat, Harriet was grateful to emerge blinking into the daylight and start striding towards home, her shoes gently trumping with each step. Sod it, she thought, she would not let herself feel overawed at the party. Just that day at school, she'd spoken to Latisha Baldock – angry, defensive Latisha, who'd been suspended last year for breaking a boy's nose – and sensitively tackled the subject of her mother's latest health problems. To the surprise of them both, hard-faced Latisha had let down her guard for once and cried actual tears in the sanctuary of Harriet's little office. She'd even allowed Harriet to hug her and comfort her, and accepted that it would be good to talk to a counsellor who could help. 'Fanks, Miss,' she'd said, tucking a soggy tissue in her skirt pocket, when she eventually left. It was like being awarded a gold medal in the Social Work Olympics. And how many brainbox authors at the party could claim that kind of job satisfaction, eh?

The party would be *fine*. It was only one evening. And if it was awful, she and Robert could giggle about it in the taxi afterwards and slag everyone else off. So there.

*

An hour later, Harriet had scrubbed and moisturized, bleached her tache into non-existence and then applied a stinky depilatory cream to de-hair her legs. Unfortunately the cream had been ancient – from the summer before, she realized belatedly – and made her itch horribly to the point where she couldn't wait the full treatment time but ended up with first one leg in the bathroom sink and then the other, hastily rinsing the burning goo straight off again and yelping the whole time. Of course, wouldn't you know it, her skin promptly sprang up with a scarlet rash, forcing Harriet to smear on gallons of EasyTan bronzing lotion in a panicky cover-up attempt. The only silver lining in the whole disastrous episode was that her daughter Molly had vanished off to her best friend Chloe's for tea, so wasn't there to snigger and post photos of the strangely orange, hairless, pit-pony-resembling limbs on Instagram. Small mercies.

What next? Eyebrows. The plucking didn't go too well first time around so she had an emergency glass of wine and tried again (even worse). Then she resorted to drawing on new eyebrows, which gave her the surprised air of someone who'd just had a dart fired into their bottom. Well, it was a talking point, she supposed. That or the death knell of any future invitations out with Robert, anyway.

'Hello? Where is everyone?'

Oh, thank goodness. Now her husband was home and he was sure to make her feel better. He would kiss her and tell her she looked sensational in a hessian sack, and didn't she know, big pencilled eyebrows were totally the in-thing this year, and he'd always adored her strong legs, however weirdly neon and shiny they might look now. 'Up here!' she yelled in reply, unhooking her red cotton H&M dress from the rail and holding it in front of her.

'What do you think?' she asked as he came into the bedroom. 'Red? Or . . .' She rummaged through the wardrobe, wishing she had an extensive collection of summer outfits she could choose from for a glamorous cocktail party. Instead, her hand fell on her faithful pink Primark wrap dress which she'd worn so often the fabric was bobbly. 'Or pink?'

Robert came over and tossed both dresses onto the bed, then wrapped his arms around her and kissed her very thoroughly. Wearing only a pair of pants and her bra, Harriet felt suddenly raunchy, especially when he started tugging at said pants. Unfortunately, they were control panel ones, with a rubbery, hold-back-the-flab top, which made them almost impossible to remove unless one was prepared to use surgical instruments and a whole can of WD40. She giggled, feeling infinitely more party-ish. 'Well, someone's pleased to see me,' she said, as he gave up on the pants and began unhooking her bra. 'What are you wearing tonight, then?'

'As little as possible,' he murmured in her ear, releasing the clip and yanking her bra from her body. Then he sniffed. 'What's that weird smell?'

Oh Lord. It was the disgusting depilatory cream, she knew it. Or maybe the pungent EasyTan bronzer. 'No idea,' she said, the wine putting fibs in her mouth. 'Robert, no . . . I need to get ready. Haven't we got to be there in, like, an hour or something?'

He was bending down, nuzzling between her breasts, which was both ticklish and erotic at the same time. Mmm, hello. 'Where?' he said.

'The party!' she laughed, stepping back so that he almost fell over. 'Your publishing thing. At the posh house. Cocktails. Mingling. Everyone saying how great you are.'

His face went blank for a moment – two, three long moments – and then he slapped a hand to his head. 'Oh shit,' he said.

Harriet, feeling slightly silly standing there in a pair of huge, unflattering, for-her-eyes-only control pants, positioned her arms over her bare breasts and bad choice of underwear. 'What do you mean, oh shit?'

'I . . .' He raked a hand through his hair and sighed. 'Oh, love. I thought I'd told you. I got it wrong, about it being a plus-one thing.'

'You mean . . . ?' Her heart beat wildly. He *hadn't* told her. There was no way she would have forgotten him telling her, not when she'd been stressing out all week about this effing party. The effing party to which she hadn't even been invited, as it turned out. And now she'd obliterated her own eyebrows and brought on a virulent leg rash for nothing! 'I'm not going?'

He shook his head and sat down on the bed. Harriet put on her dressing gown, feeling like the biggest idiot ever.

'Sorry,' he said. 'I'm such a doofus. And here you are, getting all ready . . .'

She tried to smile, although she probably still looked surprised from the stupid eyebrows. 'It doesn't matter,' she said but inside she was deflating like a punctured balloon. No cocktails, then. No party. No make-up and high heels and frock. No giggling about all the goss to her friends at work on Monday morning. ('So I was saying to Zadie, right . . .')

'It does matter. Of course it does!' He looked at her wretchedly and somehow, despite the punctured-balloon sensation, she felt her stomach flip ever so slightly at his hangdog eyes. 'Look – let's blow it out,' he said. 'Let's forget the dumb party, and go out, just the two of us, and have a laugh somewhere instead. I'd much rather be with you.'

She shook her head. 'No, don't worry, honestly.' It was a relief really, she told herself. For the best. She hadn't truly wanted to go anyway, had she? But . . .

'But you've got your sexy pants on and everything,' he said, flicking the top of the elastic (with some effort, admittedly; he'd probably broken a finger in the attempt). 'They're all Matron-esque and forbidding. I'm getting stirrings just thinking about them.'

She pulled a face. 'I'm glad someone is. I feel completely numb from the waist down. God knows how I'm ever going to get them off again.'

He made a growling noise in his throat. 'Now there's a challenge . . . Come here, gorgeous. Let's see if we can do something about that.'

Forty-five minutes later, Robert left in a cloud of aftershave and further apologies and Harriet tried not to feel too disconsolate. Oh well, she told herself, putting on her pyjamas and trudging downstairs. There would be other parties, wouldn't there? Lots of other parties. Not going tonight would give her more time to brush up on some clever things to say and hunt down a fancy dress and sparkly shoes.

She tried not to think about those fabulous white stucco houses near Regent's Park where the publisher lived – she'd been dying to have a nose around inside – and poured herself an exceedingly pokey vodka tonic instead. 'Cocktails, shlocktails,' she said, drinking it down in three eye-watering gulps.

Just as she was on the verge of nosediving into a gloomy all-by-myself mood, Molly came back from Chloe's house – 'I got a lift from Chlo's dad, don't worry, Mum' – and she was pink in the cheeks and giggly, her phone pinging with new text messages which made her eyes shine even more. Harriet felt better listening to her daughter talk about her day and the forthcoming end-of-term party the Year 10s were throwing, and was warmed by thoughts of what a beautiful creature Molly was, all long legs and Bambi eyes and big tawny hair.

She flicked on the television. The Alan Carr show was just starting, and they snuggled up together on the sofa, both cackling as Alan exclaimed theatrically about the week he'd just had. There were worse Friday nights, Harriet reminded herself as Molly leaned against her. As for the party . . . what party? She was so over it already.

Meanwhile, Robert glanced over his shoulder as he came out of Tottenham Court Road Tube station, then let himself become swallowed up by the crowd as he headed into Soho. He loved warm, grimy London on a Friday evening in summer, when everyone was in a good mood from finishing work and there was nothing better to do than sit outside your favourite pub and put the world to rights with your mates. It was at times like this he missed having a proper job and being able to clock off, bosh, on the stroke of five thirty. He even missed the camaraderie of the courier firm, the banter between the lads, the adrenalin rush as you bested a van driver, the joy of being outdoors each day rather than on the wrong side of a window. Still. He'd made his bed. He had to lie in it now.

He wandered past pizzerias and nail bars, second-hand bookshops and bondage gear haunts, past the theatres and brightly lit restaurants which were already drawing in queues of backpack-laden, selfie-snapping tourists. On and on he walked, winding his way through the busy streets until he ducked down a side road and, with a final check over his shoulder, slipped into The Loyal Hound pub, dingy and beer-smelling, the perfect place to hide. He ordered a pint of bitter and a plate of chips then parked himself at an empty table with a good view of the boxing match now starting on the TV. Just for good measure, he switched off his phone.

With a flash of guilt, he thought about his wife at home, with her party dresses returned to the darkness of the wardrobe. 'Sorry, love,' he had said, and he *was* sorry. Harriet was all good. She was cherry-red lipstick and a great bum in a pencil skirt. A woman who cried at soap opera weddings (seriously) and strung fairy lights around the bedroom, yet went out each day and fought hard for all the vulnerable children in her care. She grew flowers in the garden and collected vintage perfume bottles and could still outdo anyone on the most bad-ass curry without breaking a single bead of sweat.

Oh yes. Harriet was awesome. But right now, he wasn't sure he deserved such a woman. Right now, it was hard to look her in the eye and tell her yet another lie.

He just had to have a bit of faith, he reminded himself bracingly, posting another chip in his mouth. He had to hang in there and wait for his luck to change. And it would, any day soon. It had to.

Chapter Five

'Freya? Have you got a minute? I need to speak to you.'

It was eight thirty on Monday morning, but Freya already felt as if she'd lived through an entire week of stress. Dexter had woken up remembering too late that he had a geography test that day and had glowered and thundered like one of the volcanoes in his text book. Teddy had turned the clean laundry pile into a crumpled mess looking for his Spider-Man socks, even though there were at least five other pairs of perfectly wearable socks neatly balled together in his drawer. And Libby had casually announced at breakfast that her class was having a tea party that afternoon, and she needed to bring in some party food. With their kitchen cupboards currently home to an assortment of ageing tins – kidney beans, peach slices in syrup, the wrong kind of mushy peas – all old enough to start claiming a pension (she really must get to the supermarket, preferably sometime this century), the only thing remotely party-ish in there was a packet of chocolate digestives. Unfortunately, when presented with this option,

Libby got very cross, moaning that digestive biscuits weren't at *all* party-ish, and that everyone else's mums would have baked cupcakes with swirly icing. 'Well, if you'd just told me a bit *earlier*,' Freya said through gritted teeth, feeling her patience stretching bubblegum-thin.

'Yeah, if you'd told her earlier, Mum could have bought a packet of Hula Hoops as well. Big woo,' muttered Dexter sarcastically from where he was simultaneously woofing down most of a large box of cornflakes and memorizing a map of Central America.

Freya counted to twenty under her breath in an attempt to stop herself screaming, wondered for a few deluded moments whether she should attempt to make some icing and decorate the chocolate biscuits to look more festive – no, crazy idea, was she *insane*? – then resorted to making their packed lunches instead. Their packed lunches which – because she was in dire need of a supermarket trip – were woefully boring (leftover-roast-chicken sandwich, apple, some bits of cheese and crackers) and would no doubt show up her poor neglected children yet again compared to the packed lunches of their friends (mini salads and freshly baked sausage rolls and fairy cakes with sodding swirly icing). Aaargh. She thought viciously of her husband Victor, almost certainly still fast asleep at the residential police-training centre, and deaf to all of this, and felt very much like driving down there and setting off an air horn outside his window. Just to be spiteful. Just so that he could share the suffering.

On the way to school, she was cut up at two different traffic lights by impatient drivers, one of whom gave her the finger. Then she had to tell off Dexter, who had taken to using his own invented rhyming slang wherever possible, in this case calling the second driver a 'total Talamanca'.

'Dexter, that's enough,' Freya snapped.

'What? I only called him a Talamanca. It's an area in Costa Rica. I thought you'd be pleased I had learned something for my geography test.'

'Tala*manca*,' Teddy echoed gleefully, and Freya groaned deep in her throat. Great. And of course that would be all round the infant classes within five minutes of the day starting, you wait. Knowing her luck, there would be a polite phone call from the deputy head later that day: *Dr Castledine, nothing to worry about, we're just a little concerned about some of the language Teddy has been using lately . . .*

Just try it, love, Freya thought grimly. *And then I can guarantee you'll hear some really bad language.*

She hadn't imagined motherhood to be like this. Years ago, the summer she was pregnant with Dexter, she and Vic had been in Devon and had gone out for the day to a National Trust property – a big beautiful house by the sea with sprawling, flower-filled gardens. They'd paused for a picnic and watched, smiling, as a family had rolled down the steep

grassy hill together, laughing, then tumbled into a tangle of arms and legs at the bottom. *We'll be like that*, Freya had thought happily, one hand resting on her bump as they munched their cheese and salad sandwiches. *We'll be the sort of family that rolls down hills in the sunshine, just for fun.*

Only, as it turned out, they were the sort of family who squabbled in cars and never got anywhere on time and lurched from one laundry and party-food crisis to another.

And now she had arrived at work, trying to put the mayhem out of her mind, turning her head as usual to avoid the GOT A PROBLEM? poster (*Oh, bore off*), but just five minutes after her arrival, in had come Elizabeth, the manager of the GP practice, asking if she could 'have a word'. *Monday, you total Talamanca*, Freya thought under her breath as she tried to contort her face into something resembling a pleasant smile. 'Of course!' she replied with faux cheer.

Dr Elizabeth Donnelly was a tall, chic fifty-something woman, always immaculately turned out, with keen grey eyes that seemed to look right into you; Freya had often imagined Elizabeth's patients squirming uncomfortably as they confessed in a reluctant mumble that yes, okay, they probably did drink more than ten units a week, and no, all right, they supposed they didn't really do enough exercise, you got me there, doc.

Now that cool grey gaze was turned on Freya and she was immediately gripped by a forgotten-my-homework lurch of anxiety. Was something amiss? She'd come into work so hungover last Friday she must have reeked of alcohol but whiffing a bit hokey wasn't a crime, was it? She swallowed, trying to push down her nerves and wishing she'd thought to chew more gum and spray on extra perfume that day.

'Have a seat,' she said, gesturing to the empty chair in front of her desk.

Elizabeth closed the door and sat down with a beige cardboard file on her lap. 'I believe you saw Ava Taylor and her mother last week,' she began.

'Ava and Melanie? Yes.' Freya gave a short laugh. 'I see them pretty regularly, to be honest.'

Elizabeth wasn't smiling. If anything, she looked severe. She opened the file, removing a handwritten letter. 'And according to Melanie, when they came in last Thursday, you sent her away without a prescription, telling her Ava had –' she peered at the blue notepaper – 'a summer cold.'

Freya's heart banged hard as Elizabeth raised her head and looked steadily at her, waiting for a response. She didn't like the sound of this. Why had Melanie written to Elizabeth about her appointment? What was going on? She tried to compose herself and remember the exact exchanges of the visit. 'I examined Ava and she had a slight temperature as I recall,' she said.

'You told Mrs Taylor, and I quote from her letter, "She

has a bit of a sniffle and is probably just feeling sorry for herself".'

Freya reddened. Her own words sounded glib and heartless when repeated back like that. 'Well, you know, Melanie does tend to overinflate every ailment,' she said defensively. 'Ava was displaying cold symptoms, but seemed quite cheerful otherwise. She wasn't distressed or unresponsive.' She recalled the curious gaze of the baby as Freya had examined her, the way Ava had bounced her hands around and how it had reminded her of a piano player. That wasn't an ill, fractious baby, was it? 'I advised Melanie – Mrs Taylor – to give her plenty of fluids and some Calpol if her temperature rose any higher.' *Come on*, she wanted to say to Elizabeth. *What's your point here? Any doctor would have said the same thing. Melanie is neurotic, that's all.*

'Unfortunately, Ava must have deteriorated quite rapidly after she came in,' Elizabeth said in her unnervingly calm, measured way. 'She was admitted to A&E later that night, gravely ill, where she was diagnosed with bronchial pneumonia. She's been in intensive care ever since.'

All the air seemed to leave Freya's lungs. For a moment she felt as breathless as poor tiny Ava must have done. 'Oh God,' she said hoarsely. She *had* listened to Ava's chest, though, she told herself. She was sure she'd listened, and there had been no wheezing or any shortness of breath. Had there? All of a sudden she couldn't be certain. She'd been on automatic pilot, feeling miserable and thinking about drinking gin, she remembered guiltily.

Her mouth dry, she took a gulp of too-hot coffee, barely noticing the way it scalded. Bronchial pneumonia, *shit*. That was never good, particularly when it concerned a six-month-old infant. 'Is she going to be okay?'

'Mrs Taylor didn't go into details.' Elizabeth gave a small sigh. 'I'm afraid to say, she has made an official complaint about your conduct and the way you handled her inquiry.' She glanced back down at the letter. 'She claims you were negligent and didn't take her worries seriously. She also claims that because of your response – that Ava was healthy and merely had a cold – she delayed going to the hospital because she didn't want to make a fuss.'

Melanie Taylor didn't want to make a fuss? Christ, that would be a first. Freya couldn't help but fight her corner. 'Elizabeth, I don't believe I was negligent,' she said, trying to control the trembling in her voice. 'I gave the baby an examination, I checked her temperature and breathing, I looked in her mouth. Her chest was clear, her throat looked a bit sore – which I did mention to Mrs Taylor – but there was no evidence of coughing or rapid breathing, and only a slight fever.' She was getting into her stride now, voice rising. 'I'm sorry to hear that Ava's condition worsened so quickly, but isn't that often the case with bronchial pneumonia in infants? I'm not a fortune teller, I can't see three hours into the future when a baby takes a turn for the worse!'

Oops. She probably shouldn't have said that last bit. She'd been doing so well until then, too. Now she could feel herself getting pink in the face and rattled.

Elizabeth's gaze was coolly appraising as always. Her eyebrows twitched together in a small frown and then, after an agonizing pause, she said delicately, 'I don't like to ask this, as I'm sure it must be wrong, but Mrs Taylor has also accused you of . . . er . . . "drinking on the job", as she called it. Obviously, I am confident this is a ridiculous claim but I have to mention it to you, as your manager. She said she saw a bottle of alcohol in your handbag.'

Hot colour flared in Freya's cheeks and she couldn't speak for a moment. 'That's just . . .' She spluttered, the words refusing to be summoned. 'That's ludicrous,' she got out, crossing her fingers under the desk. 'And completely untrue.'

Oh no. So Melanie *had* seen the gin bottle sticking out like that. No wonder she had gone nuclear. Freya hung her head, unable to look Elizabeth in the eye. It was, without a doubt, the worst moment ever in her professional career. She had not been drinking on the job. Sure, she might have been momentarily tempted, and yes, she'd felt miserable enough to have a bottle of gin at hand for that evening's recreational use. But she hadn't actually drunk any at work. Ever. It wasn't as if she had a *problem*!

Elizabeth cleared her throat. 'Is everything all right, Freya?' she asked gently. 'I know you've recently lost your father, but . . .'

Freya's palms became clammy. Don't say her boss believed Melanie. Had Elizabeth noticed all those early-morning hangovers, the scent of desperation that had clung so persistently in recent weeks? Her imagination went into overdrive and she found herself envisaging random bag-checks for all staff members, a breathalyser installed in the reception area.

'I'm fine,' she stammered, trying to ignore her inner turbulence. 'Absolutely fine. Bit tired, that's all. Looking forward to going on holiday next week.'

'Of course,' said Elizabeth, ever the concerned professional. 'Well, it sounds to me as if you did all the right things and were not in any way negligent, but we do have to follow procedure, I'm afraid.'

'Right,' Freya replied wretchedly. 'Of course.'

'I'll respond, suggesting that the three of us hold a meeting to discuss what – if anything – went wrong, and how we might learn from the situation. Once Ava's out of hospital, naturally.'

Freya's heart sank like an expensive watch in a swimming pool. 'Fine,' she said, knowing she had little choice. A meeting would mean looking Melanie in the eye and saying that she had been mistaken about the gin bottle. Freya was not a great liar. She would crumble as readily as a soft digestive.

Elizabeth rose to her feet, the file close to her chest. Freya could only guess at the questions fermenting in her boss's mind. *Is everything all right, Freya? Have you got an alcohol problem, Freya? Are you having a nervous breakdown, Freya?*

'Right,' Elizabeth said. 'Well, I'll let you know her response, and if there's any news about Ava. And Freya . . .' She rested her free hand on the back of the chair. 'I'm here, don't forget. If you ever want a chat, or to take a break, come and talk to me. I lost my dad too last year. I know how hard it is.'

Tears brimmed unexpectedly in Freya's eyes. Hot, stupid tears of weakness that took her completely by surprise. Within these four walls, she had always prided herself on her competence, skill and knowledge. She wasn't used to anyone looking at her with concern or doubt, let alone having her boss sizing her up, wondering if she was still fit for purpose.

Swallowing back the lump in her throat, she turned to her computer. Brisk, efficient, in control. 'Thank you,' she muttered. *Please go now*, she thought. *Go, before I start weeping embarrassingly and pouring out all my problems. Go, while I still have some last semblance of dignity.*

Elizabeth left. As the door closed gently behind her, Freya opened her mouth in a silent scream of anguish.

Chapter Six

Robert came back from the fancy publishing party quite drunk: tie askew, face mottled, breath so alcoholic he could strip paint from twenty paces. Contrary to appearances, he assured Harriet that it had been practically the most tedious night of his life. 'Those people,' he sighed dramatically, collapsing onto the bed still fully dressed. 'What a shower of knobheads, honestly. What a complete and utter parade of giant tits.' His arm dropped across her and she rolled her eyes in the darkness, anticipating his next words with astonishing clairvoyance. 'Talking of which . . .'

Harriet, who was still rather miffed that she'd been left with a pair of itching orange legs and badly pencilled eyebrows for no good reason, moved away from his fumbling hands. 'I'm tired,' she replied.

'Oh, Aitch,' he groaned, rolling clumsily along the bed so as to spoon behind her body – a fairly ambitious feat, seeing as she was under the duvet and he was on top of it. 'Don't be like that. It was terrible. Woeful. Take pity on a husband. Spare some kindness for a bloke . . .'

Harriet snorted but he seemed to take this as encouragement because he immediately began wrestling to insert a hand under the covers. 'Where was my beautiful wife?' he cried dramatically, ferreting around hopefully. 'How I longed for my gorgeous wife! When instead I was cast adrift, alone, into a sea of intelligentsia . . .'

'A sea of booze, more like.'

'These shallow waters of . . . Mmm, hello.'

He'd somehow managed to wriggle under the covers, still fully dressed, and his hand was now resting warmly on her hip. Despite her earlier crossness, Harriet found herself thawing. There was something about drinking that transformed her husband into a sex-crazed teenager trying to hump her leg. She should be disapproving but it was actually rather endearing in a pathetic sort of way. He'd probably be asleep in two minutes anyway.

She sighed, defeated. 'Go on, then. Tell me a bit more about how awful it was.'

He didn't need any encouragement and pressed closer into her. 'The women were all monstrous. Dreadful old sexless matrons with warts and chin hair. You would have been the most bewitching creature there by far.'

'Do you think so?'

'I know so. And the food was nearly as dull as the conversation. You'd have hated it. Strange canapés, greasy little sausages . . .'

'Talking of greasy little sausages . . .' Harriet teased, reaching a hand behind for him. 'I'm joking, all right!' she spluttered as he in turn gave an indignant snort. Then she sat up and burst out laughing. 'Rob,' she said. 'Are you still wearing your shoes?'

It showed how much she loved Robert, that Harriet could shrug off small things with ease: the party invitation debacle (he *hadn't* told her she wasn't invited, whatever he claimed); the completely unbelievable fibs he'd come up with in his pretence of having a terrible night (matrons with chin hair indeed); and as for the god-awful snoring that began rumbling from his throat when he fell asleep on his back moments later, Harriet was sure that plenty of wives faced with a similar situation might have been compelled to put a pillow over that wide-open mouth and hold it there until silence fell.

Instead, she lay in the darkness, thinking for the millionth time how lucky she was to have met him and how glad she was to be beside him right now, snoring or not. Sometimes she honestly felt as if her heart was so brimful of complete and utter love for him it might just burst.

Ahh, Robert! After Harriet's first marriage had bottomed out so disastrously seven years ago – was there a woman left in London that Evil Simon *hadn't* slept with? – she had plunged into a freefall of despair, abandoning all hope of anything nice ever happening to her again. Back then, her daughter Molly was eight, and the two of them had clung together, lonely and uncertain, in their small rented flat. Harriet told herself repeatedly that she didn't need a man to mess them around and cause any more trouble, she was better off without endless dropped phone calls and suspiciously muffled conversations, and that she definitely wouldn't go anywhere near a lying, cheating heartbreaker again, for as long as she lived. Positive thinking was the key, her best friend Gabbi kept saying. (Apparently Gabbi looked in her mirror every morning and told herself, 'I love you, you're amazing, you're the greatest woman that ever lived', no doubt with adoring sincerity. She probably even kissed the mirror sometimes.)

While Harriet thought this a tad extreme, she did tentatively attempt her own version of positive reinforcement, reminding her cynical-looking reflection that she had Molly, excellent friends and just enough money to scrape by. And anyway, maybe being single wasn't quite as spirit-pulverizing as everyone said. At least she got to eat ice cream in bed, and watch trashy American reality shows without anyone complaining. *Match of the Day* could jog on, too. Men – pffft. She was so over them.

But then she met Robert – at a beginners' furniture-making class, of all places – and had to reassess her plans overnight. The class was a birthday present from Gabbi ('It'll be *full* of hot blokes, I bet you,' she had said unsubtly when Harriet opened the envelope and frowned at the voucher inside) and Harriet, who was about as competent with a hammer and saw as her eighty-year-old grandmothers, almost bottled it at the last minute. Thank goodness she hadn't. Thank goodness, too, that she'd randomly sat down next to Robert in the workshop: funny, laughing, dark-haired Robert, who helped her with the plane and took the mick out of her for squealing the first time she used the drill.

Much as she hated to admit it to Gabbi (her friend could be unbearably smug about these things), Harriet quickly found herself looking forward to Thursday evenings amidst the sawdust and wood shavings, trying to concentrate on what Liam, the earnest tutor, was saying about dovetail joints, but finding her gaze straying instead across to broad-shouldered, gorgeous Robert. She was tortured by the way his hair fell just a fraction too long and shaggy on the back of his neck; she found herself fantasizing about the day-old dark stubble like iron filings around his jaw and how it would feel against her skin. By the second lesson, she'd managed to drop into the conversation that she was single and by the fourth, when she absolutely couldn't wait any longer, she asked him out for a drink. The rest was history. When the course finally drew to an end, Harriet might not have had a decent piece of furniture to show for her efforts – her foot-stool was indeed the object of much derision from her daughter and now lived hidden away in the bathroom where it had the lowly task of supporting a small wicker basket of toilet rolls – but who cared? She'd only gone and bagged herself the loveliest man in all of London Town instead. 'Didn't I tell you?' Gabbi crowed when she broke the news. 'Didn't I say this would happen?'

Harriet smiled to herself in bed. Finding Robert had been worth all of Gabbi's smugness. It was even worth putting up with a bit of drunken warthog snoring now and then. Because just look at her now: happily married with a great daughter, secure job and a holiday on the horizon. Who could want for more?

Chapter Seven

How strange it seemed, packing only for one's self this summer, Olivia thought, folding clean clothes into the suitcase. For the last ten or eleven years, Alec had routinely travelled to Shell Cottage a few weeks ahead of her in order to work, and his subsequent phone calls always involved detailing the many things he wanted her to add to her case. 'Forgot my shaver,' he'd say cheerfully while she scribbled it at the bottom of her (already extensive) list. 'The nights are on the chilly side, could you bring my slippers?' he would remember another evening.

She would tsk affectionately and call him a hopeless old man, and ask what his last slave had died of, but she never really minded. In fact, she rather liked feeling so helpful, so needed. It was a little reminder of how indispensable she was, how tightly they were still tied together. Then, as soon as he'd finished with his novel, and had sent it off to his editor and agent, he'd be back on the phone to her at once, for one final call: 'I'm all yours, sweetheart. Come on down. I miss you.'

Silly, wasn't it, that after almost forty years of marriage, she had still felt such a frisson at his low, husky words down the telephone. She'd be all packed by then, of course, her bags waiting in the hall, the previous couple of days usually spent in an agony of limbo as she waited for her orders. Some years, his call came later than others, if he'd had to wrestle particularly hard with a book, and she would become positively agitated for him, unable to settle to her own work, or the weeding, or even coffee with a neighbour, because her mental energy was elsewhere, willing him on to succeed. Then when the phone did finally ring, and she was officially permitted to join him for their holiday – oh my goodness, the great rush of pride and joy she felt every time. 'Well done,' she would cry, more ecstatic than him, even. 'Well done, darling. I'm on my way.'

She'd glimpse him as she drove up the lane, waving both arms above his head on the terrace, almost knocking off that ridiculous straw hat he liked to wear. He'd be unshaven and dishevelled by then, of course – feral, she'd tease him – but brimming with elation, work done, time to have some fun.

She tried not to think about that now as she carefully packed the last few things: her toothbrush and toiletries, a handful of Teddy's plastic dinosaurs she'd found solemnly standing sentry around the shrubbery the other day, where he must have forgotten them, and, somewhat reluctantly, Alec's final manuscript, neatly printed and slotted into a cardboard folder. 'Do you think you could get back to me by the beginning of August?' Eleanor, his editor, had said on the phone the other day, her voice rather high and tight as if someone was slowly strangling her. 'It's just . . . we'd love to publish it for Christmas as originally scheduled but it'll have to be a very tight turnaround, so . . .'

Olivia hadn't promised anything. She still wasn't sure she wanted to read Alec's final work, knowing that there would be no further words to come from him. She was worried it might unhinge her even more.

Anyway, she could think about all of that once she'd arrived in Silver Sands. Everything always seemed easier when one was in Shell Cottage. The London house had felt like a cage ever since Alec's death, a prison of sorrow, too airless, too silent, too empty without him. It would do her good to escape.

She zipped up the case, loaded it into the boot and locked the front door, her fingers trembling on the key as she was struck by sudden apprehension about the long journey ahead and whether she could manage it after all. *Come on, Liv*, she imagined him saying to her. *Think of it as an adventure, not a problem, eh?*

But as she started the car and drove carefully down the road, she couldn't help wondering if all her adventures were behind her now. When she missed her husband so desperately, how could this summer without him contain anything other than sorrow?

To her surprise, Olivia's spirits did lift a fraction once she had left London and all its impatient, lane-cutting drivers behind. She'd taken Alec's Audi, which was much nicer to drive than her ancient Renault, and she filled the car with the swelling crescendos of a favourite violin concerto. As she headed further west, the motorway ran through rolling green hills and fields of swaying golden wheat, with distant church spires and pretty villages visible beyond. Maybe Robert had been right, she thought: despite the ever-present grief lying like a lead weight in her gut, getting away might actually do her some good. At the very least, it would mean a break from wandering about the Hampstead house alone, with the terrible sapping listlessness she'd felt in recent weeks. There would be no ringing phone or doorbell to bother her, and she could spoil herself rotten with lovely long coastal walks, a glass of wine in the garden as the sun set, and all the books and DVD box sets she'd brought with her in case of rainy days. She might even head out on a boat trip, something seasick-prone Alec had never enjoyed.

Silver Sands village seemed chilly and grey when she reached it some hours later, and she drove the final few hundred metres up the lane towards Shell Cottage feeling a quiet triumph for having actually made it there under her own steam. But then the empty terrace came into view – no Alec to greet her this year – and tears immediately pricked her eyes.

No crying, she ordered herself, blinking them fiercely away. *No mawkishness*. She would mix herself a mug of hot choco-late instead, she decided, throw on a big sloppy jumper and some sandals, and wander down to the beach. The bay would be largely empty on a day like today, no doubt, save for a few hardcore 'We WILL have fun on the beach if it kills us' holidaymakers. She would perch on a rock, sip her drink and gaze out to sea, letting the breeze blow away her troubles. The sight of the waves crashing and rolling in on the sand always helped her relax.

Reaching the driveway, she was surprised to see a small red Fiat already parked there, before realizing it must belong to the housekeeper, Katie. Good old Katie! Hopefully she'd be almost finished, leaving the house clean and hoovered, cush-ions plumped, beds newly made, like the little angel she was. No doubt Olivia would have to endure yet another earnest sympathy conversation – everyone had loved Alec, and they all wanted to tell her just how sorry they were at great length – but with a bit of luck she could get it over with quickly, then close the door and have the place to herself.

'Hello? I'm here!' she called, heaving her case in through the open front door. She was surprised to hear music playing from upstairs, then even more taken aback to see a large vase of red roses in the hall and what looked like lunch set out on the kitchen table. She stared at the ready-sliced quiche and bowls of salad, the plate of cream cakes under a protective fly cover, two empty wine glasses, and three place settings. For a crazy moment she thought she'd walked into the wrong house, the wrong holiday. Oh goodness. Was she losing the plot now?

No. Of course she wasn't. There was her cooker, the cheerful striped window blind, the knotty pine table. Everything was in its place. And yet . . .

Then came a shout – 'Dad's here! I saw his car!' – and the sound of racing footsteps. Flummoxed, she whirled around to see a boy burst into the room. He stopped when he saw her and his face froze. 'Oh.'

'You're . . . you're looking for your dad?' Olivia ventured. She'd never heard Katie talk about a husband or partner before. Or a son, for that matter.

The boy squirmed at the question but didn't reply. He was gangly and dark-haired, all sharp elbows and knobbly knees, the same sort of age as Dexter, she guessed, eleven or twelve. 'What are you doing here?' she asked gently when he didn't reply. Was he even Katie's son at all, Olivia wondered, trying to work out why he was in her house. Had he wandered down from the village, found the door open and ambled in like a stray cat?

But then she remembered the three place settings on the table, the two wine glasses. She hadn't come on the wrong day, had she? Maybe she *was* having a senior moment. But then Katie wouldn't be throwing a lunch for somebody else in her house! Anyway, she was certain Robert had said the 14th of July. She could almost hear him reading the words aloud as he had typed them: *If you could have everything ready as usual for my arrival on the . . . What shall I say, the 14th of July?*

Something was wrong here. Something wasn't quite adding up. It *was* the 14th of July today, wasn't it? All of a sudden, she wasn't sure.

Before Olivia could ask the boy anything else, Katie's voice came floating down the stairs. 'Sorry, I didn't hear you, I had the music on and – ' Then she entered the kitchen and it was her turn to look stunned when she saw Olivia standing there. Well, who had she been expecting, for goodness' sake?

'Olivia,' Katie said, her voice hoarse, her complexion suddenly pale. 'I thought . . . Where's Alec?'

Olivia stared at her, dumbfounded. Was this some kind of a cruel *joke*? 'Alec's dead,' she said, after a long terrible moment, her hands curling around the top of a chair, in sudden need of support.

Katie let out a gasp. Her hand flew up to her chest. 'He's . . . What?' Her face crumpled. 'He's *dead*? What do you mean? When?'

The boy's eyes widened and his mouth fell open. His gaze

flicked from Katie to Olivia to Katie again. 'Mum?' he said. 'What's happening?'

Tears were pouring down Katie's cheeks. 'But the email . . . He said he was coming, the usual arrangements . . .'

Oh dear. It had been such a blur, keeping track of who they had and hadn't told the sad news to. Most of Alec's peers and colleagues had heard through the publishing grapevine, of course; there had been obituaries in the broadsheets, and he'd even had a few mentions on the news channels. But somehow – terribly – they had omitted to tell poor Katie.

'The email was from Robert,' she said haltingly. 'He must have sent it from Alec's account. I'm sorry we didn't let you know earlier but it's all been rather overwhelming.' Olivia's gaze returned to the lunch set out for three on the table, then snagged on the red roses. Red roses? She looked from the flowers to Katie who was still sobbing. Her mind was suddenly too full of questions to think straight. 'What's going on?' she asked. 'I don't understand. Were you expecting someone?'

Katie said nothing, her face in her hands. The boy was still staring at her, aghast, and a terrible thought began blooming in Olivia's mind, like a bloodstain spreading on fabric, seeping larger and larger by the second. Katie really was very upset. More upset than Olivia would have anticipated. And the boy, too – he'd talked about seeing 'Dad's car' outside, hadn't he? Surely that didn't mean . . . ?

She blinked, trying to clear her thoughts. The sickly scent of the roses caught in her throat and she held tightly to the chair, giddy and unnerved. 'Katie?' she prompted. 'Tell me the truth. What's going on?'

There was an agonizing silence for a few seconds. Then Katie wiped her eyes on the back of her hands, took a deep shuddering breath and put a protective arm around the boy. 'This is Leo,' she said, drawing herself up taller. Her eyes met Olivia's. 'Alec's other son.'

Chapter Eight

It was the final week of term and the change in atmosphere at Riverdale Academy was palpable. The exams were over, the Year 11s had left with the usual fanfare and scandal of prom night, and from her office window Harriet could hear the steady *swish-thock* of Wimbledon-inspired student tennis tournaments on the courts outside. Three days left to go now, and everyone had their eyes on Friday afternoon and that glorious, yearned-for 'School's out!' moment when the building would empty one last time, and the classrooms fall silent. Woohoo! No students, no paperwork, no infuriating new directives from the government, just six weeks of peace and tranquillity, the chance to close one's eyes and think about absolutely nothing for a change, apart from perhaps where the next ice cream or cold beer was coming from. Bring it ruddy well on.

As the school's child protection officer, Harriet often had mixed feelings about the end of term. Much as she was gagging for a holiday herself, she couldn't help worrying about the students in her care who led such precarious, chaotic lives. During term-time, she was their ally amidst the mayhem, the one who had their backs and noticed when things were going downhill. But who would keep an eye on Latisha and her family problems over the holidays? Or Kwame, who'd been sofa-surfing for two months after the latest bust-up with his evangelical mother? Or Sasha, who had just confessed to Harriet that she was pregnant at the age of fourteen and scared about having become involved with a horrible gang? Sometimes she had only just made a break-through with a teenager when the holidays started and it was as if all her patient, careful work had been for nothing.

You had to have boundaries. You couldn't carry everyone else's problems around the whole time. You had to know when to switch off, close down that compartment in your mind and leave it at the office – these were fundamental rules of her job. But it was hard for soft-hearted Harriet to block out the kids in her care, especially when she'd built up some trust. Their faces would come to her over the summer and she would wonder with a pang how they were coping, alone in the wilderness of the holidays. And then, come September, she'd spend the first week or so practically hold-ing her breath while she did a mental headcount, checking up on her students, counting them all back in again.

Still. She was tired, weighed down by their problems and heartbreak, by every injustice they faced. And actually, there were some things she wouldn't miss about being here and dealing with stroppy, angry, often rude teenagers day in day out. Just that morning, Violet Parker had laughed in her face and said, 'Whoa, Miss, what's going on with them funky eyebrows, then? Was it, like, a bet or summink? Was you drunk or what?'

Yeah. A break from the personal comments would be nice.

Meanwhile, Molly and Robert were on good form and looking forward to their upcoming holiday. There were all sorts of activities laid on for the students at Molly's school this week, probably in an attempt to stop the Year 10s bunking off en masse, and today she was going on a trip to Stratford-upon-Avon with the English department. Harriet had been astonished to hear that her book-dodging daughter had actually chosen this option, voluntarily, without any kind of bribery, especially as all her friends seemed to have plumped for trips that sounded way more fun – to the Tate Modern or the Olympic Park. Secretly, she was thrilled. Could this be Robert's good influence rubbing off on his stepdaughter, inspiring her to develop a love of literature? Miracles happened, she supposed.

Robert also had a big day today – an important lunch meeting with both his British and American editors in town, at some gastro place called the Marylebone Tavern. 'We're going to wade through the entire manuscript together, chapter by chapter, and discuss how to finesse it,' he'd told her rather grandly the night before as they snuggled on the sofa in front of a cop drama on TV. (Well, he was watching it anyway. She was distracted by watching him shove handfuls of Kettle Chips into his gob and wishing she had a higher performing metabolism.)

Lucky, lucky Robert, Harriet thought now as she made herself a gritty instant coffee from the last dregs of the jar and waved hello to one of her colleagues across the staff room. It certainly seemed to take a lot of eating and drinking to get a book published, in her opinion. How the other half lived!

'Will you be coming back after the holidays?' Alison, one of the teaching assistants, had asked her the other week, only half joking. 'If my hubby hit the big time, I'd be tempted to retire and lie around on a chaise longue eating chocolate all day.'

Harriet had laughed, not taking the question seriously, but later that afternoon, when she was told to fuck off (twice) and called a fat nosey bitch on the phone by Lillie Arnold's alcoholic mother, she lay her head on the desk, wondering, as she sometimes did, why she bothered. Maybe it would be easier to turn her back on it all, simply stick two fingers up at Mrs Arnold and all those other crap, useless parents she came across who seemed hell-bent on ruining their children's lives.

It was actually quite tempting now she thought about it.

She could become Robert's glamorous assistant and drive him around to his meetings and parties. Perhaps in a saucy little uniform – he'd like that . . .

The bell rang just then, signalling the end of break time, and Harriet snapped out of her reverie. Three days left of term. She could make it.

Harriet was only due to be in school for the morning that day, with a gruelling afternoon looming, where she and a local police officer had to attend a meeting at the parental home of one of her students, to discuss the boy's welfare. The boy in question had been coming to school late every day, and had recently turned up with bruises and a black eye, and Harriet had strong suspicions that the bruising was down to his father, a known thug who'd been in trouble with the police before. The family lived in a flat near Edgware Road, but it was only when she and the police officer had been knocking on the front door for five minutes that a neighbour stuck her head out of her window and told them the family were away.

Harriet didn't like the sound of that, but unfortunately there wasn't much they could do about it now, and so she had to beat a helpless retreat.

Now what? It wasn't worth trawling all the way back to school for the last hour, so Harriet wandered towards Marylebone Road, the air sultry and smelling of diesel, deciding that she might as well seize the chance to pick up a few things for the holiday. They were due to set off for Devon at the weekend, and in all the end-of-term kerfuffle she'd hardly had a chance to think about it.

It was going to be a fantastic fortnight away, she had already decided. With Molly coming up for sixteen in November, Harriet was well aware that this might easily be the last time her daughter deigned to join them on a family holiday before she had her head turned by the joys of festival trips or mooching about in London all summer with mates instead. It seemed like five minutes ago that Molly had been obsessed by making sandcastles and moats, and collecting every last shell on the beach. Now she was taller than Harriet, and more interested in building a follower base on Instagram than any sandy constructions. Where had the years gone?

Molly had been turning her nose up at the prospect of another holiday in Devon with the in-laws, especially when her friends were apparently off to Ibiza and the Greek islands, but Harriet loved the old-fashioned seaside holiday appeal of Shell Cottage. The house was beautiful yet homely, the beach was absolutely blissful, and you could go mountain biking or horse riding or hiking and really switch off and forget about the rest of the world. Of course, to her daughter, the very thought of 'switching off' was anathema, to be greeted with undiluted horror. Molly was already stressing about the dodgy Wi-Fi but you couldn't have everything.

Anyway, Harriet had an ace up her sleeve. Next summer, when Robert's book had been published and they hopefully had money pouring in like nobody's business, they could go somewhere more glamorous themselves – Tuscany, Florida, Provence, anywhere they fancied, basically. She'd lure Molly into another holiday by promising her exotic luxury and guaranteed sunshine. Yes, of course it was shameless bribery. But if she could squeeze an extra fortnight away with her daughter, before Molly decided she was too sophisticated to be seen dead holidaying with her embarrassing mother, then bring on the shameless bribery. It would be worth every penny.

She had reached the chemist now, so walked in and began adding toiletries to her basket: suncream (hey, she was an optimist), insect bite cream (and also a realist), hair conditioner and aftersun, the shaving gel Robert liked . . .

Then a thought struck her. Wait a minute! Hadn't Robert said he was in Marylebone too today? Her local geography was pretty hazy but the Marylebone Tavern couldn't be that far from here, surely. Maybe his lunch was still going on! She felt a pulse of excitement at the notion. She could offer to meet him afterwards for a debrief over coffee, get all the goss about exactly what the American editor had said. Robert had mentioned the possibility of an American tour to promote the book, and Harriet was definitely going to invite herself and Molly along for *that*, if it happened.

Hi love, how did mtg go? she texted, the basket of toiletries awkwardly balanced on one arm as she typed. **Could meet you for coffee afterwards if you fancy it?**

His reply came two minutes later as she was paying for her purchases at the till.

Sorry, will be a while yet! Lots to discuss – but going v well. Xx

Harriet wrinkled her nose in disappointment then stuffed the phone back in her bag and handed over a twenty-pound note to the cashier. Oh well. It had been a long shot, she supposed. With a bit of luck, that American editor would be drunk by now and promising Robert that yes, of *course* his wife and stepdaughter could join him for the New York leg of the tour . . .

She rolled her eyes at her own pipe dream and left the shop. Now to bump straight back down to earth by seeing if she could hunt down a pair of shorts on the high street which didn't make her bottom look too elephantine. 'This could take a while,' she murmured to herself as she strode grimly forwards.

After a bruising hour spent wincing at the sight of her unflattering-shorts-wearing reflection in various changing rooms, Harriet decided to abandon the idea and wear long, leg-hiding skirts all summer instead, whatever the weather. Even on the beach if she had to. Never mind that Robert's sister Freya was sure to be swishing around in floaty chiffon tops and stylish tea dresses in Devon. Never mind that Olivia, Robert's mum, was the most intimidatingly elegant woman ever, even when she'd been swimming in the sea, for heaven's sake, somehow remaining luminous and poised when every-one else was soggy and tousled with salt in their hair. Never mind that Harriet's only existing shorts were a pair of denim cut-offs which were getting a bit thin between the thighs now and had a grease mark on one buttock, where she'd acciden-tally sat on a discarded chip paper at Notting Hill Carnival last year.

To hell with the search for new shorts. Everything she tried on made her look like a comedy holidaymaker, rather than chic beach goddess. She just had to hope that Olivia and Freya didn't remember the denim cut-offs from last summer and – worse – chose to comment on them. *Goodness, Harriet, they've lasted well, haven't they?* Shorthand for *Goodness, Harriet, buy yourself a new pair of ruddy shorts, will you, for crying out loud? Those ones are hanging by a thread, you cheapskate.*

No. They weren't like that, thank God. And if they did notice, they were both too well mannered to comment any-way. *And besides, Harriet,* she told herself, suddenly cross at her own self-absorption, *they'll be far too preoccupied with eve-rything else, i.e. missing poor dead Alec, to give your fat arse a second glance, for heaven's sake.* If anyone was going to be rude about her attire, it would be Molly, who seemed to think Harriet chose each outfit specifically to annoy or embarrass her.

Marylebone was one of Harriet's favourite places to browse, with the heavenly cheese shop, gorgeous boutiques and cool Scandi design shops tucked into the stately Victorian mansion blocks and Georgian houses. Yet today, she felt defeated. By the time she'd slunk empty-handed from the last clothes shop she could bear to trawl through, she wished more than ever that Robert had taken her up on the offer of coffee and a chat. He was the lovely sort of husband who could reassure a woman about her thunder thighs in a way that was actually convincing. Or else he'd just take the mick out of her for caring and turn the whole thing into an affectionate joke, somehow managing to cheer her up and make her feel devastatingly attractive to the whole of humankind before she knew it.

She wondered for the hundredth time how his lunch meeting was going . . . and then let out a gasp of excitement as she noticed that the Marylebone Tavern was just across the street. Ooh! *Quel coinkydink*, as Molly would say. Should she peer through the window? Pretend to be casually passing by and – *Oh! Robert! Fancy seeing you here! Why yes, of course, I'd love to join you for dessert. Wine, too? Ah, go on, then, why not? Hi there. Great to meet you. Did I mention I've always wanted to go to the States, by the way? Like, seriously, always?*

Better not. But there was no harm in nonchalantly cross-ing the road, was there? No harm in dawdling along slowly past the restaurant with maybe just a very quick gander inside. No harm at all, she assured herself firmly, unable to resist seeing handsome, talented Robert there in his best shirt, living the dream.

It was only when she was on the other side of the street that she noticed something odd. The inside of the restaurant seemed dull and dingy, unlit. There were no tables set up outside either – strange, on such a glorious summer's day. And then, as she drew level with the front door, she saw to her bewilderment a 'Closed' sign in the glass pane. *Closed for two weeks due to renovations*, read a printed piece of paper.

What the . . . ? She stood stock-still in the street and ·removed her sunglasses in case her eyes were playing tricks on her.

Closed for two weeks due to renovations. No. There was nothing wrong with her eyes. The Marylebone Tavern wasn't open – so where the hell was Robert?

Chapter Nine

One hundred miles or so away, around the back of a multi-storey car park in Stratford-upon-Avon, Molly was fervently kissing Ben Jamison and gasping as his hand tugged her school blouse out of her skirt's waistband. 'Oh, Ben,' she said, her breathing fast and shallow. His fingers slipped under her blouse and her nerve endings fizzled deliriously as he touched her bare skin. Then his fingertips grazed the under-side of her breast and it was as if fireworks were star-bursting inside her.

Oh. My God. No way. Was this really happening? It was amazing. *He* was amazing. And to think she'd nearly been swayed by Chloe, badgering her to go on the Tate Modern trip with the rest of their mates! She'd just had a feeling about today, though. All those meaningful looks she and Ben had exchanged across the classroom recently. She'd had an ink-ling he might like her but hardly dared hope anything would happen. Yet now . . .

'Oh,' she gasped, deliciously shivery at what his fingers

were doing, the sensation of his mouth on hers. He pressed his body against her and she could feel the hardness in his groin. She'd never actually felt a penis before in real life. She hadn't even really *seen* one, not properly, unless you counted the dodgy film she and Chloe had sniggered over on Chloe's iPad last time they'd had a sleepover. The thought of taking her clothes off and letting a guy do *that* to her had always seemed faintly gross in the past. Like, ewww. Why would you?

Now she knew. Now she got it. Talk about a revelation. Talk about a voyage of discovery! She felt as if she was journeying to a brand new place and never wanted to return. For a brief wild moment, she felt as if she would do anything he asked her to. Anything. Right here behind the car park. Nudity. Penis-touching. All of it!

There was a disapproving cough behind them just then, audible even above the drum solo of Molly's heart and her gasping breaths. Ben must have heard it too because he stopped kissing her and pulled away hurriedly. Molly noticed an elderly lady giving them a very hard stare as she walked past them a few metres away, towing a tartan shopping trolley, and her cheeks flamed.

Ben laughed softly. 'Whoops,' he said, removing his hand and straightening his tie. 'I guess we'd better get back and meet the others. Find out some more about Shakespeare.' He traced a line down the side of her face and she felt her stomach somersault. 'You're so beautiful,' he said thickly. 'Oh, the things I could do to you, Molly Tarrant-Price.'

She giggled, feeling nervous and delighted and wanton all in the same moment. 'You're not so bad yourself,' she said, unable to look at him for blushing. He was *hot*, though, with those teasing blue eyes and dark hair. Different from the boys she'd fancied before, too. For a crazy moment, she wanted to pull him close to her again, resume the kissing. But he was checking his watch and the spell was broken.

'Shit. We're gonna be late,' he said. 'Look – let's just keep this to ourselves for now, yeah?'

'Sure,' she said, trying to act cool, like it was no big deal to have been snogging gorgeous Ben Jamison with such passion. She'd already decided she wouldn't blab about what had just happened anyway, not even to Chloe. Gossip went round school so fast, the last thing she wanted was everyone whispering behind her back.

He smiled at her and the rest of the world seemed to melt away, disapproving old ladies, gossiping friends and all. Then he leaned down and kissed her again, squeezing her breast this time. 'That's just for starters,' he said, low and husky, and the breath caught in the back of her throat in another gasp of desire.

Somehow or other, Molly managed to smile in reply but the rest of her body seemed beyond control, flooded with a mad racing deluge of endorphins. Oh my God. Ben Jamison, the most gorgeous person in the entire school had kissed her and told her she was beautiful. His fingers had been on her actual body. He'd said, 'That's just for starters,' as if he wanted more.

Whoa. Head rush. This was like being in the best sex dream ever, only it was real.

Heart fluttering, skin tingling, Molly tucked her blouse back into her skirt and followed him as they went to meet the others for the backstage theatre tour. Her head was in such a whirl, she could hardly see where she was going. How on earth was she going to concentrate on Shakespeare and acting and stuff after *that*?

Chapter Ten

It had been a whole month now since Freya had answered the phone to hear her husband say those terrible words, 'Hi, love, it's me. Listen, don't worry, but I'm in hospital. I've been stabbed,' but she still found herself reliving the absolute horror all over again whenever the memory flashed into her mind.

Stabbed. Her adrenalin had spun into hyperdrive with that one single syllable, her mind freezing in panic, bile rising in her throat. Back when she'd been a junior doctor, working in the busy A&E department of the Homerton Hospital, she'd seen countless stabbings, umpteen raw red slashes and punctures, where flesh had met a blade due to revenge or passion or sheer random violence. They had stitched up and mended each one, mopped up the blood and sent them home again, knowing that there would be plenty more to come, a never-ending stream of young men in the wrong place at the wrong time, often having tangled with the wrong people.

And now Victor had been added to that unfortunate club.

Stabbed, in the line of duty. Stabbed, saving the life of his colleague Tony. Freya had burst into the accident and emergency unit that day with pure dread running through her veins. It had only been a fortnight since her father's funeral, and she still hadn't surfaced from the plunging depths of grief. Now she found herself flooded with a new and terrible fear that she was about to lose her husband too. 'No,' she begged under her breath, just in case a benevolent god might be in the vicinity. 'Not both of them. Please.'

Victor had made light of the situation on the phone, of course – 'just some nutter with a knife,' he'd said. But he was tough, Vic, a real man's man. He was one of those blokes who'd say, 'I'm fine! Barely a scratch,' if he'd fallen headfirst down a mineshaft. Until she saw the damage for herself, she was officially in panic mode, fearing the worst.

Thank goodness, then, that it wasn't until she *had* seen him and knew he was going to be okay that she discovered it hadn't been 'some nutter with a knife' at all; it had been a psychopath wielding a samurai sword – a samurai sword! – and that all kinds of horrible damage might have been done.

The story was quite something. Vic and his colleague Tony had been called out to a disturbance in the Barclays bank in town, and arrived to find a crazed-looking man brandishing a seventy-centimetre gleaming sword and threatening the terrified staff. Lee Carlson, they now knew he was called: thirty-seven, local, no previous convictions. ('A bit of a loner', according to his neighbours and former colleagues. Defaulting on his mortgage payments, according to his bank. 'Just so fucking angry with banks and shit', according to the man himself, once he'd been locked in a cell and had given a statement. Like that made it all right.)

Victor and Tony had tried to calm Carlson down but he'd been wild with rage, out of control and swinging the sword above his head. He took offence to Tony calling him 'mate' and went berserk, launching himself at the terrified young bobby without warning. Victor responded instinctively, grabbing a rack of insurance and pension leaflets and throwing it at Carlson, before wrestling him to the ground. Unfortunately, though, while the two men grappled, Carlson managed to swing the sword around, catching the back of Vic's shoulder. The stab vest had saved him from too much damage, thank goodness, but the blade had sliced the top of his arm, creating a shallow wound that required stitching. 'I've had worse nicks shaving,' Vic had said (showing off because his colleagues were present, Freya thought) but there was some bruising and tenderness as well, and he'd walloped his head pretty hard when he and Carlson went down.

Back-up had arrived moments later, the weapon was confiscated, Carlson was hauled off to the nick, and an ambulance was called for Vic. Tony, who'd escaped unscathed, was wide-eyed with shock. 'You saved my life,' he kept saying dazedly, as if he couldn't quite believe it himself. 'You saved my life, mate. The man's a bloody hero, I'm telling you.'

Since then, the 'bloody hero' had had his photo taken for the local press, and been interviewed on local radio, much to his amusement ('Just doing my job. Any officer would have done the same'). He'd also had a pat on the back from the detective superintendent and been bumped up the queue to go off to this public order training course in Gravesend, which he was absolutely thrilled about.

Freya, meanwhile, felt as if she was still reverberating from the shock. They all were. She had played down the whole thing as best she could at home, but on the day of the incident, Dexter had said over dinner, ashen-faced, 'You can die from being stabbed, can't you, if the knife goes through one of your major arteries? I saw it on *24 Hours in A&E*, Mum. He could have died, Mum! Shit!'

'The stabbing man *is* in prison now, isn't he?' Libby had asked on numerous occasions, and particularly at bedtime, however much Freya had tried to reassure her. 'He's not going to come out and get Dad, or anything, is he?'

As for Teddy, Freya had received a phone call from his teacher at school to inform her that Teddy had started a gruesome playground game called 'Stabbers', and please could Freya have a word with him about it?

Yes, Freya had had plenty of words with her gory son about it since then. She'd sat up for several nights with Libby too, soothing her after bad dreams. And she'd seen Dexter break his own non-hugging rules and lean against Victor on the sofa a few times once he was home from the hospital, as if seeking the physical reassurance of his dad's living, breathing presence. They had all been left reeling by the reminder, yet again, of life's fragility.

Freya, for her part, hadn't wanted Vic to go on this two-week course so far from home. Tormented by all the terrible parallel outcomes that left her widowed weeks after losing her father, she had wanted him right there in Oakthorne where she could keep an eye on him, where she could curl up beside him at night, safe in the knowledge that the family were all together under the same roof.

Not that she'd said as much out loud, of course. Freya was a coper. She didn't go in for weakness or vulnerability, priding herself that her upper lip was so stiff it might as well be reinforced concrete. But God, it was hard work trying to manage everything on your own while your heroic husband was away, learning how to be even more heroic – especially when she could have done with being rescued just a little bit herself at the moment. Here she was, eating dinner with the children on automatic pilot, for instance, and all she could think about was whether it would be setting too appalling an example if she mixed herself a vodka tonic right now, just to take the edge off things. Probably.

'Mum! Are you listening? I said, Libby dropped her fish on purpose. Look!'

Freya blinked and tried to re-engage with the real world instead of her drinks cabinet. 'Sorry, what?'

'You *said* if she did that again, she'd have to go to bed early. Mum – *look*! It's there on the floor! Are you going to tell her off, or what?'

Twelve-year-old Dexter could be very severe when it came to busting his younger sister for her various teatime-related crimes. Unlike Freya, who would never refuse a plate of food unless unconscious or on her deathbed, Libby ate like a sparrow – pecking up a few meagre crumbs then claiming to be full. There was nothing wrong with a delicate appetite, obviously – what Freya wouldn't give for one herself – but it was the endless list of excuses she had to contend with that wore down her sanity. Last week tears had trembled in Libby's round blue eyes when Freya had cooked roast lamb ('I don't want to eat a *lamb*! They're really cute!'). At the weekend, there had been the cup of milk 'accidentally' knocked into her plate of sausage and mash ('I didn't do it on *purpose*!') and the handful of garden peas that Freya later found in her daughter's trouser pocket ('*I* didn't put them there!'). Today, it seemed that the salmon fillet had made a balletic leap of its own accord from Libby's plate onto the vinyl flooring, re-enacting a feat of athleticism it might once have made upstream in happier times.

Victor was able to display impressively abundant patience when it came to his daughter's culinary whims but Freya, always the one to cook, felt she was being driven slowly round the bend by one excuse after another.

'MUM! You need to tell Libby off. Tell her!'

'Yeah,' Teddy chipped in, always happy to see a sibling in trouble. 'Tell her, Mum.'

Dexter was turning red in the face; he was up from his chair and pointing, enraged both by the slack parenting on display and the fact that his sister might actually get away with her transgression. A seam of self-righteousness ran through her son; his catchphrase as a four-year-old had been 'That's not FAIR!' in such thunderous tones, it was enough to make even the most hardened criminal mastermind break into a sweat of self-reproach.

Freya did not have the energy to conduct a judicial review into crimes against salmon right now, though. 'Never mind,' she said wearily to Dexter. 'Let's just finish our tea, all right? I'll clear it up later.'

Out of the corner of her eye, she saw Libby stick her tongue out at her telltale brother and smirk with triumph.

Dexter's eyes shone with outrage. 'Right,' he said, and you could almost hear the cogs whirring furiously in his brain. 'So you don't care about fish on the floor, then? Fine!' And with that, he picked up his plate and tipped it sideways, so that everything on it – salmon, noodles, carefully chopped spring onions and baby corn, sticky sweet hoisin sauce, the lot – slithered off, landing with a series of splatters. There was a percussion of falling cutlery, the fork skidding straight under the fridge. 'Tala*manca*,' Teddy breathed in shocked delight and promptly hurled a mushroom overarm across the table, not wanting to miss out on any badness.

'That's enough!' shrieked Freya, her temper reaching breaking point. The hoisin sauce and olive oil were congealing stickily; the treacly mixture already gumming up the grooves of the expensive textured vinyl flooring laid a mere three months ago. It was going to be a bugger to clean up.

'Dexter Castledine, that is not acceptable,' she yelled, voice shaking. 'Go upstairs to your room and think about your behaviour. All of you, in fact. Just get out of my sight.' Her voice rose to a hysterical shriek. 'Go!'

'What about pudding?' Teddy asked, looking mutinous. He had a sweet tooth like her – he was anybody's for a tube of Smarties.

'No pudding,' Freya said in a strangled voice. 'Just go.'

They went, and she poured herself that vodka tonic and knocked it back in a single gulp.

You'd never know to look at him now but Dexter's very existence had wavered perilously for the first few weeks of his life. Born prematurely, he and Freya had spent an agonizingly stressful twenty-four days in the NICU at the local hospital after his unexpectedly early arrival. Twenty-four gruelling days during which every emotion it was possible for a human being to experience seemed to have been ripped from within her and hung out on public display. She felt turned inside out with worry, vulnerable and frightened. *So this is what parenthood means*, she thought, frazzled on caffeine and hormones and lack of sleep. *This is how it feels to love a person so desperately that you'd literally breathe for them if you could.*

Poor Dex, so small and shrunken in his perspex bed, a tube up his nose, a woollen cap on his bald head, the soft new Babygros heartbreakingly too long on his stick-thin legs. It was the first time in Freya's life that something had gone this wrong, spinning out of her control like a car on a wet road. The experience had shocked her so fundamentally that for years afterwards she would find herself holding her son close, listening to the steady thump of his heart to reassure herself that he was healthy and strong.

Of course – wouldn't you just know it – Dexter had spent his whole childhood as if he had some kind of death wish. He was the boy at nursery who managed to scramble out of the window, landing in a shrub outside with a soft, surprised thump. He was the boy who would race nimbly to the top of the highest climbing frame in any playground, shout, 'Hey, Mum, catch me!' and throw himself off, with Freya almost having a coronary each time she had to hurtle to catch him. He was the boy who'd always answer a dare, who'd jump off the shed roof because he was bored, who'd skateboard on the ramps with all the teenagers. By dint of sheer good luck, he'd somehow made it through twelve years of robust good health and become a clever, sporty boy, albeit one with a new proclivity for hurling his dinner around, it appeared.

She'd lived through all that fear and dread, though, she remembered now, kneeling down on the kitchen floor to pick up the spilled food. The scars of the special baby unit would be there on her heart for ever after. So when, she wondered, had she become so hardened to another new mother in a panic, another woman experiencing the same sort of anxiety? She'd fobbed off Melanie with casual reassurances last week because she couldn't wait to get rid of her, so desperate was she to go home and drown her own sorrows. And now poor, tiny Ava Taylor was struggling to breathe on a ventilation unit at the children's ward, her chest concave with effort, her lips turning blue. (Freya *had* listened to baby Ava's chest, though, that day. She had! And yes, she'd been distracted, but she would have noticed a wheeze or shortness of breath, wouldn't she? Wouldn't she?)

If only Vic was home right now to talk to. It wasn't the sort of thing you could bring up on the phone, not when his new course-mates were calling things to him in the background and she had the nagging feeling he wasn't listening properly. Without him around, she was left to sink into paranoia, with fears of official warnings, talk of negligence, her spotless record being tarnished, all battering her confidence.

Is everything all right, Freya? came the voice of Elizabeth, her boss, in her head. *I know you've recently lost your father, but . . .*

Oh, go away, Elizabeth. I'm fine, all right? I am absolutely bloody fine!

She began wiping the dark smeary sauce from the lino, still on her knees. It seemed that it wasn't only her career she was failing at these days, it was motherhood too. The meal just now had been a prime example. Maybe it was end-of-term fatigue, but the children had all been pushing the boundaries lately, defiant in the face of her half-arsed mothering. Four more days and they'd be off to Shell Cottage, she reminded herself, getting to her feet and trying not to look at the bottle of rioja lolling so temptingly in the metal wine rack. The holiday could not come soon enough.

Later that evening, when the house was eventually quiet, the sky dark outside and children everywhere were fast asleep and dreaming, she crept upstairs and looked in on each of her three.

The first bedroom smelled of socks and sweaty armpits. (She really had to set Dexter straight on personal hygiene; there were only so many times you could hint gently that a person needed a shower before you had to just come out and say, 'Mate, you stink, all right?') There lay her eldest son, the bruiser, so determined to lock horns and push against her these days, now in serene repose, his dark eyelashes smudgy against his pale cheek, his body relaxed for once. The sooner she got him to Shell Cottage the better, she thought to herself. He always regressed when he was there, rediscovering the childish pleasures of sandcastle-building and playing with his siblings. She hoped he could remember how to be a boy again for one more summer at least.

The room next door was Libby's, its walls a patchwork of animal posters, dance certificates and felt-tipped drawings. Libby, as usual, had flung the quilt off most of her body and Freya bent to straighten it, and tuck it around her, smelling her daughter's sour-sweet night breath. Darling Libby and her fondness for clashing colours and Knock Knock jokes; she was quirky and unconventional and daydreamy, a million miles from the serious little girl Freya had been. The other day Freya had overheard her singing to herself, and it was only when she listened harder that she realized the song was actually 'Sex Bomb' by Tom Jones, except her daughter was singing it as 'Sex Bum', which sounded even worse. *Don't go and grow up too fast on me, lovely Libby*, she thought with a pang.

And finally, there was Teddy, their funny little surprise baby, who had been jokingly referred to as 'The Accident' for the first seven months of the pregnancy – right until they heard Dexter conspiratorially saying, 'The baby in Mummy's tummy was an accident, you know,' to his Year 1 teacher, the unsmiling Mrs Lamb. Thank goodness for accidents, though! She couldn't imagine the family without golden-haired, laughing Teddy with his love of numbers and dinosaurs, and his wonky little glasses permanently balanced at an angle on his snub nose.

Gently, very gently, Freya lowered herself onto the end of Teddy's bed and rested a hand on his warm slumbering form. She thought of Ava across town in hospital, the rhythmic suck and *sssh* of the ventilator, the stifling, too-warm temperature of the ward, and the other grey-faced parents you passed in the corridor, all bearing enormous burdens of stress. It was like remembering a bad dream she'd once had, and her hand tightened inadvertently on her son's body. *If I thought for a single minute that anyone had misdiagnosed something crucial with one of my children*, she found herself thinking, *then I'd want to kill them too. I'd be shrieking down the phone, demanding someone's head on a plate.*

A shudder went through her. It didn't feel good to have turned into the sort of woman that mothers like her despised. It didn't feel good at all.

Chapter Eleven

In hindsight, Harriet should have spotted the philandering and dalliances of Evil Simon, her first husband, a mile off. The top notes of unfamiliar perfume in the car. The ringing phone that went mysteriously dead whenever she answered it. The times he was away on shoots and the filming schedule overran yet again. (Simon was a TV producer, specializing in natural history documentaries. Unfortunately, Harriet discovered far too late that his particular speciality seemed to be human mating habits and all their variations.)

Harriet had been blind to such malarkey, though, for two reasons. Firstly, because she was obviously the most gullible, trusting numpty ever to walk the earth. And secondly, because at the time she had been increasingly obsessed with trying to get pregnant again, after three agonizing miscarriages, and she could barely think about anything other than ovulation testing kits and whether or not they should just sod it and go for IVF.

It all fell into place with shocking vividness, though, the

day she was coming back from the hospital following – of all things – yet another miserable D&C experience. She hadn't even bothered to tell him she was pregnant that time because he was away on location and also she thought that maybe, just maybe, if she hugged the secret to herself, it wouldn't feel so bad if things went wrong again. (A misguided assumption as it turned out. If anything, a lonely secret miscarriage was a million times worse.)

It was a Tuesday lunchtime. Molly was safely at school, Simon was filming in Iceland, and there was Harriet, on the bus back to their flat, numb with sorrow, one hand across her (now vacated) belly. When the bus queued at the traffic lights and she glimpsed Simon on the opposite side of the road, she thought at first it must be a hallucination, brought on by the mega-strength painkillers the hospital had given her. That couldn't be right. He was supposed to be in Iceland, filming Atlantic puffins, not loitering on a street corner, talking to some random woman.

Her eyes narrowed. A *pregnant* woman, she noticed. Some friend of his he hadn't told her about? He must have come home early from filming to surprise Harriet – lovely! He had been on his way to the flat, but had bumped into this pregnant woman he'd met ages ago and . . .

Oh my God. Wait, though. Harriet froze, mouth dry, as she saw Simon lift his hand to the woman's face and cup it tenderly, before leaning in to kiss her for several long seconds.

Not a random pregnant woman, after all, she realized, but some bit on the side; a fertile, fecund mistress. He couldn't have hurt her more if he'd slapped her about the head with an actual Atlantic puffin.

Memories of that painful day seared through Harriet's head as she stood outside the very much closed Marylebone Tavern for a full two minutes, paralysed with shock. So her second husband had clearly lied about his whereabouts, just like her first had before him.

Oh no, she thought, her stomach lurching. *Not you as well, Robert. Not you!*

She tortured herself imagining him cosied up to some thin, beautiful mistress in a strange bedroom that very moment, while she stood there, pit-pony legs and all, the sting of betrayal like mocking laughter in her ears. Then she pictured Robert checking his phone when she texted earlier – *Shit, it's the wife. Give me a moment and I'll just fob her off . . .*

The thought was unbearable. Life-shattering. And yet in hindsight he *had* been kind of secretive recently. Jumpy, you could say. He'd spin round whenever she came into the room, and often close down the browser of his laptop before she could see what he was up to. But surely he wouldn't go behind her back like that with another woman? After all the shit she'd gone through with Evil Simon, too. Robert was different. Wasn't he?

He couldn't have lied, she decided in the next minute. No way. Robert just wasn't like that. He brought her a cup of tea most mornings! He emptied the dishwasher and hung out the laundry! He noticed when she was grumpy and tired, and gave her a back rub! Surely men with such an unusual and winning combination of talents couldn't then turn out to be snakes in the grass, could they? Was that even *allowed*?

They did say that fame and glory went to a person's head, though, she remembered glumly. Alongside all the dazzling pre-publication success he'd enjoyed, who knew what temptations had been wafting themselves under his nose lately?

With Simon, Harriet had buried her head in the sand for weeks after she knew the truth, kidding herself with a foolish, naive optimism that she could win him back, that it didn't matter. There would be no such cowardice with Robert, though, she vowed. The brave and battle-scarred version of Harriet would confront him the first chance she got.

As it turned out, that evening was the Year 10 end-of-term disco, to which Molly departed in a miasma of hairspray and cheap perfume, and Harriet and Robert were left sitting outside on their small patio which passed as a garden in this part of Finchley. The night-scented stocks were just starting to release their sweet perfume, Robert was in his running gear, waiting for his dinner to go down before he took off for a brisk five-miler around the streets, whereas she had a hot date lined up with the secret carton of Ben & Jerry's Cookie Dough ice cream hidden under the bag of peas in the freezer: the reward she had promised herself for being brave.

She cleared her throat. 'I need to ask you something.' The words sounded dramatic, as if she was a character in a soap opera. 'Were you with another woman today? A lover?'

His face elongated in a gape. 'What? Where's this come from?'

'Tell me, Robert. Just tell me. Is that where you went at lunchtime, to meet a woman?' Christ, she was gripping the edge of the wrought-iron table so tightly, it was a wonder it didn't buckle and bend with the pressure.

'No! Of course not!' His eyes pleaded shock and innocence, but Simon's had too. *Stay strong, Harriet. Do not be fooled by the eyes.* 'I told you,' he went on, but there was a definite shake to his voice now. 'I went to meet my American editor. Who is in his fifties, decidedly male, with a comb-over. What is this?'

She played her trump card. 'Well, that's strange.' The tension in her jaw was making her teeth ache. 'Because the Marylebone Tavern was shut when I walked by.' She noted the flicker of panic that crossed his face, before adding, 'Closed for building work, apparently for two weeks.'

A single beat of time elapsed, then he recovered himself with impressive composure. 'Wait – did I say the Marylebone Tavern?'

'Yes, Robert. You did say the Marylebone Tavern.' She leaned back against the uncomfortable metal patio chair, barely noticing how cold and unforgiving it was against her shoulder blades. So. What did he have to say for himself now?

He put a hand to his forehead. 'I've got a mental block about that place,' he said after a moment. 'It was the *Marlborough* Tavern. You know, in Covent Garden?'

She pursed her lips. 'Right.'

'You do know, it's down that side street, not far from the Royal Opera House . . .'

No. She didn't know. She tended to have weekday lunches in the school canteen or staff room, not fancy places in the West End. But he proceeded to bang on convincingly about what he'd eaten, and the interior decor, and the meeting itself, until she put her hands up to stop him.

'Harriet,' he said earnestly. 'Look at me. I adore you. There is no other woman. I'm not Simon, okay?'

His voice rang with sincerity and she believed him. Just about. 'Okay. Good,' she said.

All the same, as soon as he set off on his run, she went straight online to see if what he'd told her checked out. Once bitten, twice shy and all that.

Right – here it was, the Marlborough Tavern, just as he'd described, with the *steak au poivre* he claimed to have eaten on the online menu, along with the crab starter. Despite her doubts, it did all stack up. It must have been a genuine misunderstanding all along, then. Oh thank goodness. Thank goodness!

She dug into the ice cream with vigour moments later, relief making her ravenous. And there she had been, tarring Robert with the same cheating brush as her ex, she thought guiltily. Next time she'd know better. Because Robert *was* better, simple as that.

Two days later, this fact was proved conclusively true yet again when Simon achieved a new low in the Worst Ever Father and All-Round Human Being stakes. Contact with her ex-husband had been sporadic, verging on non-existent, for the last ten months, mainly consisting of the occasional apologetic text when he was bailing out of picking up Molly or, worse, forgot to meet her. He had missed her school parents' evenings for three years on the trot, too busy dallying with Maya and Mia and Michelle, Sophie and Suze, Vicky and Nicki . . . Harriet had given up trying to keep track. As far as she knew, he had lost contact with Jasmine – the pregnant woman glimpsed from the bus window – as well as his now eight-year-old son, Gabriel. Molly had never even met her half-brother.

These days there was Anne-Marie: young, beautiful and – yes – pregnant. (Ironically, Simon was nothing if not fertile. He was a veritable baby machine.) And, according to the latest text, they were soon to be on the move. Just like that.

Hi all, apols for group text. Just to say, new address is below. Moving on Monday! Check Facebook page for leaving bash! Si x

There followed an address which ended, shockingly, with the word 'France' and Harriet almost dropped the phone on seeing it. France? FRANCE?! The wave of fury and hurt prompted by this new rustic address, coming straight out of the blue, left her reeling. 'What the hell?' she cried, reading the message all over again to check she hadn't just gone mad. The absolute tosser. How could he?

'What's up?' Molly asked from the end of the sofa, without taking her eyes off her laptop.

'Everything all right?' Robert asked breathlessly. He was midway through a set of sit-ups on the living room floor but paused mid-crunch to glance over.

Harriet was just about to launch into a furious rant about how absolutely awful Simon was, and why was he going off to bloody *France* when he was already so damn slapdash with his existing children, and she supposed this meant even less time spent with Molly and even fewer child maintenance payments to her . . . but she checked herself just in time. She couldn't break the news to Molly that her father was leaving the country in a shrill-voiced tirade of fury. This was a task to be tackled sensitively, sitting on the end of Molly's bed, ready to throw her arms around her in comfort. Bloody Simon. Bloody Simon!

'Harriet?' Robert prompted when she didn't immediately reply.

'Nothing,' she muttered through gritted teeth. 'It's fine.'

Lying in bed that night, she was still very far away from feeling that Simon springing this news on her in such a casual, cavalier way could remotely be considered 'fine'. It was not fine at all. It was unforgivable. Not for her sake, of course – she couldn't have cared less if she never saw his smirking face again. But Molly would be heartbroken, however hard she tried to pretend it was cool, however much she shrugged and said, 'Whatever'.

Of course, Harriet had sneaked a look at Simon's Facebook page and gawped with increasing crossness at all the photos of him and beautiful Anne-Marie, arms entwined around each other. She had also seen the photos of their prospective new home: a charming brick farmhouse in the Dordogne with its own vineyard – 'Chateau Reynolds!' as all his mates were teasing in the comments. There were green fields and a stream and proud golden sunflowers, way taller than Harriet had ever managed to grow in their tiny east-facing garden.

However idyllic it looked, though, Simon seemed to have neglected one crucial factor in all of this: he would be living in a different country from his fantastic fifteen-year-old daughter, not to mention his criminally ignored young son. Did that not bother him? Did he not feel a wrench at the thought of such distance between them? How could it be that he didn't feel the pull of his own flesh and blood, anchoring him right here in London? There was no way Harriet would ever uproot and move somewhere miles from her daughter. It would not even occur to her!

Harriet had done her best to be civil about Simon at all times in front of Molly. In fact, so desperate was she not to fall into the trap of slagging him off and making him the scapegoat for their marriage break-up (even though he was totally to blame), she overcompensated, and was often ridiculously generous about him rather than expressing her true feelings. But there were times – like now – when it was very hard to think of a single kind thing to say about him. There were times, in fact – also now – when she just wanted to smash his face in for being such a self-obsessed, daughter-neglecting twat.

Of course, he hadn't thought to contact Molly and let her know the news himself. He had that little respect or consideration for her feelings, it was a surprise he still remembered she even existed.

Going to be a daddy! was one of the captions on his Facebook page, written underneath a photo of him with his hand proudly on Anne-Marie's swelling belly. It had taken every bit of self-control for Harriet not to leave a waspish comment underneath.

Going to be? You already are, Si. Or do your other children not count any more?

She turned off the computer instead before she could start typing. It would only make things worse for Molly, she reminded herself. With a father like Simon, and all the many disappointments and let-downs this meant, her daughter already had enough problems, without Harriet adding to the burden.

Chapter Twelve

Over in Oakthorne, Freya had undergone one of the less pleasant afternoons of her career. Melanie Taylor had arrived for their meeting, as arranged by Elizabeth, but was not in any mood to sit calmly and listen to Freya's polite lines of self-defence. She was out for a scalp, shrilly listing all the reasons why Freya should be sacked for incompetence, starting with the big one: that Ava was still poorly in hospital.

'Perhaps if we all calm down a minute—' Elizabeth interrupted soothingly.

Melanie didn't want to be soothed. 'I'm not the one with a bottle of gin in my handbag!' she shrieked. Her eyes glittered with venom, the veins in her neck stood out like cords; she was a lioness prepared to go for the jugular on behalf of her injured cub.

Freya flinched in her chair. Oh Christ. She'd forgotten all about the incriminating Hendrick's bottle. The unopened, undrunk Hendrick's bottle, she wanted to protest, but she didn't dare. Not when Elizabeth had turned to look at her, a small frown rucking that pale forehead. It took every shred of composure Freya possessed to hold her head up high. 'I am a professional,' she said, even though this didn't feel strictly true any more either. 'I wouldn't dream of drinking alcohol while at work. I certainly don't have an alcohol problem.'

'We both know there was a bottle of something stashed in your bag,' Melanie retorted, so loud Freya was sure that Sanjay, the nurse next door, would be able to hear. Melanie scented blood and was not about to let this one go. 'Don't you dare insult me by lying about it. Pissed, were you? Is that why you barely looked at Ava? Too drunk to know what you were doing?'

'No!' Freya cried hotly, not daring to look at her manager's face. *Please believe me, Elizabeth*, she prayed, sweat pooling in her cleavage. It was another stifling day and she'd made the mistake of wearing a long-sleeved rose-coloured silk blouse and black skirt, somehow forgetting that the surgery was like an oven in hot weather. She could almost feel her make-up sliding down her face. 'No,' she said again, trying to sound crisp and in control. 'I was absolutely not drunk. And I did check over Ava. I listened to her chest, I took her temperature and looked in her ears . . .'

'So why didn't you tell me she was critically ill?' Melanie's voice was at shrieking pitch again. 'Why did you let her nearly *die*?'

'Let's calm down a little,' Elizabeth interjected, making downward motions with her hands.

'I didn't nearly let her die,' Freya said to Melanie. 'I wouldn't. I'm a mother myself, I've—'

'I don't care,' Melanie spat. She looked as if she wanted to fly across the desk that separated them and sink talons into Freya's eyeballs. 'I couldn't give a shit if you have children. I hope they get ill like Ava, and then you'll know how *I* feel.' She burst into a torrent of sobs, and Freya gasped, winded by Melanie's terrible words. How dare she?

Elizabeth put a firm hand on Freya's arm – the subtext: *Do not rise to this* – and said, 'Perhaps we should try this meeting again when Ava's better.'

Elizabeth guided Melanie out of the room while her bitter words thumped through Freya's head like a bad fairy's curse – *I hope your children get ill like Ava!* What sort of a mother said something like that about somebody else's child? What planet was this woman on?

She leaned back in her chair, all the fight knocked out of her, wishing desperately for one of her dad's bear hugs by way of comfort. If only. Would her father have been terribly ashamed if he could see the mess she was in right now? She could hardly bear to think about it. He had always been so proud of her.

'Are you all right?' Elizabeth asked when she returned a few minutes later. 'Don't take any notice of what she said, she's just upset. I'm sorry you had to sit through that, though, very unpleasant.'

Freya nodded, not trusting herself to speak all of a sudden.

Elizabeth gathered her papers together. 'Listen, I'm satisfied you carried out the right checks on Ava but . . . well, Mrs Taylor is clearly something of a loose cannon right now. She may want to take this further, in which case . . .' She spread her hands wide, an apologetic look on her face.

'In which case, we're in for round two,' Freya said, feeling resigned to her fate.

'Exactly. But put it behind you now if you can. You're off on holiday soon, aren't you? Well, leave all this with me and we can pick things up when you're back.'

The matter seemed to be over and Freya was about to stand up when she had a sudden flashback to being in the critical care unit with baby Dexter. Despite everything, she did understand Melanie's helpless, desperate rage. 'Maybe I should just say sorry,' she blurted out, feeling bad for the woman. Wasn't that the human thing to do here?

The words came out in a mumble but Elizabeth's eyebrows shot up as if Freya had shouted them. '*Sorry*? For what?'

'Well, for . . .' Freya ground to a halt. 'I did examine Ava properly that day, Elizabeth. I definitely did. But I know I've been a bit distracted recently. I probably wasn't firing on all cylinders. So maybe I should just—'

Elizabeth was shaking her head. Very, very firmly. 'No. I don't think that would be wise. Saying sorry is tantamount to accepting culpability. It's a tacit acknowledgement that you have something to be sorry *for*, ergo admitting you're in the wrong. Mrs Taylor could use it against you – she could sue you, twist your words . . .' Again came that shake of the head. 'I strongly advise you not to do that.'

'Right,' Freya said, feeling chastised.

'I mean, you could be putting your job in jeopardy. You saw what she was like today, flinging accusations around. And if the baby deteriorates . . .'

Bile rushed into Freya's mouth and she felt nauseous. She didn't want to think of baby Ava deteriorating. Bronchial pneumonia was bad enough for adults to fight off, but for infants there was a very real chance of death. How would she be able to live with herself if the worst happened? She suppressed a shudder. 'Okay,' she said. 'I get the picture. I'll keep quiet.'

Elizabeth nodded. 'Hopefully this will all have blown over by the time you're back from your holiday,' she said. 'And your husband's home tonight, isn't he? So put it out of your mind for now.'

Freya and Victor had met on holiday in the south of France sixteen years ago this summer. Until then, she'd only ever dated fellow med school students, all of whom had strutted round the university campus like cockerels puffed up with self-importance, God's gift to women, the sort of men who made you feel they were doing you a favour even speaking to you. That summer, Freya had just split up with a particularly arrogant specimen, Matt, and had jumped at the chance of a girls' holiday to take her mind off her feelings of rejection.

She was in a rented villa with six female friends and, as sheer bountiful luck would have it, the neighbouring villa was stuffed full of six English blokes. 'Happy holidays all round,' her friend Becky whistled, the afternoon they arrived, leaning out of the window to gawp into the grounds next door. 'Take your pick, ladies.'

Freya fancied dark, Latin-blooded Vic from the off, spying from the balcony as he dived into the next-door pool. He was the best diver by far, with his broad back and athletic body, and watching him plunge into the water left her deliciously shivery. She and her friends took it upon themselves to go next door with a neighbourly bottle of tequila that evening, and all twelve of them chatted and laughed together long into the night. The next day, they teamed up again to hire motorbikes and explore the local area and by dint of good fortune (and admittedly some jostling with her friend Cathy, who also fancied him), Freya wangled a ride with Victor. Sitting behind him, knees gripping his body, feeling the engine throbbing beneath her as they wheeled around dusty coastal roads, the scent of rosemary, lavender and hot tarmac in her nose . . . it was one of the most exhilarating and down-right erotic experiences of her life.

The first time he kissed her was a few evenings later when all twelve of them traipsed down en masse to the small town nearby, for pizza and cheap carafes of red wine. Afterwards the others left to investigate a local band the waiter had tipped them off about, but Freya and Victor exchanged a secret glance and said they'd stay for one last drink before catching up. The sky was violet-blue, darkness gradually fill-ing in the edges, and Freya felt heady with lust and sunshine and too much red wine. They were laughing about some-thing – she had no idea what, now, maybe Vic's terrible French accent which he kept putting on to crack her up – and then the atmosphere shifted, and the evening felt suspended, suddenly, as if everything else around them had melted away.

'Freya,' he said softly, and her name sounded like a poem on his lips. Then they were leaning towards each other, and his lips grazed hers – softer than she'd expected – and it was as if she'd fallen head first into him, into his kiss, his arms, his very being, as their bodies pressed together. Electricity seemed to tingle all around her; her blood thrummed, her nerve endings quivered in ecstasy. She felt like Sleeping Beauty, awoken with a single kiss, after all those wasted years of cocky med school boyfriends.

Afterwards, as they drew apart, the world seemed to have changed up a gear: the colours were more vivid and dazzling, the very air around them was charged with passion, and her heart was thumping with joy and excitement.

'Do that again,' she had demanded, half laughing, but giddy too, with the shock that one man could have such a physical effect on her entire body – on the entire world around her! She was a scientist, a doctor – she thought she knew the human form and all its vagaries. But she had never felt like that before.

She thought about all of this as she drove to the child-minder's after work, both because she was desperate to see her husband again after his fortnight away, and also because she was horribly aware of how much the two of them had changed since that first summer. Three children and house moves and work stress later, the holiday in France seemed like a mirage these days, a dream; something that had hap-pened to a more carefree person who was game for any-thing. Look at her now – in trouble at work, a bad-tempered mother, too exhausted for sex, several stone heavier . . . When was the last time they had kissed like that, with such rampant desire? Did Vic ever look back and wonder what it would have been like if he'd chosen Cathy instead, or another woman altogether?

Parking outside the childminder's, she gave herself a talking-to before getting out of the car. *Come on, Freya. Pull yourself together.* Victor the conquering hero was on his way home to them, right now. She had to make sure he was glad to be back.

'Sir Dextrous! Lady Libby-Loo! And the Tedster! Come here. I've missed you guys!'

The minute Victor walked through the front door, the children leapt on him like wild animals and he hauled them all up off their feet in a huge bearlike embrace, even though Dex was well over five foot these days. 'Cor, look at you lovely lot. Everyone all right?'

'Did you bring any presents?' asked Libby without answering the question. 'Oh, Dad, I've got a really cool joke for you. Knock, knock. Dad – knock, knock!'

'Did you get to wear riot gear?' Dexter wanted to know.

'Did you fight any more stabbers?' Teddy asked ghoulishly, bouncing up and down.

'Dad, knock, knock!'

'Who's there?' Vic replied. 'Ted, gently, mate.'

'Needap,' said Libby. 'Dad! Are you listening? Needap!'

Freya, who had just slid the joint of beef out of the oven to rest – she had done a full roast, Victor's favourite – felt her spirits lift at the excited clamour of voices. Thank goodness he was home! She had missed him so much. Everything seemed to have gone wrong without him there, propping her up. 'Hi, love,' she said, shucking off the oven gloves and hurrying over to join the group hug. 'Welcome back.'

'Hey! Great to see you,' he said, leaning in to kiss her, the children still swinging from him. 'Something smells good. I'm starving.'

'You smell good,' she replied, pressing against him. 'I'm so glad you're home. We've missed you, haven't we, kids?'

'Dad, Needap!' Libby said again insistently.

'Needap who?' Victor replied and all the children fell about laughing.

'Go to the toilet then!' Libby told him in delight. 'Go to the toilet, Dad, if you need a poo!'

He laughed too, feigning outrage. 'You naughty little madam. I'm shocked, Libby Castledine. Shocked!'

'So *are* there any presents?' asked Teddy, who could be relied upon to repeat questions as doggedly as the Gestapo, especially if presents or sweets were involved. The boy was a shoo-in for a doorstepping journalist one day, make no doubt about it. 'Presents, Dad!'

'Let him take his shoes off, kids,' Freya scolded, although she wasn't really cross. She smiled at Victor, so handsome and real and *there* in the hall once more, albeit currently under siege from their offspring. It was probably easier facing down a full-scale riot. 'So you enjoyed it, then – the course?' she asked. 'It was worth doing?'

'It was brilliant. We had such a laugh. Some of the lads there . . .' He grinned and then promptly stopped talking as if the rest of the sentence was not suitable for the ears of children. 'But we learned loads too. And yes, Dex, we did have to wear riot gear, and long shields, and practise rescuing people from dangerous situations . . .'

'Cool!'

'What about the—'

'Yes, Ted, I *did* have time to pick up a few little somethings. Now, where are they?'

'Can I have a *big* something?' Teddy asked, still capering about with demented zeal. 'Can I have the biggest?'

Freya went back in the kitchen to check on the Yorkshire puddings and make gravy. 'I thought we could make a proper evening of it,' she said as Victor came in, passing him a just-opened beer. 'I've done a roast and all the trimmings, there's an apple crumble for afters, the fridge is full of booze and there are four episodes of *The Walking Dead* saved up for us to watch. I didn't sneak so much as a minute of it without you,' she added proudly. In short, she had lined up the perfect night for them both. Melanie who? Elizabeth who? She would not even *think* about them.

But to her dismay, Vic was shuffling his feet and not looking her in the eye. 'Oh, mate – I thought I told you?' he said.

Mate? Since when had he started calling her 'mate'? She had a bad feeling all of a sudden. 'Told me what?'

'I said I'd go out with the boys tonight. It's Tony's birthday and he . . .' Victor looked bashful. 'Well, he kind of wants me there as his guest of honour, he said.' An uneasy few seconds passed. 'I thought you knew.'

Freya shook her head. 'No.' She might have been distracted recently, but she was pretty sure she'd have remembered her husband telling her he was going straight out the very same night he came home after two weeks away.

'Shit. Sorry. But . . . well, we're going on holiday tomorrow, aren't we? And we're going to spend the whole fortnight together. Yeah?'

The gravy was blurring before her eyes and she blinked, desperately trying not to cry in front of him. She needn't have worried. He had turned his attention to his phone, laughing at some text or other that had just come in. 'You nutter,' he said affectionately, typing a reply. 'This bloke on the course, Dave, funniest geezer I've ever met.'

Freya opened her mouth to respond but found she didn't actually feel like asking about Dave the geezer or hearing any hilarious stories. She stirred the gravy grimly, trying to convince herself it didn't matter, and that he was right, it was only one more night. *No worries, mate. Whatever.*

It was only much later on, when he'd vanished out again in his favourite shirt and clean jeans, and the children were upstairs in bed, that she put her head in her hands and allowed herself to cry softly in the silence of the empty kitchen.

Then she opened the celebratory champagne she'd bought specially, and drank the whole bottle herself.

The next morning brought with it a particularly vile hangover – a decidedly crap way in which to pack for one's holiday. Freya could vaguely remember a time when she had planned holiday packing far in advance, with much consideration and attention to detail – laying outfits on the bed in order to put together a 'capsule wardrobe', as the magazine articles advised, picking out jewellery, make-up, shoes for all occasions, several bikinis, toiletries in special fun-sized bottles . . .

That was back then, though, when she had time and head space to think about herself, and herself alone. So far, this year's abysmal packing list read as follows:

> *Clothes*
> *Beach stuff*
> *Swimming costumes*
> *Paracetamol*

Which was a sorry state of affairs in anyone's book.

Victor – rather annoyingly – had leapt out of bed at eight that morning, bright-eyed and bushy-tailed, despite not crashing in until the early hours. Superman that he was, he had gone out for bacon and eggs, then proceeded to cook an enormous fried breakfast for the whole family. Now he and

Dexter had headed off to fill the car with petrol and check the tyres at the garage while Freya set to work bundling the children's clothes into suitcases, cajoling Libby into packing the books and toys she might want to take and trying not to combust with exasperation when she saw that Teddy had turned his bedroom upside down looking for some long-lost dinosaur figures.

Deep breaths. Relax. Only calm, serene thoughts permitted from here on in, she told herself. On holiday the sun would shine and turn her pale skin from milk-white to double cream – the soft gold of muscovado sugar if she was really lucky. The fresh air would help her sleep deeply for once and she might finally shed those eye bags while she was at it. She would swim in the sea every day until her muscles ached. And you never knew, she and Vic might actually manage a proper conversation too for a change.

Libby burst into the room just then, wearing a red polka-dot swimming costume, a Hello Kitty woolly hat, rollerskates and some enormous purple sunglasses, and whirled around in a wobbly circle. 'READY!' she cheered. 'Ready for the holiday, Mum!'

Despite her previous despondency, Freya burst out laughing. She caught hold of her daughter's middle and rolled her closer in for a cuddle. Never mind her troubles. They would shortly be heading off to wonderful Shell Cottage and getting away from it all. She couldn't wait to see Mum and spend some relaxing time together. (Mum must be *really* relaxed, seeing as she hadn't responded to any of Freya's calls or texts the previous week.) *Deep breaths, calm thoughts*, she reminded herself. As soon as she reached Silver Sands, she'd switch her phone off too – and her worries, while she was at it.

It was all going to be absolutely fine. It *was*.

Chapter Thirteen

Olivia didn't know it was possible to experience such desolation. Since the bombshell of her husband's betrayal had detonated so devastatingly, she had felt hollowed out, numb with agony, and more alone than ever before.

Another woman. Another *child*! Another whole secret life behind her back, sneaking down to Devon on pretence of writing weekends. His charade of needing to be alone every summer so as to read through and work on his new novel in peace and quiet! Had he even *been* on all those foreign book tours he'd claimed, or was he here the whole time, sleeping with this other woman, raising this other son, in her beloved house?

She could hardly function with shock. It was as if he had punched a hole right through her heart. As a husband, Alec had been the most loving of men. As a father, he'd been tender and doting. One of her favourite ever photos showed him gazing down at newly born Freya, nestled in his arms, with a look of complete wonder and adoration. She couldn't bear the thought of him feeling like that about somebody else's child. That boy. In some ways it was even worse than him sleeping with another woman. Weren't Freya and Robert enough for him? Hadn't *she* been enough as his wife?

As for Katie, doe-eyed, thirty-something Katie, 'their angel' as Olivia had always laughingly called her – the devil, more like – she could go to hell, along with that son of hers. The son of hers, Leo, who was the mystery beneficiary in Alec's will, of course. And there she'd been, innocently assuming it was a great friend of her husband's, some beloved colleague in the publishing world. *Oh, Olivia! Silly Olivia. What will we do with you?*

Alec, Katie and Leo. Their own little family, a secret side-shoot branching off the main stem. Katie, who was two years younger than their own daughter. Katie, the housekeeper, who'd gone above and beyond her job description when it came to extra-marital duties performed for the master of the house. Katie, who had stood there in the kitchen – *Olivia's* kitchen, thank you very much! – weeping inconsolably, sobbing that she never got to say goodbye, that Leo had been left without a father, that she'd loved him so much. Olivia had felt precisely nothing at the sight of such unchecked emotion. If anything, her heart had frozen over, glistening with ice crystals.

'I thought he'd gone quiet on me because of the new

book,' Katie snivelled. 'I had no idea that . . . that he was dead!'

Olivia had heard enough. She could not stand there a second longer and listen to this woman speak about her husband as if she had any kind of claim on him. As if she had any right to grieve! 'Get out,' she roared. 'Get out of my house. I never want to see either of you again. Have I made myself clear?'

They went, both crying, the door banging shut behind them, and Olivia sank into the kitchen chair, put her head in her hands and burst into hot, gulping tears of her own. No. Not Alec. How could he? How *could* he?

Three days later, and the scene had barely changed. Her emotions may have fluctuated between shock, rage, heartbreak and despair, but the tears seemed to have flowed almost ceaselessly. Now and then she would drag herself from the chair in order to eat or sleep or make another pot of tea, but it would only take a glance at something beloved and familiar – the red knitted jumble-sale tea cosy that Alec had worn on his head during a silly dressing-up evening; the watercolour of Bantham beach he'd given her ten years ago as an anniversary present; the apple tree in the garden they'd planted as a sapling, which bore basketfuls of fruit every September – and the pain would come tearing back.

Olivia had never believed in any kind of afterlife yet found herself doing things that would deliberately annoy her dead husband were he to see her now. She drank red wine straight from the bottle and made a point of not wiping up the drops that spilled on the pine table. She took his favourite green coffee mug and hurled it out of the back door so that it smashed into a satisfying number of shards on the patio. She took a saw to the apple tree, her fingers blistering as she hacked it down and then burned it, leaving only a broken stump. And she threw his battered old panama hat far out to sea – even if she did then have a stab of conscience about ocean pollution afterwards and ended up wading in to retrieve it. She contented herself by trampling the crown of the hat into submission, the straw splintering beneath her feet, then shoving it down into the fetid depths of the dustbin. *So there, Alec. That's what I think of you and your stupid hat. And good riddance to you both!*

By the end of the week, she had reached the point of numbness. She was all out of emotional energy and could no longer feel a thing. A letter appeared through the door one morning addressed to her in Katie's handwriting but she deliberately didn't open it, not wishing to reignite all those exhausting emotions. Instead, she walked for miles along the coastal path, barely noticing the scenery, just needing to get out, away from the house and everything that reminded her of Alec. She ignored the elegant skirts and summer blouses in her wardrobe and took to roaming the cliffs in a pair of ancient cut-off jeans, and an old surfing T-shirt of Robert's she'd found in his bedroom. She stopped brushing her hair and twisted the long silvery strands up into a messy chignon, fastened in place with one of Libby's butterfly clips, left behind at Easter. Who cared what she looked like any more? She didn't. She didn't care about anything.

It came as a shock to return from a long hike one day to see a dark green Peugeot parked outside Shell Cottage and to hear children's high-pitched voices in the garden. It took her a moment to realize that the car belonged to Freya, and the children were actually Dexter, Libby and Teddy. Goodness – was it really the weekend already? She had lost track of time, forgetting that the rest of her family were due to descend for their summer break.

Her mind raced, picturing the house room by room, and how it must have appeared to Freya and Victor as they arrived. She had left the dirty crockery to pile up abandoned in the sink for days now. There were a *lot* of empty wine bottles too. The broken mug was still there in pieces on the patio, making her snarl with triumph every time she saw it, but now she imagined her precious grandchildren cutting their small pink feet on the smashed shards and felt terrible. Had she even opened the living room curtains that morning? The house probably stank too. Yesterday she had treated herself to a packet of cigarettes for the first time in years and had smoked almost all of them, enjoying the sensation of blowing plumes of curling smoke into the darkening sky. She could just imagine little Libby's jaw dropping and the scandalized '*Granny!*' when she saw all the discarded butts.

Oh dear. And poor Freya would think she was losing her marbles, finding the house in such disarray. How was she going to talk her way out of this one?

'Mum! *There* you are!' Here she came now, bustling from the house, her jaw noticeably tense even from this distance. 'Where have you *been*? I've been ringing you and texting you for ages. I even tried calling Katie to see if you were all right—'

'Ha,' said Olivia contemptuously before she could stop herself.

Freya looked startled. Olivia was not normally a sarcastic sort of person who said things like 'Ha', particularly in relation to their darling housekeeper. 'Mum . . . is everything all right?'

Olivia tried to pull herself together. The short answer, of course, was 'No' but she couldn't possibly tell Freya the news she'd discovered. She'd always been such a daddy's girl, it would destroy her to learn of her father's double life. 'I'm fine,' she said, then took a deep breath, forcing herself to smile. 'Better for seeing you,' she said truthfully. 'And where are those delightful grandchildren of mine?' She hugged Freya, trying to act as normally as possible. 'How was your journey? Let me make you a cup of tea. Ahh. I'm not sure there's any milk left actually.'

'We're okay, Mum, thanks, all fed and watered; we've been here since three o'clock. And I brought milk, it's fine.'

Olivia checked her watch: almost half past four. Another day had slipped by practically unnoticed. 'Oh. Okay, then.'

There was an awkward pause then Freya gave a bracing smile. 'Come and say hi to the kids and Vic, anyway. They're supposed to be getting their things together to go down to the beach but seem to have been sidetracked by a horrendously competitive swingball tournament. I'm expecting a full public inquiry to be called any minute if Teddy isn't allowed to win.' She put a hand on Olivia's back and steered her gently towards the back garden. 'By the way,' she added, as they walked along the rosemary-scented path, 'Katie sounded a bit odd when I rang. Said something about needing to come round and talk to us all at some point. What do you think that's about?'

Chapter Fourteen

It had not been the relaxing start to the holiday that Freya had so desperately wanted. On arriving at Shell Cottage, they found the house so messy and uncared for, she wondered for a crazy moment if a group of squatters had taken the place over. Cigarette butts littered the patio and there was a whole bottle bank worth of empties . . . Had Mum been throwing wild parties, left to her own devices? Surely she hadn't consumed them all herself? It seemed extreme, even by Freya's own increasingly low standards. Thank goodness she'd thought to stop at the nearest supermarket and pick up a few provisions on the way, otherwise there'd have been nothing to eat that night. By the looks of things, Mum had been surviving on alcohol and a few tins of beans all this time. *Like mother, like daughter*, she thought with a grimace.

Upstairs, she discovered the beds had been left unmade, there were no fresh towels laid out awaiting their arrival, not even so much as a new cake of soap in the bathroom.

Was Katie *ill?* she wondered, perplexed. Usually their house-keeper prided herself on keeping the place immaculate for them. And where the hell was Mum, anyway?

Katie sounded weird on the phone when Freya rang her five minutes later. Tearful, almost. Katie had worked for the Tarrants for years, and had always been cheerful and competent, delighting the family with surprise offerings of strawberries or a vase full of flowers or occasionally a pot of home-made blackcurrant sorbet in the freezer. She was practically part of the furniture of Shell Cottage. But this year, for some reason, she was . . . well, not *unfriendly,* but certainly a bit offhand on the telephone.

'I don't know where your mother is, I haven't been to the house all week,' she said. (Unheard of. She popped in and out most days to keep the place tidy and clean. That explained why it was such a tip, at least.)

'Oh,' Freya said dumbly, noticing with a shudder that there were two bluebottles patrolling around the sticky wine bottles by the sink. She pushed open the kitchen window and attempted to shoo them away but they dived past her, buzzing loudly. 'Is everything all right, Katie?'

Was it about money? she wondered when no reply came. Maybe Katie had asked for a pay rise, but Mum had refused and Katie had downed tools – or the washing-up brush anyway – in retaliation. She couldn't envisage this scenario, though. Her parents had always been generous people. They wouldn't have underpaid Katie, no way.

Katie eventually made a strange noise that might have been a laugh or might possibly have been a sob, then she'd made that unexpected comment about needing to talk to them all and hung up abruptly. Weirder and weirder.

And now here was Mum looking dishevelled and – Freya hated to say it – a bit manic. Her hair was loose and straggly, she was wearing fawn chinos with a grass stain on one knee, and a jumper so ancient Freya thought she remembered her wearing it twenty years ago. Oh dear. And to think she'd been assuming Mum had switched off her phone so as to get away from it all. Now it seemed as if Freya's unanswered calls and texts were due to some kind of . . . well, breakdown, possibly. She felt like the worst daughter ever for not having guessed this earlier.

'Granny!' cheered the children as Freya led Olivia around to the lawn to see them. 'Granny, I've got a joke for you!' called Libby. 'Knock, knock, Granny. Granny! Knock, knock!'

Freya's gaze, meanwhile, was caught by the sight of the apple tree – or rather, what was left of it.

'Oh no! What happened here?' she cried in dismay, but Olivia was being deafened by Libby's joke-telling (Freya hoped it wasn't one of the toilet-related Knock Knocks that her daughter favoured) and Teddy announcing gleefully how he had been carsick, and how it had gone *everywhere*, and you could still see the bits of cornflakes from his breakfast.

Nobody seemed to notice that Freya had spoken so she wandered over to the tree for a closer look. As she drew nearer she could see it had been cut, and recently too. Damp sap still oozed on the stump, like blood leaking from a wound. *Poor old thing*, she thought with a pang. All the apples they'd munched from its branches in Septembers gone by. It was the first tree Dexter had ever climbed, cheered on by all the adults as he swung nimbly from branch to branch, the biggest grin of triumph on his face as he hauled himself up. Who'd cut her down, and why? Visions of Katie running amok with a chainsaw flashed into her mind and she shook her head at her own fevered imagination.

Beyond the tree were the remains of a fire: blackened grass and a few charred logs. Freya could almost smell the applewood smoke that would have risen as the branches burned to embers. It must have been teenagers, she guessed, up from the village after exam season was over, looking for mischief. There was a fair bit of resentment towards 'second homers' in this area; every now and then they'd arrive at the cottage to discover an egg had been thrown at the front door, or find the occasional broken window. But cutting down a medium-sized tree and then lighting a bonfire was not an impulse act, was it?

She poked the stump with the toe of her shoe, knowing how sad her dad would have been to see it felled and gone. Oh, Dad. That must be why Mum looked so dreadful, of course; she must have missed him terribly the last week. If Freya had given it more thought, she'd have insisted Olivia waited until they could all come down together, sparing her the loneliness she must have suffered being here on her own. Another person she'd let down lately, she thought dismally.

'MUM! We're going to the beach!' came Libby's voice just then. 'We're going rock-pooling. Granny's coming with us!'

Freya turned to see that the children were pulling everything out of the shed – buckets and spades and fishing nets, all covered in lacy cobwebs. 'Not on your head, Lib!' Freya cried, two seconds too late.

'I've been caught! I've been caught!' squealed Libby, capering about.

'There's a spider on you!' Dexter shouted untruthfully, making her scream and fling the net off, running in circles.

'There are *loads* of spiders in here,' Ted announced happily, crouching down to examine the shed floor and prodding at one with a spade.

Olivia appeared somewhat shell-shocked by all the noise, and Victor put a hand on her shoulder. 'Are you sure you're up to coming with these mad children?' he asked with a laugh.

'Of course,' Olivia replied with a weak smile. 'It's been very quiet here, on my own. I'm glad of the company.'

'Frey? Coming with us?' Vic asked.

Freya would have liked nothing more than to join the noisy beach-going party but she was conscious of the messy kitchen behind her, the fact that their beds were still unmade, and that everyone would require feeding within the next hour. 'I'll be down in a bit,' she promised. 'I'll just get our things unpacked first.'

It was silly of her – needy, too – but it would have been nice if one single person had protested at her words, insisting that she came along with them. But nobody did. They clattered past her, laden with rock-pooling equipment, the children all talking at once, nobody so much as looking in her direction. She turned away so that they wouldn't notice the hurt expression on her face but of course none of them gave her a backward glance.

Feeling a little sorry for herself, Freya washed everything up, wiped a cloth around the kitchen and scrubbed some Charlotte potatoes for dinner. Then she tucked sheets around the beds, fluffed up the pillows and whipped clean covers onto all their duvets.

From her bedroom window, she could see them down on the beach, five stick figures clambering around on the black seaweedy rocks at the far end of the bay – even Olivia.

Instead of going to join them, as she'd promised, Freya

was hit by a wave of weariness. Sod it, she thought. This was her holiday too, and for half an hour or so, she would enjoy the peace and quiet all on her own. So she poured herself a sneaky gin and tonic, clambered into the faded canvas hammock in the garden and shut her eyes, determined to block out the world for a while.

Freya must have dozed off because sometime later, she heard a boy's voice saying, quite close by, 'Hello? Um . . . hello?'

She blinked groggily awake, disoriented for a moment until she twisted round and felt her body sway in the hammock. Hammock? Oh yes. Silver Sands. Sunshine. Ow. She should have put some suncream on, her arms were flushed hot and pink already.

'Hello?' said the voice again and she opened her eyes fully to see a boy standing hesitantly in front of her, holding – of all things – a cling-filmed plate of flapjacks.

'Hello,' she said, wondering if this was part of some stress-related dream. She refocused. Definitely flapjacks. Mmm. Had she woken up in a parallel world where she was some kind of empress to be waited on hand and foot?

'Mum said to bring these,' the boy said, shifting from foot to foot.

Something about him was familiar somehow, the shape of his nose, maybe, or those unusual green eyes. He reminded her of someone she couldn't place. 'Your mum did?' she replied, sitting up and accepting the plate, although not really understanding. 'Who's your mum, then, love? Does she live nearby?'

'It's Katie,' he said, as if she was an idiot. 'My mum's Katie.'

'Your mum's Katie? Oh!' Since when did Katie have a son? A son the same sort of age as Dexter, more to the point. How come she'd never had a mum chat with Freya? It was like finding out the housekeeper had a pet tiger back at home that she hadn't thought to mention. Freya realized she was gaping and shut her mouth hurriedly. 'Well, it's nice to meet you and thanks very much for these. We all love your mum's flapjacks.'

He didn't smile. He was an earnest little thing, all dark hair and lanky limbs. 'What's your name?' she asked.

'Leo,' he said, then shrugged. 'I'd better go.'

'Okay. Wait – is your mum all right? It's strange her not being around. Nobody's told me what's happened.'

His eyes hooded over suddenly and he scuffed the grass with one battered old trainer, shrugging again. 'I dunno.'

He did know, obviously. He must have heard Katie slagging them off or . . . or . . . Freya's mind came up against a brick wall. She had no idea why Katie had left them so uncharacteristically in the lurch. Had Mum upset her somehow?

'She's not poorly, is she? Your mum?'

He shook his head, still not looking at her. His body was held in a tense position as if he was dying to be released and get out of there. It was the same stance Dexter adopted whenever he was longing to walk away from one of her bedroom-tidying lectures.

'Well . . . thanks, Leo. I'm Freya, by the way. Please pass on my thanks to your mum and say that I hope we see her soon, will you? Can you remember that?'

Scorn flashed across his face; she could almost hear him thinking *I'm not stupid, you know.* But he merely nodded. 'Bye,' he said, and loped away abruptly, flapjacks delivered, mission accomplished.

Barely ten minutes later, something even odder happened. Victor and the children romped back from the beach, with Olivia bringing up the rear. The children fell on the plate of flapjacks like ravenous lions, and Freya was just explaining how this boy – Katie's boy! – had appeared with them, like some wonderful cake-bearing vision, whereupon Olivia caught up, heard what she was saying, and . . . well, there was no other way to describe it. Basically, she went nuts.

'Stop! Put them back! We're not eating those!' she cried, snatching the plate from Freya. 'We don't want them.'

Victor had just taken a huge mouthful and looked from Freya to Olivia in confusion. 'We don't?'

'We *do*!' Libby cried, stuffing the rest of her flapjack into her mouth before her grandmother could whisk it away.

'We really do,' Dexter said, dodging a safe distance from Olivia so that his wasn't snatched from him either.

'I love flapjacks!' Teddy declared through a huge sticky mouthful, oat clusters already welded to the sides of his lips. 'Oh, man!'

Olivia paid no attention to her grandchildren's thoughts on the matter. 'Coming round here with flapjacks, indeed,' she raged. 'Like that will change the situation. Like that makes anything better!'

'Wait – what's the problem?' Freya called, almost toppling out of the hammock in her hurry to follow her mother. Olivia was stalking towards the house, the plate held out in front of her as if it smelled bad. 'What are you doing?'

Olivia didn't stop but marched through the back door and into the kitchen, where she opened the lid of the swing bin and tipped all the remaining flapjacks inside. The sight of those treats, deliciously gooey and moreish, vanishing into the depths of litter was almost enough to make a grown woman weep.

'Mum!' cried Freya. 'What did those perfectly nice flapjacks ever do to you?'

Olivia dropped the plate into the bin for good measure and let the lid swing close.

'MUM!' Freya said again, starting to seriously worry about her mother's mental health. 'That's Katie's plate. What on earth . . . ?'

'I don't want Katie's plate in my house. I don't want her flapjacks either. And if you knew the half of it, then you would feel the same way!'

And with that, Olivia strode away again, visibly bristling, and Freya was left to stare after her, open-mouthed and deeply discomfited.

Chapter Fifteen

'Do I *have* to go on holiday with all Robert's family?' Molly groaned, collapsing across the sofa as if she'd been shot by a sniper. 'It's going to be, like, so tragically boring and tedious, Mum. Can't I just stay here?'

Do I have to? seemed to be Molly's default setting these days, especially if it involved doing anything as a family. Harriet could feel her daughter pulling away all the time, a kite on a string impatient to fly free, leaving her tedious mother far behind, alone on the ground, staring anxiously upwards into the blue.

Glancing over from where she was knelt in front of the TV, in the middle of setting up all her favourite trashy TV programmes to record while they were away on holiday, Harriet gave her daughter a stern look. 'Don't be like that! It's the beach! The seaside! And that lovely, gorgeous house.' She thought again of the fact that this might be their last holiday together and vowed to dig her heels in. No way was she going to lose this argument. Forget it, lady.

Molly remained unmoved by her mother's words. 'I don't mind being on my own,' she said, inspecting her nails (silver and jewel-adorned today), then stretched her arms languidly above her head and gave a dramatic sigh. 'Devon's just, like, so pensioner-ish and dull. And I'm telling you now, there is no way I'm sharing a room with Dexter and Libby again. It's not happening.'

'You don't have to. I told you, we're bringing the camp bed so you can go up in the attic room. Okay?'

'Good, because I'm not a total baby. Last year, Libby wanted me to play Barbies with her. And I'm, like, hello? Feminist? Libby, real women do not look like those pieces of plastic, created by the patriarchy to undermine womanhood – you get that in your head right now, girl. The place for those Barbies is in the bin – not in this bedroom. And—'

'Okay, Molls, you've made your point.' There was nothing like the self-righteous declarations of a teenager to exhaust a person, Harriet thought, however much she might privately agree with what her daughter was saying. Once Molly got on a roll you might as well give up on whatever you had planned for the next half an hour, because that daughter of hers could *talk*.

'I mean, why does Freya even give her that crap? Is she trying to brainwash her? For an educated, intelligent woman, she can be a bit stupid sometimes, don't you think?'

'Don't you dare say that to her! And how do you know

Freya even bought her the Barbies in the first place? They might have been presents from someone else.'

Molly snorted. 'No daughter of mine will ever play with dolls like that. No way.'

'Right, well, good luck to you with that one. Sometimes daughters do have minds of their own, you know. Sometimes daughters even ignore the wisdom of their poor, long-suffering mothers, believe it or not.'

Molly rolled her eyes and put her hand in the shape of a beak, opening and shutting. Quack, quack, quack. What*ever*. 'Mum, I just want to stay in London. Why can't I stay?'

And they'd come full circle. 'Because you can't,' Harriet said distractedly, selecting the series link for *The Great British Bake-Off* and the sexy detective drama she was addicted to (thank goodness the Sky box didn't judge a person on their taste).

'Because I *can't*? Is that all you can come up with? That's really lame, Mum. You'll have to do better than that. Why can't I just go to Dad's?'

Ahh. There was the rub. *Because your dad is a tosser who's heading off to France next week, perhaps? Because he doesn't seem remotely interested in you, however many times you or I text or call him?* Harriet sighed. 'They're moving, remember,' she said gently.

Molly shrugged, but the hurt was visible in her face. 'I could help them?'

It was heartbreaking, it really was, just how many times a parent could be a shitbag and a child would forgive them, in the hope that everything would change. And Simon simply didn't get that. He genuinely didn't seem to understand that he was doing anything wrong. Why didn't he care more? Why couldn't he register that their daughter had a full set of intense raw emotions, not to mention hormones rampaging around her teenage body?

Harriet found herself thinking of Molly as a little girl, back when she and Simon were still together. Molly had lived in a joyful, sunlit world, singing and dancing all the time, with umpteen imaginary friends and games. Laughing. She was always laughing. Great gurgling peals as if she found delight in every corner of the universe. She had four favourite dolls – Rosy, Posy, Pinkerbell (don't ask) and Benny – all loyal companions, with their own personalities, who went everywhere with her. But after Simon left, the laughter ceased. The imaginary friends vanished, even though Harriet asked after them longingly, probably more times than she should have. Molly stopped chattering on about everything and became more fearful, having bad dreams and wetting the bed. Then Harriet had found Rosy, Posy, Pinkerbell and Benny stuffed head down in the kitchen bin one day, along with the potato peelings and empty fish packets and old teabags, and she thought her heart might actually break.

However hard Harriet had tried to fill her daughter up

with love, Molly had never quite been the same girl again. There was a sliver of sadness and abandonment locked deep into her soul and Harriet didn't think she would ever forgive Simon for leaving it there. Not that he had any idea, of course. There was only one important person in Simon World.

'Mum?' Molly prompted now when Harriet didn't reply immediately. 'Why don't I help them?'

There were so many reasons why this was a bad idea and Harriet turned away from the screen to give her daughter her full attention. They could be here all morning otherwise and she had a hundred other things to sort out before they could load up the car and leave. 'Sweetheart, let's give them a chance to settle in, then I can sort out a date for you to go over there and spend some proper time with your dad. Maybe the end of the holidays, or even the autumn half-term. But not now. Not today when we're meant to be going to Devon in less than an hour. Go and finish your packing.'

'But—'

'Look, we're going, okay? Robert's mum is having a hard time after Alec died, so we've got to support her.'

Molly groaned, letting her head fall back so that her long hair dangled over the arm of the sofa. 'Great. Wowzers. You've really sold it to me now, Mum.'

'Don't be mean. Have a heart.' Seeing that this had exactly zero effect, Harriet redoubled her efforts. 'Come on, be positive. Two weeks by the seaside . . . You can lie on the beach, get a tan, eat loads of ice cream . . .'

'Yay. Get fat and develop skin cancer, you mean. Er, facepalm.'

'No!' Harriet tried to remember how she'd been at the age of fifteen in the hope of coming up with something even sarcastic Molly might find irresistible but all she could think of was the knicker-melting crush she and her friends had had on Paul McIver, the smouldering sixth-form boy who had worked in Woolworths on Saturdays. Poor lad, they must have driven him up the wall with all their giggling and flirting, flicking their hair and batting their eyelashes as they handed over their paper bags of Pick and Mix in the vain hope – the insane, completely deluded hope! – that he might fall in love with them across a shovelful of jelly babies.

Inspiration struck. 'You might meet a boy,' she said, arching an eyebrow. 'You might have a little holiday romance.' She grabbed a cushion and pretended to smooch it. 'Corrr. Those were the days. Mm-mmm.'

Molly was repulsed, leaping up from the sofa in an instant. 'Mum! You are so gross sometimes, do you know that? Just . . . ewww. Please never talk like that again. Seriously.'

Harriet's lips twitched in amusement as her daughter strode indignantly from the room. *Gross* indeed. She did seem young for her age sometimes, not showing the slightest bit of interest in boys or romance yet. If ever she wandered in on Harriet and Robert having a snog in the kitchen or wherever, Molly would throw a hand melodramatically across her eyes as if the very sight of affection was loathsome. 'Get a room,' she'd shudder. 'Oh, please. Can you two stop sucking each other's faces for five minutes? You're actually making me feel ill. Seriously. Vomiting now. Genuine sick in my mouth.'

Harriet finished her TV recording schedule and got to her feet. Time for one last coffee, she decided, then they'd load up the car and go. Whatever Molly might say, they were in for a wonderful couple of weeks. She would damn well make sure of it.

Chapter Sixteen

Libby had been looking forward to the holiday for AGES. She absolutely loved the seaside and was definitely going to live there when she was a grown-up. At home in Oakthorne, her bedroom was at the front of the house and all you could see from the window was the boring road outside and houses and cars, and everything seemed sort of dirty and dull. But when they stayed at Shell Cottage, the window in the children's room not only had a lovely big wide ledge that you could sit on and make things, or maybe write stories if you felt like it, but also had a view of the beach. Sand dunes and sea and sometimes little boats. When you were falling asleep, you could hear the sea saying *shhhh-shhhh-shhhh,* and she liked to imagine mermaids out there, leaping and playing and having adventures while she slept.

Libby was also looking forward to seeing Granny again. While it was really, really sad that Grandad was dead, and wouldn't be there on holiday any more (especially as he told the *best* ever bedtime stories, with proper voices and everything), Granny had always been her favourite anyway. Libby *loved* Granny.

Most grown-ups made a beeline for Teddy – *Oh, isn't he adorable? What a little sweetie! That hair!* – which was really seriously annoying, but Granny always seemed to notice Libby and have a smile for her. She remembered things, too, unlike Mum, who never seemed to listen to anything Libby said. Granny would ask, 'How did that gymnastics contest go, then? Tell me those judges gave you first prize, Libby, my darling, or I'll have to have a word with them.' Or she would say, 'How are those sunflowers coming along that we planted? Don't forget to water them!' and 'Did you and Eloise make friends after your argument? Oh, good! I *am* glad.'

Granny was the best gardener ever, too. Libby hadn't been very interested in plants and nature and stuff when she was little, but on her eighth birthday, Granny had given her a special mini gardening set with packets of seeds to plant, and she'd taught Libby to spot all sorts of weeds – chickweed and groundsel and bindweed (Granny's arch enemy, she called it) and even dandelions, which were right little buggers, excuse my language. Every time Granny came to the Castledines' house, she would jump up after ten minutes and go outside – 'I can't resist!' she'd cry, even if Mum started saying, 'Really, there's no need, honestly, you don't have to' – and Libby would always hurry out to help her.

Sometimes if it was too rainy for even Granny to want to go out, then they did baking instead: fairy cakes and scones and chocolate biscuits. Granny would sing funny old songs and let Libby do all the interesting bits like breaking the eggs and weighing all the ingredients, and she never got cross, even when the mixture was spilled.

Libby knew that Granny had been sad ever since Grandad died. The last time she'd visited the Castledines' house, she'd just sat in the kitchen the whole time, looking unhappy and old, and didn't once leap up to inspect the garden like she usually did. Even so, Libby was not at all prepared for the Granny who awaited them at Shell Cottage. Not only was she all cross and sort of wild-looking, but she didn't seem to listen to Libby when she told her about the end-of-term play and the baby strawberries she'd grown at home. Worse, she shouted at Mum (Granny *never* shouted – well, only at bind-weed and slugs sometimes), and then she actually threw a load of flapjacks in the bin! Nice flapjacks, too. Really yummy ones! Teddy wanted to go and get them out of the bin when nobody was looking and Libby was so longing to have another one herself that she only just remembered about there being germs in bins at the last second and she had to reluctantly tell Teddy that she supposed they probably shouldn't.

She didn't even cheer up when Uncle Robert arrived half-way through dinner, with Harriet and Molly, and they were all together around the table. Granny smiled a little bit but it was a strange, not-truly-happy sort of smile.

Poor Granny, Libby thought that night as she lay on the narrow single bed, listening to the faint rushing sound of the sea and the gentle snoring of her brothers. She hadn't even really laughed at any of Libby's jokes – not a proper laugh anyway. Was it because of the chopped-down apple tree? she wondered. Was she missing Grandad very, very much? What if *she* was going to die soon, too?

Libby tossed and turned, unable to drift into sleep. *Shhhh . . . shhhh . . .* said the sea soothingly and she stared up at the shadowy ceiling trying not to think about the horrible ghost story Dexter had insisted on telling them earlier, the torch held spookily under his chin.

Maybe there was something she could do to cheer up her granny, she thought drowsily. Maybe she could think of a way to make her happy again.

Shhhh . . . shhhh . . . said the sea again, and Libby closed her eyes and fell fast asleep.

Chapter Seventeen

Freya was up first, thanks to Teddy, who liked to start every morning, holiday or not, on the dot of six, tugging impatiently at his mother's arm as if he had at least twenty-seven thousand interesting things to cram into his day, and didn't intend to waste a second about it.

She made him breakfast on automatic pilot, and herself a coffee, then left him to it and padded out into the garden. The rising sun had painted the sea in glittering swathes of tangerine and fuchsia, and the dull red-wine hangover that had been her waking companion seemed to subside obligingly as she breathed in the cool, fresh morning air.

Last night, she'd had two glasses of rioja at dinnertime – 'Well, it's the holidays, isn't it?' – and both Libby and Teddy had commented when she said goodnight to them that evening. 'Poo, your breath is gross,' Libby had said, backing away and wrinkling her nose, while Teddy collapsed dramatically onto the bed, pretending to be knocked out by the

smell. 'Yuck, Mummy, don't kiss me,' he'd said reproachfully, opening one eye.

Freya had laughed it off, but her laugh hadn't sounded very convincing. She'd gone back downstairs and had another glass to absorb the sting, and then another. She could feel Harriet's eyes on her a couple of times, questioning and – she winced at the memory – concerned, even, but Freya had smiled brightly on each occasion and made a point of laughing uproariously at the next funny story in their conversation. *See? I'm fine*, was the subtext. *Nothing to worry about here!*

The wet grass tickled her ankles and clung damply to her flip-flops as she walked across the lawn, over to the destroyed apple tree stump, so forlorn and battered. Crouching next to it, she reached out a hand and touched the splintered bark. 'Hi, Dad,' she said. 'If you can hear me, that is. If you've dropped in for a visit.' The base of the tree was cold and rough beneath her fingers. 'I wish you were with us. I could do with one of our chats right now.'

She wrapped her arms around herself, trying not to think about just what an understatement this was. Since Vic had returned from his training course, he and Freya hadn't really talked at all. Well, *he* had talked, obviously: about Geezer Dave and all the other people who'd been there, and the riot training they'd done, and how he was being put forward for a Police Bravery Award that autumn, and how Tony and his wife wanted to take them both out for dinner as a thank you, and all the rest of it. The starring role of Victor's stories was inevitably Victor himself, although when it was her turn to talk, Freya did the opposite and positioned the children at centre stage. And so she had talked of Ted's first wobbly tooth and Libby's end-of-term play and Dexter's request for the new 18-rated *Call of Duty* game that *all* his friends had, apparently. 'I've told him he can't have it, just for the record,' she had added, in case this wasn't clear.

That was it, though. General conversations, nothing more. No inkling about how she really felt.

She sighed. 'I can't talk to any of the others,' she went on. 'I can't even talk to Vic, Dad. I just feel so . . . lost. Like I'm about to go over a cliff. Dad, please, if you can hear me, if you're out there somewhere, then – '

She broke off, struck by the words that were coming out of her mouth. She was a *doctor*, for goodness' sake – she knew better than anyone that when somebody's heart stopped, their brain died soon after, and it was all over. Gone. There was no afterlife, in her opinion, no heavenly postscript where souls lounged around and chewed the fat up in the clouds. And here she was, speaking to her father, who was long since dead and cremated. As if he could hear her!

The weirdest thing was how comforting it felt. How it had brought her a small shining fragment of solace, just for a few still moments.

Then the peace was broken by a delighted whoop from the house. 'Ants, Mum! Come and look at all these ants!'

Later on, after the ants had been helped outside and Teddy's trail of sugar swept up from the floor, Freya found herself with two minutes to spare while Victor supervised the children's teeth-brushing. Up in her bedroom, she typed the number for the children's hospital into her phone, wondering if they would tell her how little Ava was doing, if she was on the mend or even back home already. She knew the chances of being given this information were about as slim as a supermodel, though. Close relatives only, they would say, and Freya wasn't sure she had the necessary chutzpah to try and pass herself off as a concerned grandmother or auntie.

She deleted the number and fired off a text to Elizabeth, her boss, instead.

Hi. Just wondering if any news on Ava Taylor? Freya.

She'd only just pressed 'Send' when the two younger children burst in, Libby singing 'Surfin' U.S.A.' loudly and tunelessly as she danced around the room and out again, but Teddy in a sulk because he had been deemed too small to accompany his siblings, dad and uncle on that morning's surfing lesson.

'It's not fair! I *am* old enough!' he said as Freya pulled him in for a cuddle. His little warm body was rigid and protesting at first but then he leaned against her and a sob burst out of him. 'It's not FAIR.'

Freya smoothed down his unruly curls, which promptly sprang back up again. 'You can help me do some shopping instead. Harriet and Molly are coming too. Would you like that? You can choose *all* the puddings.'

A tear glistened in his lashes as Teddy considered the suggestion. 'Just me choosing? Not the others?'

'Just you. Whatever you like. They might even have – ' she paused for dramatic effect – 'chocolate ice cream.'

Teddy's sweet tooth made the decision. Who cared about surfing when the delights of the Co-op pudding aisle lay in his control? 'Okay,' he said.

Unfortunately, Teddy's good cheer was short-lived and came to an abrupt halt as he saw his wetsuit-clad brother and sister depart excitedly with Daddy and Uncle Rob soon afterwards. His grump lasted all the way into the Ivybridge post office, as Freya paid to put up a hand-written ad for a cleaner in their window. He sulked around the first few aisles of the supermarket too, kicking at the wheels of the trolley with his arms folded crossly around himself, his lower lip sliding right out just in case nobody had noticed he was in a bad mood. 'Tala*manca*,' Freya heard him muttering darkly under his breath. 'You total Pritt Stick.'

Dexter and his rhyming slang again. The perils of having an older brother who was a self-appointed Cockney rebel. Freya let the muttering pass without comment but felt her patience stretching thin, especially when he kicked out at a crate of apples and accidentally caught an old lady on the ankle. 'Teddy! Behave yourself!' she hissed. 'I'm so sorry,' she added to her son's victim. 'Are you all right?'

'Why don't we go and look at the ice cream now?' Harriet suggested, 'and Mummy can catch us up in a bit.' She shot a questioning look at Freya, who nodded gratefully.

'Good idea,' she replied, heaving a raggedy sigh of relief as Harriet took Teddy's hand and led him away.

Harriet was a nice woman, it had to be said. Easy to get along with. Back when she and Robert had got married a few summers ago, Freya had been quite startled by just how many female friends Harriet had – a great swarm of women, thronging protectively around the bride with wide lipsticked smiles, laughing about hen night shenanigans. The 'gal pals', as Harriet referred to them in her speech, which had been greeted by raucous cheers. Freya could see why Harriet was so popular, though. She had a friendliness about her that invited confidence, an untroubled air of a woman who saw the good in everyone.

In contrast, Freya seemed to have lost the knack of making and keeping 'gal pals', her busy schedule meaning that her social circle had shrunk like expensive knickers in a hot wash.

Her closest friend from university, Mel, now lived in Liverpool with a long-standing partner, Janie, and their friendship had dwindled to occasional emails and Facebook exchanges – 'It's been ages! We must meet up soon!' 'We really must! Definitely!' But somehow they never did.

You'd have thought that having children would be the ultimate door-opener when it came to making new acquaintances, but the school playground had always seemed a hostile environment to Freya, filled with small, tight clusters of women who all knew each other and each other's children and spent great chunks of the week at each other's houses, by the sound of things. Working full-time meant that Freya was rarely there anyway, but on the odd occasion she came to pick up the younger two, she found herself on the edge, ignored each time. Sure, she had done her best to ingratiate herself, always smiling hopefully when anyone glanced in her direction, but she had discovered too late that offering unsolicited medical advice to a parent having noticed their child's ringworm or impetigo was not the most successful way to strike up a new friendship.

Freya loaded the trolley with fruit and vegetables, fresh pizzas and garlic bread, and a couple of chickens for Sunday. Sausages. Pasta sauce. Arborio rice for a risotto with any roast chicken leftovers. Squash for the children, cereal, more tea and coffee. Cheese and yogurts and bacon. Steaks for a barbecue. Toilet roll.

She caught up with Harriet and Teddy, who were having a very earnest discussion in front of the ice cream freezer. 'Thank you,' she mouthed to Harriet, as Teddy pointed out his chosen products with the satisfied air of a boy who'd done his bit for family enjoyment and confidently predicted many well-scraped pudding bowls ahead.

'Any time,' Harriet said, ruffling Teddy's hair. 'He's gorgeous. Aren't you, Tedster?'

The gorgeous boy squirmed away and went to inspect an end-of-aisle display of summer toys: footballs, water pistols, inflatable lilos and the like. 'Gorgeous, and hoping for a water pistol, alas,' Freya said dryly, shaking her head no at him as he held one up.

Harriet smiled, then looked back at Freya. There was a delicate moment of silence, then she asked, 'Listen . . . is everything all right? Tell me to butt out if you don't want to talk, but . . .'

Freya felt her face stiffen. Was everything all right? *Well, now, Harriet,* she imagined saying, *I might have inadvertently caused a baby to die at work. I'm scared of Victor finding out what a screw-up I really am. I miss my dad desperately and am worried about Mum . . . Yeah, sure, everything's brilliant!*

She forced a rigid smile instead. 'I'm fine,' she said brightly. 'Everything's fine!'

Just then Teddy emerged from the far aisle, where he must have slipped away unnoticed. He was carrying a huge bottle of Bombay Sapphire and looking very pleased with himself. 'I got your favourite one, Mummy!' he yelled at top volume, lifting a hand to wave and accidentally letting go of the bottle, which smashed to the floor.

Oh Christ. Kill me now, thought Freya, hurrying towards him, scarlet-faced. *Just kill me now.*

Chapter Eighteen

Olivia was slumped in a deckchair on the lawn outside Shell Cottage, even though the sky was overcast and the sun defeated by thick muffling clouds. Everyone else was out, and she had found herself thinking nostalgically about summers gone by, when Freya and Robert were tiny and she and Alec had spent so much time with them down on the beach. Long golden days, laughing and playing, all enjoying their perfect family holidays together. She couldn't help looking back through a filter of melancholy, wondering if she'd ever laugh like that again.

A breeze rushed around the garden, shaking the branches of the plum tree, bustling through the long grasses as if in a tearing hurry. The lawn needed mowing, really, and the beds were becoming crowded by all the weeds that had seized upon Olivia's apathy as a chance to gatecrash the nicest borders. They had 'a man' in the village who came and maintained the garden year-round whenever the Tarrants weren't in the house, but while she was staying Olivia liked to get back on top of things herself and sink her fingers into the rich, crumbly Devon soil again.

This time she didn't feel like touching any of it, though. The sweet peas had gone berserk, a bright wigwam of colour and perfume in her sunniest border, and normally she'd be cutting bunches every day, filling vases and jugs and jam jars with the pretty papery flowers. But this year, she –

'Cooeee!'

A loud female voice jolted her out of her thoughts. Turning – rather awkwardly, thanks to the deckchair – Olivia saw that a dented silver Mini had been parked at an angle in the driveway, and then a woman came striding around the side of the house, flip-flops slapping on the ground.

'Cooeee! Anyone th—? Oh! Hello.'

The woman was in her fifties, at a guess, with a scarlet sleeveless top and a denim skirt. There was a jiggle of bingo wings going on but her legs were tanned and shapely, her glossy toenails the same shade as her top. She was chewing a wad of gum and shifted it to the side of her mouth as she flipped up Jackie O sunglasses and smiled at Olivia. 'Gloria. Hello,' she said. 'Your new cleaner.'

'My new – ? Oh. Are you? Since when?'

Olivia hadn't meant her words to come out sounding quite so unfriendly, but Gloria just laughed – a low, husky laugh that bore testament to an allegiance lasting several decades with Benson and Hedges at a guess. 'Since someone put up a note in the post office?' She waved a postcard between finger and thumb. 'Right here. Cleaner wanted for light household duties . . .'

'Oh,' Olivia said again, feeling as if she'd been caught off guard. Freya must have placed the advert, she presumed, although this woman was certainly very quick off the mark. 'I see. Well . . . do you have any references? A CV?' Her eyes narrowed. 'By the way, did you actually take the postcard out of the post office window? Only I think the idea is that you leave it there for other people to see as well.'

Gloria looked amused at the questions. She had coral-coloured lipstick, which clashed rather horribly with her henna-red hair, and about twenty coats of black mascara framing soft brown eyes. 'A CV? For a cleaning job?' she asked, a laugh bubbling beneath her words. 'You don't need O levels or – whatchamacallem – GCSEs to push a hoover round, darling. Not round here, you don't anyway.' She tapped the card impatiently against her fingers and Olivia caught a waft of cheap floral perfume mingled with Eau de Fags. 'So . . . ?'

Olivia thought about their cleaner back in London – Maria, who was meek and obedient, who tiptoed around the house like a polite shadow. She had come to them through an agency who promised rigorous checks on all their staff: visas, criminal records, previous employment history, the works. None of this turning up and brazenly asking for a job in a person's garden.

All of a sudden, she felt very old and very tired. She wasn't sure she even wanted a cleaner right now, anyway, when she was still so wounded and vulnerable. 'This is not really the way I like to do business,' she said. 'Perhaps you could telephone to make an appointment, rather than . . .' She waved a hand. 'Rather than *this* approach.'

Gloria's arms fell by her sides, the card dangling from her fingers. 'Ahh. Okay,' she said. Then she rummaged in a grubby white fringed handbag and pulled out a small pink phone. 'Right, then, let's see.' She peered at the postcard. 'I can't make out the number,' she said apologetically. 'Where are my reading specs, then?'

Olivia glared. This woman was the limit.

Failing to locate the reading glasses, Gloria held the card at arm's length and squinted. 'Tiny handwriting,' she grumbled. 'Don't suppose you could just tell me the number, like, could you? Do me a favour?'

Olivia gave her a withering look, which went unnoticed. 'Are you seriously asking me to tell you the number of my phone so that you can then ring it, and have me go up into the house to answer it?'

Gloria shrugged. 'Well, that's what you wanted, wasn't it?'

'Yes, but I didn't mean *now*, I meant—'

'Well, I'm here now, aren't I?' Another shrug. 'We could

pretend we were on the phone, if you want? If that makes any difference. I dunno, I just thought this might be the quickest way around it, like, but if you want me to sit in my car for ten minutes and *then* phone, I suppose I could . . .' She left the sentence hanging as if to say, *I'm not the crazy one here, love.*

Goodness, but she was exasperating. Olivia wished that Freya or Robert would materialize to deal with this Gloria, because she, for one, did not have the stamina today. She was just about to plead a headache and ask her to come back and talk to Freya later on, when Gloria spoke again.

'Hey, I was sorry to hear about your fella, by the way.' To give her credit, she had stopped smirking now and did look sincere at least. 'I liked his books. Me and my husband took it in turns to buy his new ones at Christmas; proper good, every time.'

The unexpected kindness took the wind right out of Olivia's sails. 'Thank you,' she managed to say tightly after a small pause.

'My husband died this year too, back in February. Came off his motorbike and cracked his head open, the dozy bugger.' Gloria's face twisted in a helpless spasm. 'So I do understand what you're going through. I'm right there in the same mess myself.'

'Th-thank you,' Olivia said again. There was another pause and then, because she was a good-mannered woman, even under extreme duress, she added, 'Sorry to hear about your husband.'

'It's shit, isn't it?' Gloria burst out. 'Proper shit. I don't know how I've got through the last few months, I really don't. But now, look at the pair of us. You need your house cleaning and I need some cash. So you could say we make a good couple. Destined for each other, like.'

Olivia snorted. Those weren't the exact phrases she'd had on the tip of her tongue. 'The thing is—'

Gloria was already talking over her. 'It's just . . . well, you could be waiting a while, that's all. If you're going to be interviewing and wanting references and all that sh – kind of stuff. And I'm not being rude but I had a peep through the front windows and . . .' She shrugged. 'Well. Not to put too fine a point on it, darl, but the place looks a bit of a tip to me. No offence, like. I'm not being rude. But—'

It was like trying to argue with a politician – a politician with only one objective in mind: win the conversation. Get what I want. Have it my way. 'Oh, all *right*,' said Olivia in defeat, putting up a hand to stem this torrent of words. Seeing as Gloria had pinched the postcard out of the post office window, they wouldn't get anyone else coming along until they'd sorted out a replacement advert anyway, and she wasn't sure she had the motivation to do such a thing herself. Besides, the woman was right, the house was a mess. What harm could it do to let her blast around the downstairs rooms with a hoover and J-cloth at least, and scrub some of the stickiness out of the kitchen? Freya had given it a half-hearted once-over the other day, but the whole house could do with a proper clean, after Olivia's negligence. She took a deep breath, hoping she wasn't on the verge of making a terrible mistake. 'Maybe I could give you a trial run. When are you free?'

Gloria beamed. She had a wide, Julia Roberts-esque mouth and good teeth; it was a nice smile despite the awful lipstick. 'Now?'

A moment passed where a series of horror-story images flashed through Olivia's mind. Gloria ransacking the place while holding Olivia hostage. Gloria casing the joint and returning after darkness with a gang of men and snarling dogs. Gloria with a hand around Olivia's throat, puffing smoke into her face . . .

Hmm. Olivia glanced at Gloria's yellowed fingers and realized that there was the clincher. She could murder a cigarette right now. 'Why not?' she said, getting to her feet. Her bones felt leaden as she stood up, and the air seemed to press down on her, thick and humid like a heavy shawl. 'I'll show you what needs doing. But first . . .' She hesitated. 'I don't suppose you could crash me a ciggy, while you're here, could you?'

Gloria beamed again. 'Of course, darling! No problemo. I'll join you.'

*

Over cigarettes on the patio – 'I daren't smoke inside, I suspect my daughter's already on the verge of checking me into rehab as it is,' Olivia confessed with a grimace – the two women chatted about this and that, and Olivia took the opportunity to find out a bit more about her potential new employee.

Gloria was fifty-eight, like Olivia, and she and her husband Bill had run the local pet shop for twenty-seven years, she said. But in the space of six months, a huge pet-shop chain had opened in an out-of-town mall, and then the big garden centre out on the ring road began selling fish tanks and hamster cages, and business had completely divebombed. When Bill died, soon afterwards, Gloria was faced with mounting debts and a business in its death throes and she had bailed out while she could. Since then, she'd taken on cleaning jobs where possible, shifts of bar work in The Dray and Horses, and she'd even done a bit of modelling at the local amateur art club.

Olivia raised a shocked eyebrow. 'You mean . . . *nude* modelling?' It was the last thing – the very last thing – she could imagine her other cleaner, shy, timid Maria, doing. It was the last thing she could imagine herself doing either, for that matter.

Gloria winked and puffed out a smoke ring that quivered between them for a few moments before it dispersed. 'Hell, yeah. Pays brilliantly,' she said. 'And it's actually kind of lib-erating to get your kit off in front of a room full of strangers.' She took a last drag from her cigarette then dropped it on the paving slab and ground it out with her foot. 'You should come along sometime if you're at a loose end. Tuesday mornings. It'll make you feel like a goddess.'

Olivia stubbed out her cigarette in the small tin ashtray that Freya had pointedly left on the patio table. She didn't like the way the conversation was going all of a sudden; the balance seemed to have shifted. Was Gloria laughing at her? 'I don't think so,' she said briskly. Time to set down a few boundaries. Rule number one: cleaners should not go around inviting their bosses to strip off and model in the nude with them, however friendly a conversation they might previously have had. They just shouldn't. 'Right. Let's get on with it, then. If you could make a start on the kitchen – floor, work-tops, cooker, everything – then I'll put the coffee machine on. How do you like yours?'

'Ooh, how I like my men: strong and black,' Gloria said with that husky laugh again. Then she picked up her cigar-ette butt and dropped it in the ashtray, wiping her hands on her denim skirt. 'Only joking.' She turned her face up to the sky. 'Sorry, Bill!' she called. 'Only messing. Go back to your fishing and take no notice.'

Olivia couldn't help feeling a moment's solidarity with the beleaguered Bill. Gloria was a force to be reckoned with, like nobody she'd ever met before. She glanced at her watch and hoped Freya would be home soon, just in case she needed rescuing. Then she gave another polite smile and opened the back door of the house. 'If you'd like to follow me?'

Chapter Nineteen

Sometime later, once the gin had been mopped up from the supermarket floor and Freya had apologized to approximately seventeen different members of staff, and Teddy had finally stopped crying, they finished the shopping and were at the checkout, packing carrier bags full of groceries. Freya could see through the glass walls at the front of the shop that Molly was perched on a wall outside, waiting for them, having tired early of the Ivybridge shopping facilities. With her phone tucked under her chin, the girl looked a picture of youth and beauty in denim short shorts and a turquoise scoop-necked T-shirt which read TOO GOOD FOR YOU.

Beep, beep, beep went the cashier's scanner. Molly twirled a lock of tawny hair around her free hand as she talked, her expression alternately coy and on the verge of bursting out laughing. A boy, Freya thought, plucking hopelessly at a new plastic bag in a vain attempt to open it up. It had to be a boy. No girl or woman ever looked that way about a mere friend.

Beep, beep, beep. Molly had her head on one side

coquettishly, a little smile playing on her lips, one of her flip-flops dangling from her toes as she murmured into the phone. The whole scene was as flirtatious and come-hither as if the boy had been right there in front of her.

Freya nudged Harriet. 'Let me guess. Important conversation with boyfriend taking place out there,' she said.

Harriet glanced over and laughed. 'No!' she said. 'Molly's not interested in boys yet. It'll be Chloe, I bet, her best mate. They're practically joined at the hip back in London.'

Before she could reply, Freya was distracted by Teddy, who was rummaging through one of the carrier bags, trying to find the multi-pack of Hula Hoops and tipping out the apples in the process. 'Oi! Fingers out,' she told him sternly. Next time she'd send Ted out on a surfing lesson with the others, too young or not, she decided. It was like trying to go shopping with a monkey, having him here.

Once they'd packed everything and paid up, Freya manoeuvred the laden trolley outside, where Molly was still on the phone.

'Don't say that! As *if*.' Giggle, giggle, eyes bright. 'No, that was *you* . . . Oh, you think so, do you?' She became aware of the others coming towards them just then and hopped down from the wall, turning slightly to shield herself. 'Listen, I'd better go. Yeah, I know you are. Course you are.' She laughed. 'Oh, all right. I miss you too. Happy now? Speak to you later.'

'Let me guess,' Harriet said as her daughter hung up. 'Chloe's got these well nice new shoes and she had to describe them to you, stitch by stitch, because they're, like, so totally amazing and awesome.'

Molly beamed. 'Something like that,' she said, but Freya was not wholly convinced. She would have put money on that phone conversation being with a boy. Maybe that was how teenagers spoke to each other these days, though.

As they walked to the car, Harriet and Molly fell into stride ahead of Freya and Teddy. Molly really was gorgeous, Freya thought with a sigh for her own lost youth. Her skin was flawless – translucent and radiant; she had high cheekbones, a luscious wide mouth and that great sweep of long caramel-coloured hair. How did Harriet dare let her walk around London unchaperoned, when she was so ripe and beautiful? Even in Ivybridge, you could feel the stares from teenage boys and men alike, heads turning, tongues practically hanging out in the Co-op car park. Freya would want a full burqa and bodyguard for Libby if she blossomed into such a peach, along with a sign around her neck reading *Hands Off. Out of Your League. Her Father is Six Foot Two and a Policeman, I'll Have You Know.*

To Freya's surprise, the hallway at Shell Cottage was absolutely sparkling when they arrived back half an hour later. She stood there for a moment, barely noticing the plastic handles of the shopping bags cutting into her fingers, as she gazed around at the transformation. The black-and-white-tiled floor, which, only a few hours ago, had been coated in a fine powdering of sand, strands of dried grass and general sticky grime, positively gleamed. The mirror – previously smeared with fingerprints and thick with dust – shone with the light from the open front door, reflecting Freya's own surprised face back at her.

Further into the house, the kitchen now resembled something from a Flash advert. The worktops had been cleared and all the toast crumbs wiped away, the pile of washing-up had vanished, and a load of laundry tumbled obediently around the washing machine. The floor shone, the hob was newly spatter and grease free, and a damp cloth hung tidily over the shining mixer tap, as if taking a rest from all its hard labour.

It was only the scent of bleach and cigarette smoke hanging in the air that convinced her she was not in some kind of dream world or hallucination. *Whoa*, as her kids would say. Mum had certainly been busy while they were out.

'Wow!' Harriet said, almost cannoning into her as she came in. 'Has Katie come over, do you think?'

Freya set the shopping bags on the floor, still marvelling. 'I don't know,' she replied, just as Olivia appeared and jumped to see her daughter standing there.

'Oh! You're back. I didn't hear the car.'

'We've only been here ten seconds. We were just saying how lovely it looks in here. Has Katie been round, or did you get stuck in yourself?'

'Neither. This is all down to Gloria. Our new cleaner.' Olivia's lips twitched suddenly. 'Our nude-modelling, former pet-shop-owning, widowed cleaner. Who's done rather a good job so far, I have to say.'

Freya was trying to compute all of those adjectives at once but it was no use: her mind was blown. 'The nude-modelling . . . ?'

'Of course, she only had time to do in here and the hall today. Something about going to see a man about a dog. Whether it was pet shop related or coincidental, your guess is as good as mine, but there you have it. She'll be back tomorrow to do the living room and bedrooms.' Olivia gestured to the laundry. 'And I put this lot on,' she added, looking uncharacteristically proud of herself.

'Right.' Freya rubbed her forehead, still not feeling quite up to speed on the strange turn of events. *I go out to the shops, I leave you for a few hours and this is what happens?* 'Well . . . great,' she added eventually. As long as the house was cleaned by somebody, it made no odds to her who that person might be. And there was still time to patch things up with Katie and bring her back into the fold, after all. Yes. She'd check out this strange-sounding Gloria, and if there was any kind of dodginess afoot then Freya would dispatch her and phone Katie, begging if she had to.

She went out to get the rest of the shopping, still puzzling it all over. She hoped Mum was okay. The whole thing sounded very odd indeed.

Chapter Twenty

Dinner that evening was a huge plateful of Aberdeen Angus steak burgers, slightly blackened and all the better for it, in Harriet's opinion. She had cooked an entire bag of Jersey Royal potatoes, adding lashings of creamy Devon butter and sprinkling them with mint snipped from the garden, while Freya had assembled a salad.

Harriet had enjoyed spending some time with Freya and Teddy that day. She had always found Freya rather distant in the past. Perfectly nice, don't get her wrong, but just the tiniest bit cool and offhand, not what you'd call super-friendly. Perhaps Harriet was being paranoid but she had wondered a few times previously if Freya looked down on her, secretly thinking she and Molly weren't good enough for the likes of Robert. Mind you, Harriet had always felt kind of shambolic and inferior to the Tarrants full stop, because they were so clever and well-off, basically, and because so many people judged single mothers and often not in a good way. It was difficult not to be ultra-defensive about these things.

Anyway, it had been rather an eye-opener, their shopping trip, because for the first time ever, Freya had seemed kind of vulnerable. Fragile. She definitely wasn't her usual composed self, that was for sure. Harriet had tried asking if she was okay but Freya's face had closed up like a clam. *I'm fine*, she'd said at once, but it was not a convincing response, especially as she turned bright red and practically burst into tears ten seconds later when Teddy went and dropped that gin bottle. Harriet would keep a weather eye on her for the time being, she decided.

Over dinner, the surfers were in high spirits with tales of dramatic megawaves and theatrical tumbles, as well as moments of triumph for them all. Robert, who always became pathetically competitive whenever Victor was around (much to Harriet's dismay), boasted of riding an eight-footer, although nobody else seemed to have witnessed this.

In contrast, Olivia still seemed out of sorts, barely joining in with the conversation, which ranged from a discussion about who was going to win the family swingball championship this summer (Teddy was most vociferous in anticipating personal glory, although Harriet caught the distinctly unsporting glint in her husband's eye which said, *Over my dead body*) through to a period of whinging about why the children had to eat lettuce when it was like *leaves* and it wasn't like they were *giraffes* or anything, and then finally (and thankfully, if the tired snap in Freya's voice was anything to go by) onto what everyone wanted to do the next day.

A hike was mooted – by Robert, of course, who had to go and suggest a really hard walk on Dartmoor, the sort attempted by professional mountaineers for charity slog-athons, just to prove how he fit he was. Much to Harriet's secret relief, this was shot down first by Dexter, who declared scathingly that walks were boring, and then by Molly, who said, with withering sarcasm, 'Er, hello? We can *walk* in London. And there'll be no signal at all on Dartmoor!'

Harriet gave her a look. 'We are not here solely for the phone signal,' she said primly, hoping that nobody thought her daughter too bad-mannered. And then, ignoring the muttered 'You're telling me' that came from her beloved, added quickly, 'We could go kayaking.' They'd all enjoyed this the summer before. It had been like Swallows and Amazons, setting off down the river in convoy, Alec with a pirate hat on his head, shouting 'Yo, ho, ho and a bottle of rum!'

'Yeah, kayaking!' Libby said, her face lighting up. 'Granny, you could come too. Remember how last time we—'

But Olivia didn't look as if kayaking was uppermost in her mind, as she suddenly pushed her plate away, knocking over the salt pot. 'I can't do this any more. I just can't. I have to tell you,' she said, her mouth buckling as if she were in pain. Everyone turned towards her except Teddy, who was enjoying the fart noises he was making with the ketchup bottle way too much, and Molly who was surreptitiously typing a text on her phone under the table.

'Stop that, Ted,' Freya hissed. 'Mum, what's wrong?'

'Tell us what?' Robert asked. 'Are you okay?'

'Do you want to hear one of my jokes, Granny?' Libby asked kindly. 'Knock, knock.'

'Not now, darling,' Freya said urgently. 'Mum? What is it? Are you unwell?'

Olivia took a deep breath, one pale hand clutching her throat, then looked from her daughter to her son and shook her head. 'We need to talk,' she said. 'It's . . . It's something bad. I thought I could keep it from you, but I just can't pretend any longer.' She got to her feet rather unsteadily, abandoning the rest of her dinner. 'I'll be in the snug,' she said, and left the room.

Talk about going out on a cliffhanger. Freya and Robert looked at one another and rose from the table wordlessly, food abandoned, as they hurried to follow her. Harriet gazed at Victor, who shrugged blankly. 'Eat up, everyone,' Harriet said in the deafening silence that remained.

'So are we going kayaking, or not?' Teddy wanted to know, unmoved by all the drama. A huge splurge of ketchup burst out of the bottle and drowned what was left of his salad. 'Whoops,' he said innocently.

'Can I leave the rest of my tea?' Libby added in the next breath. 'Can we get down from the table?'

Victor was gazing back at the door through which the Tarrants had all departed. 'Er . . . yeah. Sure,' he said distractedly, which both children claimed as their answer, Teddy giving a fist-pump and Libby sliding down from her chair before he could change his mind. Her siblings quickly followed.

Molly looked up from her phone and did a double take. 'Where did everyone go? What's going on?'

Harriet spread her hands wide. 'That,' she said, 'is the question.'

Whatever the announcement was, it was taking a while, Harriet thought as she finished the washing-up and then poured herself a glass of Pinot Grigio. Seeing Victor out in the garden with the children, Teddy hoisted up on his shoulders and all of them laughing as they attempted a game of badminton doubles over the washing line, she poured him one too. 'Sustenance right here when you need it, Vic,' she called, taking both glasses up to the patio table on the terrace.

He was nice, Victor, she thought, watching the scene as she sipped her wine. Tall and broad, with cropped dark hair and lovely olive skin (she was sure he'd already tanned a shade darker from being on the beach today), he had a directness about him that she found pleasing, a way of looking at you when you spoke as if he were really listening to your every word, mentally noting down each detail in his little policeman's book. You could tell he was good at his job too – he was always fair to the children, never losing his cool with them, even during Olympic-standard bouts of bickering and She-started-it-No-*he*-started-it fisticuffs.

Seeing him with his brood like that gave her a pang for all the babies she'd never quite had, the big family she'd always wanted. Some things just weren't meant to be, though. She'd accepted that long ago and was grateful for Molly and Robert at least. They were enough for any woman.

A few minutes later, Victor lowered Teddy to the ground, pleading exhaustion, and came up to the terrace, grinning. 'Good one, thanks,' he said, taking up the glass of wine. 'That's exactly what I need right now.'

'I wonder what's going on inside,' Harriet said as he sank into the chair beside her. 'Olivia and the others, I mean. Have you got any clue what all of this is about?'

'Not the foggiest. Olivia seemed pretty on edge, though. She has done since we got here. Definitely not her usual self.'

'Yeah.' Harriet hesitated. 'Actually, I was wondering . . . is Freya all right at the moment? She doesn't quite seem herself either.'

Victor looked surprised at the question. 'Freya? Sure, why?'

'Oh.' Back-pedal, back-pedal. 'It's just . . . Nothing, really.

Must be the social worker in me, worrying about everyone, that's all.'

Victor shrugged. 'No need to worry. You know Freya – the ultimate coping machine. She's always on good form.'

Harriet didn't quite know what to say. Was he for real? He was married to Freya and yet couldn't see what Harriet had noticed – that she was really fragile and stressed out. She was packing away the booze, too. Last night, she'd drunk so much, Harriet was amazed she could get upstairs to bed in one piece.

Before she could reply, though, the back door of the house banged and then Freya and Robert came marching up the path towards them, tears rolling down Freya's face. 'Well, she doesn't seem all that happy now,' Harriet murmured, before jumping to her feet. 'What's happened? What's wrong?' she cried.

Freya reached the terraced area and flung herself into one of the chairs, her back deliberately turned to the children. 'Oh my God, Vic,' she said. 'I can't believe it. I just can't believe it.'

'What? Is your mum okay?' he asked, reaching out for her. 'What did she say?'

'It's Dad,' said Robert, catching up, white-faced. 'He had an affair.'

Harriet's jaw dropped open. Had an *affair*? No way. Not Alec. He was devoted to Olivia. His face had softened with love every time he so much as glanced her way! 'No,' she breathed. 'Shit. No wonder your mum's been looking so upset.' She clapped a hand to her mouth, feeling almost as sad as if it had been her own parents. 'Oh my God. I'm so sorry. I always thought they were, like, the happiest couple in the world.' Robert sat down next to her and she wrapped her arms around him. 'What a terrible shock.'

'That's not all.' Robert looked at Freya, who was still pale and weeping. 'There's a child,' he said heavily. 'Our half-brother.'

'And I've met him,' Freya spluttered. 'The kid with the flapjacks; Katie's son. I even thought he looked familiar!' She scrubbed at her eyes furiously then turned to Victor with real pain in her face. 'And all this time we had no idea. No clue whatsoever that there was a cuckoo in the nest. An extra kid brother!'

It wasn't long before their mother's distress filtered down to the bat-like ears of the Castledine children, and their badminton game was abandoned, racquets dropped to the lawn. 'Why is Mum crying?' asked Teddy uncertainly, hanging back and staring.

'Mum!' cried Libby, loping across the grass. 'What's the matter?'

Freya pushed her tears away and smiled a wet and very

artificial smile. 'Nothing, darling, I'm fine. It's just . . . hay fever.'

'But – ' Libby didn't look convinced but Victor rose to his feet and headed her off before she could say another word.

'Mum's fine,' he said, 'but you grubby lot all need a bath or shower. Teddy! You're up first, mate. Come on.' He glanced back at Freya. 'I'll get this lot washed and ready for bed.'

'Ready for *bed*?' Dexter said indignantly. 'It's not even seven o'clock!'

'Well, clean at the very least,' Victor said, herding the three of them towards the house with impressive aplomb. 'Chop chop. Quick march. You can have some pudding once you're in your pyjamas, if there's no mucking around.'

Once they'd gone, Harriet looked from Robert to Freya, both of whom seemed to have lost the power of speech. 'I am so sorry,' she said. 'What a shock. And your poor mum too.'

Freya nodded miserably, draining Victor's glass of Pinot in a single mouthful, and Harriet seized an opportunity to offer some practical help. 'I'll get more wine,' she said, dashing inside.

By the time she had located the bottle and extra glasses, Robert was loitering at the back door. 'I need to go for a walk,' he said, raking a hand through his hair. 'Clear my head. This is completely nuts.'

Of course. This was Robert's answer to everything: to move, whether it be walking or running or cycling, just working his body, hard and fast, to try and relieve the build-up of stress. 'Do you want me to come with you?' she asked, remembering Freya weeping up on the terrace and now presumably alone. 'Because . . .'

He shook his head. 'I'd rather be on my own,' he said. 'Whereas Freya . . .'

'Yeah.' *Whereas Freya should definitely not be on her own in this state. Got it.* Harriet gave him a hug. 'Okay, well, take care, all right? Don't go too far. Make sure you come back again.'

His lips smiled briefly but his eyes were sad, so sad. 'I'll be back,' he said. He must have been *really* sad because he didn't even do an Arnold Schwarzenegger impression as he said the words.

Meanwhile, Freya was pink-eyed, her face swollen and puffy from tears, so Harriet hurried back up to her and poured her a gigantic glass of wine. 'Here,' she said. 'Get that down you. What a shitty bit of news to hear.'

Freya gulped. 'Yes,' she said. 'Yet another shitty piece of shitness in Freya Castledine's shit-tastic shitsville life.' And with that, she drained the glass in two swallows and filled it up again.

Whoa. Okay, then. So Harriet had been right. Something *was* troubling her sister-in-law, just as she'd suspected.

'Do you know what?' Freya said before she could respond to this declaration. 'You're the first person in this whole family who has actually asked me, am I all right. Yeah. You! The only one. Mum hasn't noticed. My own husband hasn't noticed. Too busy rescuing everyone else to remember I'm even here. But who's left to rescue me? Nobody, that's who.' Her mouth trembled and she twisted her fingers in her lap. 'And then today, in Ivybridge Co-op, you asked me, was everything all right. The only one to ask. And I said . . .' She began to cry again. 'And I said yes, everything was fine. But it isn't. It isn't fine at all.'

Harriet reached out and put a hand on Freya's. 'What's going on?' she asked softly. 'Tell me.'

It was as if she'd uttered an enchantment, some kind of code that unlocked Freya. Because out it all came: how worried she was that she'd screwed up at work. How desperately she missed her father, and how this latest bombshell had completely rocked her adoration of him. But also – saddest of all – was that she felt she couldn't talk to anyone about it, because everyone was under the illusion that she was some kind of superwoman who could manage everything flung at her without breaking a sweat.

'And I can't,' Freya sobbed, draining another glass of wine.

'I can't manage any of it any more. And I don't know what to do.'

Harriet hugged her, feeling desperately sorry for her. The 'coping machine' Victor had called her. Her own husband, and he hadn't even picked up on any of this! She knew that Olivia, too, had leaned heavily on her daughter since Alec's death – the whole family had, until Freya, quite naturally, had reached breaking point. And now look at her: defeated and unhappy and crying all over Harriet's shoulder.

'Oh, lovey,' Harriet said, feeling Freya's body heave with so many pent-up tears. 'Oh, Freya. Don't worry. Get it all out.'

Get it all out was exactly what Freya did for several minutes, while Harriet just held her and rubbed her back as if she were a tired child in need of comfort. Eventually, Freya took a long, shuddering breath and pulled away, blowing her nose and trying to control herself. 'Sorry,' she mumbled.

'Don't be,' Harriet said. 'You really needed that, I can tell.'

'I really did,' Freya said. She looked exhausted all of a sudden.

'I think everyone's taken you for granted recently, haven't they?' Harriet said. 'Good old Freya, she won't mind doing this for me. Good old Freya, she's brilliant at juggling everything, she can handle it if I add one more thing to her load.' She risked a joke, gently elbowing the other woman.

'It's your own fault, you know. You're too bloody fantastic at everything. They've stopped remembering that you're a human being as well, and that actually you're all juggled out.'

Freya nodded. 'Yeah,' she said, but she didn't smile.

'You need a break, that's all,' Harriet said. 'This hasn't been much of a holiday for you so far, has it?' She thought quickly. 'But Rob and I can take the children out if you and Vic need some time together. And obviously forget about things like cooking and chores – the rest of us can get stuck into that. Maybe you just need some time off to sleep, read, go swimming . . . whatever you want. But . . .' She cleared her throat, suddenly feeling self-conscious. She and her sister-in-law had never been particularly close, after all. 'But you don't have to keep on coping if it's too much for you. You don't have to struggle along alone. I think your mum and Victor would be shocked to find out how low you've been feeling. And I'm here. You can bend my ear any time, all right?'

'Thank you,' Freya said but Harriet wasn't sure she was even listening any more because her eyes had gone very faraway. 'I keep thinking about all the lovely things Dad ever did for me, you know? Coming to pick me up from university early one winter when I was ill. Making the most beautiful speech on my wedding day. The way he'd ring up, just for a chat, and his voice always sounded as if he was smiling. I really loved him. So much.'

'Of course you did. I know you did. He was such a wonderful man.'

'But to hear that all this time – ' her voice shook – 'he was carrying on with *Katie* . . . I mean, she's younger than me. Don't you think that's gross? I'm not sure I'd be able to believe it, if I hadn't seen that boy with my own eyes. Leo.' She grimaced, real pain on her face. 'He looks so like Dad I should have guessed right then. But you don't expect such a thing to ever happen, do you?'

'No,' Harriet agreed, trying to imagine how she would feel if she discovered her father had been carrying on with her friend Gabbi, or someone else her age. It was quite difficult, admittedly, as her dad, a leading entomology professor, tended only to have conversations about a) insects or b) cricket, but all the same. The very notion made her queasy. 'That is gross,' she agreed. 'And really upsetting.' She held up the empty bottle. 'I'll get more wine.'

By ten o'clock, they had sunk the best part of two bottles of Pinot and the dark garden seemed to be sliding around them, like a fairground waltzer. There was still no sign of Robert, or of Vic, who Freya predicted had probably nodded off while reading one of the younger two a bedtime story. A silver crescent moon floated in the velvety blackness of the sky, and you could hear the gentle rushing of the waves down in the bay. The perfect summer evening, except of course it wasn't.

'So what are you going to do?' Harriet asked, slumped back in her rattan chair, her feet tucked under her for warmth. It was starting to get chilly but she felt too drunk to go inside for a blanket or a jumper. 'About everything, I mean. You are going to talk to Vic, aren't you? I really think you should.'

Her words were slurring, her lips floppy, but Freya sounded even worse. 'No,' she said, shaking her head. 'No. Can't talk to him. Just can't.'

'You can,' Harriet argued. 'You have to. You have to tell him what you've told me. He's got no idea how you feel, you know. I asked him tonight, what's wrong with Freya? She doesn't seem herself. And he said, nothing's wrong.'

Freya snorted. 'That figures.'

'Which is why you have to tell him. Really! He'd be devastated if he knew all of this.'

'Devastated if I knew all of what?' came a voice, and they froze for a moment before spotting Victor's shadowy figure through the darkness, very much awake and striding up the path towards them. How long had he been listening there? 'Sorry,' he said. 'I dozed off on Ted's bed. What's going on?'

'Nothing,' Freya said immediately.

'Freya . . .' said Harriet.

'I said nothing!' Freya snapped, and lurched up onto her feet. 'Leave me alone!'

And then in the next moment, she had taken off and was running a drunken zigzag through the garden. 'What are you doing?' Victor shouted after her. 'What the hell's wrong with her?' he asked Harriet, when no reply came.

Harriet felt very drunk and very cold and very tired. 'Just . . . go after her,' she said, seeing Freya vanish through the gate that led down to the beach. 'Just go, Victor. She's not a coping machine, whatever you think. She needs you. Go!'

Chapter Twenty-One

Another son in the family. A kid brother, a third of his age. Holy Christ. Nobody had seen that one coming, thought Robert in bed that night, when he had finally returned to Shell Cottage and trudged up the dark staircase. Nobody had had the faintest.

Beside him, Harriet slept fitfully – it was languidly muggy, even now at two o'clock in the morning – but Robert's brain was still whirling; there was no way he was going to sleep a wink.

He stared up at the ceiling, feeling hollow with sadness. Your parents weren't supposed to let you down so badly. The mask wasn't supposed to slip. Perhaps he was too trusting but his mum and dad – particularly his dad – had always seemed superhuman in Robert's eyes, proper grown-ups, the like of which he was still aspiring to emulate. And yet Alec had failed them all, twice as it turned out – once with this affair with Katie (Katie! She was *their* age, for crying out loud, it was almost perverse!) and then again with Leo, Robert's all-new half-brother, blinkingly shoved into the hot Tarrant limelight.

Well, good luck to the lad. Really, good luck to him. If he was expecting any kind of open-arm welcome from Olivia, he would have a long wait. And what if the story broke in the media? What if the world got to hear that Alec Tarrant, devoted husband and father, had had a secret mistress and love child? Nobody would want that kind of attention, least of all a kid. Being Alec Tarrant's son was a curse and a blessing, as Robert knew all too well. What was more, in his experience, being Alec Tarrant's son led you to do some very stupid things.

Robert had mused upon the strangeness of having a famous father many times, right from when his teacher at junior school pulled him up for poor spelling. 'What would your dad say about that, then, hmm?' she had asked, raising an eyebrow.

To the nine-year-old Robert, who had until then enjoyed a certain cachet in the playground for having a dad in the public eye, this was like being drenched with a bucket of cold water. The realization that this was how it would always be – he would be judged against his dad his entire life – was devastating. How could a small boy ever measure up to such a giant of a man? How could anyone?

Other adults were kinder. One English teacher had written *Like father, like son!*, at the bottom of one half-decent essay and drawn a smiley face in red pen. His girlfriend, Emma, back when he was twenty-two, had gratifyingly never heard of Alec Tarrant, and assured Robert that he was miles better looking anyway. But such cases were few and far between, compared to the hordes of people who immediately made judgements about him, once they knew his name. The conversation usually travelled along the same well-trodden tracks.

You're Alec Tarrant's son? Oh wow! Do you write yourself? (No.)

God, that must have been amazing, growing up with him. Did he tell you really cool bedtime stories? (No.)

Are you tempted to have a go at the old writing thing yourself? (Well . . .)

So what do you do, then? Something creative as well? (I'm a cycle courier – or sales executive, or whatever else he was doing at the time.)

Oh. Right! Well, nice to meet you. Any chance you could get me your dad's autograph?

It was enough to drive you nuts, frankly, particularly the way the exchange would invariably end with the other person's thinly disguised pitying looks, their polite smiles and sudden hurry to leave. If he hadn't been Dad's son, nobody would have cared that he was a so-called underachiever.

Instead there was the most unbearable pressure from having this colossus in the family, this global success, loved by millions – and trying in vain to live up to him. Freya had been smart to pursue a career in medicine, so completely different and admirable in its own right that she never had to put up with the direct comparisons. Robert, though, hadn't managed much of a career at all. Nobody had ever said so to his face, but he knew that the rest of his family had always seen him as the weak link.

'I do worry that Robert will never achieve anything, if he doesn't change his attitude,' he'd once overheard his father say to his mother one evening, not realizing Robert was in earshot. He'd ducked out of the room, face burning, hating the patronizing, almost sorrowful expressions glimpsed on their faces, but the words had already branded themselves onto him, like a terrible prophecy.

Robert will never achieve anything.

Robert will never achieve.

Never. Never. Never.

Last year, he reached a tipping point. He'd had enough of being the weak link. He was done with having to listen to the triumphs of Mum, Dad and Freya, and feeling as if he had nothing to offer in return. Perhaps the balance was swung by being married to Harriet, who was always telling him he was just as good as the rest of his family. Perhaps it was one too many 'So are you a writer too?' questions. It was also the feeling of, well, why not? How hard could it really be? Would sitting down at a laptop every day and tapping out a few sentences seriously be more laborious than cycling miles around London as a courier, weaving through black cabs and buses, dodging one accident after another? Come on. No way. More pertinently, it might just shut everyone up for a while.

Sure, Robert could remember how his dad would lock himself away for hours on end to write, eventually emerging with his hair standing on end where he'd raked through it incessantly. He would growl and glower, complaining bitterly about how he'd never finish this blasted book, and he was done for this time, he had run out of steam – but such moments seemed to fade into insignificance beside all the publication celebrations Robert remembered: the flowers and champagne, the parties and speeches and fan mail. For a while there had even been a deluded female stalker who kept appearing in their garden, wild-eyed and pressing love notes against the window. (Robert had been fifteen at the time and found the whole thing mildly erotic. He'd been quite disappointed when his mum eventually called the police and had her bundled away.)

Harriet gave a little snore beside him just then and Robert rolled over for the hundredth time, kicking the covers off his feet. The shock of his mother's announcement was giving way to a growing curiosity about Leo, this surprise new half-brother. Freya had said he was the spit of Dad, now she thought about it. *I knew he reminded me of someone!*, she'd cried in anguish. Robert had missed Alec very badly. Who wouldn't want the chance to see this half incarnation of a lost one? You couldn't ignore that, could you? It wasn't the kid's fault he'd been born into such secrecy.

Yet if he did make contact, Olivia might never forgive him. She would see it as a betrayal, a taking of sides. 'We are the Tarrants,' she had said imperiously at the end of their conversation, clutching his and Freya's hands. 'We are Alec's family. Not them. And they never will be. So don't you forget that. He might have broken our hearts but we are still the Tarrants and we are united.'

The meaning had been implicit. *Do not go near them. Shun them both.*

Robert shut his eyes, willing sleep to descend, if only to muffle the conflicting thoughts that churned through his brain. Then came the thorniest question of all. Had Alec loved the boy more than him?

Chapter Twenty-Two

The next morning, Freya woke to find herself still half-dressed under the covers, with the unpleasantly gritty feeling of sand in her hair. Her head pounded as if someone had been at it with a mallet and the skin on her face was tight and dry. Then a series of unwanted memories from the night before dropped into her mind, like struck matches illuminating dark corners of a room.

Oh God, yes. Mum's face at dinner. The quaver in her voice as she broke the news. Dad's affair with Katie, his secret second family tucked away in Silver Sands village, right under their noses for all these years.

She clutched at the pillow, feeling as if the underpinnings of her world had just collapsed again. Last night, she'd been in freefall, plunging helplessly from drink to drink, plummeting towards oblivion with no safety net left beneath her. And . . . something else. Something else had happened.

The door burst open and she heard Libby's voice. 'Mum! Look what I made! It's a reverse twist pattern – Molly showed me how to do it.' Her daughter's wrist was shoved under her nose, the fair freckled skin adorned by a lurid bracelet made from coloured rubber loops. Loom bands, she thought they were called. The big craze at school for the last term.

'Lovely,' she croaked, but almost immediately Libby was recoiling, her freckled face twisting as she stared.

'What's that in your hair, Mum? That green thing?'

Freya had no idea what her daughter meant. 'I . . .' she began uncertainly.

'Is it *seaweed*? Oh my God. It IS. Mum, you've got seaweed in your hair. That is so weird.' She took a step back, then bolted for the door. 'Dex, come and look, Mum's just woken up and she's got *seaweed* in her hair. Seriously!'

Oh help. World, please swallow me up now. Thunderbolt, strike the house and blast me away. Cringing, Freya tentatively put a hand up to her hair, with no idea or memory of what her daughter could be talking about. Her hair felt matted and sticky, then her fingers landed on something slimy and she gingerly picked it off and brought it down for a closer inspection. Yes. Libby was right. A dark green thread of seaweed had been nestled against her scalp all night. Shit. How had it even got there?

She shut her eyes, letting the dizzying blackness swing mercifully into her head. *Go away, world.* If only she could somehow stop time for a while and stay here in this cool dim room, unmoving in the rumpled sheets, until she felt able to face the day.

But the door opened again just then and in came Victor in his dressing gown, bearing two cups of coffee.

Her head thumped. Victor. She vaguely remembered running away from him towards the beach the night before but everything else was fuzzy. Blurred. Christ, she must have been wasted. Trashed, even by her already diabolical standards.

'Morning,' said Vic, leaving a mug on her bedside table. He, unlike her, smelled fresh and clean. He had already showered; tiny water droplets still clung to the dark mat of hairs on his legs. She, in contrast, had never felt more unclean. Never so ashamed.

'I . . . I'm sorry about . . . what happened,' she said, her voice sounding small and broken. She still wasn't quite sure what *had* happened, but that was probably enough of a reason to apologize, she figured.

Vic sat down on the bed beside her and said nothing for a moment. 'I know you had a shock last night, Frey, but . . .'

He left the sentence hanging in mid-air and Freya winced, wondering how on earth it might end. A fragment of memory bloomed in her mind like a photograph developing: her, lying weeping on the beach, the cold, granular sand against her face.

'But what?' she said miserably.

'But you were completely out of control. I mean, *completely*. I've never seen you like that.'

She swallowed, unable to look at him, scared of the disapproval she would no doubt see there. She wanted to touch him, for him to put his arms around her and tell her it was okay, but he was sitting so stiffly, so rigid, she knew that was not going to happen. 'What . . . what did I do?' she asked hesitantly, almost immediately wanting to cover her ears. Did she really want to hear the answer?

'You can't remember? Seriously?'

She shook her head. She was a dreadful human being. The worst.

'Well, you ran all the way down to the beach. You were upset about your dad.' He sipped his coffee, eyes hooded. 'Then you decided to go swimming. Fully dressed and totally pissed. It was freezing cold and almost pitch-black. If I hadn't been there, Frey . . .'

Oh God. A shiver went through her. She dimly remembered the shock of the icy water now, tussling with Victor as he tried to haul her out. Seaweed in her hair. Sand on her skin. Shame swept through her. Dark, damning shame. 'I'm sorry,' she said, but her teeth had begun chattering and it was hard to get the words out. 'I'm really sorry.'

He sipped his coffee, still not looking at her. 'You could have died, Freya,' he said. 'You could have drowned. If I hadn't been there . . .'

She shut her eyes wretchedly. Hadn't she wanted to be rescued by him? Hadn't she wanted someone to notice she was unhappy? Not like that, though. Not in a way that meant her husband could barely look her in the eye afterwards. 'I'm sorry,' she blurted out. 'I realize that. It was a one-off, it won't happen again, I've just been under a lot of stress.' She thought she might actually vomit with mortification.

He looked at her at last, looked at her as if he didn't even know her. 'Freya . . . I think you are drinking too much.'

'Yes.' Her voice was barely more than a whisper.

'I'm sorry, I know it's a horrible thing to say, but that's the truth. Even the kids were saying as much last night.'

A hot tear rolled down her face and her throat was so tight and clenched she couldn't speak.

'And in the sea . . .' He shook his head. 'It all could have gone so badly wrong. Irreparably wrong. You know how strong the current gets, you know how cold the temperature drops.'

'Yes,' she mumbled. And she *did* know, of course she knew about hypothermia, and survival rates, and just how brutal the current could be. Her parents had drummed it into her from an early age, incessantly, repeatedly, just like she and Vic had told the children: you can't take a chance with the sea. It's bigger than you, it's stronger than you. Rule number one: respect its power and know when to stay out of the water.

'Vic, I'm sorry,' she tried saying again, but he was already speaking, not seeming to hear her.

'I don't know what to say, Freya,' he said unhappily and his gaze slid away. 'I just don't know any more.'

Freya had never experienced quite such depths of self-loathing as she stood in the shower ten minutes later, washing the seawater from her hair and skin, watching another strand of seaweed twist around the plughole with the foaming shampoo suds.

You could have died, Freya, she heard Victor say accusingly as she towelled her hair dry afterwards. Her head ached with the roughness of the action and she could hardly catch her own eye in the mirror for the wave of hot shame that cascaded over her once again. Just imagine. The children would have woken up to discover their mother was dead, seaweed-hair and all. The thought of their shocked, tearful faces was like a punch in the stomach. How could she have been so stupid? How could she have let herself get into such a state?

When she finally slunk through to breakfast, she felt as if everyone must be staring at her, but Libby was busily making another bracelet under the tutelage of Molly, Dexter was glued to his iPod, Teddy was lying on his front arranging a series of pebbles into a line, and none of them gave her a second glance. Over at the worktop, Harriet looked as if she'd just got up too; still in pyjamas, her hair dishevelled.

She popped a couple of Nurofen from a packet and tossed them down her throat with a shudder. Seeing Freya, she slid the blister pack along to her. 'Morning,' she mumbled huskily. 'Bloody Nora. My head.'

'Thanks,' said Freya, accepting the packet. She felt embarrassed for having blurted out all her problems to Harriet the evening before too. What must her sister-in-law think of her? 'Listen, I'm sorry about . . . last night,' she said in a low voice, tucking a wet curl of hair behind her ear. 'Me blathering on for hours like that.'

'Don't be daft,' Harriet said. 'There's no need to apologize for anything.'

Freya threw two Nurofen down her throat and washed them down with the last dregs of her coffee. 'Thanks,' she mumbled.

'How much did you guys have to *drink* last night anyway? Jesus! What was all *that* about?' Molly asked, looking up disapprovingly.

'Fifty, I bet,' Ted replied gleefully. '*Fifty* drinks. Jesus!'

Freya felt herself turn scarlet but Harriet merely rolled her eyes. 'Don't pay any attention to Goody Two Shoes over there,' she said. 'We are on holiday, thank you very much,' she added, addressing her daughter. 'Adults are allowed a few drinks on holiday. And God knows we need it, after days on end spent with our loved ones. That's you lot, by the way.'

'Charming,' Molly replied, tossing her hair. 'Well, as long

as you keep setting me a good example, then . . . Oh, wait. You don't. Role model failure.'

Harriet groaned. 'I can't cope with crushing teenage wit and acerbity today,' she said, rubbing her eyes. 'I am weak and vulnerable.'

'Ha. Well, if this is your mid-life crisis, then you've only your bad-ass self to blame,' Molly said heartlessly, passing the bracelet back to Libby. 'There,' she said in a friendlier voice as she ran a finger along the colourful pattern. 'See?'

You could see genuine awe shining in Libby's eyes as she gazed up at her cool older cousin. 'Thanks,' she said, slipping it onto her wrist and turning it this way and that. 'It's bad-ass,' she added daringly.

When was the last time Libby had looked at her so admiringly? Freya thought with a pang, remembering how her daughter had recoiled from her in bed, freaked out by the seaweed. Colour burned in her cheeks at the thought. Even the kids had noticed her drinking, according to Victor, and that felt like the worst kind of judgement of all.

How had it all gone so wrong? She had tried so hard to be the perfect wife and mother, juggling her schedule and begging favours from colleagues so that she could go to school assemblies and PTA meetings. She had tried too hard, if anything, desperately overcompensating by spending hours creating Gruffalo and dinosaur costumes for fancy dress parties in the vain hope that her children would love her for it and other parents would notice and approve. The last thing she wanted was for anyone to accuse her of being a part-time mum just because she had a demanding full-time job. And she had worked damned hard to protect that image this far, to keep all those different plates spinning merrily.

But in the last few weeks, the plates had come crashing down one after another. Dad. Work. The children. Her marriage. Somehow she had become a woman who felt better when there was a bottle of gin in her handbag; a wife who threw herself recklessly into the sea because she was so drunk she couldn't control herself; a mother whose children pulled faces because she stank.

Every way you looked at her, she was a failure. An embarrassment. A screw-up.

Hands shaking, Freya poured herself a glass of orange juice and pushed some bread into the toaster, stepping closer to Harriet, who was slathering two slices of toast with butter and marmalade.

Harriet shot her a look. 'About last night,' she began tentatively, but Freya was too embarrassed to let her progress even a syllable further.

'It won't happen again,' she interrupted, forcing brightness into her voice. 'I'm sorry to have bored on at you for so long. From now on, I'm on the wagon so there won't be any more bad behaviour from me. Brownie's honour!'

'Have we *got* any brownies?' Ted asked with sudden

interest. (What was it with kids and their acute sense of hearing when it came to certain words? Freya marvelled.)

'No, dumbo,' Libby said, kicking him. 'Brownie's honour is, like, when you make a big important promise. Mum, when am I starting Brownies anyway? You did say I could, ages ago.'

'Um . . . I'll ring the Brownie lady when we're back home,' Freya said, wishing it was possible to have a private conversation without young ears tuning in for a change. She wasn't sure she could cope with a 'big important promise' when it came to drinking either. The very words 'on the wagon' made her feel anxious the moment they fell from her lips. No cheeky wine while she made dinner? No gin and tonics on the terrace? It was a horrible thought. A scary thought. Even at eight thirty in the morning.

Harriet merely turned kind brown eyes on her. 'Well, I'm here, okay? Any time you want to talk. You know that, don't you?'

'Sure,' Freya mumbled. And then, because she couldn't bear the sympathetic look on Harriet's face any longer, she turned away abruptly and addressed her children, who were all still tousle-haired and in pyjamas. 'Right, you lot! Go and get dressed, then brush your teeth and hair. Now, please! We're all going kayaking today, remember. Chop, chop!'

Kayaking. Even thinking about swaying around on a boat made her want to puke. But her words had the children cheering and leaping up immediately (a miracle in itself) so that was some small blessing at least.

Freya buttered her toast doggedly. Today was a new start, she vowed. A new, sober start where she pulled herself together and made everything all right again.

Chapter Twenty-Three

Libby had been doing her best to cheer up Granny but so far things hadn't gone very well. Down at the beach, she'd found the most beautiful shiny pink shell which she had saved especially to give to her (Granny loved seashells; she had a whole jar of special ones up in the bathroom). Libby had washed the shell with squirty soap and then dried it gently on one of the towels, so that it even smelled nice, but before she could give it to Granny, Teddy found it and threw it out the window, trying to hit Dexter on the head.

Libby had punched him, Teddy had squealed, and down in the garden, Dexter was yelling that he was going to kill Teddy. Then, amidst all the ruckus, Libby heard Granny say, 'What on earth is wrong with those children? For heaven's sake!' in a very peevish, grumpy sort of way, which meant that the shell had actually just made her feel worse. Libby had gone down and searched all around the garden, but she never saw that shell again. Stupid Teddy. He was really lucky Libby wasn't the sort of sister who did mean things like throw a person's *dinosaurs* out of the window, even though she very badly felt like doing it.

Next, she decided to pick Granny some flowers. She cut a huge bunch of colourful sweet peas, and put them in a pretty vase of water, meaning to leave them by Granny's bed as a nice surprise. The children weren't usually allowed to go into their grandmother's bedroom but Libby was sure nobody would mind this one special time, so she crept in on tiptoes, being super-quiet and careful. Unfortunately, though, she didn't notice Granny's slippers on the floor, tripped over them, and ended up tipping the vase and its contents all over the bed. She gave a sob of anguish and tried to dry the bed with Granny's old hairdryer but of course Mum walked in on her – 'What on *earth* are you doing?' – and got really cross and didn't seem to understand that she was only trying to be kind.

Libby was starting to feel that everyone was in a bad mood on this holiday. Mum didn't even want to listen, she just told her off in a shouty, impatient sort of way and then insisted Libby help her make up the bed – as if she didn't have enough to do right now, honestly, it's just one thing after another with you kids – until Libby's face felt very hot and her eyes went swimmy and her throat went all tight and sore. What was wrong with all the adults? Even Uncle Robert kept going off and talking on his phone all the time when he thought nobody was looking.

Then, the next day, they were all set to go kayaking but nobody had mentioned Granny, and Libby felt really sad that they were going without her, because kayaking was so much fun, it would cheer up anybody, even the saddest little sad granny. And so she went up to the bedroom and knocked ever so quietly and gently on the door – 'Granny? Granny, are you coming with us?' – and she was only trying to be nice *again*, but then Mum was there, looking all tight-faced and pulling her away, saying, 'Libby, for the last time, stop badgering your grandmother, just leave her to sleep, all right? You can see her later.'

'She's not a badger, she's a girl,' Teddy said from downstairs and Libby threw her shoe at him, just because she was sick of people telling her she was doing the wrong thing all the time, and because Teddy was really totally annoying sometimes.

Badgering your grandmother! She wasn't completely sure what badgering meant but the way Mum said it was not good. Like Mum was cross with her again. Well, Mum was just cross all the time lately, and Libby was getting fed up with it. Maybe if Mum tried a bit harder to be nice and cheerful herself, then Granny would feel happier too!

Libby sighed as she and her brothers clambered into the

car a few minutes later and began their usual argument about whose turn it was to sit in the middle seat. She wasn't about to admit defeat yet, though. She would think of a way to make Granny smile again, and that was that.

Chapter Twenty-Four

The Tarrants and Castledines drove in convoy to the kayaking safari centre near Kingsbridge and were soon kitted out in life jackets. Unfortunately there were only three double kayaks available as well as one pedalo, and some scrapping ensued about who went with who, and in what. 'Well, I was kind of hoping to be partners with *you*, Ted,' Harriet said quickly. 'And I know Uncle Rob wanted to go with you, Dex.'

'We'll leave these losers behind, right, Dexter?' said Rob, holding one hand up, and his nephew grinned and high-fived him. 'Too right,' he said.

Libby sidled closer to her adored cousin. 'Can I go with you, Molly?' she asked shyly, and Harriet replied at once.

'Perfect! Yes, of course you can, Libs. Can't she, Molly?'

'Sure,' said Molly, who didn't look quite so thrilled at the prospect.

'Wait – so that means . . .' Freya had lost track of who was going with whom.

'So that means you're with Vic,' Harriet said. Was Freya

imagining it, or was there a glint in her eye? 'Tell you what. Why don't you two take the pedalo for a nice relaxing cruise around, while Rob and I chaperone these tearaways on the kayaks? Is that okay with everyone?'

'Yeah!' the kids yelled, all grabbing paddles at once, patently glad not to be stuck in the infinitely less cool choice of river craft.

Freya looked at Victor, feeling as if they'd just been played, but Harriet was already bustling the children away. It would be a job trying to convince any of them to go in the pedalo with her now. 'Looks like it's just me and you, then,' she said after a moment.

He nodded, his face hard to read. 'I guess so.'

The next few minutes were spent double-checking everyone's life jackets were put on correctly and giving Ted strict instructions that started 1) No jumping in, and ended 17) No pushing anyone else in. Despite Freya's best efforts to delay the moment that she and Victor were contained within a small space together, the children were all eager to get in their kayaks and start paddling, and were soon on the water and shouting competitively at each other that they were so going to beat the others, you just wait. Seconds later, they were splashing away amid hoots of laughter.

'And then there were two,' Freya said apprehensively, clambering into the pedalo, which swayed beneath her weight. *Just me and my husband, who thinks I'm an alcoholic. What fun we'll have!*

She knew why Harriet had done this, of course. Despite the horrible wine-misted haze that shrouded most of last night's events, she could distinctly remember Harriet telling her, several times, that she needed to talk to Vic. That he'd be devastated if he knew how she'd been feeling. 'Devastated' was perhaps taking it a bit far – he'd looked at her as if she repulsed him just a few hours ago – but she knew deep down that the conversation needed to be had, cards laid on the table. She had to reveal what a mess she'd been, how she'd been freefalling for the last few weeks, silently and unnoticed until she'd almost plunged to a watery demise last night. It didn't promise to be an easy conversation, that was for sure.

It was another warm day, with barely a breeze to stir the overhanging willows lining the sides of the river. The pedals seemed stiff and creaky at first but Freya and Victor soon settled into a rhythm and began cruising along the creek at a fairly leisurely pace, miles behind the others, who were already vanishing at speed into the distance. Just as Harriet had envisaged, no doubt.

Freya tried to drink in the beauty of the wide, meandering creek, rumoured to be the home of kingfishers and nesting swans, as well as offering possible sightings of herons and otters, according to the pamphlet they'd been given. She couldn't concentrate, though, not even on soothing thoughts of otters and kingfishers, as she pedalled along, one hand trailing in the cool green water. 'Vic, I've got something to say,' she blurted out before she lost her bottle. 'Last night . . . I know it got kind of out of hand and you're pissed off with me, but I need to explain.' Her nerve failed her and her mouth dried up, then she remembered Harriet's earnest brown eyes. *You have to tell him*, she'd said. *You have to!*

'I'm just . . . struggling right now,' she went on, feeling as if every word was an effort to drag out. 'I can't cope. One of my patients is probably going to sue me. I miss Dad. You getting stabbed totally freaked me out. I . . . I . . . It's just too much. I'm losing the plot.'

Victor stopped pedalling in surprise. 'What?' he said. 'Say all that again?'

Freya's pulse was racing; she tried to calm herself with a deep, slow breath. *Otters*, she reminded herself. *Kingfishers. Swans.* 'Everything's gone wrong this summer,' she confessed. 'Since Dad died, I've found it really hard to cope. I—'

He shook his head as if her words made no sense. 'But you've coped really well,' he told her. 'You've held it together, you've run around looking after your mum, you've got on with everything like you always do.' He stared at her, baffled. 'That's what you do, Freya. That's who you are – coping queen extraordinaire.'

She winced, reminded of her old nickname from the sixth

form – the Ice Queen – given to her by Johnny Dodds, when she wouldn't kiss him at the Christmas disco. *Ice Queen.* Back then she'd prided herself on her cool detachment, her need for nobody and nothing, certainly not Johnny Dodds and his red face and slobbery lips. But maybe she'd taken things too far. Maybe the Ice Queen should have let herself thaw a long time ago.

A sob was building in her throat but she forced it back down. 'No. Well, yes. I suppose it looked that way from the outside.' She hung her head. 'I didn't let it show, that was all. Inside I've been a total mess. I've been frightened. I've been sad – oh, so sad, I can't even put it into words. But I just numbed the pain with . . . with booze, I guess, and did my best to keep up appearances.'

He said nothing for a moment and the pedalo drifted into the riverbank with a dull thump, jerking them forward in their seats. He shoved them away from the edge and they began pedalling again. 'I didn't realize,' he said, so quietly it was hard to hear him over the splashing water. 'I didn't know.'

'I'm going to change,' she said quickly. 'I'm not some complete lush or addict.' She bit her lip, hating the fact that she was even saying these words. 'I don't have a problem or anything, I swear. I'm going to stop drinking from now on anyway. Knock it on the head.' Again came that terrible acid fear at the thought of boring soft drinks every evening, herbal teas and cordials, instead of blurring the day's troubles away with an enormous kick-arse gin. God, it was going to be hard. The thought of having to be so strong and resistant night after night after night . . . it seemed a Herculean task.

'Blimey, Freya, I . . .' He sounded bewildered. 'I didn't realize things were so bad. I had no idea you were feeling like this.'

No. And that was the nub of it, right there: his shock that there might actually be something wrong. Like Harriet had said, it *was* probably her fault too, of course, for maintaining this illusion, for letting the world believe that she was perfectly competent and had life under control. She gazed unseeingly out at the green water. These days everything seemed to be her fault, one screw-up after another. Was there anything she had got right recently?

'I've been pretty good at covering up,' she said eventually. 'It was only really coming here that made me realize how much. I . . . I've let everyone down, Vic. I've let myself down.'

She risked a glance sideways; he was staring straight ahead as he guided the pedalo around a curve in the river, but looked absolutely stricken. 'You haven't let anyone down, Frey. Don't say that.'

'But it's true. I've messed up work, my job's on the line. You said yourself, the kids have noticed that I'm drinking too much. How do you think that makes me feel? An absolute failure, that's how.'

He was silent for a moment, digesting. 'What's actually happened with work?' he asked eventually. 'You keep saying you've messed up but you haven't said how. Why don't I even know about any of this?'

'Well . . .' She took a deep breath and haltingly told him about Melanie and Ava, and then, lowering her eyes penitently, about the gin in her handbag (did he still think she didn't have a problem now? she wondered). 'I haven't heard anything back from Elizabeth,' she said shakily at the end, 'and I can't help fearing the worst. I'm scared, Vic. If Melanie wants to take it further, and I end up going to some kind of tribunal . . . I mean, I don't think I did anything wrong, but what if they don't see it that way? I could lose my job.'

He had gone very quiet since she launched into her little spiel, she thought in anguish. She began pedalling again, but the soles of her pumps were wet and slipped off the pedals. She wished he would say something. Why wasn't he saying anything?

Finally he spoke. 'I wish you'd told me this before,' he said. 'Why did you let me go on thinking everything was fine?' He gave a hollow laugh. 'Some detective I am, when I can't even spot what's happening under my own roof.'

'I'm sorry,' she said again, her voice wobbling. She could no longer remember why it had seemed so important to maintain the illusion of control, other than for her own sense of pride. Because here was her husband looking at her as if he didn't recognize her and she felt worse than ever.

They pedalled along in silence for a while and she felt sick with the feeling that she'd let things reach such a crisis point. Where did they go from here? she wondered. She no longer had the faintest idea.

Chapter Twenty-Five

Leo Browne had never been very good at maths (it was his worst lesson by a mile) but even he could add up two and two to make four.

It had all been so strange and horrible, the day that he and Mum found out about Dad. Leo had been excited about seeing him again – they both were. Mum had put on perfume and spent ages making Dad's favourite banoffee pie (she had even grated chocolate sprinkles over the top), and they'd both woken up really early, as they always seemed to do when Dad was coming back to Devon.

Leo felt buzzy and jittery while they waited for him to arrive. 'Ants in your pants,' Mum said whenever a car went by and he rushed to the window to peer out. Then she put on some music and they both sang along to a song they liked, and Leo made her laugh by doing some cool dance moves. Then she dumped a pile of clean towels in his arms and told him to hang them up in the bathrooms – 'Come on, hurry up, we want the house to be nice for him, don't we?'

Yes. Leo did want that. He wanted it to be perfect, so perfect that Dad would think, actually, do you know what, I like it better here with Katie and Leo than I do in boring old London. He was in the downstairs bathroom, hanging up the soft blue towels, and just resting his face against them a bit, because they were still so fluffy and warm from the drier, when he heard a car pull up and peeked behind the net curtain to see Dad's Audi in the drive. His heart gave this gigantic trampoline bounce of joy.

'He's here!' he shouted, running out at once. But he'd got it wrong, as it turned out. Because Dad wasn't there at all. And Dad wouldn't ever be there again either.

Everything turned weird so quickly. It was like a video slowing down, like a bad dream, like he wasn't even really there, just watching it from somewhere else. That woman – Olivia, Mum said she was called – told them that Dad was dead, and it was like a bomb went off in Leo's head. Boom. BOOM.

Dead, she said. *Dead*. What?

No, he couldn't be. She must have got it wrong. Dad was coming to Devon – they had been counting down the days. Leo was going to tell him about being picked for the school cricket team, and how he'd gone out sailing last week and they'd caught loads of mackerel and . . . There was so much stuff he had stored up to say. And Dad would ruffle his hair and give him a bear hug and later they would go out in the garden and Dad would bowl nine hundred cricket balls at him so Leo could practise his batting and . . .

Dead, she'd said. *Dead*. And he couldn't help thinking of that sinkhole they'd been shown on a news clip at school, the way the ground had just caved in one day, with houses, cars, people, even a bit of road, all swallowed up in the hole. Next to him, Mum was crying, tears spilling through her hands, but Leo felt as if he was in a sinkhole of his own, that the kitchen floor had just given way beneath him, and he was falling, falling, falling. Plummeting through the earth. His whole body had gone sort of stiff and frozen, like it had when Mr Dale, their neighbour, was hit by a car when he was crossing the high street, and just lay there looking broken, while people started screaming.

Mum put her arm around him as if she could tell how he was feeling, and he felt her taking a really deep, scared breath, before she said, 'This is Leo. Alec's other son.'

Then it all went crazy. Bad crazy. Olivia clutched at her hair as if she wanted to rip it out and yelled at them, really yelled at them, to get out of her house, to go, to get out right this minute, now!

They fled. Out to the car and then back home, where they tumbled into their small house, the terrible truth still beating at them like stormy rain. Mum was shaking. She had gone really pale, like she was ill or something, and Leo had tried to make her a cup of tea but he burned his hand and started to cry too. He wasn't sure if he was crying more about Dad or because his hand hurt so much but somehow he and Mum ended up sitting on the kitchen floor together, arms around each other, both crying at once, their tears mingling in little rivers down Leo's neck.

Leo didn't like thinking about that day. Since then, he had locked it away in the very back of his mind, like a secret in a box. He had even imagined turning a key in the box and hurling the key into the sea, never to be found again. He didn't want to remember any of it – *He's dead, he's dead, he's dead* – all the shouting, all the crying, that horrible empty ache inside him, like he hadn't had any breakfast or lunch.

But it was hard to completely block it out. Bits kept leaking back to him. The sinkhole feeling sometimes crept up on him when he didn't expect it, and he had to hold tight to the nearest thing because he thought he might lose his balance and fall. He dreamed of Dad, of one last game of beach cricket, one last bear hug, one last wrestling match on the sofa, and would wake up with his face wet where he'd been crying in his sleep. He and Mum had their own private good-bye ceremony where they drove out together to Pemberley Point, one of Dad's very favourite places, then wrote chalk messages on big stones and threw them out to sea. Mum wrote *I always loved you.* Leo wrote *I miss you, Dad.*

Back home again, Mum made them another banoffee pie – they'd left the first one at Shell Cottage – and said this one was just for them now, but Leo didn't feel hungry, even though banoffee was usually his number one pudding, like Dad. Mum's mouth went all trembly and turned down at the corners so he quickly ate some anyway and said it was really nice, but it just sat in his stomach like a hard ball of sadness. All he could think about was how much better it would be if Dad was with them too, eating banoffee pie and telling Mum she was a baking genius. 'Your mother,' he would say to Leo, 'is a goddess of a woman. Don't ever forget that. An absolute goddess.'

It was confusing, as well as sad. Dad hadn't been ill, had he? He might be older than Leo's friends' dads, but he wasn't *that* old, he wasn't doddering about with a stick and a hearing aid or anything. So why had he died like that, without any warning? Why was that even allowed to happen? When his friend Toby's grandad had died, he'd had cancer for months, and Toby was always going to visit him in hospital after school. Had Dad been in hospital too? He hadn't sounded ill last time Leo spoke to him. Anyway, Mum would have said something. She definitely would have. Maybe something else had happened – like Mr Dale being hit by a car?

Leo felt his eyes get hot just imagining Dad lying crumpled in the road, like Mr Dale had been. One of Mr Dale's legs had bent right back and you could see the bone sticking out, white and shocking and wrong.

Maybe he was better off not knowing what had happened.

He definitely wasn't about to ask Mum. Every time Leo mentioned Dad's name, she started crying again.

Curiosity got the better of him eventually. Plus something about the whole episode was bugging him, something he'd missed. It was as if he already knew but was being stupid or slow, but that was mad because he *didn't* know. How could he? Even though he tried to ignore it, the 'something' kept tapping away at the back of his mind, like Marcie Grayson from over the road, who was always knocking at their house, wanting Leo to come out and play. (No way. Marcie was the most boring girl ever. Leo always pretended he hadn't heard her knocking until Mum got fed up and shouted, 'Leo Browne, will you answer that door for goodness' sake, we both know it's for you,' and then he had to use all his Jedi mind powers to come up with an excuse really quickly while he was walking to the door.)

So he sneakily borrowed Mum's laptop and googled Dad, to see if he could find out what had happened. Just so that he would know.

Click, click, type, type, type. Click.

Pages of text sprang up on the screen and Leo leaned forward breathlessly, his eyes scanning the sentences.

Distinguished novelist Alec Tarrant has died at the age of sixty-four, following a sudden heart attack at home.

A heart attack. Not a road accident, at least. He let out a long, shuddering breath and read the words again. A heart attack at home. Dying the next day, at the beginning of June, according to the newspaper website. Again, he had that weird sensation, that there was something important right under his nose, something his brain hadn't quite caught up with. It was like when you were trying to remember spellings for a test, and you knew there was something you'd forgotten, some double letter or weird i before e thing, or . . . He scratched his head unhappily. *Think, Leo. Think.*

He clicked through to another website, one he'd looked at many times before – the Wikipedia page about Dad.

Alec Tarrant is married to Olivia, and has two children, Freya and Robert, it said. Words he'd read over and over again, his fingers hovering on the keyboard, wondering if he had the nerve to add in the extra, unwritten line.

He also has a ten-year-old son, Leo. And a girlfriend, Katie. He really loves them and they love him back. A lot.

'Why can't we just *tell* people?' he had grumbled, more than once, when Mum told him they had to keep Dad their special secret.

'Because while it's secret, we get to keep him,' Mum had replied, stroking his hair. 'But if everyone else finds out our secret, then Dad might not come back. The others might not let him. So we stay quiet, Leo. That's the rule.'

Leo wasn't dumb; he understood that, loud and clear, and was so scared by the threat of Dad vanishing from their lives, that he *had* kept quiet and held the secret tight to himself all this time. Sometimes he typed the words into the laptop – *Alec Tarrant is my dad!!!* – but he deleted them straightaway. He had never told anyone, not even Max, his best friend. He had kept the secret. Not that it mattered any more, seeing as Dad was dead, and that screaming Olivia lady knew the truth anyway now.

It still didn't seem real, that Dad was gone, that they wouldn't be seeing him again. He had been dead for over six weeks now – Leo had counted on the calendar – and they hadn't even known! The last time Leo had spoken to him, he –

Then Leo went cold all over. That was it. That was the weird thing that had been bugging him. The beginning of June, he'd died. The 7th of June – it said so, in the newspaper.

His heart began to pound. The last time Leo had spoken to him was on the 6th of June – he remembered because it was the day after Max's birthday. Max had been given a puppy, and Leo had asked Mum if he could have a puppy too, and Mum had said, 'Well, I'd better talk to your dad about that when he comes down,' in a twinkling, smiling sort of way, as if to say, she would actually quite like a puppy too.

But Leo hadn't been able to wait that long. And so, when Mum wasn't in earshot, he had picked up the phone and carefully dialled Dad's London home, feeling all shivery because he knew he wasn't supposed to. He was breaking the rule.

Dad had been surprised to hear him. Surprised in a not

very good way. 'How did you get this number?' he had asked. 'You mustn't ring this number again!'

And Leo was just about to say sorry, and he'd be really quick, and he just wanted to tell him about Max's puppy, which was the cutest, softest Golden Retriever called Poppy, but then Dad made a strange noise, like he was choking.

'Dad?' Leo said cautiously. He almost whispered it because he felt scared. Then there was a thump and a loud clatter, and he heard a woman shouting in the background – 'Alec? Alec!' – and Leo quickly hung up, feeling really, really guilty.

He would not tell Mum, he had vowed, slinking into his bedroom and shutting the door. He hoped Dad wouldn't be too cross next time he saw him. But then he'd forgotten all about the phone call because Max sent him a message on his iPod – **Mum says you can come over to play** – and Leo was so keen to see Poppy again, that he'd dashed downstairs at once.

But now it came back to him. The choking sound Dad had made, the thump as if he was falling to the ground. As if he was having a heart attack in his own home. Everyone knew you could have a heart attack if you were really, really angry, didn't they? 'Don't have a heart attack, love,' Mum had said sarcastically just the other day, when a driver had beeped and shouted at her for not indicating to turn right at the traffic lights or something.

Two plus two. Two plus two. Leo had phoned up when he

wasn't supposed to – he had broken the rule – and Dad had been so furious with him that he'd had a heart attack and died. *How did you get this number? You mustn't ring this number again!*

Dad had died, and it was Leo's fault. Two plus two made four, and that was a fact.

Leo lay back on his bed, feeling sick with shame and fear. He thought of the policeman who'd come in to talk at school last term, how he'd impressed on them that bad people always got caught and thrown in jail. 'Trust me, guys, you don't want to end up in there,' the policeman had said sternly, shaking his head.

Leo didn't want to go to jail. He didn't want to leave Mum. But what would she say when he told her? She would hate him for the rest of her life!

His stomach twisted. He couldn't remember ever feeling so awful. He could never tell Mum. He could never tell anyone.

He gave a sob of anguish, and then, because he didn't want Mum to hear him, he pulled the pillow over his head. 'I'm sorry, Dad,' he said, his voice cracking on the words. 'I'm so, so sorry.'

Chapter Twenty-Six

'Morning! And how are we today? Here – thought you might like these. Fresh from the allotment an hour or so ago and proper delicious too. Shall I put a brew on, then? Oh.' Gloria paused for breath. 'Are you all right?'

In the maelstrom of torment of the evening before, Olivia had somehow forgotten about Gloria, her unorthodox new cleaner. Yet here she was, thrusting a Tupperware box brimful of scarlet strawberries into Olivia's hands, taking two steps into the hallway then stopping dead to look suspiciously at her.

Olivia, clutching the strawberry box and gaping like a grounded fish, became conscious of two things at the same time: firstly, that she was still wearing her nightie, had no make-up on, and unbrushed hair. And secondly, that Gloria did not seem particularly au fait with the concept of discretion, and it would probably be all round the village by the afternoon that Olivia Tarrant was having a nervous breakdown. She wished fervently that she hadn't answered the door in the first place but the house was empty and Gloria had pressed her finger on the bell for such a long time, shouting, 'Cooeee? Anyone in?' through the letterbox, that Olivia couldn't bear it a second longer.

In contrast to Olivia's dowdy night attire, Gloria looked ready for anything, wearing a faded denim jacket slung over a cerise-pink sundress. She had a vivid streak of turquoise eyeshadow shimmering on each eyelid and parrot-feather earrings swinging from her ears. She was gazing closely at Olivia with those toffee-coloured eyes, clearly wondering why this well-spoken woman ('posh' she probably called her) was still undressed at eleven o'clock in the morning.

'Thank you,' Olivia forced herself to say. 'I'm fine. How kind of you, these look delicious.' Alec had loved strawberries, she found herself thinking, then was pierced by a sudden memory springing unbidden to mind: of being newly-weds and lying on a picnic blanket in a cornfield, feeding each other plump, juicy strawberries under a cloudless blue sky, bare legs companionably entwined. Had he fed strawberries to Katie, too? Placed them on her lips and watched her small white teeth bite through the flesh?

Stop. Just stop. 'Let me make you a cup of tea,' she said briskly, walking ahead into the kitchen, trying not to think about how dreadful her bed-hair must look from behind. *Olivia Tarrant, just pull yourself together, for goodness' sake.* She thought of her mother: a woman who, until her dying day, had always been fully made-up and perfumed, a woman who would have refused, even if faced with a firing squad, to allow any person outside the family to ever glimpse her in nightwear. She was a woman who'd lived through falling bombs, rationing, poverty and her beloved brother dying on a battlefield in Normandy. She wouldn't have caved in to misery like Olivia; she'd have kept her head up, her powder dry, and come out fighting.

Olivia found herself standing a little straighter, spine stiffened. 'I thought perhaps you could tackle the bedrooms and upstairs bathrooms today,' she said to Gloria, with a new, resilient so-what-if-I-*am*-in-my-nightie? set to her shoulders. 'You'll have to take us as you find us, I'm afraid – the children are rather messy but they *are* on holiday, so we don't feel we can be too strict with them.'

She was getting out the tea things when Gloria touched her on the arm. 'Look, love, tell me to mind my own business but . . . are you sure you're all right? Only . . .' Her voice trailed away, uncharacteristically uncertain.

Never explain, never apologize, Olivia reminded herself. *And never, ever, show weakness.* 'I'm fine,' she replied. 'Do you take sugar?'

The shower must have been piped straight from a spring of magical healing water that morning, because when Olivia emerged from its drenching, she felt miraculously better, as if her dreadful night's sleep was but a distant memory. She smoothed scented body lotion into her skin and dressed in a crisp white blouse with short sleeves and a broderie anglaise trim, teamed with a cream linen skirt. Then she blow-dried her hair for the first time since she'd arrived in Devon so that it fell into a neat silvery bob, and carefully applied mascara and a touch of lip gloss. There. The old Olivia was back, in the mirror at least, if not quite in spirit.

The question now was what to do with the rest of the day. She'd vaguely heard voices and doors earlier that morning, and remembered Robert saying something about a kayaking trip. Libby had tapped tentatively at her bedroom door at one point – 'Granny. Granny?' – and Olivia, aware that she hadn't been the most doting grandmother of late, had opened her mouth to reply when she heard Freya hissing that they shouldn't disturb her, that they should leave her to sleep. Soon afterwards, the front door banged shut and then she'd heard one car drive away, followed by the other. They were long gone now, wherever they were.

The house already smelled of fresh air, hot hoover and cleaning spray as Olivia made her way downstairs, her hand sliding lightly down the old wooden banister. A montage of images turned in her mind: of all the times she'd walked up and down this staircase over the decades, first as a young bride with pink cheeks and a shy smile, and then through all the stages of wife, mother, granny, and now, finally, old widow. She remembered tinsel threaded through the wooden struts of this staircase during the Christmases when the children were tiny, then lengths of ivy and white fairy lights as her taste grew more refined. She had carried drowsy babies up and down these stairs, soft, warm heads lolling against her shoulder. She had herded sandy toddlers up to the bath, wincing at the debris left in their wake, and stood at the bottom, hands on hips, calling up during the teenage years that it was eleven o'clock and a glorious day, Freya and Robert absolutely had to get up right *now*, otherwise she was coming up there to drag them out! (Kind of ironic, when she was the one emerging bedraggled and unkempt this morning at eleven o'clock, but never mind. That was the circle of life, she supposed.)

Olivia wandered out into the garden, feeling at a loss for what to do with herself. All dressed up and nowhere to go, she thought, slipping into her deckchair again and folding her hands in her lap. She didn't feel like reading or swimming or walking today; she couldn't face tackling the garden or baking anything for afternoon tea. She certainly wasn't about to start wading through Alec's final manuscript for his editor, as she'd half promised. Why should she do him any favours now?

She leaned back, feeling every single minute of her years: the permanent ache in her lower back, the click of her knees and, when her gaze fell to them, the liver spots on her hands.

I'm getting old, she thought. Sixty next year and before she knew it, she'd have turned into one of those bitter, shrewish old biddies, telling children off in the street and writing letters of complaint in green ink to the local newspaper. The sort of woman that the rest of society ignores, barging past in a hurry, too busy to notice.

She glared up at the sky. *And it'll be your fault, Alec. It's you who's driven me to this. Are you happy now?*

She must have dozed off again because it seemed like no time had passed until she became dimly aware of the scent of Marlboro and that citrus-scented perfume Gloria seemed to favour. 'Mrs T? Olivia? I'm off now. All done.'

Olivia opened her eyes blearily to see Gloria before her, cat-eye sunglasses on even though the sky was quite overcast. She sat up a little straighter (not easy in a deckchair), feeling self-conscious to have been caught napping in the middle of the day. Gloria must think she was such a feeble old thing. 'Thank you,' she said, realizing that her knees had splayed outwards while she dozed, and pulling them tightly together. She gave a little nod, meaning *You are now dismissed* but Gloria didn't budge.

'I was just wondering . . . Well. We haven't actually talked about money yet.'

'Oh. Yes. You're right. Sorry about that.' She tried to

remember what they'd paid Katie but Alec had always taken care of that. *Payment in kind*, she thought, flushing. 'Er . . .'

Gloria named a figure that she received for another cleaning job with a questioning shrug. It was considerably less than Olivia paid the domestic help agency for Maria, her Filipino girl, so she nodded. 'Fine. No problem. If you could come to us Monday, Wednesday and Friday for a few hours each time, that would be marvellous. Nine thirty in the morning?' She would make sure she was up and presentable next time, she vowed.

Gloria was still hovering. 'So . . . about the money, then . . .' she said expectantly.

'Ahh. You want paying now? Right.' She had brought her handbag outside with her – you couldn't be too careful these days – and dipped a hand in to find her purse. 'Here,' she said, counting out the notes. 'Thank you.'

'Thank *you*.' Gloria tucked the money into a small silver purse which had sequins falling off one corner. 'Well, I'll be off then.' She hesitated. 'Left you on your own, did they? The family?'

Olivia shrugged. 'They've gone out in boats, I think. I was . . . tired.'

Gloria pushed her sunglasses off her nose and up into her hair. 'Got any plans? I was going to go for a bit of a spin, spend some of my hard-earned wages.' She held up the purse then shoved it into her jacket pocket. 'Come with me if you like.'

The suggestion was so unexpected, Olivia found herself floundering for a polite way to say no. 'Well . . .'

'You ever been to the Lobster Pot on Ennisbridge beach? Only opened a month ago and they do the best lobster burgers you've ever tasted.' She kissed the tips of her fingers theatrically. 'The owner's a mate of mine, he'll give us a discount if we ask nicely.'

Olivia was partial to lobster although she couldn't remember ever trying a lobster *burger*. It was just the sort of thing Alec would have turned his nose up at, she thought . . . which promptly made her mind up. 'Yes, all right,' she said. Why not? She had nothing else lined up to while away the hours. She levered herself up from the chair, feeling an unfamiliar thump of excitement at her own daring. 'Let's go.'

Not five minutes into the journey through the winding lanes of south Devon and Olivia was fearing for her life. Gloria was a wild and reckless driver, careering round blind corners without turning a hair let alone changing down a gear, loud music blaring all the while. What a way to end her life this would be, Olivia thought despairingly as Gloria stamped on the brake to make an emergency stop when they flew round another bend to find a trundling tractor in their path. What would the children say if they received a visit from a policeman later that day – *Very sorry to inform you . . . passenger in a silver Mini, driven by a lunatic, slammed into a tree when the driver lost control, both died at the scene . . .*

'You okay, there? You've gone very quiet,' Gloria bellowed over the racket. (Even calling the noise 'music' was stretching things in Olivia's mind.)

The fear must have been naked in her passenger's eyes because Gloria abruptly switched off the stereo – thank goodness – and took her foot off the accelerator a fraction. 'It's my driving, isn't it?' she chuckled. 'Sorry, love. Do you want me to stop? You look as if you're about to chunder.'

Olivia had never heard the word 'chunder' before but was pretty sure she knew what it meant. She was pretty sure she was close to 'chundering' right now too. 'I'm fine,' she said through gritted teeth, trying to stop herself from pressing her right foot too obviously against the floor of the car, her reflexive braking reaction.

'Bill always used to call me the Getaway Driver,' Gloria went on, coasting over the brow of Longdown Hill, her hair flying back in the wind. 'He said I drove as if I was trying to get away from a bank heist with sacks of money in the boot.' She hooted with laughter at the memory then gave another sidelong glance at Olivia. 'Cheeky bastard. He was one of those stickler drivers, you know, braking through the gears and whatnot, letting other people go ahead of him, hands at ten to two on the wheel at all times.' She flicked on the indicator and turned right down a lane, and Olivia found herself praying that this one would be a little wider than the one they'd just careered along. 'But opposites attract, right?'

'So they say.' There was a pause as if Gloria was expecting Olivia to respond with some similar nugget about her own relationship but Olivia had never been in the habit of woman-to-woman confessionals about Alec. Their marriage was their own business, in her opinion, not something to be served up in palatable slices for other people to pick over and devour. She folded her hands in her lap and stared out at the dense green hedgerows, so high in places it felt as if they were speeding through a leafy tunnel. There were worse ways to die than in a fast car on a summer's day, she supposed. And at least if this was her last day on the planet then the pain she was feeling for Alec would be over.

They rounded another corner and then the land seemed to drop away, a whole new vista unfolding of a sapphire sea and its crescent of biscuit-coloured sand. 'I never get tired of this view,' Gloria said cheerfully as they headed down through the small village of Ennisbridge. 'Lucky old us, eh? Even on a cloudy day, it's the business. Right. Here we go, just over on the left. One of those pop-up restaurants. Very fancy. I hope you're hungry!'

Olivia's family hadn't come to Ennisbridge beach all that often, favouring their own Silver Sands Bay, which was prettier and far more convenient. Ennisbridge was more touristy, with a bus service that brought in day-trippers, and a parade of small hotels, souvenir shops and cafés. And now it was home to the Lobster Pot, an unlovely bunker of a building with white-painted breeze-block walls and a corrugated iron roof. In front of it were set barrels for tables, each with parasols for shade, and stools that had been fashioned out of upturned crates with vinyl seats on top.

Very fancy, Gloria had said, but the two women clearly had different notions about what 'fancy' actually entailed. Thanks to Alec, Olivia had dined at the Ledbury in London and Le Bernardin in New York, neither of which had had a breeze block or an old crate in sight. What on earth had possessed her to say yes to this magical mystery tour? she wondered, as Gloria hurled her car into a parking space and yanked on the handbrake. Maybe moping about back at the house would have been the more sensible option on second thoughts.

Out of the car, though, Olivia could smell chips and garlic – and yes, definitely lobster – mingled with cigarette smoke, coconut tanning oil and the briny scent of sea. Despite the absence of sun, the air was warm and sultry with a fresh breeze occasionally ruffling in, and the waves made a pleasing rattle-crash as they rolled into the pebbly shore. Ah well, they were here now, Olivia thought, and she was actually quite hungry by this point. She had barely eaten any dinner the night before and had only drunk a single coffee that morning.

'This is nice,' she said politely, but Gloria was already bust-ling forward, matily slapping the back of a broad-shouldered guy with salt and pepper hair perched at a table and calling a cheerful hello to the two men working behind the counter of the shack.

'Hey, *compadre*! How's the head this morning, eh?' She turned back to wink at Olivia, then indicated Mr Broad Shoulders, who was wearing a faded green T-shirt and had a copy of some motorbike magazine open in front of him. 'We had a bit of a session last night, didn't we? Jägerbombs and karaoke. Lord, it got messy, all right.' A husky laugh bubbled out of her at the memory. 'Olivia, this is Mitch, Ennisbridge's answer to Mick Jagger, last seen rocking out to a mash-up of – what was it? Motörhead and Britney Spears. Hmm. And Mitch, this is Olivia, my new . . .' She was about to say 'boss', had her lips shaped to speak the word, then seemed to change her mind at the last minute, and said 'friend' instead. 'We've come for lunch. Some of us have been working since seven o'clock and are starving.'

Olivia flushed, first because she hadn't done a stroke of work in days, and second because Mitch was staring at her curiously and she felt very out of place, the stiff in a Jaeger outfit rather than the cool chick doing Jägerbombs, whatever they might be. 'Hello,' she said, conscious of the clipped tone to her voice.

'Hey, Glor,' Mitch said, slipping off his stool to give her a hug. He was in his late fifties, like the two of them, Olivia guessed, and dwarfed diminutive Gloria by at least a foot. 'Olivia, nice to meet you,' he added, turning his smile on her. (He had a lovely face, she found herself thinking in surprise. Craggy and weather-beaten now, he must have been a heart-breaker in his day, with Slavic cheekbones and pale blue eyes that reminded her of the sea on a cool day.) 'Don't let Mrs here lead you astray, will you? She's trouble in a tight dress, this one,' Mitch said, then grinned and stepped back as Gloria pretended to cuff him. 'Enjoy your lunch, ladies. I've got to head off unfortunately. Those Jägerbombs won't pay for themselves now, will they?'

'See you soon, handsome,' Gloria called after him as he strode away, and he raised a hand in salute without turning. 'He's an artist,' she explained to Olivia, rather admiringly. 'Kind of famous around these parts. That's the life, eh? Party all night then get up at midday for some chips, before sauntering off to your studio to *draw*. All right for some.'

Olivia wasn't sure whether to be disappointed or relieved that Gloria's friend had left as she settled herself gingerly on one of the stools. *In for a penny, in for a pound*, she told herself. This was a new experience and certainly better than slump-ing in a deckchair like a past-it geriatric, her brain cells gradually silting up.

Gloria ordered their food – a burger and chips for her, scal-lops and chips for Olivia – then spent several minutes leaning over the bar, gossiping with the chef, her behind sticking out as she did so. Olivia turned her gaze upon the beach which, despite the lack of sunshine, was crowded with families and sunbathers, the sea awash with lilos and dinghies and shrieking wave-jumpers holding hands. She smiled at the sight of a group of children nearby who were burying their father in the sand with great gusto. Good times.

'Here we are,' said Gloria, returning just then with tall glasses of home-made lemonade, clinking with ice and half-slices of lemon.

'Thank you,' said Olivia, who was both parched and ravenous by now. She sipped the lemonade and found it cool and refreshing, then her gaze was caught by an inky blue mark on Gloria's upper right arm as her companion shrugged off her jacket. 'Is that a tattoo?' she blurted out and immediately felt embarrassed. She must seem such an ingénue to Gloria.

Gloria looked amused at the question and swung round so that Olivia could see the design in its entirety: a dandelion clock, with a few loose seeds hanging like tiny gossamer parachutes as they floated away up towards her shoulder. Olivia had always written tattoos off much in the way she had breeze-block burger joints: not very classy and (frankly) not very nice. Not the sort of thing that a person like her would ever contemplate. But she found herself having to rethink her prejudices. She had expected to see something tacky and clichéd on Gloria's arm: a red rose, a skull, perhaps her and her husband's names entwined in dark lettering, but the artistry of the dandelion clock had taken her by surprise, being fragile, pretty and . . . yes, even feminine too.

What a snob, she thought, suddenly cross with herself and her preconceptions. 'It's lovely,' she said, eyes still on the delicate lines of ink. 'Really lovely.'

'Have you got one?' Gloria asked, rummaging in her hand-bag for a cigarette and snapping her lighter to produce a yellow licking flame.

'Me? No. It's not really my . . . No.'

Gloria drew on her cigarette and puffed out a stream of smoke, then offered the packet to Olivia. 'Why not? Scared of the pain? It's not as bad as you think.'

'No, I – ' She fumbled for the right reply but spread her hands helplessly. Scared of pain? Definitely not. She'd gone through childbirth twice over and had gritted her teeth throughout each time, barely making a sound. 'My husband always hated them,' she said in the end as Gloria gazed steadily at her, waiting for an answer. 'So . . .'

'So what? He's not here any more, right?' Gloria's lower lip twisted in awkwardness as soon as she realized just how blunt she'd been. 'Sorry,' she added hastily. 'That came out wrong. Bill never liked them either. Oh, it was all right for a *bloke* to have tats, he reckoned, but not a woman.' She patted her arm with a grin. 'I had this done after he died. Not as a way of disrespecting him or anything. Mitch talked me into it. Having a tattoo changes you, he told me. Gloria with a tattoo will be a different person from broken-hearted, bereaved Gloria who is financially up shit creek.' She rolled her eyes. 'So I did it.'

'Are you and Mitch . . . together?' Olivia found herself asking.

Gloria gave a roar of laughter. 'Together? No, love. Just friends. No, he's the tattoo artist. He's the one who did it for me.'

Handsome Mitch was a *tattoo* artist? For some reason Olivia had imagined him splodging oil paints into wild sea-scapes on huge canvases, not creating something as finely beautiful as the floating dandelion head. Had his thick fingers really worked such delicate lines? She must have looked disbelieving because Gloria laughed.

'He does bloody big dragons and Harley Davidsons for other people, mind. Whatever floats your boat. I've always loved dandelion clocks, though. The way you see the seeds drifting on the breeze, flying free, to who knows where.' She chuckled. 'Your nicest flower bed probably, or a good bit of lawn, knowing my luck, but never mind. It seemed like the right design for me, that's all.' She nudged Olivia. 'You should get one.'

'Oh, no,' Olivia said at once. 'I couldn't.'

'Couldn't you?'

'Well . . .' Olivia floundered. Of course she couldn't. Offer up her bare skin to be punctured by a tattoo artist's needles? The idea was ridiculous. Imagine her children's faces! 'Did it work like Mitch said it would?' she found herself asking. 'I mean, did it make you feel better?'

'A million times better,' Gloria told her. She touched the tattoo with her fingertips. 'It's hard to explain but I just felt . . . new. Different. Like the version of me that I truly wanted to be.' She rolled her eyes. 'Gawd, listen to me. Hippy nonsense.' She waved a hand self-consciously. 'Sometimes a change is as good as a holiday, as they say. You know.'

Olivia wasn't sure she did know, especially as this holiday had turned out to be memorable for all the wrong reasons. Mercifully, their food arrived before she had to reply, though, and goodness, it looked wonderful: miniature silver buckets stuffed with salty skinny fries, scallops served in the shell with garlic and flecks of chilli, and Gloria's burger which turned out to be pieces of lobster crammed into a golden brioche, and came with its own tiny jug of garlic butter. As the chef placed the final dishes on the table – a small jam jar of juicy red tomato relish and a dish of green salad to share – he bid them, 'Enjoy your food,' and left them to it.

Oh my. Olivia would never judge a pop-up breeze-block restaurant on appearances again. The scallops were deliciously fresh and cooked to perfection, the fries crunchy and moreish, and the relish properly tangy, with the tomatoes tasting as if they'd been picked just that morning. The sun poked itself tentatively out from where it had lurked behind the clouds until now, and Olivia felt her spirits lift. Sitting here with good food and – yes – good company, however unconventional, felt much more like a holiday. It reminded her, too, that she was most definitely alive.

So there, Alec, she thought defiantly, dabbing her lips with a paper napkin. I won't let you destroy me. *Look how much fun I'm having without you. Just look at me go!*

Chapter Twenty-Seven

A few days after the kayaking trip, Molly lay back on the creaking camp bed and stared up at the sloping ceiling of Shell Cottage's attic room. Poky and hot, home to about a million industrious spiders and with so little floor space that she was always tripping over her suitcase, this was not exactly the bedroom of any self-respecting teenager's dreams. Nor for that matter was this holiday.

So far this week, she had made approximately five thousand loom-band bracelets with Libby and played *Minecraft* with Dexter for a whole rainy morning; she had feigned interest in Ted's pebble collection and listened to all his many tedious dinosaur facts; she had kayaked and hiked (under duress), and then yesterday she, Mum and Robert had cycled all the way to Salcombe and back, stopping for a pub lunch and a nosey around the swanky yachtie shops ('Swanky with a silent "S",' Robert had said, eyeballing the price tag on a T-shirt with a look of horror). She had eaten a cream tea too, even though she knew it was, like, a million calories and would give her spots. But she'd had enough of being here now, and badly missed her friends. She missed Ben even more. Next year, she was either staying at home or going to go to Dad's, and that was that. Whatever Mum said.

She twisted her phone in her hand. She still hadn't heard back from Dad. What was he up to? she wondered. How was life working out for him and Anne-Marie in France? He had posted a picture on Facebook recently which showed him raising a bottle of beer in the air as the sun set beyond the mountains in the background. There was another one of Anne-Marie looking vastly pregnant in a sundress and bare feet, standing on the terrace of their knackered-looking farmhouse and laughing. She had very white teeth, Anne-Marie. White teeth and thick, glossy black hair. She was going to have the cutest baby ever, probably. A cuter baby than Molly, anyway, who had been a skinny, shrunken egghead for the first six months of her life.

Would Dad still love her when he and Anne-Marie had their cute French baby? Would he even remember her, back in London, spots on her chin, slogging to school on drizzly autumn mornings? Her friend Chloe barely saw her dad these days, not since he'd married again and had two other children. He had taken his new family off to California this summer, while Chloe and her mum, Jan, were left in their small flat in Finchley. The paint was peeling off Chloe's bedroom wall where damp was getting in but Jan had been off work for six months with depression and they had no chance of moving anywhere nicer. When she spoke about her dad, Chloe didn't sound bitter or even angry, just sad. Resigned to the fact that he loved these other kids more than her. Molly had often thought, quite fiercely, that if she ever saw Chloe's dad again, she would give him a piece of her mind.

She hoped her own dad wasn't about to flake out and go crap on her. He wouldn't, would he? He'd always made such a fuss of her whenever they met, taking her out for grown-up dinners, buying her things she wanted, pressing twenty-pound notes into her hand when she asked for money, even letting her have a glass of wine one afternoon in a pub garden last summer. ('For God's sake, don't tell your mother, or I'll never hear the end of it,' he'd said with a wink.)

Yes, okay, so he wasn't the most reliable father in the world. He hadn't been to any of her school concerts for years, even though he always promised he'd be in the audience. He sometimes even forgot to turn up when they'd arranged to meet at weekends – 'Oh bollocks. Love, I'm so sorry,' he'd say when she rang him, having waited half an hour already, heart sinking. Mum had got really cross after it happened the third time and actually insisted on waiting with her after that, until Molly pretended she was meeting Chloe instead and didn't tell her where she was really going.

Molly didn't mind anyway. Well, not that much. She always hated sloping off home on her own when he didn't show, but then he would be so super-apologetic and nice when she spoke to him afterwards that she couldn't help forgiving him. 'I'll make it up to you, Molls,' he said, and he always did. Mostly.

But it would be ages until she saw him again now that he lived in France. She'd taken for granted him being a few miles up the road in Mill Hill; she liked being able to slope round to his flat every now and then, particularly if she had the hump with Mum about something. Dad was always on her side, whatever happened. He would make her a coffee (which she didn't really like, to be honest, but she drank it anyway) and give her a hug, and then they'd watch some boring sport thing on telly together (even though she didn't really like watching sport either), and within minutes she'd be feeling better again.

The girlfriends – well, she could take or leave them. Dad was handsome and charming, it was no wonder women flocked around him like pigeons over a croissant. He was also incapable of speaking to a woman – be she the waitress serving him or a lady in a shop selling him a newspaper or whoever – without leaning in a fraction and giving her this kind of *look*, a look that said, *I am really, deeply interested in you and everything you have to say*.

He did the look on Molly too, of course, but then he *was* really interested in her and everything she had to say. And if she turned up unexpectedly at his flat and there was a woman round there, Dad always sent the woman packing so that he could be with Molly instead. 'You're top banana around here, kid,' he said to her. And while Molly wasn't that thrilled about being called a banana (she hated bananas and their evil smell), it gave her a warm glow knowing that she was top of Dad's list, above all these random women who fell in love with him.

Apart from Anne-Marie, it seemed. Anne-Marie must have placed some kind of voodoo enchantment on him because in the space of a year, she had moved into his flat permanently (that had never happened before), got herself pregnant and persuaded him to up sticks and move to bloody France, miles away from Mill Hill and miles away from Molly. These days Molly was pretty sure that Anne-Marie was top banana, not her.

In her darkest moments, Molly had fantasized just a little bit about Anne-Marie tripping over her stupid terrace in France and falling down the mountain, breaking her elegant tanned neck. Maybe that would stop her smiling quite so many toothy smiles.

There was a knock at her door and Dexter pushed his head in. 'We're going to the beach in a bit. Dad's going to blow up the lilo so we can go in the sea with it!'

Molly forced a smile. 'Cool.' Then because she couldn't face another conversation about *Minecraft*, she held up her phone. 'Just about to make a call, so . . .'

'Sure,' he said, vanishing again.

The door banged behind him and she dialled Dad's number, feeling bad about her horrible Anne-Marie-down-the-mountain thoughts.

'You have reached the answerphone of Simon Reynolds. The signal isn't great here so I might not get this for a few days. But leave me a message and I'll get back to you when I can.'

There was a laugh in his voice, as if he couldn't care less that the signal was terrible, as if he didn't really want to hear from anyone anyway. When the beep sounded, Molly drew a breath in to speak, but then all of a sudden, she wasn't sure what she wanted to say any more. So she hung up instead.

She lay there for a moment, unable to stir herself into excitement over the thought of going to the beach with a lilo. Out of habit, she clicked Ben's name on her phone with the usual stab of longing. She couldn't help herself. Ever since she'd been forced on this dumb holiday, he'd been in her head non-stop. His slow, sexy smile. The way his eyes fastened onto hers, making everyone else around them blur and vanish. His low rumbling voice, muttering dirty, suggestive things into her ear. Lord have mercy! as Chloe would say. It was enough to make a girl *ache*.

She threw her arms around her pillow, remembering how they had snogged in the book cupboard of her English class-room on the last day of term, her back pressed against piles of copies of *Macbeth* and *Of Mice and Men*. She actually *burned* inside with yearning when she thought about taking her clothes off in front of him and . . . well, you know. Doing it. If she was brave enough to ever go through with it, that was. (Would it hurt? Would she make stupid noises? Would he laugh at her if she made stupid noises?) She just wanted to feel like a woman. A proper sexual woman. She had never even *thought* like this until he had gazed at her, gimlet-eyed, across the classroom two weeks ago, and then brushed up against her in the corridor afterwards, disturbingly close. It was like receiving an electric shock; the hairs on her arms actually stood on end, her stomach seemed to drop away in sudden desire.

Oh, Ben. *Ben!* Maybe she should just drop him a quick line, a teeny, casual 'hi' so that he would think about her. Should she? They'd chatted on the phone and swapped flirty messages a few times but she'd heard nothing in the last couple of days. Was it too keen of her to text him again?

So boring here. Wot u up 2? she typed, then frowned. No, that sounded moany. Babyish, even. She deleted it with a sigh.

I miss u, she typed but hesitated again, fingers hovering above the keypad. Too needy. Way too needy. Boys hated clingy girls, didn't they? 'Klingons' they called them at school, like something that needed to be peeled off and flicked away. She didn't want Ben to think she was a clinger.

She wanted him to be reminded she was fun. And sexy. And still interested.

Hey, she typed, then pressed send before she could stop herself. Then she threw herself back on the bed, heart thudding. A second later, her phone buzzed and she almost stopped breathing, clammy fingers skidding over the screen in her haste. Oh. Just Chloe.

Why aren't you here?? Loz having party 2nite. Everyone going. Inc Niall!!

Molly's heart sank. Gutted. Their friend Lauren had been promising to throw a party all summer. Why did she have to pick a date when Molly was stuck here in the middle of nowhere? Typical! She felt a rush of annoyance with her mum, for dragging her on this stupid holiday against her will, for taking her away from her friends, for not being nicer to Dad to stop him from moving to France with smiley, pregnant Anne-Marie. And now she was going to miss the best party of the year. Great!

'Molls? Molly?'

Huh. Speak of the devil. There was the Evil Tyrant Motherlord herself, bellowing up the stairs. Molly paid no attention, instead thinking glumly about how, if she was at home, she and Chloe would be talking about the party this minute and what they were going to wear. Actually, they'd probably be trying stuff on in Zara that they couldn't afford and then going to buy cheaper versions in Primark. Chloe would be getting in a state about Niall, this lad from the sixth form that she'd fancied for, like, ages, and—

'MOLLY! Where are you?'

I am in hell, Molly thought, but then her phone buzzed again with another text and it was from Ben. **Hey**, it said. **Miss u x**

A smile slid across her face and warmth spread through her body.

'Where *are* you? MOLLY!'

I am in heaven, Molly thought. *I must be in heaven.* Then, still smiling, she rolled off the bed and shoved the phone in her shorts pocket. 'Did you call me, Mother dearest?'

He missed her. *He missed her.* Maybe being away wasn't so bad after all. Didn't they always say absence made the heart grow fonder? She liked thinking of him pining away for her, unable to concentrate, counting the days till she was home and back in his arms . . .

Yeah, yeah, steady on.

As Dexter had said, they were all going down to the beach and Mum had this whole speech planned about how Molly had been indoors the entire morning and it was a beautiful day and she needed to get fresh air and Vitamin D, and . . . Oh, whatever, Mum – Molly had switched off by that point. She was in such a good mood about the 'miss you' text that she couldn't be bothered to argue. 'All right, all right,' she said, pulling a face. 'Don't give yourself laryngitis, Mum.' Even fresh air was better than listening to her mother when she went into one.

Down at the bay, Molly spread out their large turquoise beach towel and frowned through her sunglasses at her phone. Surprise, surprise: barely any signal. (Poor Devon teenagers. How could they stand it, living here with such crap phone coverage?) She thought longingly of London and Wi-Fi and of messages from Ben piling up in some celestial traffic jam, unable to drop into her phone, and felt like thumping the sand. She didn't but she must have made some noise of exasperation because Mum pushed up her sunglasses to peer sideways at her. 'Everything all right?'

'Yes, of course, everything's completely amazing and spectacular, why wouldn't it be?' she replied witheringly, tucking her hair up into a bun before it got loads of sand in it. Then she pulled off her T-shirt and shorts to reveal her new white bikini, and flumped onto her front before anyone could see her stomach. If she had to be down here, she might as well top up her tan, she supposed.

'Marvellous,' Mum said sarcastically. 'Well, just as long as you're happy.' Then she spread out a towel alongside Molly and put her nose in a magazine.

It was only the two of them on the sand right now – the others were already by the water's edge, pumping up the lilo and a dinghy that Robert had found at the back of the garden shed. Molly squinted crossly at her phone and turned the Wi-Fi on then off again in the hope it might encourage her phone to try a bit harder to find some kind of signal. Yes – two bars! Thank you, patron saint of heartsick teenagers. She twisted her head and shoulders sideways, and tilted the phone to shield the screen from prying eyes. **I miss u 2**, she typed, then added a sadface emoticon.

Her phone buzzed a second later. **Bn thinking about u.**

He was thinking about her! Get in. She felt her insides turn to liquid, imagining a picture of her face in a thought bubble floating above his head.

What r u thinking?? she typed, feeling giddily, ridiculously happy.

Bzzzz. **About kissing u. About doing it again.**

Her heart pounded. Her body felt swimmy, as if her blood was rushing through her veins too quickly. Her fingers flew over the screen. **Mmm. Sounds good.**

What r u wearing? came his swift reply.

Bikini . . . she typed back recklessly, adding a winking face. Her mouth quirked in a smile, anticipating his expression as he read it.

'What are you up to, over there?' Harriet asked, and Molly jumped.

Shit. The Motherlord's bad-daughter radar was obviously working well today. 'Just chatting with Chlo,' she said from behind her hair.

Bzzzz. **Send me a photo**, his reply instructed, and Molly felt her body flush with heat. A photo? How was she going to get away with that, when she had the Parent Police less than a metre away? Unless she rolled onto her side, maybe, but even then – she was lying down, and everyone knew that was, like, the least flattering angle ever for a photo.

A worrying thought struck her. He did mean a photo of her *face*, didn't he? Or was he after some pervy cleavage shot?

'What's she up to?' asked Harriet.

A new text buzzed in. **I'm waiting . . .**

'Hmm?' Molly asked, distracted.

'Chloe. What's she up to, over the summer? Is she going away, or . . . ?'

Molly couldn't concentrate on the conversation. 'Um . . . dunno.' She did know, of course. She could practically recite Chloe's diary for the next month ahead, they knew each other so well. But all she could think of was Ben's text.

I'm on the beach! she typed apologetically in the end. Surely he'd get the message that she couldn't just start snapping pictures of –

Bzzzz. Oh my God. Her eyes nearly popped out at the photo that had just appeared. Seriously? That surely wasn't what she thought it was.

Her face flamed as she tilted her phone away from her mum's prying eyes and out of the glare of the sun. Whoa. Yes. It *was* what she'd thought: his pink, swollen . . . Molly's mouth went dry. His willy. His tackle. His tent pole. Oh God, she didn't even know what she should call it. Penis sounded like you were in a biology lesson. Willy was a word that five-year-olds used. Knob? Cock? She and Chloe had once giggled over a film where the female characters had referred to one male character's . . . equipment . . . as his schlong. It had been a running joke between them for a while; they'd both used it as their new favourite insult. 'What a total schlong,' Chloe would mutter about Mr Dobson, the deputy head, whenever he bollocked them about their skirts being too short. 'He is such a schlong-head,' Molly might moan about Jackson West, an annoying boy in the year above, who was always squeezing girls' bums when they went by in the corridor.

She imagined herself typing *Nice schlong* back to Ben and a hysterical giggle rose in her throat. No way. She couldn't. But what should she do?

'Molls, have you got any suncream on?' her mum asked just then, and the phone slipped out of her sweaty fingers, landing on the towel.

No. Don't look, Mum. Help. Quick. She snatched it up and closed the image, her breath hard and fast in her lungs. Bloody hell. Lying on a beach could be surprisingly stressful.

'Mollypops? Speak to me. Shall I put some cream on your back for you?'

She didn't care about suncream. She didn't care if the sun fried her skin to the colour and texture of crispy bacon. She quickly typed **gtg** – got to go – and turned off her phone before things got any more complicated. 'Yes please, Mum,' she said.

Harriet came over and knelt beside her, rubbing luke-warm coconut-scented cream into her back and shoulders. All Molly could think about was the photo, though. That pale, thick penis rising from the forest of dark hair. It was freaking her out. It actually made her feel a bit scared. She had been innocently thinking about holding Ben's hand and kissing, gazing into one another's eyes. Schlong photos were another thing altogether.

'It's a lot easier to do this now you're grown-up,' Harriet said, rubbing circles into Molly's shoulders before smearing the last of the cream down the tops of her arms. 'There. All done.' She laughed. 'Dear God, the palaver of getting sun-cream on you when you were little. I had to chase you round the flat before you'd let me put any on. Do you remember?'

Molly smiled faintly but for some mad reason her mum's words made her want to cry all of a sudden. They made her want to be a little girl again, squirming out of her mother's reach, shrieking that the cream was too cold, too ticklish. Back then, that was all she had to worry about. 'Yeah,' she said, an unexpected lump in her throat. 'I remember.'

And now Ben probably thought she was a little girl too, abruptly ending the conversation as soon as he pinged his naked penis into her inbox – so to speak. How uncool she was. How prim and proper. He probably thought she was frigid, and being a fridge came a close second to being a Klingon in terms of undesirability, everyone knew that.

Molly didn't mean to give such a heavy sigh as her mum moved back to her own towel, but she must have done because then Mum was pushing up her sunglasses again and staring at her. 'Are you sure everything's all right, love?'

And oh, how she wanted to tell her. Oh, how she wanted to ask so many things. (Did they all look like that? Was sex really painful? How should you reply when someone sent you a schlong photo?) But in the next moment Libby ran up, screaming and dripping water everywhere – 'Hide me! Hide me!' – because Dex was charging up the beach after her, his arms laden with wet, slimy seaweed, and the moment vanished.

Up jumped Mum, dropping her magazine onto the sand – 'Don't you dare! Libby, get behind me!' – and then she and Libby and Dexter were all laughing and running around on the sand together. Part of Molly wanted to join in too but then she thought of Ben, and what he might say if he saw her racing around squealing with the others. He really would think she was a baby, then. Maybe she should seize the opportunity to take a quick cleavage photo to send back to him instead?

She hesitated, not really wanting to. No boy had ever seen her bare breasts before; she didn't want the first time Ben saw them to be on the screen of his phone. It wasn't very romantic, was it? And what if he thought they were a bit . . . weird, or something? Too small. Too girlish. It might put him off her. He might laugh about the picture. He might even show his mates and snigger. But if she didn't text him a photo, then he might think she wasn't interested. Maybe she should just bite the bullet, get it over with . . .

Splat! All of a sudden, something wet and slimy landed on her back. Shrieking in shock and horror, she leapt up to see Robert – bloody Robert! – pelting away from her with a big, dumb grin on his face. Ben forgotten, she abandoned her phone and set off in pursuit. She'd worry about what to do later on.

Chapter Twenty-Eight

At last, Harriet thought, as she traipsed up the sandy steps back to the house later on, a rolled windbreak under one arm and a canvas bag full of sandy towels in the other. A lovely afternoon on the beach where everyone seemed happy. Robert was laughing again. Freya had thrown herself into a game of beach cricket for the first time all holiday, and miraculously Molly had actually put down her phone for five minutes and joined in too. Nicest of all was when Olivia appeared on the sand with a box of ice lollies for them, to be enthusiastically mobbed by the whole family. Harriet had almost forgotten what her mother-in-law looked like with a smile on her face. A tremulous smile admittedly, and a wan face, but still. This was progress.

The bombshell about Alec had been so devastating that Harriet could foresee the reverberations continuing for weeks to come but after several subdued days when Robert, Freya and Olivia all had faces as grey as the overcast sky, she felt as if they were now picking themselves up again, and peering around the scorched ground to see what was left of their lives. Besides, there was something about being back on a beach with kids that made everyone remember how to have fun. However deflated you might be feeling, by the time you'd had a seaweed fight, lilo races, beach cricket and helped with the construction of a huge sand fortress complete with an intricate set of moats, it was almost impossible not to feel the blackness lifting away like gulls on the breeze.

Later on, she and Robert had swum out to the point together and floated on their backs, saying nothing for a while. The sea was cool and deep but the sun warmed their faces, casting broken streaks of light across the water as they lay there companionably. 'It's going to be all right, you know,' Harriet ventured after a few minutes had gone by, and he reached out through the water and took her hand, squeezing her fingers in gratitude.

It *would* be all right. Of course it would. Harriet hadn't survived years of single motherhood by being a pessimist. *It'll Be All Right* would be carved on her gravestone, she had said the words to herself and her loved ones so often. *We've got each other. We'll get by.* If you kept on telling yourself, you did actually start believing it in the end, even though you might be down on your luck with mice scratching beneath the floorboards and mould sprouting on the wall. Even when – in Robert's case – your father turned out to be a bit of a shit, and not Captain Awesome after all. If years of social work had taught Harriet anything, it was that human beings were often way more resilient than they thought. People could get through extraordinary times of stress with the support of loved ones.

The worst was over, Harriet thought, as she pushed open the gate that led into the garden. The truth about Alec was out and even though it would take them all time to get over the shock, to recalibrate the family lines in a different shape, at least they were here together for another week, and could lean against each other for that time. With a bit of luck, there would be no further dramas, and everyone could take a breath and regroup. And at least they were in the most bliss-ful surroundings for some rest and recuperation. Silver linings . . .

Back in the house, everyone scattered. Olivia announced that she was going to cook dinner that evening, having bought some fresh fish and salad earlier. She was even going to dig up some new potatoes from the garden, having aban-doned her vegetable patch for the entire holiday so far. (More progress. *Good for you, Olivia*, Harriet thought, seeing her heading off purposefully with the garden fork.) Victor took charge of carting all the beach equipment over to the shed, Molly vanished off upstairs, glued to her phone again and Robert bagsied the first shower. Meanwhile the younger chil-dren played on the lawn together, Libby arranging the shells she'd collected in size and colour order, while Dexter and Ted gently tipped up the bucket they'd brought from the rock pools, releasing a couple of crabs to begin a sideways scuttling race. 'Make sure they go back to the beach later on,' Freya called, seeing them. 'Or they might end up in Granny's cooking pot.'

Harriet and Freya busied themselves shaking the worst of the sand off the towels and hanging up wet swimming costumes to dry. The sun was still warm in the garden, even though it was almost five o'clock, and Harriet loved the sensation of it on her bare arms. She breathed in the scent of suncream and seawater, mingled with the fragrance of Olivia's yellow velvety roses and the white trumpet-shaped nicotiana flowers which gave out such a glorious evening perfume. The smell of summer, she thought cheerfully. If only it could be bottled, she would wear it year-round.

Fair-skinned Freya had a newly sun-pinked nose, Harriet noticed, and a mass of freckles on her face and shoulders. Her hair was frizzy from the sea, and fell around her face like a blonde candyfloss cloud. They hadn't had the opportunity to chat much recently but she had noticed Freya had kept to her word about being on the wagon. She looked less haggard for it too.

'I'll put the kettle on,' said Harriet, when the last pegs were snapped into place. 'Fancy a brew?'

'Definitely,' said Freya. 'That would be great.'

No sooner had they stepped inside, though, than Robert's

phone began ringing from where he had left it on the work-top on his way up to the shower.

'I'd better get that,' Harriet said, 'just in case it's some-thing important. Probably Hollywood calling about film rights or something. I'll see if I can wangle us two parts as extras, Freya. Be right back.' She pressed the answer button and walked quickly out of the room, into the dingy cool of the snug. 'Hello, Robert's phone?'

'Is that Robert Tarrant?'

'Er . . . no.' Harriet pulled an are-you-serious? face into the mirror above the mantelpiece. Did she sound like a man? 'It's his wife. Can I take a message for him?'

'Sure. It's Nick from YourBook International. He left a message, wanting a quote for self-publishing his novel? If you could just tell him – have you got a pen there? – that we would charge the following fees. For the complete package – editorial work, cover design, formatting – our prices start at . . .'

Harriet, hunting around for a pen, stopped short, sud-denly confused by what this man was on about. Charges? Prices? He must have got it wrong. 'Wait. Hang on. Someone else is publishing it,' she explained. 'And *they're* paying *him*. He's already sold it around the world!'

There was a pause and the man gave a little embarrassed-sounding cough. *Yeah, and you should be embarrassed, pal,* Harriet thought, shaking her head. It had to be some kind of scam, and she'd just caught the guy out. Fees indeed. Wait till she told Robert!

'Sorry, maybe I've made a mistake,' the man said in the next moment. Harriet could hear him clicking something. 'Robert Tarrant? Seymour Street in London N2? Yeah. He contacted me a few days ago and we chatted through some options. I'm going to put all of this in an email if that's easier, only I thought, having spoken in person yesterday, I—'

Harriet frowned. This was too weird. Robert had phoned the guy? She must have missed something crucial here. 'Oh, sorry. So . . . you're from the publishers, then?' she guessed. 'Or the literary agency?'

Another pause. 'We're a reputable self-publishing firm,' he said, as if speaking to a particularly stupid child. 'We've been established for three years, and have lots of very satisfied customers.'

Customers. Now they were back to fees and charges again. So how did that work? Surely the author wasn't a *customer*? Robert was being paid shedloads of money, he had told her, promising holidays to America and a new car, just as soon as the first portion walloped into the bank account. So why was this man talking about prices and packages and customers? 'I think I'd better get him to ring you back,' she said in the end, defeated. She finished the call and sank into the nearest armchair, the dusty velvet tickling the backs of her bare legs. Something wasn't right here. She felt as discombobulated as she had standing outside the closed-up Marylebone Tavern the other week. The story didn't quite stack up.

Her gaze fell to Robert's phone, still warm in her hand, and her skin prickled with the sense that something fishy was going on. Harriet did not like being made to feel a fool.

The phone buzzed just then, making her jump, and she glanced down to see that a new email had arrived. *Nick from YourBook International*, she read – the man she'd just spoken to, from the self-publishing firm. She clicked on it before she could stop herself. One can of worms, open for business.

Dear Mr Tarrant, Thank you for your email, blah blah. She skimmed through it, wincing at the prices he was quoting, until she reached Robert's original email below. As she saw his email address followed by the subject line *Self-publishing query*, her hands began to shake.

She shouldn't be reading his private emails. This was not her business. She should stop right there, take her beak out, switch the phone off.

Yeah, but actually, a voice inside her head pointed out, *it is your business if there's something dodgy going on. It's absolutely your business if he's stringing you along. Wouldn't you say?*

She looked away, not wanting to believe he had been keeping secrets from her. He wasn't that type. Was he?

She cocked an ear as she heard the boiler rumble off, and guessed he must have just stepped out of the shower. He'd be towelling himself dry now and throwing on some clean clothes. Give it a minute and he'd be running downstairs to see what everyone else was up to. If she was going to read his email, she'd have to hurry up about it.

It was now or never. Now? Never?

Sod it, she decided impulsively. She was going to look. Look and be damned. She scrolled down, her eyes skimming through the words, fast and guilty.

> Dear Sir/Madam, My name is Robert Tarrant and
> I am an aspiring author. Having decided against
> conventional publishing routes, I'm writing to inquire
> about self-publishing possibilities. I have completed
> a novel of 90,000 words and am now interested in
> getting a quote for editorial work, a cover design
> and—

'There you are! I was wondering where you'd got to. Here, this is from Freya.'

Harriet jumped as Robert walked into the room, bearing two steaming mugs of tea. He was wearing shorts and a clean white T-shirt, and his hair was damp around his face. With the guilt of being caught spying on him, her hands gave an inadvertent jerk and the phone slipped out of her fingers and into the velvety depths of the armchair.

'Is everything all right?' Robert asked, setting down the mugs and perching on the edge of her chair. His solid, muscular thigh pressed against her arm and she flinched away. *Do not touch me.*

'You had a phone call,' she said, her tongue feeling thick in her mouth. *Here goes nothing,* she thought, her fingers clenching in her lap. *Here goes marriage number two.* 'A man from a self-publishing company. He wanted to give you some quotes, how much it will cost to have them produce your book.'

Beside her, she felt him freeze. 'I—' he began, but then her temper snapped.

'Don't bother telling me any more lies,' she said, getting up and away from him. She was positively crackling with rage. 'I've had it with lies. Do you or do you not have a publishing deal? Do you or do you not have a literary agent, an editor, an American publisher, Uncle bloody Tom Cobley and all the rest of them?' Her voice had risen to a shout but she no longer cared. Let the Tarrants all hear. Let them know what a snake their precious Robert was! 'You don't, do you?' she said contemptuously. 'The whole thing's been a bloody fantasy from start to finish. For fuck's sake, Robert!'

He still wasn't looking at her, guilt written all over him. *Not even bothering to think up an excuse this time,* she thought angrily. *Well, that was a first. Not so creative now, eh, Robert? Not so proud of yourself now!*

'No,' he mumbled eventually. He actually looked as if he might puke right there on the faded oatmeal carpet. 'I don't have those things. But – Harriet! Wait!'

Oh, no. Was he for real? Harriet was not about to wait and listen to any more bullshit. He clearly thought she was the dumbest halfwit alive for believing him in the first place. 'I'm not interested,' she snarled, voice shaking. 'I don't want to hear another word. I can't even look at you right now.'

Rigid with anger, she marched out of the room and straight through the house, crashing the front door behind her. *Fuck you, Robert*, she thought furiously. *Fuck you and your big fat lies.* He'd spun this whole web of deceit, and he'd let her believe it for weeks, for months. When all along, there was no glittering fairy tale of success, there was no contract or glory. *Shit, Robert. What were you playing at? Why did you do this? And how the hell did you ever think it would work?* There she'd been a few weeks ago, toying with the idea of giving up her job, becoming a lady of leisure supported by him! Thank God she hadn't!

She jumped into the car and began speeding away from Shell Cottage, the first sobs gulping out. First Simon and his lies, then Robert and his. Was there something about her that attracted these lying bastard husbands? Did she have the word 'Mug' tattooed on her forehead or something? How could she have fallen for it all over again?

Chapter Twenty-Nine

Everyone had seemed so delighted when Robert announced that he was quitting the courier job in order to write his first novel. It was almost as if they'd been waiting this whole time for him to come to his senses and jolly well get on with it already.

Alec had clapped him on the back, Olivia's eyes had become soft with pride and even Freya had grinned and said, 'Watch out, Dad, you've got competition.' Yeah, right.

For someone who'd always been his number one cheer-leader, Harriet hadn't been *quite* so enthusiastic when Robert told her what he was planning, instead fretting about their finances and how they would manage without his regular salary. 'I know you'll write an amazing book, but I just don't earn enough money for all three of us,' she'd said anxiously. 'Maybe you could go part-time with the courier firm for now, so that you're still bringing something in?'

Unbeknown to his wife, though, Robert had already handed in his notice following a row with his bell-end boss,

Keith. There was no way he was going grovelling back there, asking for a part-time job. He'd been cut up in the bus lanes by enough aggressive London drivers to last a lifetime; in the last week alone, two of his mates had been knocked down on deliveries. One had a broken collarbone, the other a broken wrist and concussion. It was a dangerous job unless you had the recklessness and quick wits of youth, and Robert felt he'd been living on borrowed time for the last year or so. He was an accident waiting to happen and he and Fate both knew it.

'Don't worry,' he told Harriet, assuring her he would cash in a trust fund that should keep them afloat for the year. 'And if I don't sell the book, I'll get some other kind of work,' he promised. 'But I have to try, Harriet. I have to give it a go.'

So off he went, flexing his fingers like a boxer before a fight, and typed *Chapter One* on the blank page. Characters bloomed in his mind. Plot twists and turns came to him when he least expected it. He introduced a clever science-fiction element, and a heart-stopping heist scene. His word count grew steadily, day after day after day. Thanks to his double-line spacing and a judicious choice of large font, he'd reached one hundred pages within the first month.

He wrote more. He changed his mind about the science-fiction element. He added a comedy romance sub-plot. He killed some of the characters when he couldn't decide what to do with them. He made the beginning funnier. Then he made it darker. Then he deleted the entire first chapter and decided the comedy romance wasn't quite so comic after all. Maybe black humour and sarcasm were more his style?

In the meantime, he began sending out sample chapters and a letter of introduction to various agents and publishers. He deliberated whether or not to mention his father but eventually vetoed the idea. He didn't want to ride on anyone else's coat-tails. He wanted his talent to shine out from the submissions pile, for him to be admired for his writing, rather than for the branches on his family tree. Unfortunately, as the replies began trickling back, he wondered if his lofty principles had been such a good idea after all.

We found the writing muddled, one editor said. *The plot seemed far-fetched to the point of farce*, said another. *The characters need development. The style is overblown and, at times, a little pretentious.* Some editors didn't even offer a word of feedback, instead sending a proforma thanks-but-no-thanks.

Each brush-off was a kick in the gut, bringing the terror of failure ever closer. He cursed himself for boasting of his writing plans in the first place. Why hadn't he attempted this in secret, so that nobody else need know of his endless rejections? Now he had to put up with a steady flow of innocuous, hopeful questions and each time he replied in the negative, he felt himself dying a little more inside.

So, how's the great novel progressing? Pretty well, thanks. Really enjoying it. (He wasn't enjoying it. He hated it. Why was he putting himself through this stupid charade at all? He was starting to relate to the Jack Nicholson character in *The Shining*. Any day now he'd be taking to the door with a pickaxe, bellowing 'Heeeeere's Robbie!')

Can I read some of it? Sure, when it's finished. (No way. Not until he had a cast-iron guarantee of publication, anyway. He had been forced to let Harriet read a few scenes when she wore him down with eager requests but there was no chance of his father or anyone else getting a look-in. Dad would recognize his inadequacy within two sentences even if Harriet didn't.)

What's this masterpiece called, then? What's it about? Oh . . . er . . . I don't actually have a title just yet. I guess you'd call it literary fiction with a twist. (The twist being that it was shit.)

'Any dirty bits in this novel, then?' Harriet purred in his ear one night in bed, and then, when he confessed no, not really, it wasn't that kind of book, she'd clambered on top of him and growled that perhaps they could make one up now, together. No bloke in his right mind could turn down an offer like that. Of course, he'd duly conjured up a particularly filthy scenario there and then. (*See? You can be creative when you put your mind to it!* he assured himself afterwards when they rolled apart, panting.) It didn't half make him feel a bastard, though.

One Sunday back in the spring, Robert, Harriet and Molly were at the Tarrant home in Hampstead for the usual roast chicken and trimmings when Alec cleared his throat and said,

'I told my editor, Eleanor, that you were writing a novel, Robert. She said she'd be very interested in taking a look when you're ready.'

If anybody noticed Robert's silent gulp of panic, they didn't show it. He fully expected lightning to strike him down when he politely replied, 'Thanks Dad, that's great. I'll definitely send it to her, when it's ready to submit.' What he didn't mention was that he'd already had his sample material rejected by Eleanor with the damning line 'It just didn't convince me, I'm afraid'. Thank goodness Robert had had the foresight to send in the chapters under a pen name. The last thing he wanted was for Eleanor to mention it to Alec during one of their working lunches. *Oh dear, I'm afraid I had to reject your son's work. Really not up to scratch, sorry. Looks like the writing gene skipped a generation!*

Whenever he considered the horror of such a scenario, Robert's skin crawled. Bad as he felt about lying to his old man, it was preferable to that, at least. But then he upped the ante when Harriet came back from work one night a few days later and asked in that still hopeful, bright voice, 'Any news on the book, then? How's it going?'

He was just sick of mumbling that there was no news, not yet, and seeing the light die in her eyes. Sick to the back teeth and tonsils of it. And so this time he heard himself say, 'Well. Actually, there is a bit of a news. A publisher rang me up today, wants to meet me to have a chat.'

Harriet had screamed. She'd actually *screamed*, her hands clasped either side of her face like a joyful version of the Munch painting. 'No way!' she cried, eyes sparkling. 'Rob! Oh my God, that's *amazing*! So they must really like it, then, this publisher? They must be interested, surely?'

He could have stopped it right there if he'd had his wits about him, reined himself in so that he'd have room to manoeuvre further down the line. But he'd had such a depressing week with all those rejections that he simply couldn't resist the temptation of indulging himself with fantasy, trying it on for size. 'Yeah. He said he loved it,' he replied recklessly. 'Said he's never read a debut so good.'

Oh man. Why did he have to over-egg the pudding with lie upon lie? Because for a few minutes while Harriet kissed him and squealed and told him how proud she was, he almost believed it himself. That was why. Because it allowed him to daydream, to imagine what it would feel like if this was actually true. It felt damn good already, in that suspended moment of pretence. It felt amazing.

Afterwards there was no going back, though. He had dug himself a hole and was firmly entrenched. In recent weeks, he had invented an editor – Richard DuLac (fiercely clever and cutting edge) – and given himself an agent to boot (the butt-kicking and brilliant yet sadly fictitious Jake Greenaway). He had conjured up meetings and contracts from thin air, boasted of likely bestseller status and foreign deals. At night he lay in bed, agonizing over his deceit and worrying about how on earth he could extricate himself, but each day the lies just kept on flowing, particularly since his father had died, the one person who might have blown his cover ('I've never heard of Richard DuLac,' he would have said, terrifyingly. 'What publisher did you say he was with?').

Grief-stricken as Robert was by Alec's death, there was still a tiny cynical corner of him that had breathed a very small sigh of relief at his father's untimely demise. Yes – relief. It was a blessing that his dad had never discovered the unpleasant truth: that his son was a liar. (Did that make him the worst son ever? Probably. Just like he was the worst husband too.)

Like father, like son – liars and deceivers both, he thought grimly, in the ringing silence that followed Harriet's departure. Bad blood passing down the line from one to the other. And now look what had happened. The facade had collapsed. The deceit beneath was revealed. He felt like the Wizard of Oz after his unmasking: a fraud, disappointing everyone.

What an idiot he had been. He'd clung to blind faith this whole time that someone somewhere would still publish his novel and that he could get away with his lies. But as email after email came in, all rejecting the novel and him in the same old brief, polite, screw-you format, he had become increasingly desperate. Time was ticking by, everyone expected to see an actual book with his name on it within a matter of months. How was he going to get out of this mess? He toyed with stories about the publisher going bust, Richard DuLac falling under the number 73 bus, the manuscript becoming destroyed somehow – anything to put the brakes on the runaway train of his so-called literary success and clamber down from it without losing too much face.

Then he'd learned about self-publishing and thought he'd found his rescue plan: he'd pay for a load of books to be printed so that he could show them to Harriet and his family, maybe even have some made up in foreign languages in order to continue the pretence of going international . . .

But now that Harriet knew the truth, the game was up and she despised him. The runaway train had crashed straight through their marriage and plunged off a cliff. It was surely only a matter of time before everyone else knew, too: Molly, Mum, Freya, Victor . . . The thought of their incredulous looks as they learned what a waste of space he really was . . . It was excruciating. They wouldn't understand. They would stare at him as if he wasn't right in the head. *What, so there is no book deal? So it was all a load of bollocks? You actually made the whole thing up?*

Harriet's words kept flashing into his mind. *The whole thing's been a bloody fantasy from start to finish. For fuck's sake, Robert!*

He pushed his hands through his hair and wondered if he'd ever be able to make this up to her, if there would ever come a day when she could smile at him with love in her eyes again rather than undiluted contempt. Right now, it was hard to imagine. Right now, he felt as if he was at the bottom of a hole, unsure whether he'd ever be able to scramble out of it. And for what? Stupid male pride. The sinking feeling that he hadn't been quite enough for his wife, his parents; that he hadn't measured up in the eyes of the watching world. It was pretty pathetic, really.

Sickened by his own weakness, he shoved his telltale phone into his pocket and staggered to his feet. Then he slipped out of the house, wondering how long he had left before everyone knew what he'd done.

Down on the beach, for the first time in his life, Robert considered just walking into the sea and giving himself up to the tumultuous waves, letting them drag his body into the undertow and thrash it against the rocks. It would be a way out, at least. An apology.

Chapter Thirty

'Here we are,' said Gloria, parking the car. 'South Devon's best-kept secret. I bet you never even knew this was here, did you?'

It was the following day and Olivia, none the wiser as to her son's disintegrating marriage, had come out with Gloria again following the morning's cleaning session. As she clambered out of the passenger seat, legs like jelly, she gulped in the briny air, thoroughly relieved to have survived another white-knuckle driving experience with her new friend. The woman turned a simple car journey into a bone-shaking rollercoaster ride where your life flashed before your eyes with each blind bend. Mercifully – miraculously – they had arrived in one piece this time.

'The perfect hidden cove,' Gloria had suggested earlier as she scrubbed the cooker to within an inch of its life. Olivia, who had taken to cleaning alongside her in a companionable sort of way (and why not? Lounging around was too boring for words), wiped the toast crumbs and spilled cereal flakes off the kitchen table, replying, 'Sounds good to me.'

The words came back to haunt her as they duly bounced down a bumpy single-track road for what felt like miles. Just as Olivia was about to query Gloria's inner satnav – was this *really* the right way? – they rounded a corner and the land dropped away before them, with the sea a sparkling carpet of blue laid out for their admiration. 'Oh my,' Olivia breathed, and then, before she could brace herself, they had stopped and Gloria was yanking on the handbrake, the little car quite alone on this deserted stretch of grassy headland. It was as if the rest of the world had simply vanished and left them to it.

Olivia gazed apprehensively at the vertiginous cliff-drop before them. 'Goodness me,' she said. 'All these years I've been holidaying in Silver Sands, and no, I had absolutely no idea this was here.'

Gloria gave a pleased-sounding cackle as she got out of the car then rummaged in the boot for a faded canvas bag and slung it over her shoulder. 'Not many people do,' she said. 'Me and Bill found it quite by accident one day. He was lost, of course, even though he said he knew where he was going. It's a bit of a scramble down, mind, but once you get there . . . heaven!'

'A bit of a scramble' was a generous way of phrasing it. Olivia felt as if she was taking her life in her hands for the second time that morning, as she clambered down the rocky slope, her sandals feeling perilously flimsy against the limpet-encrusted boulders. There was no path as such, just a tumble of stones with the occasional grassy clump to hang on to. *I'm too old for this*, she thought, heart thudding in panic, when her foot slipped and she had to clutch at the nearest rock to stop herself falling. Below her, Gloria yelled out 'Hey!' in surprise as a scatter of stones was dislodged and went pattering down past her. Olivia dimly registered the pain of the rock's rough edge scraping her skin and how she seemed to be clinging on by her fingertips. She was still there, though, hanging on. Today was not the day she plummeted to her death, apparently. She hoped.

'You all right up there?' Gloria called out, seeing her frozen in position. 'Trying to knock me out or something?'

Olivia gave a shaky laugh. 'Whose stupid idea was this again?' she called back, tentatively lowering her foot to the next rock. She was braced for another slithering slip, another shower of falling stones, but to her great relief the boulder felt firm and solid beneath her weight.

Gloria let rip another cackle. 'Gets a bit easier further down, don't worry,' she said. Olivia heard her land on the sand below with a soft thud. 'There. Keep going. You've almost made it now.'

Olivia could feel sweat breaking out along her hairline as the sun's hot midday rays beat against her with unflinching intensity. If Freya or Robert could see her now, they'd be up in arms, she thought with a sudden urge to giggle. Freya would be calling the coastguard to send round a helicopter, Robert would be shinning down in some doomed rescue attempt, yelling at her not to move, don't look down, Mum, just keep still!

Not such an old biddy after all, she thought with a rush of pride as she felt Gloria's hand on her waist, helping her take the last steps down. There! And now that she was here on the sandy floor of the hidden cove, she was so glad she'd done it, even if her legs had gone to jelly all over again. What a place. What a find! Sheltered by high curving cliffs, there was no wind at all in the crescent-shaped inlet, just a stretch of pale yellow sand and the sea, foaming up the beach towards them. High above a kittiwake soared, its wings silhouetted against the blue.

'It's gorgeous,' she breathed. 'It's perfect.'

Gloria looked pleased. 'Good, isn't it?' she said. 'And best of all, I've never seen another person here, in all the times me and Bill came down. It's like having your own private beach.'

Olivia took off her sandals and let her bare feet sink luxuriously into the warm, powdery sand. It was so quiet. So remote. You could just about see the bonnet of Gloria's Mini up on the headland if you stretched your head back but there was no other sign of civilization in sight.

Then a thought struck her. An image of the straw beach bag containing her swimming costume and towel, still neatly tucked in the passenger footwell of Gloria's car where she'd left it. 'Oh dear,' she said. 'Slight problem.'

Gloria merely shrugged when she heard the news. 'Not to worry. Nobody will see us here anyway,' she said, heaving a large bamboo mat from her bag and unrolling it on the sand. 'Go crazy and skinny-dip if you want to swim. Me and Bill used to do it all the time.'

Olivia tried to hide her embarrassment at the suggestion, feeling as prim and proper as a Victorian nun. 'Oh. Well. I'm not sure,' she said, feeling her face flame. Honestly. Gloria might be able to throw her clothes off and swim about naked but Olivia . . . No. She couldn't. Nobody had seen her body since Alec and it would feel horribly exposing to reveal all so brazenly in public. Every time she showered or bathed, she was aware of how pale and wrinkled she had become, of how she sagged and pouched in all the wrong places nowadays. When one was approaching sixty, nudity was simply not the done thing.

Gloria gave a hoot of laughter. 'Well, if you're not going to, I am,' she declared, and pulled her sleeveless cyan shirt-dress over her head. Olivia averted her eyes but not before she saw Gloria's magenta bra and black lacy knickers go flying off onto the bamboo mat. 'Last one in's a rotten egg!'

called Gloria, and then she was pelting away down the sand, bottom wobbling like twin caramel blancmanges, shrieking for joy.

SPLASH. In she went, launching herself at the waves, arms outstretched as if embracing a watery friend. Up went another squeal. 'Jesus, it is *cold*. Makes you feel alive, though. Come on in!'

I couldn't, thought Olivia as Gloria waved from the sea, then surface-dived like a frisky bum-baring dolphin. *I absolutely couldn't.* Turning away, she wiped each foot free of sand before gingerly stepping onto the bamboo mat and sitting down. Gloria, meanwhile, was windmilling her arms through the water, sending up fountains of spray that glittered like crystals against the blue sky. From the lack of tan lines on Gloria's body, Olivia suspected she was a frequent nude sunbather and swimmer. Oh, to be so carefree and liberated!

'Come on. Seriously! It's lovely when you get used to it. Refreshing. Blissful!'

Olivia shook her head, smiling and wishing she could be so bold. It did look lovely, to be honest. A memory came to her – one she hadn't thought of for years. She and her sisters when they were in their teens, swimming naked in the millpond of the farm along the road, while all the farmhands were getting in the corn. She remembered the paleness of their bodies in the cool green water, the dreamy, weightless sensation of swimming without a single stitch to cover you.

They'd splashed one another and laughed at each other's lolling breasts and floating pubic hair as they lay on their backs. It had been a glorious day. Birdsong and duckweed and the prickly sensation of the dried grass when you came out, dripping. She could almost hear the peals of girlish laughter now.

The sun felt hotter than ever all of a sudden and Olivia slipped off her cardigan, folding it carefully on the sand. She had on a fawn-coloured shell top underneath which was light and cool. Gloria cheered approval as she saw Olivia remove the cardigan, clearly thinking she was about to join her in the water. 'I knew you'd do it,' she crowed. 'Come on, get 'em off.'

Olivia was about to shake her head again – no, Gloria had misunderstood – but there was something about the way her friend had cheered that made her think twice. *I knew you'd do it!* Like she had faith in her. As if she didn't think Olivia was a fuddy-duddy Victorian nun at all, as if she knew about the day at the millpond. Gloria was fully expecting her to strip off and wade in. So . . . what was stopping her?

She glanced up at the cliff behind her. Nobody there. Back as a teenager, she hadn't hesitated for a moment, stepping out of her slip and knickers before pinching her nose and jumping straight into the delicious cool water. Had she even been the first one in, the most daring of the sisters?

She smiled. Yes. She was pretty sure she had been. She

could even dimly remember urging her sisters to join her, just like Gloria was now.

The sun was casting sparkles on the water. So enticing. So refreshing. And before she knew it, Olivia was standing up, unzipping her skirt and undressing. Doubts skittered across her mind when she was down to her bra and pants: Freya's voice, *Mum, what on earth are you doing?*, the notion of hikers up on the cliff path peering down through binoculars, a yachtsman tacking round from the next bay . . .

Oh, who cared? Flesh was flesh. Life was short. And besides, the sea looked absolutely marvellous. She unhooked her bra, dropped her knickers and stretched her arms up to the sky. 'Here I come!'

Chapter Thirty-One

Unbeknown to Olivia, she wasn't the first to leave Shell Cottage that morning. Harriet was already long gone.

After a night of tossing and turning, punctuated by angry dreams, she had left Molly sleeping peacefully in the double bed and tiptoed out before anyone could stop her. She hadn't seen Robert since the catastrophic phone discovery the evening before – and frankly, nor did she want to. Following her meltdown in the car, loudly shouting and crying like a maniac, she had eventually returned to Shell Cottage with takeaway fish and chips, scooping up Molly en route, and driving them both out to Pemberley Point for a carbohydrate bender. When in doubt, eat. That particular mantra had got her through her first divorce, anyway. It seemed as good a time as any to wheel it out once more.

'By the way, you're sleeping in with me tonight,' she had announced, much to Molly's surprise. They were sitting out on the headland, the sea bashing against the cliff face below.

It felt a suitably dramatic place to come, given her state of mind. 'Robert's going up in the attic.'

Molly lay back, faintly green around the gills, having monstered a huge battered haddock and chips. 'How come? What's going on?'

Harriet licked her salty fingers. She was completely stuffed already but couldn't bring herself to stop eating. 'What's going on is that Robert is a . . .' she began and then somehow managed to shut her mouth before she came right out and uttered the words 'complete knobhead'. She wiped her fingers on the grass, uncertain how much to confide. 'He's . . . got a headache,' she said in the end. Molly didn't need to know the contents of their row, she decided. Not yet anyway.

Molly didn't seem suspicious, thankfully. 'Okay. Cool,' she said, shrugging. 'As long as you're not snoring and farting all night anyway.'

Harriet thought of this charming daughterly reply now as she got into the car, and smiled briefly despite her lack of sleep and the black cloud she was under. **Gone out for a few hours. Ring me if any problems, love Mum**, she texted Molly quickly, before starting the engine and heading out towards the coast road. Molly would probably sleep in till midday anyway, given half a chance, and Harriet would no doubt be back before she even stirred. In the meantime, it was a relief to leave everything else behind. She didn't have a clue where she was going, but she knew for certain that she wanted to get away from her husband for the time being. And good sodding riddance, too!

Quite honestly, she had felt like a puppet with cut strings since finding out his dirty little secret, she thought, accelerating away. She wasn't sure what to do with herself or how she would ever pick herself back up again. All she knew was that she was hurting, very badly, winded with shock and burning with humiliation. It wasn't just the fact that he had lied about his so-called publisher, it was all those other lies he'd told too. The glamorous party to which she had been mysteriously uninvited, the envy-inducing lunches and meetings. Hadn't she known there was something dodgy about the Marylebone Tavern mix-up? She should have trusted her instincts all along.

After their takeaway last night, Harriet had been sorely tempted to bundle her and Molly's things into the car and flounce off back to London like a raging adolescent. When this sort of disaster struck, she wanted all her mates around her with a crate of wine and a lorryload of Dairy Milk, so that they could get stuck into a proper cathartic They're Such Bastards bitchfest.

The adult in her was just about able to resist this temptation though, recognizing wearily that oh, bloody *hell*, she and Robert were going to have to sit down, she supposed, to talk the whole dreadful situation through, like proper grown-ups. It would be hideous, she could tell already. He, no doubt, would try and cobble together more excuses and lies to explain his shameful behaviour while she scowled and sat on her hands to avoid punching him in the nose. Bloody Robert! Why did husbands, however nice they initially seemed, always end up being such utter cocks?

Bollocks. And she'd thought he was the one, too. The key that fitted her lock, the perfect match, two halves of a whole. She'd even used the word 'soulmate' about him in her wedding speech. 'Arsehole mate, more like,' she sneered to herself, hunching over the steering wheel as she put her foot down and nipped past a trundling milk lorry. 'Without the "mate", that is.'

Realizing she was way over the speed limit, she slowed down and tried to calm herself by dwelling on the beautiful, serene landscape around her. It was a staggeringly gorgeous morning; even she, in her toweringly crap mood, could appreciate that. Not yet eight o'clock, and the sky was still faintly pink around the edges from the sunrise, with just a few rose-tinged wispy clouds like puffs of icing sugar. Mind you, if there was any justice, there'd be a massive thunderstorm now instead, with booming crashes and bangs and a biblical downpour. And Robert would be struck by a bolt of jagged lightning and . . .

She wrinkled her nose and let out an exasperated sigh. No. That was the problem. Even after what he'd done, even after all those lies, she didn't want him struck by a bolt of lightning, or any other means of death. She just wanted the situation to miraculously unhappen, to rewind nine months and talk him out of this whole stupid book-writing idea in the first place. Oh, sure, he wanted to live up to his dad, he wanted to make everyone proud – she got that, loud and clear. But couldn't he have just helped old ladies across the road, like normal people did? Remembered his mum's birthday on time, done some voluntary work at the local animal shelter, cleared snow off their neighbours' stretch of pavement . . . the sort of nice, thoughtful thing he already did, in fact, for crying out loud. Why wasn't that enough for him? Why had he felt so compelled to stick his neck out in the hope of impressing the world?

Honestly. Parents and children, expectations and hangups. It was always so flaming complicated, so fraught. Thank God she didn't have that kind of relationship with Molly. Thank goodness *they* could always be straight with one another.

The thought cheered her a little. She still had Molly. Whatever happened, whichever prat of a bloke messed her about, she had her daughter and that was enough for Harriet. If it came to the crunch, they could go it alone again, even if it meant the two of them moving back to a smaller, cheaper flat, even if they had to put up with mouldering walls and mice under the floorboards like last time.

They would manage. They didn't need one crap ex-husband or the other. They didn't need anyone or anything at all!

Mind you, saying that, she couldn't half do with a kick-ass coffee right now. And a bacon sandwich would definitely hit the spot too. She also quite fancied phoning her friend Gabbi and having a good, long whinge to her. Every broken-hearted, angry woman should have sustenance and friends in her hour of need. She drove on in search of where she might find them.

Chapter Thirty-Two

Since the Pedalo Ride of Despair, where Freya had confessed all to Victor, she had made a few big decisions. The first was on the drinking front. As she had vowed to Harriet, she was going cold turkey, cutting it out for good, bosh. Three days later, she was proud to say that she hadn't touched a drop. Going to bed stone-cold sober was a novel experience and the first couple of nights she had lain there, head buzzing with spirals of thought, unable to switch off her brain without the dulling tether of alcohol. Waking up without the jarring ache of a hangover was worth it, though. She felt alert and energized each morning now, ready for anything, even child-wrangling. Well, well. Who knew?

Of course, it was early days, and she definitely wasn't kidding herself that stopping drinking was going to be easy. It had become a habit for her, a crutch on which she had leaned far too heavily. Just the night before, Olivia had opened a bottle of port and the smell was enough to make Freya salivate. She and her dad had loved a drop of port after a large dinner, especially on Christmas Day. But in the next second, she remembered the seaweed-in-hair moment when Libby had stared at her with such reproach, and she poured herself a glass of orange juice instead. *No. Don't go back there.*

Thankfully Freya was the sort of person who saw things through when she put her mind to it. She had a steel rod for a spine; determination ran through her veins. 'I can do this,' she said to Victor, doggedly drinking her juice.

'I know you can. If anyone can, it's you,' he said.

Her second decision concerned Victor. Their conversation on the pedalo had been cut short when they rounded a corner and saw that Teddy – of course – had fallen in the water and was currently drying off on the riverbank along with Robert, who had leapt in to haul him out. 'I went swimming!' Teddy cheered, waving his hands above his head. 'Don't worry, I didn't lose my glasses!'

Since then, there hadn't really been the moment for another heart-to-heart with her husband. They had been courteous to each other, kind, even. He was keeping an eye on her, she could tell, his gaze flicking to hers more often than usual, putting a solicitous arm around her as they sat out on the patio *en famille* in the evening. She couldn't help worrying a little about what he was *not* saying, though. After Dad's secret affair, and now Robert and Harriet seeming to have had a bust-up, this holiday was fast turning into the

Hunger Games of Tarrant relationships. Would any of them survive the fortnight?

She *wanted* their marriage to survive, that was the key thing. And so decision number two was most definitely to find a way to get their relationship back on track. She would build up the courage to talk to him properly and find a way to muddle through.

Decision number three was the one she was about to tackle now, though, and it involved an apology she should have made two weeks ago.

Don't, her boss Elizabeth had advised when Freya had first suggested it. *Saying sorry is tantamount to accepting culpability. Mrs Taylor could use it against you – she could sue you, twist your words. You could be putting your job in jeopardy.*

Freya had gone along with her boss's instructions at the time, not wanting to risk her career in any way. But the decision had weighed heavily on her conscience this whole time. It had not felt honourable or honest. It went against Freya's personal code of right and wrong to duck an apology. And so now, this morning, it was time to change that and make the call.

For once, the house was quiet. Mum had gone off with Gloria, who seemed to have transformed from Gloria-the-cleaner into Gloria-the-new-best-friend, judging by the way both women had been cackling as they clambered into Gloria's clapped-out Mini together. (Freya was *delighted*!

Mum had never really gone in for female friends before. 'I prefer to spend time with your father,' she'd always said, and Freya had never quite voiced the *Yes, but . . .* that rose to her lips each time.) Victor had taken the children down to the beach with the bodyboards (and Teddy's armbands); Freya had promised to join them just as soon as she'd made this call. Neither Robert nor Harriet were anywhere to be seen and their car had gone (maybe they had taken out a Heartbreak Pedalo of their own), although Molly was still in the house, judging by how long the shower had been running just now.

Meanwhile, her phone waited silently beside her. The sooner she got this over and done with, the sooner she could head down to the beach with the others. *Come on, Freya. Do the right thing.*

She perched on the edge of the bed, suddenly nervous. What if she did end up losing her job because she'd said sorry, and a court viewed that as guilt? When she'd talked it through with Victor the night before, sitting up on the patio with their glasses of lemonade (lemonade!), he'd told her gruffly that it sounded as if she didn't have anything to apologize for anyway. 'It wasn't your fault the baby got ill. You said yourself, you made all the right checks at the time.'

'I know, but . . .'

'Just do what you've got to do, Freya. Follow your instincts.

If you want to apologize, do it, and we'll deal with the consequences, whatever they are, later.'

Do what you've got to do, Freya. It was good advice. Time to stop prevaricating and act. With a shaking finger, she dialled Melanie's number and waited. *Ring ring. Ring ring. Ring ring.* Freya's breath tightened in her lungs. Then the voicemail message kicked in.

This is Melanie, I can't take your call right now. Leave me a message after the beep and I'll get back to you.

Leave a message. Ugh. Freya hadn't considered having to leave a message. She thought about hanging up in a moment of panic, but Melanie's phone would surely store her number. No. Deep breath. Do it.

BEEP. 'Er . . . Hello. This is Freya. Doctor Castledine. I'm just ringing to say that I really hope Ava's on the mend and you're okay.' Another deep breath. 'I hope you don't mind me calling you. My boss actually advised me not to, but . . .' Her mouth dried and she had to force herself on. 'Well, look, I just wanted to say that I'm sorry. I wasn't at my best the day that you came in. I'm not making excuses; I should have been more on the ball. So I'm sorry if I let you down.' She wanted to cry all of a sudden. She wasn't even sure what she was saying any more, let alone whether or not this was the right thing to do. 'For what it's worth, I genuinely didn't see any signs of serious illness when you came in. My mind might have been elsewhere but I would have noticed, I promise you that. I'm on holiday right now but I've been thinking about you and Ava. Maybe we could have a chat when I'm back in Oakthorne.'

She had run out of words. 'That's it, really. Forget doctor–patient, I just wanted to reach out as a human being and a mum, and say all of this. I should have said it sooner, so I'm sorry for that, too. Okay.' Wrap it up now. She would be cut off any second. 'Well, take care anyway. Bye.'

She pressed 'End call' and collapsed backwards onto the bed. Had she even been coherent? She hoped she had sounded sincere, at the very least. She hoped, too, that Melanie would accept her apology in the spirit it had been made and not let rip at her again.

Freya exhaled noisily. Christ, doing the right thing was exhausting. But that was one important job crossed off the list, one amend hopefully made. Now for some quality time with her loved ones, as the magazines liked to call it. Or trying not to mind when your six-year-old attempted to give you a wedgie on a public beach, as she preferred to think of it.

There were three main bedrooms on the first floor of Shell Cottage: her parents' room, Freya and Victor's, and the room shared by Rob and Harriet. Her children were wedged into the box room at the back, up a small flight of stairs, whereas Molly had been sleeping in the attic room.

The house had seemed silent earlier, bar the long-running shower, but as Freya walked along the landing, she heard voices from Rob's room and paused in confusion. Who was the male voice she could hear talking to Molly? Oh, right. She must have the call on speakerphone or something.

Freya was not generally a nosey person but as she passed the bedroom, an overheard phrase stopped her in her tracks.

'You would, if you loved me,' the male voice said.

The words instantly triggered a warning bell in her head. Oh, what? How many millions of manipulative men had said *that* to women over the centuries? And now here was some lad trying it on with poor innocent Molly, by the sound of things. *Don't give in to that kind of bullshit, Molly*, she thought fiercely, gripping the bannister and cocking an ear to hear the girl's response.

'Well . . . I don't know. I mean . . . I should check with Mum.'

'No. Don't tell her. Don't tell anyone. This is our secret, Molls. If you tell anyone, I won't see you again. Do you understand? If you tell anyone, it's over.'

Freya felt the hairs prickle on the back of her neck. *The sly little bastard*, she thought to herself indignantly. She had a good mind to charge into the bedroom, snatch the phone and have a few words with this jerk herself. She tiptoed towards the open door and peered through the crack along the hinged side.

Molly was sitting on the bed speaking into her laptop. Ahh, Skype, then. She was fully dressed at least, but sounded subdued as she replied. 'Okay. So . . . what's the plan, then? Where are you staying?'

'It's called the Ennisbridge Hotel. Only a couple of miles from you, I checked. Double bedroom. Just the two of us.'

Freya put her hand up to her mouth. Oh my goodness. Did Harriet know about this? She would bet anything she didn't have a clue. 'Boyfriend?' she had laughed the other day at the Co-op. 'No, not Molly!' Harriet worshipped her daughter. If she had the faintest idea that this kind of conversation was taking place, there was no way she'd have left the house that morning.

'Here,' the male voice continued. 'I've just texted you a link to where it is. You can't miss it, though: right on the seafront, big white building. We can be together at last, just me and you.' Freya heard him laugh, low and throaty. 'I can't wait to see those tan lines in person, babe.'

Molly giggled but through the crack in the door, Freya thought she could see a nervous light in the girl's eyes. *Christ. Don't do this, Molly. Don't go!*

'Okay,' Molly said. She blew a kiss to the screen. 'I'm on my way.'

Freya immediately scuttled back to her room, heart thumping, as she heard Molly shut the laptop and then, moments later, hurtle down the stairs. What should she do?

She couldn't let Molly go off and meet this boy without trying to get hold of Harriet. In fact, she couldn't let her go at all. Yes, eavesdropping was awful, and yes, Molly would probably hate her for interfering, but Freya had to stop her step-niece before she did anything she regretted. Call it women's intuition, call it a mother's sixth sense, but she didn't like the sound of this guy one bit.

She hurried down the stairs but the front door had already slammed and when she reached the porch and opened it, she was just in time to see Molly vanishing out the drive on a bike, pedalling hard.

Shit. Now what?

Well, ring Harriet, that was what. Track her down and send her racing over to the Ennisbridge Hotel. How long would it take Molly to get there on her bike? Half an hour, tops. There was no time to lose.

Back in her own room, she grabbed the phone and dialled her sister-in-law. It rang and rang and rang, just as Melanie's phone had done earlier, and then once again, she was greeted by a voicemail message. *Hello, this is Harriet, leave me a message and I'll call you back. Byeee!*

'It's Freya,' she said urgently. 'Look – this might sound odd but I couldn't help overhearing Molly just now. She was talking to some boy, arranging to meet him at the Ennisbridge Hotel. He sounded really slimy – he was trying to push her into it. Maybe you know all about this but I just got a bad feeling. Um . . .' Oh God. How she wished Harriet had picked up the call. Where was she? 'Let me know if you get this in time. She's on her way to meet him now – I've just seen her heading off on a bike. Okay, ring me back. Hopefully talk to you in a minute.'

She paced around the room, feeling stressed. What if Harriet had no signal, and didn't receive the message for ages? By the time Harriet's phone alerted her to her daughter's plight, it could all be too late. Freya envisaged Molly walking innocently into the hotel reception – walking headlong into danger, possibly – and let out a groan. Hadn't she thought herself, that day at the supermarket, that her stepniece was jailbait? The way every bloke had turned and looked at her, even middle-aged blokes, old enough to be her father, for heaven's sake . . . Molly was like a ripe golden peach, just waiting to be plucked. *I can't wait to see those tan lines, babe.*

Well, not on my watch, mate, she thought grimly. Glancing out the window, she could see Victor and the children, already setting up camp for the day on the beach. Ten forty-five, and the sand was fast filling up with families and sun-worshippers, but her eye picked them out immediately. There was Vic, using a rock to hammer in the poles of the windbreak. (*Corrrr*, she thought, with an unexpected flicker of lust. Even from this distance, she could see how the muscles rippled in his back.) Beside him Teddy was digging a hole, while Dex and Libby were in their wetsuits, scampering down to the sea with the bodyboards. She could almost hear their laughter.

Freya ached to join them. Ten minutes, she'd said. But Harriet still hadn't replied to her call, and Freya knew she couldn't turn her back on Molly and the creep in the hotel. No woman could.

She fired off two quick texts.

Vic, something's happened with Molly – I'll be a bit longer than I thought. Sorry. Will explain all later. xxx

Harriet, me again. I'm going to follow Molly and make sure she's all right. If you get this in time, Ennisbridge Hotel – big white one on seafront. Love Freya x

Then she hurried downstairs and into the car. Much as she respected the sanctity of young love, Molly was fifteen and her boyfriend shouldn't be putting her under pressure, she thought as she drove away. She'd give this teenage Lothario a flea in his ear and send him packing, then they could all get on with their lives again.

Chapter Thirty-Three

Molly cycled along the path, heart thumping. Above her head, the trees waved leafy branches, casting dappled shade on the ground, and birds sang merrily. Molly hardly noticed, though. A unicorn could come prancing out of the under-growth, and it would barely register. All she could think about was Ben Sex Bomb Jamison. Ben, Ben, Ben!

Waiting for her at the hotel. Ben. Taking her hand and leading her up to the bedroom. Oh, Ben. Kissing him in the lift. Ben! (Was her breath okay? She'd have to quickly chew some gum once she'd locked her bike up.)

He'd booked them a double bedroom. *Ben*. He wanted to see her tan lines . . .

Oh God. That was the scary bit. Well, the first scary bit of several scary bits. Taking her clothes off in front of him. Or would he rip them off passionately, like they did in romantic films? (Mum would kill her if she came back with ripped clothes. Aargh. Mum would kill her *full stop* if she had the faintest idea what Molly was up to. Thank God she had gone out for the day, according to that text.)

Then, after that . . . Well. It was obvious he wanted to do it. How could they not do it, when there was a bed there? When he had paid for a hotel room and everything? He had basically paid all that money so that they could do it. What if he didn't think she was worth it? What if he asked her for some of the money back??

A few stolen kisses at school was one thing. Getting physical and horny in Stratford-upon-Avon – yep, that had been good, too. The flirty texts and phone calls – she could handle those. But a hotel room for two . . . It seemed like a massive leap forward. A huge, serious, no-turning-back leap.

A bird suddenly flapped across the path and Molly jumped, almost losing her balance on the bike. Stupid bird, trying to kill people. Stupid bird, getting in the way of her romantic, epic sex mission, and the course of true love!

She hoped it was true love, anyway. Did he love her? She knew his texts off by heart, she'd read them so many times now, but he'd never actually said those three little words. (Yet.) Instead he'd said

1) He was *crazy about her.*

2) He fancied her.

3) He wanted to see her naked. (HELP.)

4) He couldn't wait to be alone with her.

5) He thought she had nice boobs. That was after she'd

daringly sent a photo last night – a selfie in just her bra and knickers. If she was completely honest with herself, she'd been kind of hoping he'd reply saying, 'My God, you are beautiful. I am bewitched,' that sort of thing, but instead, he'd texted back, **Ur tits look amazing**, which wasn't quite as romantic. Still, at least he hadn't sent any more schlong photos. That was something.

Oh help. The schlong. She was going to actually see the schlong. Would he expect her to touch it? Would he expect her to . . . you know, kiss it? Or put it in her mouth? Boys wanted you to do that, everyone said so. A blowie . . . although you weren't actually supposed to *blow*, according to Jasmine Barrett in the year above, who'd done everything with her boyfriend, she reckoned.

Yes, love, but have you stayed in a hotel with him? Molly thought, arching an eyebrow. *I think not.* Jasmine was going out with Olly Goodings, who had really bad acne on his forehead anyway. He was a mere child in comparison to Ben.

She emerged from the woodland, and the path curved down so that it ran alongside the main road. *Ennisbridge 1 mile*, said a signpost and her skin felt hot.

One mile until she was with him again. One mile until they were up in that bedroom. She hoped she wouldn't be all hot and sweaty by the time they arrived. What if she smelled horrible? Had she put enough deodorant on that morning? She was in a T-shirt and shorts, and an old pair of faded pink

Converse, with a broken lace that was knotted together on the left side. She'd been in such a hurry to leave, she hadn't even thought about make-up or jewellery. Suddenly she wished she had dressed up a bit for the occasion, maybe put on a nice dress and jewelled flip-flops. It wasn't every day you lost your virginity, was it? She could have at least made herself look presentable.

A shiver went down her back. She and Chloe had often discussed what it would feel like to actually DO IT. To have sex. To have some bloke's penis shoved up inside you. (Ugh.) When you put it like that, Molly wondered how the human race ever continued. Jasmine Barrett said that it really hurt the first time. Like, serious actual pain. And she'd bled all over Olly's mum's sheet, and it had been totally embarrassing.

What if Molly bled on the hotel sheet?? Nightmare. She would die of embarrassment. She and Chloe had been so paranoid about bleeding when they lost their virginity that they'd actually signed up for a school horse-riding day, because everyone said that riding a horse broke your hymen. It was bollocks, though. It hadn't worked *and* she'd been given the most stubborn horse ever, which kept stopping dead and refusing to budge, however hard she pleaded.

There was Ennisbridge ahead, a clutch of white-painted buildings nestled against a beach, with a tiny harbour full of boats. The cycle path ended and Molly moved gingerly to join the cars who were already queuing back up the hill. Shit. Nearly there now.

By the time she was returning uphill this way, she would no longer be a virgin, she thought breathlessly. She'd have done it, with Ben. She'd be a woman.

Fucking hell. It was terrifying. She wasn't sure she actually wanted to be a woman any more, to be honest. She and Robert had swapped beds last night after he and Mum had an argument about something, and Mum had been crying in bed, when she thought Molly was asleep. It was all a bit weird. When Molly asked what was wrong, Mum hadn't wanted to tell her, just said in this sad sort of voice, 'Don't worry. It'll be all right. It's fine.'

Not that Molly was thinking about her mum right now. *Go away, Mum. You are not invited into my head today. Not invited and not welcome.* If Mum was here, she'd only –

NO. Stop. Think about Ben instead. Gorgeous, charming, handsome, funny Ben who had chosen her, yes, her, Molly Tarrant-Price, to share his hotel bedroom. He'd come all that way for her.

Her knuckles tightened on the handlebars. Losing your virginity wasn't a big deal anyway, she told herself. It would be a relief to get rid of it. Imagine going back to school in September and telling Chloe and her other friends, *Yeah, I did it.*

They would all be agog, mouths dropping open like trapdoors. *No way. What? Seriously? Who with?*

Ahh. She braked, as the hill wound steeply down into the centre of town, and remembered that she wasn't meant to tell anyone. *If you tell anyone, I won't see you again. Do you understand? If you tell anyone, it's over.*

God, it was complicated, being in love.

She'd reached the seafront now and braked to a stop by an ice-cream van. Bunting fluttered across the street, from lamp post to lamp post. The sea winked and twinkled in the sunshine. There were families everywhere, making slow progress towards the beach, laden with buckets and spades and lilos. Old people deliberated in front of postcard racks in the souvenir shops, while toddlers drummed their feet in buggies and whinged for an ice lolly. A bunch of teenagers went by, the boys all with their shorts hanging halfway down their bums, and Molly watched scornfully as she saw them lope into the amusement arcade. They seemed so immature compared to Ben.

Seagulls screeched as they sailed across the sky, and she could smell pasties and coffee from a nearby takeaway shop, mingled with the tang of diesel from a motorboat setting off to sea. Everyone else was just getting on with their holidays on this bright, sunshine-filled day – an ordinary summer morning, down at the seaside.

It might be ordinary for them, she thought, but meanwhile, she had a sex mission to attend to. The love affair of the year just waiting to explode into life. She chained her bike to the prom railings feeling fluttery, excited, completely bricking it. Then she took a deep breath and strode along the front. *Ennisbridge Hotel, here I come.*

Chapter Thirty-Four

The sheer numbing cold of the sea took your breath away for the first minute but after some brisk swimming back and forth, Olivia quickly acclimatized. And then she was laughing out loud in utter delight. My goodness. It was heavenly! 'Oh, Gloria,' she said, floating on her back, the water lapping gently under her arms, 'you are a breath of fresh air. Never in a million years would I have done this without you.'

It was true. Gloria had completely turned this holiday around. Olivia had envisaged slogging her way through three weeks of moping and misery, particularly after Katie's devastating secret. Instead, the woman doing a splashy front crawl a few metres away had shaken everything up, and in a good way. In less than a week, Olivia had had to rethink her preconceptions on a number of things: tattoos, lobster shacks and now skinny-dipping. Life was full of surprises – good ones as well as bad. Just look at her now! She felt unmoored, set free, joyfully floating here like some geriatric mermaid as if this was what she'd been destined to do.

Gloria beamed and smoothed her hair back from her face. 'Never a dull moment,' she said. 'That's what Bill used to say.'

'Well, he was a lucky man,' Olivia told her. 'I hope he appreciated you.'

To her surprise, Gloria's smile slipped a fraction, like a cloud passing over the sun. 'Ha. Maybe. Does any man really appreciate his wife? I mean – truly. I'm not sure they do.'

In the past, Olivia had always shied away from those confessional all-girls-together conversations where husbands inevitably came in for a slating but there was something about being naked in the sea that made you forget your inhibitions. 'Mine didn't,' she heard herself saying and shrugged, the water sliding from her shoulders. 'Mine played me for a total fool.'

Gloria raised one of her severely plucked eyebrows and considered Olivia. 'You don't strike me as a fool,' she said. 'Far from it.'

Olivia let herself sink down in the water until the balls of her feet touched the soft mud of the seabed, then pushed gently back up again, relishing the feeling of buoyancy. Gone were her aches and pains, her stiff knees, her tired old feet. 'I didn't think I was a fool either,' she agreed, 'but somehow my husband got away with having a mistress and another son while I was looking the other way. Thirteen or fourteen years, it must have been going on. So not only a fool but blind as well.'

Gloria's mouth fell open for a moment before her expression changed to one of thorough indignation. 'Flaming Nora,' she said and whistled. 'Seriously? Now that's devious. That's proper greedy. Straight from one of the pages of his books, that kind of behaviour. Catch me buying another of them now? No chance.'

Olivia said nothing, letting her body drift downwards again, while she thought of the still-unread manuscript, untouched and gathering dust in a bag in her bedroom. She hadn't gone online to look at her emails since arriving in Devon but she would lay money on there being a few marked 'Urgent' from Alec's editor, Eleanor, by now. Urgent, indeed! They were talking about a novel here, made-up words on a page, not a building on fire or a volcano about to blow. Let Eleanor email away and get her knickers in a twist. She'd be in for a long wait, that was all Olivia could say.

'Tell me about Bill,' she said, not wanting to think about Alec or Katie or Eleanor any longer. 'Was he the love of your life?'

She was expecting the usual toothy smile on Gloria's face but again came that muted expression, the clouding of Gloria's eyes. 'Well, I thought he was,' she said cryptically and gazed out at the horizon for a few moments. Then, to Olivia's consternation, a tear trickled down her friend's cheek and into the sea. 'Sorry. Always reminds me of him, coming here.'

'You don't need to say sorry,' Olivia replied at once. 'I'm sorry for asking. Silly of me.' She knew only too well how the smallest thing could set a widow off, memories waiting to ambush you around every corner. 'Do you want to talk about him, or . . . ?'

Gloria shook her head. 'No, I'm fine,' she said. 'Just having a moment, that's all.' She rubbed her arms theatrically. 'Brrrr. Think I'm going to get out and warm up again. There's a flask of coffee in my bag. What do you reckon?'

'Sure,' Olivia said. She recognized subject-avoidance when she heard it; she was an expert herself, after all.

Taking your clothes off and swimming in the sea was one thing, but it was even more daunting to walk out again, completely naked. All the water pouring off your wet body to start with, and then the terrifying prospect of facing land as one emerged. Needless to say, Gloria didn't seem fazed for a second, and strode ahead confidently, arms swinging, towards the refuge of the bamboo mat. Olivia, by contrast, had one arm clasped across her goosepimpling breasts, and the other covering her privates.

'Looking on the bright side,' Gloria said, drying herself quickly, then passing the damp pink beach towel to Olivia, 'at least we won't be sitting around in wet costumes all afternoon. Nothing worse than that, in my book.' She put on her bra and dress, and Olivia hugged the towel around herself.

'Absolutely,' she said, sinking down onto the mat. Her bare legs glistened with water and her muscles felt stretched. The warm air encircled her like an embrace and she twisted her hair up, squeezing out the drips. 'That was wonderful,' she added. 'It reminded me of being a girl. I'm starting to think that women of our age should behave recklessly more often, you know.'

Gloria grinned. 'Sounds like a T-shirt slogan right there,' she said. She rummaged in the bag for a thermos flask and brought out two plastic mugs as well. 'The Reckless Women Club. We should make badges. Or get matching tattoos.' She winked and then went plunging back into the bag to produce a white paper bakery bag with two fat jam doughnuts inside. 'Here. Get one of these down you.'

'Jam doughnuts. Now you're talking. I'm always prepared to be reckless when it comes to jam doughnuts,' Olivia said, taking one and biting into it. 'Thank you. For all of this. You thought of everything.'

Gloria passed her a steaming mug of coffee. 'All part of the service.' She held her own mug aloft. 'To being reckless women!'

'To reckless women everywhere!' Olivia echoed. Coffee had never tasted so good. She gazed out at the rich deep blue of the sea, a million golden sparkles on its surface. *You'll never guess what I've been doing*, she imagined saying to Freya when she returned to the cottage, and felt happier and younger than she had done for years. Contrary to popular belief, life could still be fun when you were widowed, she marvelled. It was a revelation.

Coffee drunk, doughnuts munched, they lay back in the sun for a while, soaking up the warmth, like two old lizards on a rock, Olivia thought drowsily. Now, this felt *good*. Much as she adored her children and grandchildren, much as she'd always enjoyed family holidays down at Shell Cottage, this was something just for her for a change. Miles away from the house, from the heartbreak, from Katie, she felt as if her energy was being restored, charged up by sunshine and relaxation. *Olivia Tarrant, you're going soft in the head*, she scolded herself in the next moment. But still. There was something to be said for getting away from it all, that was for sure.

'So what are you going to do about this other woman?' Gloria asked after a while. 'Want me to shove her off a cliff for you?'

Olivia gurgled with unexpected laughter. Every conversation she'd had about Katie recently had been accompanied by fraught, angry tears and hurt offspring. Lying here and actually being able to laugh made the whole messy situation slightly more bearable. 'Better not,' she replied. 'My son-in-law's a detective. My recklessness doesn't go as far as seeing either of us locked up behind bars.'

'And there's a kid as well, did you say?' Gloria remarked

and Olivia heard her snapping her lighter and then two quick puffs of a cigarette. The smoke hung in the air like a small fragrant cloud.

'There's a kid as well,' Olivia confirmed. 'Leo, he's called.'

Gloria coughed on her cigarette. 'Oh right, Leo Browne? Christ. And *Katie*. I know who you mean now. He's a nice lad. Used to come in my pet shop every Saturday and mooch about, stroking the hamsters and giving them all names. His mum was allergic so he wasn't allowed one of his own.'

Olivia rolled onto her front, not really wanting to hear about Leo and his devotion to small rodents. The more the boy was coloured in with details – hamsters, allergies, 'a nice lad' – the more he began to take shape in her mind as a real person. As Alec's son. Living and breathing. Crying in her kitchen.

'So what are you going to do?' Gloria asked again.

The question was like a scalpel poking at a wound. Olivia shrugged, her good mood shrivelling at the edges. 'I'm not sure,' she confessed. 'Katie's tried a few times to build bridges but . . .'

'You're not ready for bridges,' Gloria finished for her. 'Fair enough. Plenty of time for bridge-building.'

If I actually want to build any bridges, that is, Olivia thought doubtfully. Given the choice, she would rather sever all ties, turn her back on what had happened and slap thick black paint over that part of her memory. Bridges were overrated.

Gloria rolled over too, and blew a perfect smoke ring that hovered in the air for a moment before wispily dispersing. 'It's bloody annoying, when the one you love surprises you after they've gone, isn't it?' she said, in commiseration. 'Inconvenient too. You can't have it out with them and make them answer for what they did. You can't ask them why, or how could you, or what the hell were you thinking? Inconsiderate bastards.'

Precisely. Olivia couldn't have phrased it better herself. 'Quite. *And* they leave you the mess to deal with on your own, just when you're feeling at your absolute worst,' she agreed. Then the full portent of Gloria's words trickled down into Olivia's subconscious and she eyed the other woman across the bamboo mat. 'Go on. You might as well tell me. What did Bill do?'

For a moment, Olivia thought she'd overstepped the mark, pushed too hard. It was none of her business what had happened with Gloria and Bill, after all.

She was just about to apologize and retract her question when Gloria spoke. 'He died in a road accident,' she said, puffing another smoke ring. 'It was a wet night, him on his motorbike, the front wheel must have skidded. Went straight into the path of this Land Rover, the driver couldn't do anything about it. First thing I know is the next morning when two coppers are knocking at my door, hats in their hands, the works.'

'Oh, Gloria,' Olivia said, picturing the scene.

'Accidental death, the coroner said. But . . . Well . . .' Gloria heaved a sigh. 'I just don't know, Liv. He'd been depressed for a few weeks before then – our business was going under, things were looking bleak.'

'I remember you saying.'

'We'd had a bit of a row too. Just a silly one about whose turn it was to fill up the car. Of all the things! Petrol, for heaven's sake. But I wouldn't leave it. I kept on at him. Even got a receipt out of my purse to prove it had been me who'd paid last time, like the annoying old cow I am.' Her mouth quirked in a miserable twist. 'He lost his temper, anyway, we both did, and then he stormed out. It wasn't unusual for him not to come home when we had rows, he'd often go drinking with a mate and kip over, come slinking back the next day. Not this time, though.'

Olivia reached over and took her hand. 'I'm so sorry,' she said helplessly. She and Alec had had fairly tempestuous rows on occasion. Didn't every married couple? What dreadful bad luck for Gloria and Bill, never able to make up again.

'Yeah,' said Gloria, a heaviness in her voice. 'But then that afternoon a text comes through, and it's from him. And I'm, like, what the hell, because I've just been told he's dead, but the signal's so shit around here, it can sometimes take hours for a text message to get through, especially if the weather's bad.'

Olivia's heart clenched. 'Oh gosh. What a horrible shock.'

'I know, right? Total shock. First I have this, like, euphoria that he must still be alive, that there's been some terrible mistake. Then I'm confused – wait. How can that be? But then the penny drops. Ahh. No. He's not alive, it's just a delayed text winding me up from beyond the grave. So *then* I'm like, oh my God. He was texting to say sorry. His last words will be that he's sorry we had a row and that he loves me and I was totally right about the petrol.'

She pulled a face but her mouth was resolutely down-turned and Olivia had the sinking feeling that Bill's last words were nothing of the sort. 'What did the text say?' she asked gently. Gloria seemed to have run out of steam.

'It said . . .' Gloria stubbed her cigarette out in the sand and chucked it into her empty mug, her expression grim. 'It said "Sorry, love, but I can't go on like this." That was it. And ten minutes after he sent it, he was dead.'

Olivia winced. 'Oh no. So you think . . . ?' She couldn't bring herself to finish the question. Poor Bill. And poor, poor Gloria. It was just heartbreaking.

'Yep. Not "accidental death" at all. Not that I told anyone about it, mind. Couldn't face them all knowing.' She looked sidelong at Olivia. 'You're the first person I've told, actually.'

Olivia still had her hand around Gloria's and she squeezed it tightly, at a loss for what she could possibly say. 'I'm so sorry,' she said again eventually, the words seeming inadequate. 'That's awful.'

'Yes,' Gloria said, 'but what can you do? Life goes on, doesn't it? The world keeps on bloody well spinning, whether we want it to or not.' She gave a snort. 'And for us reckless widows left behind, we have to just pick ourselves up and carry on. It's that or go into full nervous breakdown mode, anyway.'

Olivia nodded. 'I think I've done a bit of both recently. It's hard. Especially, as you say, when they surprise you like that. Selfish sods.'

'Yeah,' Gloria agreed, sounding a bit more like herself again. She propped herself up on her elbows then shook a fist at the sky. 'You selfish old twat, Bill! You inconsiderate ball-sack!'

Before she knew it, Olivia was doing the same. 'You cheating prick, Alec Tarrant!' she heard herself screeching. 'You smooth-tongued weasel! You lying snake in the grass!'

'YEAH!' Gloria yelled, before catching Olivia's eye and snorting again. The snort became a laugh and then the two women collapsed into giggles, shoulders shaking, tension released.

'Tune in next week for the latest episode of *Two Streaking Madwomen in Devon*,' Gloria said, still laughing, 'when the madwomen gatecrash a beach party.'

'The madwomen get arrested for indecent behaviour.'

'The madwomen bust out and go joyriding.'

'The madwomen go to expensive restaurants and run off without paying.' They could hardly speak for laughing now.

'And then toddle off and enjoy a nice cup of tea in front of the wrestling,' Gloria finished, wiping her eyes. 'Oh, you do make me laugh, Liv. I'm glad our paths crossed this summer.'

'So am I, Gloria,' Olivia said, feeling slightly hysterical from so much laughter. Her stomach muscles ached but in a good way. 'So am I.'

Chapter Thirty-Five

Robert had barely slept up in the attic room the night before. His mind had churned and circled, unable to be stilled, with everything coming back to Harriet and her face when the penny dropped. The bewilderment. The shock. And then, worst of all, the contempt. He would never forget the contempt, for as long as he lived.

You piece of utter shit, her eyes said. *How could you do this to me?*

She had reeled, open-mouthed, for a long, terrible moment before storming out of the house. She had then vanished for the entire evening with Molly, reappearing only to defiantly stuff a white plastic bag full of vinegar-smelling fish and chip wrappers into the kitchen swing-top bin.

'Is everything all right, Harriet?' Freya had asked, looking concerned, but Robert could tell that Harriet was so boilingly angry that she barely trusted herself to speak, other than a gritted-teeth 'Yes'.

The next thing he knew, his clothes had been taken out of

the wardrobe in great armfuls and dumped unceremoniously back into his suitcase, along with his toiletries, alarm clock and the thriller he was halfway through, before the whole lot was carted off to the attic room. It was the least he deserved, he supposed.

Up in the attic he had stewed all night, cursing his own stupidity for having blown the best relationship of his life. And all because he had been too proud to admit to his failings! The worst thing was, Harriet was the one person who wouldn't have thought any less of him for it. Harriet would have hugged him and told him, Never mind, declaring that books were overrated anyway, give her real life any day – give her a real fabulous *husband*, even better, and, corrr, come here, let me cheer you up . . . *I* still think you're the best thing since squeezy Marmite . . .

She would, as well. He could imagine her saying almost those exact words, just as he'd have said them to her had their situations been reversed. She'd have comforted him, and he'd have got over the rejections, then moved on to something else – a job that he actually liked and was good at, for starters. Because that's what loving wives and husbands did for each other – they held hands through the disappointments every bit as much as they celebrated the triumphs. He'd never met a woman who was so loyal and so cheerleading as Harriet. Why hadn't he appreciated just how good and precious and special their relationship was back at the time? Why had he fucked it all up?

Today, Harriet had got up earlier than everyone else and gone out, taking the car with her. For a moment he had feared the worst, agonizing that she'd driven home and left him for good. In a terrible flash of foreboding, he envisaged returning to Seymour Street and finding the locks changed, a huge sign up in the front garden: LIARS CAN JOG ON. NOT WELCOME HERE.

No, he reminded himself thankfully, seeing Molly's spotted raincoat hanging in the hallway as he came downstairs for breakfast. Harriet wouldn't have left without Molly. And *she* was definitely still here, judging by the row of bikinis hanging bone-dry on the washing line, the vanilla-scented perfume and Clearasil in the bathroom, the jumble of sandals and flip-flops abandoned in the hall.

For as long as they remained at Shell Cottage, the onus was on him to somehow make it up to her and show just how sorry he was. He would get down on his knees and beg for a second chance if he had to.

With no car and no desire for company, Robert decided to take himself off for a long walk in the meantime. He wouldn't come back again until he'd worked out his next move: a way to make it up to his wife. There must be *something* he could do to make her love him again. He just had to think hard enough.

It was another perfect summer's day and the roads were empty. All self-respecting holidaymakers would be at the beach by now, he supposed, staking out their patches with windbreaks and towels, snapping open folding chairs, trying to keep their picnics cool and sand-free in the shade. If he hadn't gone and messed everything up, they might have been there again too, the sound of the surf rushing deliciously in the background, Harriet flicking through a magazine, teasing Robert about his awful shorts (he loved those shorts) and asking him to put cream on her back.

He thought longingly about the feel of her soft, warm skin beneath his fingers and cursed himself all over again. *Idiot, idiot, idiot*, every footstep seemed to say instead as he walked dismally along.

Silver Sands village wasn't large by anyone's standards – a few streets of houses, the post office, the bakery, the pub, the newsagent's run by the same elderly couple who'd been there when Robert was a boy (he was convinced some of the stock was the same too, especially the crappier souvenirs at the back of the dusty shelves). It was a quiet place, with little traffic. Most people tended to go further along the coast to Ennisbridge or Bantham, preferring the bigger, more touristy beaches to be found there. In Silver Sands, you were lucky if you saw the local bus trundle by more than once a week.

Talking of which . . . He narrowed his eyes. Maybe he was about to glimpse this rare and endangered vehicle again sooner than expected. He'd reached the end of the village now, where the bus stop stood, inconveniently after all the houses had ended. You never usually saw anyone there but today a dark-haired boy waited with a small suitcase by his feet, anxiously scanning the horizon.

Robert glanced around, wondering if a parent or friend was in the near vicinity, but the streets were deserted. Strange. The boy seemed quite young to be heading off on his own – ten? Eleven? Maybe he was older than he looked. It was hard to tell with kids nowadays.

He shot another look at the boy as he walked closer. There was something familiar about his face. The green eyes, the freckles, the way he held himself so stiffly, back straight, like a soldier.

A thought struck him. Wait. Could this be him, Leo? His half-brother?

Curiosity got the better of Robert. 'Excuse me,' he said, reaching the bus stop. The boy flinched, his hands curling protectively around the handle of the suitcase. He'd obviously been told not to speak to strangers. 'I don't suppose your name is Leo, is it?'

The boy eyed him warily. God, it *must* be Leo. He really looked like Dad, right from the way he cocked his head to that suspicious well-who-wants-to-know? glint in his eye. Actually, now that Robert was standing right in front of him, those green eyes looked kind of bloodshot, as if he'd been crying.

'I'm Robert.' He held out his hand gravely. The boy didn't move. 'And I know you've probably been told not to talk to strangers but I'm not completely a stranger. Or rather, I'm not, if you're Leo.' He pulled a face. He was getting this all wrong. 'I'm Robert Tarrant. Alec's grown-up son? And if you're Leo, then that makes me your big brother. Kind of.'

Leo – if it was him (it *had* to be!) – looked worried but didn't speak.

Robert dropped his hand, feeling awkward, and leaned against the lamp post. 'I always wanted a brother,' he said, which was true.

Leo glanced down and scuffed the floor with his trainer. 'Are you the policeman?' he asked in a low voice.

'Am I the . . . ?' Oh, he meant Victor. 'No, I'm the other one.' The unsuccessful one, in other words. The loser! Robert changed the subject quickly. 'Where are you off to, then, with that case?'

Now Leo looked positively anguished. 'Nowhere,' he mumbled, looking past Robert in the direction of oncoming traffic. Not that there was any, of course.

Robert studied the timetable. The buses from here went up to Ivybridge but only ran twice a day, midweek. He glanced from Leo to the times listed, then back again. 'You know, you could be waiting here a while, mate,' he said gently. 'The next bus is at three o'clock. That's . . .' He checked his watch. 'That's four and a half hours away.'

Leo slumped at this news. He looked as if he had all the cares of the world on his shoulders.

'Where were you going to, anyway?' Robert asked again. A thought occurred to him. 'Does your mum know you're here, waiting for the three o'clock bus with a suitcase, by the way?'

A tear rolled down Leo's cheek and he kicked at the dust as it plopped to the ground. He shook his head.

'Oh, mate. What's up?' Robert vividly remembered being that age, and the passionate feelings that could be aroused by some injustice or slight. He'd once marched out of the house himself, having left a note declaring that he'd run away because it wasn't fair that he had to tidy his bedroom before *Doctor Who*. He'd ended up in the park for the longest ninety minutes of his life, sitting on a bench and feeling increasingly sorry for himself, until Olivia found him and gave him the biggest hug ever, shortly followed by the biggest bollocking. *And* he'd missed *Doctor Who* after all that. 'Were you running away?' he asked.

Leo didn't say anything but his lower lip trembled – a dead giveaway that Robert had hit on the truth. 'Look,' Robert said, 'there's not another bus for hours, you know that now. There's only one thing to do, if you ask me.'

'What?'

'Let your big brother take you to the pub and buy you a drink. And then tell me what's happened.'

The Haystack pub was yet to open when they arrived, so they wandered further along to the newsagent's, Robert carrying the suitcase, and bought two cans of pop instead. Then they sat on the wooden bench outside the pub and cracked them open in the sunshine. 'So, first things first,' Robert said. 'Where's your mum today?'

'Cleaning,' Leo said, chugging back his lemonade thirstily.

'And she thinks you are . . . ?'

'She said she'd be back just after eleven. She left me on my own. I *am* nearly twelve, I'm not a baby.'

'Right. But you were hoping to be gone by the time she came home. Was that the plan?'

'Yeah.'

'Did you have an argument or something?'

Leo shook his head, eyes to the ground.

Robert elbowed him. 'Come on. I'm your brother, remember. You can tell me. Brothers can tell each other anything.'

Leo bit his lip and for a moment, Robert wasn't sure he was going to get anywhere. But then the boy asked with great solemnity, 'Do you promise you won't tell that policeman?'

'What, Victor?' God, this sounded serious. It crossed his

mind for a split second that he might regret becoming involved. But the kid was looking at him so beseechingly that there was only one possible answer. 'I won't tell him, if you don't want me to.'

Leo looked down at the table, then searchingly up at Robert, then all around, as if to check that nobody else could possibly hear. Bloody hell. What had he *done*?

'It was my fault,' he mumbled eventually. 'I . . . I killed him.'

Holy cow. What on earth . . . ? Was the kid some sort of psychopath? Robert tried to keep his cool. 'What do you mean? Who did you kill?'

Leo squeezed his eyes shut for a moment and two fresh tears spurted out. 'Dad,' he said unhappily. 'I'm really sorry, Robert. But I think I killed Dad.'

Robert choked on his Coke. Of all the answers he might have been expecting, that was the very last one. He put down his drink and looked Leo in the eye. 'You didn't,' he said kindly. 'I'm telling you that for a fact. He had a heart attack. He was unfit, he ate too much and he definitely drank too much. His heart couldn't cope any more. That's what killed him, Leo. Not you.'

Leo scrubbed at his eyes. 'But . . . I rang him. And that was one of the golden rules. Mum always said, Don't ring your dad. Even if you really really want to.'

Robert didn't quite get Leo's point. 'So you did ring him, and . . . ?' he prompted.

Leo nodded, his thin shoulders hunched. 'I just wanted to talk to him,' he said in a whisper. 'I missed him.'

It was hard not to feel angry at Alec just then. Angry that he'd never been able to give this boy quite enough of himself, because, selfishly, he'd split himself across two families, even though most people considered one family to be ample. And now look at this boy, so pale and upset, blaming himself because he'd made one single phone call. Because he just wanted to speak to his dad!

'Of course you missed him,' Robert found himself saying. 'It must have been horrible, not being able to chat to Dad when you wanted to. But one phone call isn't the end of the world. It certainly didn't kill him.'

'He shouted at me,' Leo mumbled.

'Well, he did a lot of that,' Robert said. 'He shouted at me all the time when I was your age. But he still loved me. Even when I was really naughty. Even when I borrowed his car and crashed it into the wall.'

'Did you really?'

'Oh yes. I was a bit older, mind – more like sixteen. Showing off in front of my mates, like a prat. It was a really flash Audi, as well, brand new. My God, he was absolutely livid. I was grounded for a whole month.'

Leo smiled a little bit, then looked anxious again. 'The

thing is,' he said, 'he was really cross when I rang. And I think that gave him the heart attack. Because then he sort of made all these weird noises and I heard Mrs Tarrant – your mum – come over and she was really upset and worried, shouting his name like something really bad had happened.' He bowed his head. 'So I just hung up. And then the next thing I know, he's dead. Because of me.'

'Oh, mate.' No wonder he had looked so stricken. No wonder he didn't want Robert to tell Victor about it. He must have been bricking it ever since. 'It wasn't your fault, you know,' Robert said gently. 'I absolutely promise you. He was going to have that heart attack whatever happened, whether you phoned up or not.'

'Yes, but—'

'No buts. Really – I'm serious. No buts. Look at me, Leo. You didn't kill him. Okay? It wasn't your fault. And I'm saying this, brother to brother, man to man, all right? Don't worry about it. Do not worry about it for a single extra minute. That's an order.'

Leo said nothing for a moment. Then his lower lip wobbled again, and he burst into sudden, chest-heaving tears, his face in his hands. Poor little lad, Robert thought. Poor kid! He'd obviously been freaking out about this the whole time.

Robert put an arm around him and pulled him into a bear hug. 'Hey,' he said. 'Think about it this way. Dad died knowing that you loved him so much, you couldn't bear to keep the rules any more, that you were bursting to share your news with him.' He tousled Leo's hair, feeling a rush of affection for the kid. 'I think he'd have liked that, you know.'

Leo scrubbed a grimy fist in each eye socket. 'Really? Do you really think so?'

'I know it,' said Robert. 'I promise you.'

Once Leo had dried his eyes and blown his nose, Robert glanced at his watch and saw that it was nearly eleven o'clock. 'Look, your mum's going to be home soon, and then she'll be worried when you're not there,' he said. 'Why don't we go back there together? I'd like to say hello to her anyway. I always liked your mum.'

He'd even quite fancied her one summer, he remembered, when he was about twenty-five. She was pretty and shy, with bobbed chestnut hair and an upturned nose. She sang as she stripped the sheets off the beds; she smelled nice whenever she passed him on the stairs. Great bum in a pair of shorts, too, as he recalled. She must already have fallen in love with Dad, by then, of course. God, that could have been messy, if he'd actually dared try anything with her.

Leo perked up a bit as they made the short walk back to his house, telling Robert about his friend's new puppy, his undying support for Exeter City, his feelings about starting secondary school in September (they had to wear a tie! He didn't know how to do it! And the uniform made everyone look a right wanker, apparently). It was only as they turned into the cul-de-sac of boxy modern houses, all with identikit net curtains at their small mean windows, that he went quiet. Fair enough. Every boy knew that mums went mental if their sons weren't exactly where they'd left them.

Seconds later, they arrived at Leo's house and Katie burst from the front door looking frantic before they'd even had time to knock. 'For Christ's sake, Leo!' she cried, grabbing hold of him and then smothering him with a hug. Her voice was a mixture of anger, fear and all-consuming relief. 'I was just about to come out looking for you. Where have you been? I didn't know what to think!'

'I was with Robert,' Leo said, muffled against her chest.

It was only then that Katie clocked who else was standing in her neat front garden. 'Oh,' she said. 'Robert.' Her expression became defensive, her arms still around Leo as if unsure of Robert's motives.

'I found him by the bus stop,' Robert said, putting down the suitcase a little awkwardly. 'We've had a good chat, haven't we, Leo? Sorted a few things out. He's all right now.'

Katie's eyes flickered from Robert down to Leo in a suspicious sort of way. 'Bus stop? What were you doing at the bus stop?' she asked her son. Then she turned to Robert, her voice becoming shrill. 'Two hours, I left him, that's all. He *is* eleven. And it's difficult in the school holidays. I mean, I still have to work.'

Shit, did she think Robert was having a go at her? Questioning her parenting? Luckily Leo spoke up before Robert had to defend himself. 'I was going to run away,' he muttered, pulling at one ear and staring at his feet. 'But Robert changed my mind. He said I should come back.'

Katie's chin looked a bit wobbly when she noticed the suitcase and the fight went out of her at once. 'Thank you,' she said. She hesitated. 'Don't suppose you've got time for a coffee, have you?'

'I'd love one,' Robert replied.

'That was nice, what you did,' Katie said, as Leo went straight through to the back garden and began kicking a football at a goalmouth he'd chalked on the shed. 'Talking him round, I mean. Your dad was always saying what a great guy you were.'

The compliment was so unexpected – and so utterly welcome – that Robert couldn't speak for a moment. 'I actually always felt kind of a failure, compared to Dad, to be honest,' he confessed, with a rather fake-sounding laugh.

Katie passed him a mug of instant coffee and they went through to a small bright lounge which was decorated almost entirely with photographs of Leo, drawings by Leo and certificates commending Leo for football, running and his position on the school council. It was stuffy in there and she pushed open the two front windows before she replied.

'Well, he didn't think that.' She sank into the faded blue corduroy sofa, tucking her bare feet up underneath her. 'He admired your determination. Said he loved your spirit – how easy-going and happy you were. Honestly!' she added, seeing the disbelieving look on Robert's face.

Robert cradled his mug in his hands. The words were like a soothing balm, a surprise gift, right when he needed it most. With recent events being the way they were, though, he wasn't sure he could receive such compliments without feeling a fraud. 'Well, I dunno about that,' he said, shrugging.

'I do. You're dyslexic, right? Yeah, and he was so proud of how you slogged through all your exams, determined not to give up, getting to university and everything. Wasn't it you who ended up teaching English somewhere really exotic?'

'Well . . . it was Poland, just for a few weeks, but . . .' Borscht, and three extra jumpers, ice inside the windows of his dorm, it had not been remotely exotic, merely another stop-gap scheme of Robert's while he attempted to work out what the hell to do with his life.

'There you go! See – how would I know all of that, if he hadn't told me?'

Robert smiled, but it was a sad sort of smile. 'I'm not sure he'd be all that proud of me now,' he admitted. 'I've made a hash of things lately. Got myself in a bit of trouble.'

It was hard to read Katie's expression. 'Well, we all do things that perhaps we shouldn't,' she said. 'That's life, though, isn't it? I never expected to get pregnant when I was twenty-three, let alone . . .' She spread her hands helplessly. 'Let alone cause so much friction in your family. But I loved him, Robert. I really loved your dad. And I made the decisions I did back then because that love for him made everything seem worthwhile.'

Robert nodded. 'I get that.'

'I mean, you do what feels right at the time, don't you?' Katie went on. 'If you've mucked things up as you say, I'm sure you didn't intend to. Just as I never intended to upset your mum or anyone else.' There was a moment's pause. 'I wouldn't act the same way now,' she said, with a sidelong glance. 'I wouldn't get involved with a married man, not when there were kids involved. So I'm sorry I've caused trouble and . . . and heartache. I feel bad for your mum, and all of you, I swear. At the time, I was just caught up in the romance of it. I didn't think this far ahead.'

Robert wasn't sure what to say. Was she asking him for forgiveness? 'It's never easy,' he said diplomatically.

Katie gave him a half-smile. 'No. Which is why we all end up making a hash of things, like you said, at some point or other. But then again, at the end of the day, I wouldn't change anything either, because I wouldn't have Leo otherwise,' she said. 'And he's my world.'

'He's a great kid,' Robert agreed. 'A really nice lad. You must be so proud of him.'

Katie smiled. 'I am. Even when I can hear him thumping that effing football against my shed every five seconds.'

They both laughed because the dogged *thud-thud-thud* was still audible despite them being here at the front of the house.

'I'm glad we had this chat,' she said, looking shy all of a sudden. 'I don't want to be enemies.'

'We're not enemies,' Robert said. 'We were never enemies. Mum's just upset, that's all. She feels betrayed by him – we all do, a bit. We thought he was the greatest man alive before . . . all this. You know.'

She nodded. 'Of course. I understand. But don't forget – he thought that you were the greatest too. If I've learned anything about being a parent, it's that even when your kids mess up or do something they end up regretting, you still love them.' She eyed him meaningfully over the mug. 'And he loved you. Very much.'

It felt as if a great load had been lifted from Robert's shoulders as he hugged both Katie and Leo goodbye a short while later, and promised to be in touch soon, for a tie-tying lesson, some penalty shoot-outs and whatever else they might want from him. Dad had loved him, he thought, walking away from the house with a new spring in his step. Dad had been proud of him. Even though Robert had known this deep down, it meant a lot to have another person, an outsider, validate him in this way.

The only thing was, now he felt more of a fool than ever for spending so long lying to everyone when, as it turned out, there hadn't been any need. So how could he put things right?

Chapter Thirty-Six

Having stumbled upon a friendly little beach café down in Hamstone, Harriet had never been more grateful to sink into a chair outside on the big open terrace, and tuck into a full English breakfast and two delicious cups of coffee. So much for heartbreak making you skinny and tragic – well, not in Harriet's book, it didn't. She had probably put on half a stone already since Robert's bombshell last night, and there would only be more comfort eating to come. She'd gone up two whole dress sizes after Simon walked out. The bastard.

Still, sitting here in the new-washed morning, seeing the sea rushing hypnotically in and out just metres away, she was actually starting to feel vaguely human again, for the first time all day. There was something about leaning back in the early sunshine, having polished off a huge breakfast, and watching the surfer dudes in their wetsuits leap acrobatically through the waves, that cheered a woman right up. Especially the bare-chested surfer dudes with their sculpted muscles and

taut thighs. Mmm. *Good work, lads*, she thought apprecia-
tively. *Good show.*

The man from the café came out just then and collected
up her breakfast plate. 'Can I get you anything else?' he
asked.

Harriet was positively stuffed but then again, she *had*
just been royally shafted by her formerly beloved husband
and was therefore entitled to have anything she damn well
wanted. Besides, she had always found that pastries were
very helpful when it came to absorbing hurt feelings. 'Well
. . . I wouldn't mind another coffee, please,' she said. 'And
did I spy some almond croissants at the counter in there?'

'You did indeed. Shall I bring one out with your coffee?'

'Yes please.' And then, because she didn't want him to
think she was always this greedy, added, 'I *am* on holiday.'

'Absolutely! You're on holiday and it's a glorious morning
to sit and admire the view. I'll be right back.'

Harriet blushed as he walked away, wondering if there
was an undertone to his words about admiring the view. Had
he noticed her watching the surfers like some saddo middle-
aged pervert? She picked up her phone and cupped a hand
around the screen to shade it from the sun. She would ring
Gabbi for a chat, she decided, to prove to the café man that
she did actually have a life other than perving over surfers.

Ahh. And then again, maybe she wouldn't, she realized,
peering at the screen. There didn't seem to be any signal.

'The reception's terrible around here,' a male voice said just then, and Harriet looked up, her eyes popping out on stalks because one of the surfers was striding up the café steps, his wetsuit stripped down to his waist, tousled shoulder-length hair dripping onto his hunky bare chest.

'Oh,' she said, flustered. (Bloody hell. He was fit as a butcher's dog, as Gabbi would say. Was this some kind of celestial reward sent by the Betrayed Wife Goddess?) 'Right. Thanks.'

'It comes and goes,' he went on, grabbing a towel that had been left hung over the terrace railing. 'Sometimes if you stand on a table, jump up and stretch your arm out and . . . Nah, I'm joking.' He grinned and towelled his hair and face, and Harriet had to try very hard not to gaze up and down his bod while his eyes were covered.

She looked out to sea instead. 'Nice day for it,' she said, tilting her head to indicate the surf. Then she blushed violently, aware of the innuendo in her words. What was wrong with her? Heartbreak was turning her into a sleazeball as well as an eating machine. But he was smiling back at her, periwinkle-blue eyes twinkling naughtily, and she found herself giggling. Oh well. She needed cheering up right now, and she was far too old for him anyway. He was never going to take her cheesy lines seriously. 'Sorry. That came out wrong,' she added. 'Don't take any notice of me.'

He raised an eyebrow. He really was very handsome, it

had to be said. 'It's always a nice day for it, if you ask me,' he replied, in such a flirtatious manner that she giggled again, as if she were twenty years younger. (She *felt* twenty years younger all of a sudden. The sun had gone to her head or something.)

The café man emerged just then with a fresh pot of coffee, a sugar-dusted croissant and a folded copy of the *Guardian* under one arm. 'Just in case you wanted something to read,' he said, setting it down on the table in front of Harriet. 'Morning, Joe. Coming in for a coffee?'

Surf hunk Joe looked from the café man to Harriet and then back to the café man. 'I might stay out here for one, mate, if that's all right with you. Don't want to go dripping on your floor or anything, do I?'

The café man looked disbelieving but didn't comment on this display of apparent consideration for his floor. 'Coming right up.'

'Mind if I join you?' Joe asked, sliding into the seat opposite Harriet before she had a chance to say no. Like she was going to anyway.

'Of course not,' she said, trying to sound cool, although inside she felt positively fluttery. She racked her brain for something witty and clever to say – what? what? – but then her phone had to go and choose that moment to detect a faint bar of signal and rang, like the attention-seeking little git it was. She decided to ignore it. A fiver said it would be

Robert anyway, with a plaintive Where-are-you?-Can-we-talk? call and she certainly didn't want to engage in one of those right now. Let him stew. Let him agonize. Let him think a bit more about what a complete and utter twat he had been. She would contact him, when she was good and ready, thank you very much – although that could be a while, now that the Goddess of Betrayed Women was rewarding her in such a glorious and unexpected way.

'Buzz off,' she muttered to her phone, shoving it deep in her bag without even bothering to look at the caller. She kicked the bag further away from her – *Do not ruddy well disturb* – and then sat up a little straighter in her chair in the hope of disguising her pot belly. 'So,' she said, flashing her most dazzling smile at Joe. 'Tell me about surfing.'

Thank you, universe, she thought, half an hour or so later, when Joe had scoffed a huge brown-sauce-smothered break-fast and she'd put away not one but two almond croissants and her third coffee. *I owe you big time for that act of mercy.* Sod her belly, tight as a drum, forcing its way unprettily over the waistband of her shorts. Sod the vague feeling of seediness that she was sitting here, a married woman, flirting with a handsome stranger. The seedy feeling was worth it, as was every last calorie, for the brief, fabulous pinch of time when she'd forgotten all about Robert – and every other living human being for that matter – whilst chatting and laughing with this god of a man, bronzed and honed, and mere inches across the table from her.

So what that nothing would ever happen with him? So what that she knew she'd eventually have to peel herself away and return to her trouble-riddled real world? It was bliss, sheer bliss, to flirt and banter in the sunshine by the beach. Exactly what she needed to make her feel human again.

'How come you're down here all by yourself, anyway?' he asked her once their plates had been taken away, and she'd (reluctantly) requested the bill.

Ahh. And there was reality knocking against the window: time's up. How she wished she could reply with something romantic and thrilling – that she was making a fresh start down by the seaside, that destiny had brought her here, some other made-up tosh. Instead she sighed a little and traced the spilled sugar crystals around the table with her index finger.

'Had a row. It was either come down here or hurl myself off the nearest cliff.' Oh God, that sounded melodramatic. She didn't even mean it, either. Like she'd ever do anything so rash when she had Molly to care for. 'I'm joking,' she said quickly. 'Well. About the cliff thing, not about the row.'

'A row,' he repeated. 'Ahh, right. Is that who keeps ringing your phone, then?'

'My phone?'

'Yeah, it's been vibrating against my foot every now and

then through your bag. We must be having a good reception morning for once.' His mouth twitched. 'That's if it is your *phone* that's vibrating, of course.'

She laughed at the smutty glint in his eye but hauled her bag back towards her all the same. God, Robert must be getting desperate if that was him, making so many calls. It *was* Robert, wasn't it? She had a flash of panic that something was wrong with Molly, that she'd been rushed to hospital while Harriet had been lounging around here, ogling the local talent. She delved into the bag. 'It's probably just – ' she began as her fingers closed around the phone. It buzzed almost immediately with a new text and she leaned over the screen to examine it.

Three missed calls from Freya. Freya? Maybe it was some awful medical thing. The text was from her too and Harriet read it – then leapt to her feet in alarm. Oh my God. Molly. She thought she might throw up.

'I've got to go,' she said.

Come quickly. Ennisbridge Hotel. I think Molly's in trouble.

Words guaranteed to stab through any mother's heart with so much fear, angst and guilt; it was a wonder that Harriet actually made it back into her car. Her hands shook violently as she turned the key in the ignition, and she thought for a moment she might not be up to the job. Wished, for a second, that Robert was there to drive them both instead, to reassure her that everything was going to be okay.

No. Don't think that. She could manage fine without him. And now was not the time to be thinking about him anyway. *Deep breaths, Harriet. Control yourself. Do not crash the car.* She had to keep her cool and get herself over to Ennisbridge right this minute, without crumbling or crying or freaking out.

But it was difficult after hearing Freya's anxious voicemail messages one after the other, saying that she'd overheard Molly making arrangements with some boyfriend or other – and worse, that she was on her way to meet him in a hotel. Right now! A hotel! While her back was turned! While Mother of the Year Harriet had been flirting idiotically with a twenty-something surf hunk over almond croissants.

Christ, Harriet, you stupid wazzock. Priorities, for God's sake. What were you thinking? How could this have happened?

Scorching along the road, she beeped anyone who dared dawdle along in front of her, overtaking recklessly, cutting up other drivers at junctions. Someone gave her two fingers, someone else flashed their lights reprovingly at her but she couldn't have cared less. *Sorry, love. Bore off. You are nothing to me but six feet of machinery between me and my precious daughter. Possibly between me and my daughter's virginity. So take your flashing lights and bloody well stuff them up your arse, all right?*

Shit. *Shit*, Molly. What the hell? Where had this come from? Why didn't Harriet even have a clue about this boy?

And since when did Molly go all secretive on her, and live this double life? Harriet would not have believed someone if they'd said Molly had a boyfriend. No. She actually would have laughed at the suggestion. Molly? Bless her, but no. She was far too naive. Way too innocent. She still had a cuddly bunny rabbit in her bed, for heaven's sake! She still put her hair up in bunches sometimes! She was a girl, not a woman. And that was fine. Why should any teenage girl feel they had to rush these things, if they weren't ready?

Oh Molly. She wished she'd thought to just ring her before leaping into the car and heading off. Her phone was back in her bag in the footwell, but she was driving too fast and furiously to start leaning over to try and fish it out now. *Wait for me, love*, she thought desperately. *Just hang on. I'm coming. Don't do anything daft. Please!*

Who *was* this boy, anyway? Who the hell was he, booking hotel rooms and arranging things on the sly? Wait till she got her hands on him, that was all Harriet had to say. Freya's last message had assured her that she was heading down to Ennisbridge, in order to give this lad 'a flea in his ear' and make sure Molly was okay. Well, Harriet would give him a lot more than that if she caught up with him. She would be so ferocious that his skin would blister. If he thought he could try it on with her fifteen-year-old daughter, then he jolly well had another think coming.

If she could get there in time, that was. If! Still six miles from Ennisbridge and now she was stuck behind a sodding tractor on a single-track bit of road. Harriet thumped the steering wheel and yelled every last expletive she could think of at the chugging, trundling farm vehicle. Why had she come all the way down to Hamstone anyway? She should not have left Molly on her own in the house. Her mother instincts should have been better; she should have known somehow, a sensor in her head, the daughter radar picking up signals . . . Oh, where was that sodding 'Rewind' button when you needed it?

She just had to hope there was still time. What if she was already too late?

Chapter Thirty-Seven

Hurry up! I'm in reception, eagerly awaiting your arrival
. . . Ben texted as Molly hurried along the prom, and she
felt her legs turn weak and watery at the promise of him
there, in the flesh and so close, waiting for her. Drumming
his fingers, perhaps, glancing up hopefully every time the
door swung open . . .

Oh my God. And then there it was, the hotel, less than
twenty metres up on the left: a large white-painted building
on the corner, just as Ben had described it. She thudded to
a stop, fighting the feeling of disappointment that their
romantic rendezvous point actually looked more like a big
old house than the glitzy hotel Molly had pictured in her
mind. A seagull was pecking at some dropped chips on the
pavement outside and there were grubby net curtains at
the windows. Oh, so what? she told herself. Big deal! She
wasn't a snob. It could be a bus shelter or a cow barn and
she'd still be excited to see Ben there.

Excited if slightly terrified, mind, but whatever. She'd got this far and she wasn't a bottler. It couldn't hurt *that* much, surely, otherwise nobody would ever bother doing it twice. And she did love him, didn't she? She certainly didn't want him to go off with anyone else. *Let's do this.*

Molly hadn't ever stayed in a hotel before. A few bed and breakfast places with Mum and Robert, a youth hostel on a school trip to Wales, a campsite with Mum in a leaky tent back when they were skint. She had imagined that hotels would be full of butlers and maids, chandeliers and silver cutlery, kind of like in *Downton Abbey*, only on a larger scale. When Ben had told her they were booked into a hotel, she'd envisaged a vast crisp bed, a massive TV and room service arriving under those big silver domed covers . . . Maybe the Ennisbridge Hotel wasn't going to be quite so posh, though, she thought, stepping cautiously through the propped-open front door. She found herself in a small, poky hallway with an empty desk and chair in front of her. *Ring for service* said a small card propped against an old-fashioned bell. What, seriously? Molly wanted to giggle at the idea of her standing there ringing a bell. Yeah, right. Like that was going to happen. Now, where was Ben?

There were rooms leading off to the right and left of the hall, and she poked her head around the one on the right. It was a rather fussy-looking lounge with dusty velvet sofas, a huge sprawling fern in one corner and a bookcase full of peeling hardbacks that probably hadn't been read by a single person for at least fifty years. But that was all irrelevant because there, too, was Ben – Ben! – unfolding his long legs and standing up.

'You made it,' he said with a grin.

Her heart gave an enormous flip. 'I made it,' she said. And then – yes! – just like in her dreams, he was walking across to greet her, and then grabbing her in the most enormous smoochy kiss, and it was all just so blissfully romantic and beautiful. His hands roamed up her body and her breath felt shallow in her throat. Oh my God. This was it. They were here together, in Devon, in a hotel. This was really happening!

'You look beautiful,' he said, touching her face. 'Oh, Molly. You're amazing.'

She could feel herself blushing, her whole body one huge blush, suffused with the heat of her blood. It felt weird seeing him, and not being in school uniform, almost like a dream, being in this musty-smelling hotel together, miles from London. 'Thank you,' she managed to say, her legs trembling.

'Just relax,' he said, his voice low and whispery. 'We're going to have fun together. Loads of fun. Shall we go up to our room?'

Molly gulped. *Our room.* All of a sudden, her feet felt heavy as if she might not be able to drag them across the carpet. But she could hardly back out now, could she? Not when he'd come all the way down to Devon to see her. She swallowed, trying to act cool rather than the bag of nerves that she really was. 'Sure,' she said. 'Although . . . Maybe we could . . .' She cast her eye around hurriedly, wanting to delay their departure. Just for a few minutes until she felt ready and brave. She saw a half-drunk glass of Coke on a side table, where Ben had been sitting. 'I wouldn't mind a drink,' she said tentatively.

He placed one hand over her breast and squeezed it, slowly and deliberately, his eyes on her face the entire time. 'We'll order up room service,' he told her, and pulled out a key from his pocket. 'Shall we?'

This was it. Now or never. Her lips parted to reply but her mouth was so dry. 'I . . .'

And then in the next moment, there was another voice in the room. 'Hey! Oh no, you don't, pal. Get your hands off her this minute. Now!'

Molly swung round and – holy *fuck* – there behind them was *Aunty Freya*, like a pantomime genie appearing from out of nowhere. What? For real? Molly wondered if she might be dreaming for a second but no, it was definitely Freya, her hair wilder and corkscrewier than ever, striding forward with her handbag so purposefully that Molly actually thought she was about to wallop Ben with it.

'Er . . .' Molly stammered in alarm, as she and Ben unclinched themselves. Talk about a passion-killer. This was a passion-annihilator. What the . . . ?

Ben, meanwhile, stared from Molly to Freya. 'Who the hell are you?' he asked Freya, then rounded furiously on Molly. 'Is this a joke? I told you not to tell anyone.'

'I didn't!' squeaked Molly, taking a step back, but Freya wasn't deterred. If anything, she looked like she might very well punch Ben.

'I could ask you the same question,' Freya replied tartly. 'Who the hell do you think *you* are, sneaking around with a fifteen-year-old girl?'

Oh shite, thought Molly, the romance of the scene evaporating before her eyes, like blight on a rose, a glass heart trampled by a jackboot. She was going to be in so much trouble for this. She should have known nobody else would understand their love! But before Ben could even answer, in came a shrieking hellcat – *Mum!* – barrelling into the room with such force and ferocity that the walls practically quaked. 'Molly!' she cried, making a beeline for her and almost squeezing the life out of her with a wild embrace. Jesus. Hysterical mother alert. Now she was definitely in the shit. But then, as her mum's arms tightened around her, she was struck in the same moment by how safe she felt, and how relieved she was, deep down, to have been rescued at the last second. Embarrassingly, she almost wanted to cry.

'I'm sorry, Mum,' Molly began saying but was almost deafened in the next moment when Mum let out a yell of shock upon recognizing Ben. 'Mr *Jamison*? What on earth . . . ?'

'I can explain,' Ben mumbled, hanging his head, but Mum was on a total roll now. She let go of Molly and advanced on him, eyes blazing, squaring up to him like a boxer.

'You're her English teacher, you dirty old sod. She's *fifteen* years old! What the frig do you think you're doing? Wait until the headteacher hears about this. And the police!'

Everything happened really quickly after that, like a film that had been set on fast-forward. Mum went on ranting, her voice rising shrilly – 'Is this what you do, prey on young girls? You piece of shit! You pervert!' – while Ben collapsed into the nearest armchair and put his head in his hands. 'Please don't tell the head,' he said, his voice muffled. He didn't look at Molly. 'I don't want my wife to know.'

'I bet you bloody don't,' Freya said with disdain, just as Molly cried, 'Your *wife*?' He still wasn't looking at her and she felt heat rush into her face, a huge lump of hurt sticking in her throat. He'd never said anything about a *wife*!

'Welcome to womanhood, darling,' her mum said in the most awful, angry voice. She glared at Ben; Molly had never seen her face look quite so ugly with hatred. 'Spoiler alert: they're all tossers at the end of the day.'

'I'm ringing the police,' Freya said. 'This is appalling. You realize you've broken the law? Christ, man, pull yourself together. Snivelling isn't going to help you now. You're finished, end of story. You're history.'

'Ben,' said Molly in a low voice. *'Ben.'*

Still he didn't raise his gaze to hers. 'Don't speak to him, darling,' Mum said, as Freya said, 'Police, please,' into her phone and began rattling off what had happened.

'Please, Ben,' Molly said desperately. Even though she was secretly kind of relieved that she hadn't had to go through with it – sex with him, her thirty-something teacher, in this weird-smelling hotel – she was devastated too. Sorry for him, even. He looked broken and haggard. No more swagger. No more charming smiles, white teeth and suggestive looks. Now he seemed to have shrunk in the space of a few minutes, his forehead lined, a sheen of grease on his top lip. He'd seemed so handsome at school, striding around with an armful of exercise books, reading them Wilfred Owen poems and becoming so choked up with emotion that his voice had caught on the last lines. She had fallen in love with him there and then, swooning in her bedroom later on over the hidden depths of sensitivity, wisdom and compassion that little catch in his voice implied. A man who was unafraid to show his emotions – hell, yeah. *Emotion me right up, Mr Jamison*, she'd thought dreamily.

And then he'd caught her eye once, twice, three times in class. He'd asked her to stay behind one lesson – something about a book he thought she should read – and touched her arm, unbearably softly, just with his fingertips. She had gasped and turned red (and had then gazed yearningly, romantically at that same patch of skin on her arm for the rest of the day, unable to believe it didn't still bear the imprint of his touch). She had even had a go at reading the poetry book he'd lent her, although in all honesty, poetry was so not her thing and she didn't have a clue what poets were wittering on about half the time.

But he'd kindled something in her. Something hot and exciting and unquenchable. English lessons became the golden hours of her week at school, the hours that sped by fastest, where she drank in the sight of him, her heart fluttering like a million butterfly wings whenever he glanced her way. God, he was beautiful. He was just so manly and knowing and clever. A million miles away from all the spotty jerks in her year, with their bobbing Adam's apples and disgusting Lynx miasma. Compared to Mr Jamison, they were practically babies who knew nothing.

Yet now – at last – he was looking up and his gaze was cold and unpleasant. 'You had to go and open your mouth, didn't you?' he said sullenly, and she felt sick inside, that this was all her fault, that he hated her now.

'Ben, I swear I didn't tell anyone,' she cried in anguish, tears pricking her eyes, but Mum was already flying at him. 'Don't you dare,' she hissed, pointing a finger in his face. 'Don't you dare even *look* at her any more, or you'll have me to answer to, sunshine.'

Freya hung up her call and came to stand by Mum in solidarity. 'The police are on their way,' she said.

Molly couldn't stop staring at Mr Jamison, head bowed, sniffing into his hands. Mr Jamison, who had a wife at home – a wife who hadn't got the faintest idea that Molly even existed. Mr Jamison, and the naked texts he'd sent her, and the dirty phone calls, and his fingers touching her body in Stratford. All of a sudden she couldn't wait for the police to get there. She felt repulsed, even to be standing in the same room as him.

The police came and escorted Mr Jamison away while a crowd of curious holidaymakers watched outside. 'Shame on you!' Mum yelled as he was pushed into a police car, much to Molly's mortification. Glad as she was that Mum and Freya had turned up like they had (how had they even *known* to anyway?), there was something about having your mother yell things, publicly, in the street, that was never going to be not embarrassing.

'Oh, Molly,' Mum said, and looked as if she was going to start crying again as the police car drove away. 'Why didn't you say? Why didn't you tell me? You stupid bloody girl! Have I taught you nothing? Didn't it occur to you that you might be getting yourself into danger?'

Mum had never called Molly a 'stupid bloody girl' before. She'd never said anything so horrible to her, ever, and Molly badly wanted to dish out some cool, snarky answer about having a *private* life, thank you very much, and nobody told their mums anything *anyway*, and *God*, Mum, it was hardly *danger*, but she lost her nerve and then – even more mortifyingly – the shock of what had just happened hit her, and she burst into proper gulping tears herself. How had it all gone so horribly wrong? She would have to go to the station later to be questioned about what had happened, the police officers had said, and even though Mum had promised she'd be with her, and Freya had said Vic – a policeman himself, of course – could help out if she wanted him to, Molly still couldn't quite get her head around it. All she kept thinking about was Ben's face, and the ashen look in his eyes as the police arrived and told him he was under arrest. Under arrest!

'I was scared,' she blubbed. 'I wanted to tell you, Mum. I did! But he said . . . he said . . .'

'I heard him,' Freya said, putting a consoling arm around her. 'Oh, sweetheart. I'm sorry to have eavesdropped, but I heard your conversation with him this morning. That's how I knew you were here.'

'Well, *I'm* not sorry you eavesdropped,' Mum said a bit tearfully, putting an arm around her on the other side so that Molly was like the filling in a middle-aged woman sandwich. 'Thank Christ you did, Freya. Thank heavens!'

'He was putting a lot of pressure on you, I heard him,' Freya went on kindly, which just made Molly cry even harder. 'And unfortunately, men say all sorts of things like that if they think they might have a chance of getting their leg over.

When you reach our age, you know better, but we've all fallen for it in the past ourselves. Come on, darling, you're okay, there's no real harm done.'

'I'm sorry I shouted. You just gave me a fright, that's all,' Mum said, rubbing Molly's back. 'The fright of my bloody life. I'll have grey hair by the time this holiday's out, you wait.' She kissed her head so hard and fiercely, Molly thought she might get whiplash.

'Sorry, Mum,' she mumbled. 'And thank you for coming to get me. Both of you. I'm actually sort of glad you did.'

And then they were all hugging each other and even though it was, like, *soooo* embarrassing, and Molly would totally die if anyone from school ever saw her do anything like that, it was also weirdly nice. Even if Mum never let her out of her sight again and grounded her for ever – she was *so* going to ground her once she'd got over the shock and the hugging had ended – Molly had a feeling that everything might just be okay.

Only one thing was puzzling her. Why was Mum being so down on men when Robert was, like, the nicest, funniest man ever?

Chapter Thirty-Eight

The three of them were all so charged with adrenalin after the teacher-pervert was taken away that nobody was in any hurry to get back in their cars and leave the scene of the crime. Harriet was tearful and shell-shocked, thanking Freya repeatedly for what she'd done, Molly was subdued, and Freya . . . Well, Freya felt quietly proud of herself for once, for having done something really, really good at last. It was a bloody great feeling. Thanks to her, disaster had been averted. Thanks to her, they were all sitting safely on the prom now, with takeaway cups of tea and a bag of iced buns for the shock. And would she have acted so quickly if she'd been groaning with a hangover that morning? Probably not.

Maybe, just maybe, this was some divine kind of recompense, a sign that good things came to those who drank lemonade. Or something.

Besides all of that, she was just glad to have been able to help Harriet, when her sister-in-law had been such a good friend to her on this holiday. Now they were bound together, battle comrades who had both been there for each other in their hours of need. Freya wasn't used to this sort of kinship with another woman, the sensation of a friend 'having your back', as Vic would say. That felt pretty bloody brilliant, too.

In all, the whole experience was a definite reminder that life was short, she thought, getting back into her car after the buns had helped revive them. In a few years, it might be Libby falling in love with the wrong man and cycling off for clandestine meetings (God forbid). Dexter was already talking longingly about motorbikes (over her dead body) and Teddy had told her matter-of-factly the other day, first milk tooth in hand, that he knew the tooth fairy was only a story, and could she just give him the pound now, please? The years were passing, the children were growing up fast and one day a summer would come when all three of them would rather be off doing their own thing, having adventures, falling in love. This morning had been a wake-up call, she realized, starting the engine and driving away. She had to make the most of these precious summer months while they were still together, because you never knew what might be around the next corner.

As she dropped a gear to climb the steep hill up and out of Ennisbridge, a memory tickled at the back of her mind and she smiled. *Oh yes*, she thought to herself, banging the steering wheel in the triumph of a good idea. *Thank you, subconscious.* Now she knew exactly what to do that afternoon.

'Wheeeeeeeee!'
  'Aaaaarrrgghh!'
  'Watch out!'
It was later that day, and she had brought Victor and the children out to the very same National Trust house they'd visited all those years ago, with the big beautiful house, gorgeous flower-filled gardens, and the best hill she'd ever seen for rolling down like lunatics.

They had grass in their hair, green smears across their clothes, and – 'I've broken my glasses!' cried Teddy in excitement, poking his finger through the now empty bit where a lens had once done its duty. But none of it mattered. None of it was important, compared to the raucous shrieks of laughter that floated through the summer air, as they each tumbled down and down and bumpily down. Raucous, shrieking laughter was the very best sound in the world today.

And actually, she thought with a grin, rolling down a hill, holding hands with your husband or child in a wobbly human line, seeing the world twist and rotate at dizzying breathless speed . . . Well, that was up there with the best sensations in the world too. It felt like pure, undiluted happiness, in fact; an espresso of joy.

'Listen, Frey . . . I just want to say I'm sorry,' Vic said, as the children raced back up the hill for their tenth roll, leaving just the two of them dishevelled and giddy at the bottom. 'I'm really sorry I didn't notice that you haven't been yourself lately.'

'It's all right,' she said, leaning forward and plucking a clump of dried grass from above his right ear. 'It's fine.'

'No, love. It's not fine. I've been so wrapped up in what happened to me that I stopped seeing what was happening to you – or anyone else.' Now it was his turn to lean over and gently tuck a daisy into her hair. 'And I'm sorry. I'll make it up to you, all right? I promise.'

She smiled at him – a tentative smile of hope. She had a feeling that they had turned a corner together, that they were going to be okay. And then – 'WHOOOOAAAAAA!' – down tumbled Libby in a flurry of screaming and flying plaits straight into Victor, and they were all laughing again.

Afterwards, when everyone was too weak and giggly for any more rolling, and the subject of ice creams had been raised by several hopeful voices, Freya glanced over and saw a couple on a bench nearby smiling across at them. *We've become that family*, she thought, smiling back. *The family I always wanted us to be, right back when Victor and I came here that first summer's day, all those years ago.* Sure, they would still have their bickering, door-slamming moments and laundry panics and homework dramas ahead, she wasn't kidding herself that any of the chaos would miraculously cease. But in years to come, she and Victor would be able to look back on this afternoon and think, *We got it right that day*. It would become a proper, lovely, gold-tinged memory for all of them.

'Let's go and track down some ice creams,' she said, to wild whoops of delight.

Chapter Thirty-Nine

Once they had finished at the police station, Harriet drove the two of them back, Molly's bike strapped onto the roof rack. She kept glancing sideways at her daughter along the way. It was as if a mask had slipped – a mask on her own daughter's face – revealing this beautiful young woman in place of the little girl Harriet had seen there all this time. How had she failed to notice? Somehow, in the blink of an eye, Molly had transformed into a semi-adult who fell in love and plotted secret getaways. Who had almost gone to bed with Mr Sleazebag Jamison.

Harriet could weep at the very thought of that creep getting his hands on her daughter. And she a child protection officer, too. Well, she hadn't exactly done a brilliant job of protecting her own child. She had failed dismally, in fact. Thank goodness Freya had been there, she thought for the hundredth time.

That afternoon, back at Shell Cottage, Freya disappeared off with Victor and her children, while Harriet and Molly felt the need to stay close together. Harriet was reminded of penguins huddling against one another for comfort and protection from battering storms, as the two of them set up sun loungers in the garden beside each other and lay there, two penguins eating ice creams in the sunshine, reassured by the other's presence. She kept having to resist reaching out and touching her daughter, just for the physical contact, just because she was there. She never wanted to let her out of her sight again. Not until she was at least thirty, anyway.

Molly looked pale and wrung out, and Harriet felt a twist of sympathy for her. Even though she'd been boiling over with rage back there in the hotel, fists clenched as if she might actually deck the sleazoid and bust up his shifty, weasely face, her heart had cracked a little at the agony apparent in her daughter's shocked expression. She wasn't sure that crack would ever heal over. Mothers always felt their children's pain; this was just how it was. 'How did it all start, then – with you and him?' she asked gently. 'Do you want to talk about it?'

Molly's eyes hooded over and for a moment Harriet thought she would pull down the shutters and mumble that no, she did not want to talk about it. She did not want to talk to Harriet about anything, ever again. She was probably embarrassed that her mother and aunt had dragged her away and kicked up such a loud, shrill fuss in public. Was the door now closed to future confidences and confessions? Would Harriet be frozen out for her crime of compassion?

'He was just really nice to me. At school,' Molly said eventually. 'He made me feel . . . special.' She winced, obviously aware that this was no longer the case. 'And it was exciting too. Having to keep the secret.'

Harriet's heart ached with the memory of what it was like to be fifteen and in love. That delicious soup of feelings, so vivid and intense, so all-consuming. The girls at the school where she worked were always coming into her office, starry-eyed, throwing themselves into a chair and pouring their hearts out about this boy or that. 'He is so *fine*, miss. I am well in love.' She knew this. She saw it every day. So how on earth had she failed to notice her own daughter going through this electrifying experience herself?

'When a boy – or a man – starts making you keep a relationship secret, it's not generally a good sign,' she said gently. While she didn't want to alienate Molly by being patronizing, there were some things a girl had to know.

Molly licked a drip from the bottom of her ice cream and nodded. 'I can kind of see that now,' she admitted, her face doleful. 'I just didn't want to get him into trouble.'

'I know you didn't. Because you cared about him. Because you – ' Ugh, it was hard to get the words out. 'Because you fell in love with him. And I'm sorry that he wasn't the person you thought he was. I'm so sorry he hurt you, Molls. It's the pits, I know.'

'I wanted to tell you,' Molly said, her chin trembling in that telltale trying-not-to-cry way. She'd never been one for big emotional scenes, Molly. Ever since Simon had left them, she'd always made a point of toughing everything out. 'I really did, Mum. But . . .'

'But you knew what I'd say,' Harriet finished for her. They both knew what Harriet would have said – she'd have exploded with shock and outrage, called the headteacher to have Mr Jamison sacked, then contacted the nearest nunnery to see if they took in wayward teenagers.

Molly nodded. 'I knew you'd tell me not to go.'

Got it in one, kid. And the rest. They were silent for a while. Harriet had reached the point of her ice cream where the melting–licking ratio hung drippily in the balance and she ended up cramming the rest of it into her mouth in one inelegant gulp.

'Are you going to tell Dad?' Molly asked nervously.

Simon. He hadn't crossed her mind at all while she was hurtling towards Ennisbridge, fearing for what was happening. It had been Robert she'd longed for – unflappable, practical Robert who was so good at making everything all right. Apart from when he was constructing elaborate parallel lives woven from lies and bullshit, of course.

Harriet considered the question. Was she going to tell

Simon? He was out in France now, playing happy families. Happy new French families. What could he do about Mr Jamison, if she told him? What *would* he do, more to the point. Nothing, probably. Big fat nothing. Give Molly earache down the phone about it for twenty minutes then forget it had ever happened. Not like Robert, who'd have just hugged Molly and . . . anyway, she wasn't thinking about Robert.

'I won't if you don't want me to,' she replied, once the huge lump of ice cream had vanished, very coldly, down her throat. She reached over – because resistance was no longer an option – and tucked a stray golden tendril of hair behind Molly's ear. Just to touch her. Just as an excuse to brush her fingers against that beautiful, beloved face. A face she never wanted to see looking so confused and heartbroken for as long as she lived. 'I think this can stay our secret, don't you? Secrets between mums and daughters are always fine. So long as you promise not to try running off with any other teachers. Mr Bennett, for instance. Or Mr Montague.'

Molly laughed but then the tears sprang free from her eyes and she was crying again and rubbing a bare arm against her face, her ice cream choosing that moment to slither off its stick and onto the grass. 'Oh, lovey,' Harriet said, shuffling closer and rubbing her back, just as she had done when Molly was a colicky baby, or when she was poorly with a tummy bug. Just as she would do forever more, if Molly wanted her to. 'Oh, darling. You're all right. It'll be all right.'

She rummaged in her shorts pocket and found the paper napkin from earlier at the beach café – *Don't think about the surf dude right now*; she'd punish herself for that later – and passed it to Molly, who took it gratefully and blew her nose.

'Sorry,' she said, after a moment. 'I don't know why I'm crying. It's stupid.'

'It's not stupid. You really liked him. God, I remember being your age and crying my eyes out when this pop star I liked got married. I mean, *that's* stupid. I never even knew the guy. You are perfectly entitled to cry. As loudly and dramatically as you like. Go for it, I say. Let rip.'

Molly gave her a rather watery smile, just as Harriet had been hoping. 'Thanks, Mum,' she said. She blew her nose again. 'I don't think Dad would care anyway. Not now he's got this other kid on the way.'

Harriet was so used to trotting out niceties she didn't even believe in when it came to her ex-husband that the usual platitudes appeared obediently on the tip of her tongue, ready to be wheeled out once again. *Of course he cares. Of course he loves you. He's just busy, that's all. But I'm sure – no, I KNOW – he's always thinking about you, wherever he is.*

Simon, you twat, she thought instead. *I'm sick of making excuses for you. You don't bloody deserve a daughter like Molly, you fuckhead.*

'The thing about your dad,' she said, before she could stop herself, 'is that he cares about himself more than anyone else.

Unfortunately. I am sorry I didn't fall in love with a better man. He is not the father you deserve.'

Now it was Molly's turn to reach out and pat Harriet, gently and affectionately, on her arm. 'Oh, Mum. I know that. It's okay, you don't have to pretend to like him any more. Because at least we've got Robert now, who's brilliant.'

Harriet pinched her lips together, not wanting to break her daughter's heart all over again with the news flash that actually Robert had also been kind of a twat recently. Now was not the time. Not while she was already so fragile and broken. 'Hmm,' she said non-committally, casting around for a new topic of conversation.

But Molly's eyes were narrowing. Something seemed to have clicked in her mind, a memory making a reappearance. 'What's going on with you and Robert, Mum? Where is he today, anyway?'

No. She couldn't do it yet. Not until she and Robert had properly talked, like adults, and brought about some kind of conclusion, happy or otherwise, to the situation. 'I'm not sure what he's up to,' she replied breezily. 'We had a bit of an argument last night but – ' She hesitated, not wanting to lie. But what else could she say? 'We'll sort it out.' *One way or another*, she reflected grimly.

What a summer this was turning out to be, she thought, as they lapsed into silence, sun spots dancing before her eyes. She'd never known a holiday like it. They had come to Shell

Cottage a happy little unit of three – or so she'd assumed at the time. But since then, secrets had emerged so deep and so earth-shattering, their happy family had been fractured and left reeling.

Chapter Forty

'I didn't tell you, did I?' Gloria said, as they reluctantly got back in the car and left the Cove of Reckless Women behind. 'Mitch was asking about you last night in the pub. Seemed very interested.'

'Mitch?' Olivia felt herself blush like a teenage girl. 'The tattoo artist?'

'How many Mitches do you know? Yeah, the tattoo artist. That gorgeous, kind, handsome, talented tattoo artist. Asking about you.'

Ridiculously, Olivia's heart spun a little pirouette. 'Oh,' she said, feeling – well, there was no other way to describe it – flustered. Flattered. She remembered Mitch all right. The slanting planes of his face, those intense sea-blue eyes that had drawn her in so bewitchingly. 'That's nice,' she said, 'but . . .' Gracious, it was quite absurd to even be *having* this conversation. 'But really I don't think . . .' She couldn't get the words out. 'Oh,' she said again in the end.

Gloria gave a hoot of laughter. They were heading for

Shell Cottage because, after Gloria's confession about Bill, and the revelation that her tough, sparky new friend was secretly every bit as wounded as she was, Olivia hadn't thought twice about inviting her to come back for dinner that evening. There was some puff pastry in the fridge that she'd been planning to use as the base of a tomato and mozzarella tart, and she was sure she could stretch it out for another person if she made extra salad and a dish of rosemary potatoes.

'*Oh*,' Gloria teased, mocking Olivia's response. 'Is this the start of a little holiday romance, I wonder? Because he's a great guy, you know. You could do a lot worse. A *very* nice man.'

Olivia almost choked at the suggestion. Much as she liked her friend, she wished Gloria had more than a passing acquaintance with the concept of subtlety. 'Gloria! No! Absolutely not. No. A holiday romance is definitely not on the agenda this summer.'

Gloria pursed her lips, slowing fractionally at a junction before swinging the car round into a too-fast right turn. 'I seem to remember you saying something like that about skinny-dipping,' she teased.

'Yes, but—'

'You know what they say. If you fall off a horse, the best thing to do is get straight back on.'

'Alec was not a horse!' Oh, the woman was impossible! It was like being back at school and being teased for supposedly making eyes at Edward Granger in the year above.

'And wouldn't you like a bit of no-strings fun? A summer fling? God knows I would. I'd jump at the chance. I'd jump the first sexy man that raised an eyebrow my way, to be honest.'

'I am a grieving widow,' Olivia retorted, her words coming out rather more piously than she'd intended.

'Yeah, you really looked like one this afternoon,' Gloria teased. 'Come on, Liv. You're on holiday. Have some fun!'

'I *am* having fun,' Olivia retorted, 'but—'

'Have some more fun, then. Have some sex fun. And on that bombshell,' Gloria added hastily, glancing over and seeing that Olivia had turned puce, 'I will now shut up before you withdraw your offer of dinner. Subject closed. Lips zipped.'

'Thank goodness for that,' Olivia said, folding her hands primly in her lap and staring out of the window. All the same, though, Gloria's words lingered in her head for the whole way back. And her thoughts did keep annoyingly returning to Mitch's slow, wide smile, his dark shock of hair, his tanned, strong body.

Olivia Tarrant! she chided herself eventually. *You wouldn't!* But perhaps the Cove of Reckless Women was still exerting some mystical power over her, because the very next thing she thought was, *Oh, wouldn't I?*

It occurred to Olivia as they parked outside Shell Cottage that she hadn't spent much time with her family recently. She felt, in particular, that she'd rather neglected her daughter in the last week, especially since the revelations about Katie. Hopefully it didn't matter too much, though: Shell Cottage was such a quiet, peaceful sort of place where nothing much ever happened; she'd have heard if anyone needed her. They'd probably all had a lovely, relaxing time without her.

All the same, she must make more of an effort, she vowed as Gloria yanked on the handbrake with her usual neck-rattling vigour. There were only four days left of the holiday, and she was determined to set aside more time to do family things, Granny things, take everyone for a lovely afternoon tea, perhaps, or out to Dartmouth Castle – that was always a good day trip, and Teddy in particular would love the shop that sold wooden swords and other weapons.

First things first, though: they were all going to have a nice evening together. There was wine to slide into the fridge, potatoes to scrub and pastry to roll. 'Come on in,' she said to Gloria, pushing open the front door. 'Tonight, you're our guest. Welcome to the madhouse.'

★

Olivia had only been joking when she said the word 'mad-house' but it wasn't long into dinner that her words came back to haunt her.

The tomato tart was a success, Gloria chatted away to the family as if they'd been friends for ever (she was even the recipient of about twenty Knock Knock jokes from Libby, which she answered with great humour and patience) and Freya looked cheerful as she told them all about their after-noon. True, neither Robert nor Harriet spoke more than a word or two and Molly didn't seem quite herself either, but on the whole, it felt a pleasant enough evening.

But then Robert cleared his throat. By now he had pol-ished off the best part of two large glasses of red wine and there was a strange sort of recklessness about him, Olivia observed in concern. 'I've got a few things to say,' he began baldly, and Harriet immediately looked away.

Oh dear. Had they fallen out? Their body language had been terrible since the meal began, Olivia realized, noticing belatedly that Harriet had seated herself at the opposite end of the table to her husband. She felt a pang of guilt for her day larking around in the sea with Gloria while some kind of domestic had clearly occurred.

'The first thing,' Robert went on, 'is that I saw Katie today.'

Olivia's knife and fork clattered right out of her hands.

'Oh, Robert,' she said weakly. *Not now, not tonight*, she thought.

'Who's Katie?' Teddy asked in a loud whisper. One of the lenses was missing from his glasses, Olivia noticed, giving him a faintly piratical air.

'That lady that used to clean the house,' Dexter replied. 'Remember, last summer, she let us slide down the stairs on the bed sheets?'

'Hush,' Freya told them. 'Maybe we should talk about this later, Rob.' She looked meaningfully at the children. 'When little ears aren't flapping.'

'My ears don't *flap*!' Ted said indignantly.

'They do when I flick them,' Dexter said, demonstrating.

'I don't want to hear anything about Katie now anyway, thank you,' Olivia said tightly.

'Ow!' Teddy cried, shoving his brother.

'Look, just hear me out,' Robert said. 'I spoke to her and Leo, and—'

'I really think later would be better,' Freya said again, more urgently this time.

'Robert, *please*,' Olivia begged. She couldn't face talking about Katie and Leo tonight. She didn't think she'd ever be able to face it, frankly, but especially not when the subject was sprung on her without warning.

'Maybe you should respect how your mother feels about this Katie person,' Gloria put in sternly, and everyone looked at her in surprise, apart from Olivia, who gave her a small smile of gratitude.

Robert shrugged. 'All right. In that case, I'll move on to the second thing I wanted to say.'

He took another slug of red wine, draining his glass, and Olivia braced herself.

'I'm a fake,' he said bluntly. 'I'm not remotely proud of it, but there's no two ways about it. I've deceived you all. I've been a complete dick. And I'm sorry.'

'Robert!' Olivia cried, shocked that he was saying such things in front of children and a guest. What was wrong with him? She glanced at Freya, who looked equally startled. Harriet, though, had narrowed eyes and a pinched mouth. She knew all too well what this was about, Olivia realized with a lurch. And by the expression on her face, she fully agreed with Robert's self-assessment and the 'complete dick' judgement too. Oh dear.

'Ted, Libby and Dexter, you may leave the table,' Freya said quickly, sensing worse to come. *Everyone* sensed worse to come, judging by the expectant hush that had descended. 'If you go right now, you're allowed to watch TV in the living room.'

Round-eyed and gawping, Teddy looked as if he'd much prefer to stay right here and learn some more rude words, courtesy of Uncle Robert, but Freya added, 'Now please, Teddy,' with such chilling authority that he reluctantly peeled himself off the dining room chair and scuttled after the other two.

Barely had they left the room when Robert went on, the words rattling out like machine-gun fire, as if he was worried he'd lose his nerve if he stopped to take a breath. 'I've lied to you all. I'm so sorry. But there is no novel. Well, there is, but it's shit, and I don't have a book deal. I don't have an agent or a contract either or . . . or anything. I made it all up. Because I'm a dick.'

A clamour went up. '*What?*' cried Freya, incredulous.

'I don't understand,' Olivia said.

'Does this mean we're not going to America?' Molly asked in dismay.

'No, sweetheart,' Harriet replied. 'And there's no money either.' She gave a hollow laugh and made limp jazz hands. 'Yay.'

'No way,' Molly said, mouth falling open. 'Oh, *man*. So we're skint again?'

Harriet shrugged, turning her face away, but not before Olivia saw the wounded light in her eyes. She recognized the how-could-you? anguish visible in her daughter-in-law's body language; it was how she'd been feeling most of the summer.

Oh, Robert, she thought in despair. Was it really true? No book deal? No glittering career? Maybe there'd be no wife any more either, by the look of them. She couldn't make sense of it. Harriet was the best thing that had ever happened to her son. What had he been thinking?

Robert's jaw clenched – you could almost see him absorbing the hit – but then he nodded. 'I'm sorry,' he said. 'I should have told you. Things . . . Things got out of hand.'

'So you made it all up?' Freya asked, her forehead creasing. 'The stuff about your editor and the foreign rights? None of it's true?'

Robert shook his head. 'None of it's true,' he said.

There was a moment's silence and then Gloria pushed her chair back and rose from her seat. 'I think that's my cue to pop out for a fag,' she said tactfully, and left the room.

Olivia was still trying to get her head around her son's extraordinary announcements. Was Robert drunk? Had he gone mad? 'But *why*?' she asked him in bewilderment. 'Why did you feel you had to lie?'

'Because you all think I'm a failure!' he burst out. His hands balled into fists at his sides; rage bristled from him. A peaceful, easy-going boy, she'd hardly ever seen him angry but now it was bursting up from him like a volcano. 'You always have done. I've never lived up to the Tarrant name, have I?' His lip curled as nobody spoke immediately. 'It's all right, you don't have to be polite, I know I was never good enough for you.'

'Nonsense!' Olivia cried, stung. 'That's simply not true!'

'Of course you're good enough!' Freya added in the next breath. 'Why are you saying all this, Robert?'

'You were good enough for me,' Harriet added woodenly. 'At least you were until this happened.'

Robert's face was grey as he wrestled with a whole gang of inner demons. 'Well, now you all know the truth,' he said bitterly. 'And for what it's worth, I'm sorry. I got carried away. I just wanted to impress you. Be successful.' He gave a harsh laugh. 'So that turned out well, anyway.'

Oh, Robert, Olivia thought again. He'd been the most sensitive little thing as a child. He'd cried all the way back from primary school once because another boy had called him stupid for getting his sums wrong. 'But I *am* stupid,' he had sobbed pitifully, burrowing into Olivia on the safety of her lap once home. 'I *must* be stupid.' And here he was, a grown man and still putting himself down.

'I have never thought you a failure, Robert,' Olivia told him. 'Not once. You're a kind, good person. You always have been. Look how you've helped me through your father's death. I couldn't have asked for a better son!'

'I don't think you're a failure either,' Freya said. 'Not at all! I—'

'You don't have to say all of this. It's fine,' Robert interrupted dully. 'Really. I don't want a Help Robert the Fuck-Up support group or anything. I just wanted to tell you. To say yes, I did fuck up. Yes, I have done the last thing I ever wanted, which is wreck my relationship with Harriet. Yes, I am ashamed of myself. And yes, I know Dad would be too.' He rubbed a hand across his face. 'I'm sorry for lying to you all. Deeply, deeply sorry. I don't expect you to understand or forgive me or – ' he turned pleadingly to Harriet – 'or feel you can love me any more. I wouldn't blame you.' He walked towards the door. 'Once again, I'm sorry.'

He left the room and they all looked at each other, speechless.

'Bloody *hell*,' Molly said, breaking the silence. 'Did that actually just happen? I'm telling you, after today, I'm never going to get married. Seriously – *never*!'

Chapter Forty-One

Freya made her excuses and slipped away from the dinner table as soon as possible. While she might not agree with what her brother had done, she knew only too well that desperation could lure you down strange roads, ones you might normally avoid. When you lived in a permanent state of dread that everyone else would find you out to be no good, then any escape route, however crazy, could seem a bright idea at the time.

The grass was cool beneath her bare feet as she padded across the garden in search of him. The sun was starting to sink through the sky, like a penny falling in slow motion through water, and the day's warmth was gradually leaching away from the ground. Robert was down at the bottom of the garden on the creaky old swing seat, staring out at the beach and swigging red wine straight from the bottle. She could smell it as she approached and the sharp, fruity scent made her stomach clench. Oh, for a delicious gulp of Merlot, to ease her way through what was almost certainly going to be a difficult conversation. She could picture it, scarlet and viscous in a large full glass; she could feel the weight of it in her hand, the taste on her tongue . . .

But no. Not tonight. And not for quite a few nights to come either. That way was closed for the time being.

'Rob. Mind if I join you?'

He shrugged as if to say he couldn't care less, and she perched on the seat beside him, feeling it rock and sway with the extra weight. There were spots of high colour on his face from the drink and the drama, and as a veteran of both those things this summer, she felt a renewed kinship with him.

'I remember sitting here as teenagers one summer,' she said when he didn't make any attempt at conversation. 'Do you remember? Sneaking Dad's fags in secret and nearly puking up in tandem. Bleeurgh. Green faces a-gogo.'

He didn't reply, although she thought his lips twitched in a tepid smile. She took that as her cue to venture further down memory lane.

'And us two hiding here once, when we were much younger, and Mum was insisting we had to have baths.' The memory came to her out of the blue, of them crouched low on the padded seat, trying not to giggle or make any other sound as Olivia's voice rang out around the garden. 'And Dad telling us bedtime stories, with us in our pyjamas. "Just one more chapter, Dad, pleeease!"'

She shouldn't have mentioned their dad, or telling stories,

because Robert immediately stiffened and drew away from her. Idiot, Freya. Running before you were walking. Maybe it was time to tackle things head-on instead.

'Listen, about all of that,' she said quickly, before he could make excuses and leave. 'For the record, I've never thought you were a failure. No – listen, hear me out. For as long as I can remember, I've wished I was more like you – laid-back, confident, able to get on with everyone.'

He snorted, looking unconvinced.

'I'm serious! What I wouldn't give to be less neurotic and uptight, less of a social bloody misfit compared to you.' She hoped he could hear the conviction in her voice, because she meant every word. 'I went into medicine because Mum and Dad wanted me to, basically. I've always done the safe, nerdy, traditional thing. Whereas you—'

'Whereas I lurch from disaster to disaster because I'm not as clever or successful as *you*,' he said bitterly, upending the bottle again and swigging out of it.

'*No*,' she said. 'No, Rob. You made a mistake with the book thing, granted. But at least you tried! You gave it a go. Most people are too chickenshit to take that kind of a risk.'

'Too sensible, you mean.'

She tried again, concerned that she would never lift him out of his black mood at this rate. 'Anyway,' she said bracingly, 'work stuff isn't the be-all and end-all, is it? You've got Harriet and Molly . . .'

393

'I'm not sure I have any more.'

'And you're a good person. You're kind! Who else has made the effort with Katie and Leo? Not me. Not Mum. We've been in total denial. We've been too scared and freaked out, instinctively shunning them rather than doing the mature thing – the *right* thing – like you, and dealing with the situation. You've got bags of – what do they call it? – emotional intelligence. Whereas Mum and I are more like emotional cripples.'

There was a pause and then he shrugged. 'I felt sorry for him. Leo, I mean. He's only a kid.'

Freya thought of that solemn little boy she'd met with a plate of flapjacks in his hands – her half-brother! – and felt a wrench inside that she'd barely given him a second thought, with everything else going on. 'Good for you, Rob,' she said. 'Our little brother.'

'I know.'

'He looks like Dad, doesn't he?'

'Yeah. He's a nice kid. And Katie's had a hard time too. We really need to get Mum to see that.'

Freya nodded, although she knew it wouldn't be quite so simple an undertaking. 'Give her time,' she said. 'She'll come round eventually. It's been a massive shock for her.'

Neither of them spoke for a few moments, with just the rhythmic creak of the seat's hinges and the faint roar of the sea down in the bay below breaking the silence. A car engine

started and then faded away – Gloria leaving, presumably
– and then came Victor's voice telling Teddy off about something or other. She wondered what Harriet was doing right
now and how she felt about Rob's deceit. Poor, trusting
Harriet, with a headstrong, impassioned daughter to cope
with, and now a husband's lies on top of everything else. She
must be in pieces.

'Look,' she said in a low voice, 'I've messed things up this
summer too. I know you might think I'm this perfect person,
but I'm not, Rob. I'm really not. I—'

'There you are!' came their mother's voice just then. And
down the path she bustled, a cream cardigan thrown around
her shoulders. 'Robert, dear, I've been thinking. About what
you said.'

Freya heard him stifle a groan. *I've been thinking* had been
their mother's catchphrase for much of their teenage years;
it tended to precede notions about them getting paper
rounds or Saturday jobs, signing up for homework clubs or
doing more to help around the house. You could almost hear
the *Here we go again* in Robert's head.

'Hi Mum,' he said, somewhat dutifully. 'Welcome to the
swing seat of doom.'

'Robert, now listen, don't be like that. Feeling sorry for
yourself, I mean. Everyone makes mistakes. And I'm really
sorry that you felt you had to pretend that—'

He held up his hand, clearly not wanting to go over everything again. 'Mum. It's fine. You don't have to say anything. Please.'

'But I've had an idea. That's the thing. Dad's last manuscript – why don't you finish writing it?'

'What?' That took him by surprise. It took both of them by surprise, actually. With everything else that had happened over the summer, Freya had completely forgotten about this half-completed manuscript that Dad's publishers were so keen to get their hands on.

'Dad's manuscript,' Olivia repeated patiently. 'His last book. Goodness knows how many hysterical emails that editor of his will have sent me by now, I dread to think. But you could finish it. You could be his co-author. He would have loved that.'

Freya gasped. Of course. The perfect solution. 'That is genius, Mum. Yes!'

'No.' Robert shook his head. He was so drunk now it seemed to take him an effort to stop shaking it again. 'Definitely not. I'm not good enough.'

'But you *are*. Of course you are!' Olivia and Freya chorused. It would be lovely, Freya thought. Father and son collaborating, the old master and the young apprentice . . .

Robert merely laughed – a short, scornful noise lacking in any humour. 'Mum, I'm really not. Genuinely. Every last publisher in the country has said so. Nobody thought I was up to scratch.' He sighed and scuffed at the ground again. 'I tried, all right? I gave it my best shot. But at the end of the day, I failed. So let's not bodge up Dad's last book and tarnish his reputation out of some well-meaning attempt to make me feel better. Honestly. It's time for me to look for a different job.'

Olivia sagged a little but nodded. 'Okay,' she said quietly. 'I understand.'

Freya moved up so that she was in one corner of the seat, leaving space in the middle. 'Why don't you sit down, Mum? Join us.'

Robert shuffled over to the other corner so that there was enough room and Olivia gingerly squeezed in between them. 'This is nice,' she said after a while, as they rocked there, all three of them gazing out at the bay. The sea was turning a deep rose-pink and the beach was deserted, save for a few last sandcastles still standing proud against the tide. Olivia reached out and took their hands so that they were linked in a line. 'Well, now. We three are having a peculiar old summer, aren't we?'

'It's memorable, I'll say that,' Freya replied dryly. What with Dad and Katie, Mum losing the plot, her nearly drinking herself to a watery death, Molly's near seduction and now Robert's revelations, it was not at all the relaxing holiday break that any of them had been hoping for. She squeezed her mum's hand, feeling glad for this moment together at least. 'But we've got each other, right? We've still got each other.'

'We've still got each other,' Olivia echoed, squeezing back. 'And we'll face the future – and whatever happens next – together.' Her eyes misted over a little. 'This has been the strangest summer of my life. But if getting to know Gloria has taught me anything, it's that you can live through the worst, and still come out smiling. We'll get there, I promise. All three of us, we'll get there.' There was a pause. 'By the way,' she added, 'I've been wondering about getting a tattoo. What do you think?'

Freya hadn't felt so close to her mother and brother since they'd held hands at Alec's funeral two months ago. They all talked honestly about how they'd struggled ever since, and vowed to look after one another better from here on in. It felt good – as if they'd wiped the collective slate clean and could forgive each other's mistakes, and move on. Then, later that evening, just after she was coming downstairs from kissing the children goodnight, Freya's mobile started ringing. *Melanie Taylor*, she read on the screen, and her stomach gave a lurch.

Oh, Christ. Now she really badly wanted a drink. A vat of wine to paralyse her brain, to make this all go away. And even though waiting for a reply had been fraught and full of dread, now that the call had finally come, she was so scared of what

Melanie might say that she was sorely tempted to send it directly to voicemail.

Be brave, Freya. Take the medicine. She had just confessed her drinking problem to her mother and brother, after all. She could handle this on top.

She slid her finger across the screen to answer the call, her mouth dry. 'Hello? Freya Castledine speaking.'

'Hello, Doctor Castledine, this is Melanie Taylor returning your call.'

Freya sat down on the bottom step, her heart banging in her ribcage as if she'd just run around the block. 'Hi,' she said, her voice barely a whisper. 'How are you? How's Ava? I hope you didn't mind me ringing earlier.'

'Ava's fine. She's much better. She came home yesterday and is eating and drinking like it's going out of fashion.'

Freya's throat felt so tight for a moment that she couldn't speak. Ava was fine. She was back home. Eating and drinking. Oh, thank goodness. Thank goodness! 'I'm so pleased,' she said, hearing a sob in her voice. The breath whooshed out of her with sheer relief; she felt light-headed and dizzy with a burst of happiness. 'I'm so glad to hear that, Melanie.'

Melanie had sounded formal and clipped until that moment but then her voice softened a tone. 'Me too,' she said. 'It's been . . .' It sounded as if she might be swallowing back a sob herself. 'It's been a nightmare.'

'I'm sure. I can imagine. And for what it's worth, I am

truly sorry about that day. If I missed anything. I mean, I honestly don't think I did, but—'

'I'm sorry too,' Melanie said, and Freya was so surprised she stopped mid-sentence. 'I'm sorry I took it out on you. I said some horrible things. I was just scared, that's all. Really scared. But it wasn't your fault.'

It wasn't your fault. Never had words sounded so God-given, so merciful and downright wonderful in one's ear. It wasn't her fault. Freya had to press her lips together for a moment, fearful that she might break out into full-blown tears. 'Thank you,' she said eventually. 'Thank you for saying that. I really appreciate it. But seriously, don't worry about the things you said. You wouldn't be a mother if you weren't prepared to fight for your child. I completely understand.' She let out a long, shuddering breath, feeling a weight of tension leave her body. 'Thanks for letting me know anyway. I'm so glad Ava's okay.'

'You're welcome.' A thin mewling cry went up in the background. 'Oh, I'd better go, there's madam now, just woken for her bedtime feed.' She hesitated as if she wanted to say something else, but then the crying went up a notch and she must have changed her mind. 'Goodbye, then, Doctor Castledine.'

'Goodbye, Melanie. Take care.'

Freya clicked off the call and leaned back against the stairs, clasping the phone to her chest as if it were a lucky charm, a talisman, a love letter from a sweetheart. Not a person remotely given to superstitious whims, she nonetheless felt very much like offering up some kind of prayer to the universe all of a sudden, for granting her this reprieve, this day of redemption. 'Thank you,' she murmured, shutting her eyes and breathing in sheer, blessed relief. 'Thank you, thank you, *thank you*.'

Chapter Forty-Two

'Why didn't you *tell* me?' Molly cried, just as soon as they'd left the dinner table. 'God, Mum, why didn't you *say*?'

Harriet topped up her wine glass, feeling numb after the dinner table revelations. Everyone else had left the room, except for her and Molly, still there with untouched puddings in front of them. So now they all knew, she thought dismally. Now they all knew Robert had been lying for months, living in this crazy fantasy world of his, and everyone would be eyeing her marriage from the sidelines like it was some kind of disaster area. Which, let's face it, it was. Full-blown carnage. A motorway pile-up. A meteor strike.

She hadn't been able to bear looking at Olivia or Freya, not wanting to see expressions of pity or even contempt. She certainly didn't want to pick up What-the-hell?-And-you-*knew*-about-this? vibes from them either. (Cringe.) 'I was going to tell you,' she replied wearily, twisting the stem of her wine glass between her fingers. 'I wanted to. But I figured that you'd had enough going on today without yet another drama to add to the load.'

'I can't believe it. I don't understand, Mum. Why would he make it all up? And keep on lying like that? Why?'

Ahh, the very questions that had been seething tumultuously through Harriet's head since the night before. She still wasn't sure how to reply. Because he's a psychopath? Because he's deranged? Because real life – and us – weren't enough for him? 'I don't know, love,' she said despondently. 'I've been trying to figure that one out for myself.'

Molly's heart-shaped face twisted. 'I really liked him, though,' she said. She looked as pained as Harriet felt. 'I really, really liked him, Mum. He was always so nice to us. And funny. And kind. I thought he was a good person.'

'Me too, Molls. I thought he was the bee's knees. And the bee's elbows, ankles and arse and all.'

Molly leaned her head against Harriet, who slid an arm around her in response. They sat there like that for a moment: mother and daughter, the betrayed, the ones left behind. Harriet couldn't help thinking of how they'd clung together when Simon left, how they'd even shared her bed for a few weeks because they both felt so bereft without him. History repeating itself in the cruellest possible way.

'What are you going to do?' Molly asked after a while. A hank of her long hair was pooling, soft and ticklish, on Harriet's arm. 'Are you going to . . . split up?'

There was a catch in her voice and Harriet was pierced by a shard of terrible, awful guilt that this was somehow her fault, that she'd mucked things up for the both of them yet again; unable to hang on to a husband for longer than five minutes. But she'd never asked Robert to be anything other than he was! She'd never pushed him to be more ambitious or reach for a target he couldn't achieve!

The question hung in the air between them. Were they going to split up? Oh, help. When would Harriet feel like a proper grown-up who knew the answers to all the difficult questions? 'I don't know,' she said again, with the hopeless feeling that she was failing her daughter once more.

'Mum. Talk to me properly. How do you feel about him? Do you still love him?'

'I . . .' The question took her by surprise. 'Um . . .'

'It's okay, you know. Say what you want to say. I'm not a baby any more, Mum, you don't have to keep hiding things from me because you're worried I'll be upset.'

Harriet blinked and looked at her daughter: this clear-eyed, caring girl-woman who knew her better than anyone. For all these years, Harriet had been the defender and protector in their unique, close relationship. For so long, Harriet had stood in front of Molly, shielding her from troubles as best she could. But now the scales seemed to be tipping, and here was Molly stepping forward and coming to stand beside her, announcing her arrival as comforter and adviser in return. Maybe Harriet didn't have to hide unpalatable truths quite so furtively any more. This girl beside her – this young woman – knew a thing or two about love, after all.

'I do love him,' she found herself replying slowly. The words took her by surprise and she said them again. 'Yes. I do still love him. And not just for me, but for you too. What he's brought to our little family. All the good times we've had together. But—'

'You don't have to think about me in all this,' Molly interrupted. 'Yeah, I really like him too – liked him, anyway – but I'll be gone in a few years, won't I? It's what you think about him that counts. Whether you can trust him any more.'

Harriet nodded. That was the big one. *Should* she trust him? Others wouldn't. Others would send him packing, show him the door. Would it be very weak of her to give him a second chance? Did that make her even more of a sucker? 'You're right,' she mumbled.

'But for what it's worth,' Molly went on, 'I don't think he's a nasty person. I don't think he was lying in an evil way, like Dad did.'

Harriet opened her mouth to protest – still automatically leaping to Simon's flimsy defence – but Molly went on before she had the chance. 'With Robert . . . I think he lied because he wanted to impress everyone. Not because he was trying to trick you or hurt you.' She shrugged. 'It's still pretty lame, let's face it. But he does love you, Mum. Even though he knows he totally screwed up.'

'When did you get so wise?' Harriet said, marvelling at this super-smart advice-dispensing daughter who seemed to have all the answers, right when she had precisely none herself. She squeezed Molly's hand. 'Thank you, lovey. I think you're right, to be honest. I need to talk to Robert and get things straight again although – ' she glanced over her shoulder at the door, through which he had strode earlier, full of drink and self-loathing – 'probably not tonight. But tomorrow. I'll talk to him tomorrow.'

Molly seemed to approve of this. 'I know he's been a bit of a jerk, Mum,' she said, 'but maybe you shouldn't be too hard on him. He's just a bloke, remember.'

Harriet laughed, and then Molly did too, and they hugged each other tightly. But Harriet's smile didn't last for long. Somehow or other, she and Robert needed to get to the bottom of why he'd been such an idiot – and where the two of them might go from here.

Whether it was straight to the divorce courts, or into last-chance saloon, she still had no idea.

Chapter Forty-Three

'You're singing, Granny!' cried Libby the next morning at the breakfast table.

Olivia, stirring porridge at the hob, glanced round to see her granddaughter with a bowl piled high with chocolate cereal, beaming across at her. 'What, darling?'

'You're singing again,' Libby said. The sun had brought out all her freckles, Olivia noticed, and her hair was fluffed up from being in bed. There were only the two of them up in the house so far; the rest of the family were obviously still sleeping off the fraught events of the day before. 'You always used to sing when you were cooking but you haven't lately. Not for ages. And today you are!'

'Today I am,' Olivia realized, smiling back at the little girl who looked so triumphant to have noticed this. 'Today I'm singing – who knows what I'll be doing tomorrow. Juggling, maybe. Ice skating.'

'Sliding down the bannisters,' Libby said, eyes lighting up at the idea. 'Oh, Granny, why don't you try it? It's really fun.'

Olivia laughed. 'I think I'll stick to singing for the time being,' she said, abandoning the porridge for a moment to come round and hug her granddaughter. Bless her for noticing the change in her grandmother, when Olivia's mind had been elsewhere for so much of the holiday. It was time to put that mistake right, at least. 'I was thinking,' she went on, 'maybe later today, me and you could do something special together, just us two. Anything you like – apart from sliding down the bannisters, that is.'

Libby was warm and soft to cuddle, and her hair smelled of strawberry shampoo. 'Can we make cakes?' she asked hopefully. 'We haven't made cakes in ages. Proper ones with icing and sprinkles.'

'Good idea! Cakes with icing and sprinkles it is,' Olivia said. 'This afternoon at . . . let's see. Three o'clock? Then everyone can have one for afternoon tea.'

'And it's just me, not Dexter or Teddy, isn't it?'

'It's just you, not Dexter or Teddy,' Olivia promised. 'I'll do something nice with them tomorrow instead.' She planted a kiss on Libby's head. 'By the way, I'm pretending I haven't seen all the chocolatey cereal you've got heaped up there. Or perhaps it's my weak old grandmotherly eyes that are playing tricks on me.'

Libby giggled and shoved in a spoonful guiltily. 'Are you coming to the beach today, Granny?' she asked.

'Not today, darling. I've got a couple of important things to do first.'

'And then we'll bake the cakes at three o'clock?'

'You bet we will.'

'Brilliant, Granny.' Libby beamed again. 'Knock, knock,' she said.

'Who's there?'

'Dunnap.'

'Dunn – ' Olivia broke off and laughed. 'Oh, no, Libby Castledine, I'm not falling for that one.' She poured her porridge into the bowl and added extra sugar, just for the hell of it. 'Now then, three o'clock on the dot, I'll see you back here with clean hands and an apron on. Do we have a deal?'

Libby held out a warm pink hand. 'Deal,' she said solemnly.

After breakfast, Olivia washed and dressed herself, combed her hair and carefully applied her favourite lipstick. She exchanged a tentative smile with the woman she saw in the bedroom mirror, hardly able to believe it was almost three weeks since she'd come to Shell Cottage. She felt a completely different person from the widow who'd arrived then, weighed down by grief and the lonely, desperate feeling that life held precious little to look forward to. Back then, she'd known nothing of the storm about to break, of course; had no idea of the shock that waited for her down in the kitchen of this very house. Ignorance, while not exactly blissful, had been a protective bubble, blinkering her from the rotten core at the heart of her marriage. And for a short while after arriving here, she'd lost sight of the valuable things she still had left to cherish: her daughter, her son, her glorious grandchildren, her gardening business . . . so much that was worth treasuring. What was more, she'd forgotten how to smile, let alone have fun.

But that had all changed. It was as if a new Olivia had been born. An Olivia who had emerged from the sadness, who was singing in the kitchen again, who had remembered just how much she cared about her family. She had been shocked to hear the night before what had been going on under her nose recently: Freya's drinking (poor, unhappy Freya!), Robert's turmoil, and then the dreadful story of what had happened – or almost happened – with pretty young Molly yesterday. They all needed her, she realized. She still had a purpose. Now it was time to step up and get on with life again, with the same grit and bravery that the rest of her family had shown.

It wasn't all doom and gloom, of course. She had also made a brand new friend, who made her laugh so hard she worried for her pelvic floor, and who spurred her on to do the most ridiculous, extraordinary things. She had become a woman who dared to hope that there may yet be good times ahead of her and was no longer quite so scared of the future. She refused to be scared of the future!

That was why she had stuffed the bundled sheaf of paper – Alec's last novel – into a canvas bag and put it, and herself, in her car. 'A couple of important things to do,' she had said to Libby. Now there was an understatement if ever she'd heard one.

The first important thing was to read the blasted manuscript, of course. She could easily have done this at home, sat in a deckchair, or on the sofa in the living room if it was too breezy outside, but she knew that such a scenario would inevitably lead to a stream of interested questions and speculation from the rest of the family. ('Is it any good?' 'What do you think of it so far?' 'What are you going to do about it?')

She didn't want any of that. She needed peace and quiet, a chance to settle into the book and give it her full attention without glancing over her shoulder every time she heard approaching footsteps. So she started the engine and drove away from Shell Cottage and along the coast road as far as Ennisbridge. That would do, she thought, turning down the narrow, winding lane that led down to the heart of the village and the seafront itself.

She parked the car, locked up and headed off with the canvas bag of papers in search of somewhere quiet to sit and read. It was a humid sort of day, with very little wind, and she was thirsty already, the bag weighing unexpectedly heavily on her shoulder. She glanced down at the beach, where she could see the Lobster Pot opening up, and thought for a moment of Mitch, Gloria's friend. Would he be there today? Would it be very obvious if she took the manuscript and parked herself at one of the tables in the hope of seeing him again?

Yes, Olivia. Obvious and naff. Have some dignity, for goodness' sake.

She went instead to a vintage tea room just off the seafront, which had splendid eau-de-nil wallpaper printed with a repeating gold feather design. Antique gilt-painted bird cages hung from the ceiling, the tables were laid with smart white cloths and there was an old dresser against one wall with mismatched crockery. It reminded Olivia a little of the coffee houses where she and Alec had met, back in their courting days, and she decided that this made it the perfect venue for today's task.

She settled herself into a corner table, ordered a pot of tea from the henna-haired waitress in a 1950s frock, and set the manuscript on the table in front of her. *Okay. Right. Here we go, then.*

Her hand hovered above the first page but her fingers made no contact with the paper. She was surprised by how apprehensive she suddenly felt. Alec's last book. Once she had finished reading this pile of paper, there would be nothing new of his ever to read again. His life's work – over.

The finality of it stopped her hand and she sipped her tea, pondering the matter. Despite everything, she *was* curious to take a peep. Alec had always been so precious about his work, so superstitious about not letting anyone read a single paragraph until he was completely satisfied with what he'd written. She didn't even know what this book was about.

Well, she thought. Only one way to find out.

She set her teacup back on its saucer, then picked up the first page, took a deep breath and began reading. *Chapter One . . .*

Alec's books were all thrillers along a similar theme. He had his world-weary Belfast-born detective, Jim Malone: a maverick chain-smoking gumshoe, engaged in a running battle with the more traditionally minded detective superintendent, although Jim's quick wits and magpie-like brain always managed to solve the crime and bring about justice by the closing chapters.

Alec and Jim were like brothers, he used to say when he appeared at festivals or did broadcast interviews. Jim was like the dark side of Alec, he explained, who said and did all the things that he, Alec, was too fearful or socially responsible to dare do himself. 'This way I get the best of both worlds,' he would say, smiling his charming smile. (Olivia could picture him now, leaning forward confidentially, eyes twinkling, giving the impression it was the first time he'd ever admitted this information to anyone.) 'I stick by the rules and toe the line, yet I can indulge this other side of my personality and allow Jim to get into all kinds of trouble, so I don't have to.'

Olivia gave a small snort of derision, remembering this now. How he'd had the front to say, many times over, that he had stuck by the rules and toed the line, she'd never know, when he had his mistress and son tucked secretly away in Devon. Maybe he was more like Jim than he'd cared to admit.

She soon became engrossed in the novel. The plot centred around a shady Russian oligarch whose money had come from human trafficking. Two young women had been found dead and the net was starting to close around the prime suspect. What interested Olivia more, though, was the sub-plot, which described Jim cheating on his long-standing (long-suffering, more like) wife Margaret, with a younger woman, Katherine.

As Olivia read on, she no longer heard the sounds of the café around her – the tinkling of the bell as new customers came in, the hiss and gush of the coffee machine, the chatter of other women on nearby tables. She was deeply in Malone's world now: trudging through rainy streets in search of the next clue, meeting Katherine in dingy bars and then slinking home to Margaret, sick with guilt as he lied to her about where he'd been. Her breathing almost stopped as she got to the part where Malone berated himself for his own weakness. Margaret was the best and most loyal woman alive, after all, Jim reasoned. She had stood by him through the ups and downs of his career. She understood him like no other person on earth! So why – why – was he risking it all for this younger woman, who had bewitched him with her youth and beauty? What was wrong with him that he couldn't be satisfied with his wife? How he hated himself at times!

Olivia's hands shook as she turned the pages. Previously Jim Malone had never been one to indulge in such soul-searching. Was this Alec on paper, spilling his guts about his divided loyalties? And how would Jim – and Alec – resolve the dilemma?

She munched through a toasted sandwich at midday and ordered another pot of tea as she read on, becoming impatient with the Russian oligarch plot, uninterested in the poor dead women, obsessed only with Jim Malone's love life. And then, on page two hundred and twenty, it was Jim's birthday and he had an epiphany. Margaret brought him breakfast in bed (she did the best ever Eggs Benedict, apparently; at least Jim appreciated her for that much) then surprised him with tickets to see the London Philharmonic Orchestra at the Royal Festival Hall that evening. In short, she was the thoughtful, loving wife she'd always been. (*Quite*, Olivia thought dryly, wondering where this was going.)

Katherine, meanwhile, seemed to have forgotten it was

Jim's birthday altogether. The only thing he received from her was an emailed photo of a positive pregnancy test. *And Jim felt a rushing sensation of doom*, Olivia read, *like a condemned man hearing the judge read aloud his punishment.*

Olivia dropped the manuscript as if the pages were red-hot and sat back in her chair, only just remembering to breathe. Of course, Jim was a fictional character, this wasn't an autobiography, but it was impossible not to interpret his reaction as that of her husband. Had Alec felt the same way, that Katie's pregnancy test had trapped him into a relationship? Was this whole book some kind of coded message to her, and to Katie? Surely he wouldn't have been so cruel. Surely he wouldn't have been that crass?

As the pages began to dwindle to a close, the paragraphs became scrappier, the sentences crafted with less care. At the end, Alec had left a series of notes to himself, a kind of 'thinking aloud' in print.

Katherine loses the baby – Jim's secret relief. They split up and he returns to Margaret, feeling he just made a lucky escape. Jim's guilt drives him to – ?? How can he make it up to M?? Holiday somewhere romantic – Italy? South of France?

Olivia dizzily remembered Alec making a similar suggestion to her shortly before the heart attack. 'We should go away together later this year,' he'd said. 'Just the two of us, somewhere sunny and romantic, a proper holiday. What do you think? We could go to Italy, perhaps. The south of France . . .'

The room seemed to be spinning around her. What did all of this mean? Had he been planning to leave Katherine – Katie, rather? Was the holiday suggestion prompted by guilt, as it had been for Jim?

She stared blindly at the paper, her heart gradually returning to its normal pace. Well, one thing was for sure, she realized, there was absolutely no way she could send this book to Eleanor at the publishing house. Have the literary reviewers and wider book-reading population speculate on just how much of the novel was based on real life, picking over her marriage with a gossipy eye? Certainly not. Some things had to remain private, and that was that.

Then again, she realized in the next moment, Jim had chosen Margaret, ultimately, hadn't he? Jim had *loved* Margaret, while Katherine had been a passing dalliance, one he was pleased to be rid of. Perhaps there was some crumb of comfort to be had from this.

For a few quiet moments, she sat and absorbed this interpretation and its wider implications. *So I win*, she thought. *In that case, I win, Katie.*

But the victory felt hollow, as if it wasn't much of a victory after all.

'Can I get you anything else?' the henna-haired waitress

asked, appearing at the table and picking up the empty teapot and milk jug.

Olivia shook her head. It was almost two o'clock and she still had her other 'important thing' to do. 'No, thank you,' she said. Then she stuffed the manuscript back in her bag and headed out to the car, her mind still turning.

Olivia had never actually been to Katie's house before but they had her address for Christmas cards, and she knew vaguely where the street was. Thinking of Alec sidling up this same street to sneak a visit to his other family left a nasty taste in her mouth. Jim going behind Margaret's back. Alec and Katie. Would she have guessed anyway, reading the novel, if she hadn't already found out?

No, she decided. Olivia had always been too trusting; she'd believed everything he'd ever told her. Some might say that was her downfall, of course – but in hindsight, she was glad she'd lived her life that way. Imagine how exhausting it must be to mistrust your husband, to check up on his every night away, to drive yourself mad, wondering how many hearts he was shattering around the country while you weren't looking.

She had loved him. Why would she have doubted his word? That approach to marriage only led to misery, she was certain.

Still. Here she was now, about to confront Alec's long-standing mistress, which was not exactly a situation that arose out of wedded bliss either.

Her nerve failed her as Katie's house came into view, down at the end of the street. She recognized Katie's car outside, a small red Fiat, and noticed that the front door needed painting, and the garden needed weeding. (Had Alec ever helped out around the place? she wondered wretchedly. He wasn't the most handy of men – he'd rather pay someone else to fix things and decorate – but he might have shown willing with the odd job now and then, she supposed.)

Don't think about that now, she ordered herself. *Just do what you came to do, then leave.*

'Oh,' said Katie when she answered the door to Olivia a few minutes later. A whole series of emotions flashed across her face – shock, anguish, apprehension, before she finally settled on defensiveness. She folded her arms across her chest and leaned against the jamb, subconsciously – or maybe deliberately – blocking the entrance. 'Hello.'

'Hello,' Olivia replied, trying to keep her composure. 'I was wondering if we could talk. Is now a good time?'

Katie glanced over her shoulder and Olivia could hear the sound of boys' laughter floating out from one of the rooms. 'Sure,' Katie said, after a moment. 'Come in. We can sit out in the garden, away from the rabble. It's my day off work today,' she added unnecessarily, as she led Olivia down the narrow hallway and into a small pristine kitchen at the end. 'I feel obliged to have everyone else's kids here, when I'm not working, because so many mums look after Leo for me on the other days.' She was babbling and must have realized it, because she pulled herself up short and gave a quick, awkward smile that lasted a whole two seconds. 'Sorry. You don't need to know that. Can I get you a drink of something?'

Katie poured them both tall glasses of elderflower cordial and they ventured out to the garden, where a bench stood under a cool, shady canopy of scrambling passionflower, its exotic white and purple flowers humming with bees.

'This is nice,' Olivia said politely, casting a professional eye around the small garden as Katie dragged over a patio table for their drinks. There were hollyhocks and sunflowers, bright orange Californian poppies, and a glorious sprawl of rudbeckias, their golden faces upturned to the sky. She'd missed spending time in gardens, she thought, with a sudden pang for her neglected flower beds at Shell Cottage and home, not to mention her work back in London. Her two beleaguered members of staff had shouldered the entire workload since Alec's death, she remembered guiltily. She would make it up to them, she vowed, planning to get stuck in again just as soon as she was back. By then, of course, it would all be about the weeding and dead-heading, and thinking ahead to brown paper bags full of crackling bulbs, hardy annual seeds to choose and plant, staking all those overblown cosmos and dahlias and . . .

First things first, though. She'd come here for a reason and now Katie was sitting and looking expectantly at her, and she had to get started.

'I just wanted to talk to you,' she said. 'To make some kind of truce. I've come to terms with – ' she gestured mutely at both Katie and the house, words not seeming sufficient – 'with . . . what happened. I realize that what's done is done, there's no use crying over spilt milk, and all those other insufferable clichés. You and I, we've both had Alec's children, we both loved him. We're bound together now, like it or not, so at the very least we should be civil to one another.'

By the look of relief on Katie's face, she had clearly been expecting Olivia to put up more of a fight, start shouting at her again, probably. 'Yes,' she said earnestly. 'And . . . look, I'm sorry. He was your husband. I should never have got involved in the first place, it was wrong of me, I was swept away. Selfish.' Her mouth twisted, defensiveness creeping back in. 'But then, like I said to Robert, of course I'm not *that* sorry, because I wouldn't have had Leo otherwise. And he's the best thing that ever happened to me.'

Olivia softened. She had always liked Katie, after all. 'Of course he is,' she said. 'I understand that.'

Katie hung her head, looking down at her lap. (Such lovely brown legs she had, Olivia thought with a stab of envy. No wonder Alec had been tempted by a younger model.) 'For what it's worth,' Katie went on in a low voice, 'he always did love you more. I know he did. I'm not just saying it to make you feel better, but I knew all along he was never going to leave you for me, or anything. That was never an option.' They both watched a red admiral butterfly as it fluttered past, alighting on the sprawling buddleia that had elbowed its way over the fence from next door. 'He felt bad for cheating on you,' she continued, sounding sad. 'At times he said he loathed himself for being so weak.'

The irony wasn't lost on Olivia. Hadn't she just sat and read this entire story in the tea room, from Jim Malone's point of view? The guilt, the self-loathing, the conflict of loyalties?

'That must have been nice for you,' she said dryly.

Katie looked up anxiously, still wary that she might be under attack, but gave a rueful smile when she realized Olivia was being sarcastic. 'I loved him,' she replied simply. 'I was willing to take being second best if it meant I could still . . . you know. Be with him.'

Olivia nodded. She did know. Alec had always made a room feel brighter, an occasion more fun. If her and Katie's roles had been reversed, she might well have settled for being second best herself. He was just that kind of man you wanted in your life, the kind of man who lent you an added lustre simply by being beside him. 'It was hard not to love him,' she conceded. 'Impossible, probably.'

Katie nodded, eyes sad. 'Yes.'

There was a pause while they both sank into memories. Happy times. Laughter. Then Olivia gave herself a shake and said with her usual briskness, 'Look. We're never going to be the best of friends but we can put aside our differences, can't we? Alec would have wanted his children to know each other and stay in touch. So . . .' She took a deep breath. 'So I was wondering. Our holiday's almost over and we always have a big family barbecue on the last evening. Maybe . . . Maybe you and Leo could join us this time?'

Katie's mouth quivered. 'I'd like that,' she said, clearly trying to hold her emotions in check. 'I'd really like that. Thank you, Olivia. We'll be there.'

'Right,' Olivia said, unsure whether to feel pleased or trepidatious. The wife and the mistress, their children together. Would it ever stop feeling so awkward? Probably not, but she knew they had to try. They had to make an effort, like it or not. 'Well, in that case, we'll see you both there,' she said, then paused. 'I'm glad we've talked,' she added, rather in a rush. 'I have been dreading this conversation, I have to say.'

'Me too,' Katie said.

They looked at each other with new-found understanding. 'But we're grown women, aren't we?' Olivia went on. 'We're experts at dealing with difficult things that come our way – including extraordinary men. And we can go about this with our dignity intact.' There was a brief moment where Olivia imagined they were both remembering that ugly shrieking scene in her kitchen, where there had not been a shred of dignity to be had, by her in particular. That was the past, though, and they were moving on. They could airbrush the worst moments out of their collective history, she decided, saying goodbye and walking away from the house with a little wave.

There, she thought. *There, Olivia. You did it.*

And now she felt positively triumphant for having dredged up her bravery in order to confront the woman who had been her rival, the woman she'd have been well within her rights to consider an enemy for life. But no, Olivia had risen above; she'd been a better person. So that was two difficult things achieved in the space of a day. Just wait until she told Gloria!

She got back into her car feeling as if she'd just come through a long dark tunnel and out into sunshine on the other side. Even better, her next task was going to be a truly joyful one: baking cakes with her granddaughter. She started the engine and drove away without looking back. There might even be some more singing, she thought to herself with a smile.

Chapter Forty-Four

Libby had had a really good day. After breakfast, she'd made a daisy chain out of twenty-two daisies from the lawn and even Molly had said it was cool and took a photo of it on her phone.

Then they had gone to Bigbury beach and they'd ridden over to the island on the big wobbly sea tractor, which was so exciting, she and Teddy had bounced up and down in their seats. 'It's like riding an elephant,' Mum had said, laughing. They'd had a picnic on the beach – egg sandwiches, which tasted really yummy if you pushed in bits of salt and vinegar crisps ('Poo!' said Teddy, wrinkling his nose), flaky sausage rolls from the bakery and round red apples.

And then, best of all, they'd come home to find Granny in the kitchen, wearing her apron and getting out the cake-making ingredients. Teddy had wanted to help too but Granny had said, sorry, darling, but she was going to bake just with Libby today, they could do something nice together the next day – and Libby had felt all fizzly inside with happiness that Granny had remembered.

They weighed and mixed, they sieved and whisked, they set out the paper cake cases in trays and Granny let Libby spoon in the mixture, dollop by dollop. Then, while the cakes were baking in the oven, Libby reached into her shorts pocket, remembering something she'd put there earlier.

Her cheer-up-Granny plan wasn't really necessary any more, she thought, glancing over at her grandmother, who was humming to herself as she scrubbed the mixing bowl and wooden spoons at the sink. Granny seemed to have made herself happy again all by herself, without Libby's help. Still, earlier that day, Libby had thought of the perfect present to give her grandmother, and now seemed like the right time.

'I've got something for you,' she said, hiding the perfect present in her fist and holding it out. 'Here.'

'Whatever could it be in there?' Granny said and peered at Libby's folded-up fingers. 'Let me guess . . . A lovely new spade for the garden?'

'No,' Libby giggled.

'A beautiful red dress and some high heels, so I can go dancing?'

'No!' Libby gurgled.

'Oh, you haven't gone and splashed out on a snazzy silver sports car when it's not even my birthday?' Granny guessed.

Libby laughed. 'No,' she said. 'It's . . .' She opened her hand to reveal the small brown pip on her palm. 'It's a new apple tree for the garden. Well. Not yet. But one day.'

Libby had expected Granny to smile but instead her mouth went all wonky and her chin gave a wobble. 'Oh, darling,' Granny said in a chokey sort of voice, and she gave Libby such a sudden, fierce hug that Libby almost dropped the apple pip. 'Oh, my darling girl. That is the best and nicest present ever. Will you help me plant it when the cakes are out? Shall we do it together?'

'Yes,' Libby said shyly, from the depths of the enormous perfumed Granny hug. It felt lovely in there: squishy and safe and warm. She had forgotten how much she had missed Granny hugs. They were awesome. 'Yes please.'

Chapter Forty-Five

Harriet shared the double bed with Molly for a second night and they both slept deeply. Neither of them stirred until it was nine thirty the following morning, when Robert came creeping into the room laden with a tray of coffee and pastries, and a hot chocolate for Molly.

'Morning,' he said quietly, setting the tray down on the bedside table next to Harriet.

She opened her eyes and blinked, taking a few seconds to jigsaw together the pieces of what was happening. Robert. Breakfast. Last night. The stupid non-existent book deal . . .

'Morning,' she said, rubbing her eyes and sitting up. Harriet always looked dreadful first thing: creased face, flat hair, general air of dishevelment. Having Robert wake her like this made her feel at an immediate disadvantage.

'Freya told me what happened,' he said. He looked pretty good for the hangover he must have, she thought, with a flash of irritation as she took in his freshly showered hair, and the mint-coloured T-shirt which brought out the green of his

eyes. 'About Molly, I mean.' He shook his head, words bursting indignantly out of him as if they'd been pent-up inside all
night. 'Jesus Christ, I couldn't believe it. Is she all right? Molly,
are you all right?'

Molly shifted slightly under the cover. 'She's fine,' she
muttered. 'A bit pissed off to be woken up so bloody early
but—'

'Language, Molls,' Harriet said automatically.

Robert was pacing up and down in agitation. 'I could
bloody kill him for this. I could punch his fucking face in.
Mr sodding Jamison, how dare—'

'Language, Robert,' Molly chided.

'Sorry. But . . . *shit*. I can't get my head around it. Thank
God you got there in time. Thank God everything's all right.'
He paused, mid-pace, to peer closer at Harriet. '*Are* you all
right?'

There was an angry part of Harriet that wanted to put a
hand on his chest and push him away, sneering, *What's it to
you, Robert? Like you're even allowed to ask me that any more,
when you've been lying to me for the last three months?*

But confusingly, there was also this other part of her that
just wanted to be folded into his arms, and to tell him gratefully that yes, she was all right now, but oh, it had been her
worst nightmare, the most horrible series of events . . .

She didn't do either. She felt paralysed by not knowing
how to respond. This was Robert, the man she'd loved and

aligned her life with – and yet, it wasn't the same Robert any more. This was Robert mark 2, the one that had revealed himself so shockingly as flawed and faulty. As the man who had lied and lied.

'I'm fine,' she mumbled, not looking at him.

'I'm so sorry I wasn't there,' he said, arms dangling helplessly by his sides. 'And I'm sorry about everything else too. I've done a lot of thinking since then.'

Molly pulled the pillow over her head. 'Too weird,' she groaned. 'Too awkward. Please don't start talking about feelings in front of me. I'm serious.'

Robert looked chastened. 'Sorry,' he said again. 'Of course. It's a conversation for me and your mum to have when – if – she wants to.' His eyes pleaded silently with her and Harriet felt her anger wavering before she turned her head resolutely away. *Don't look into those eyes*, she reminded herself. *Do not be swayed.*

'Harriet?' he prompted, waiting awkwardly for her reply.

I know he's been a bit of a jerk, Mum, but don't be too hard on him, Molly's voice piped up in her head. *He's just a bloke, remember.*

'Maybe later,' she mumbled, sipping her coffee. His gaze, when she could bring herself to meet it, was sad and repentant.

Well, and rightly so, she thought defensively, as he nodded and left the room, pulling the door shut behind him. Sad and repentant was no more than he deserved, and she was not about to start feeling sorry for him just because he gave good puppy-dog eyes and brought pastries. A husband shouldn't deceive his wife like that, end of story.

She grimaced, wishing she could follow her daughter's example and pull the pillow over her head. Instead she needed to think very hard about what she should say later on in this big serious chat they needed to have. She had to weigh up the best possible outcome for her and Molly – and, not to put too fine a point on it, whether that involved Robert or not.

Right now, though, she couldn't face any major decisions. First things first – there was a large sticky Danish pastry within reach, and a bloody good cup of coffee. Food first, love life later, she told herself. When in doubt, eat.

They needed a nice day today – a fun, happy, holiday-ish day, after the trauma and shouting of yesterday. They definitely needed to get away from Robert and his kicked-puppy eyes too, so that she could clear her head and think straight. And so after breakfast, Harriet packed up a picnic and then she and Molly drove out to a stable yard near Tavistock for a lovely long hack across the moors. There was something about jolting along on horseback on a summer's day, the wind in your hair, the land unrolling green and wild before you, not to mention laughing childishly with your daughter about your horse's enormous genitalia, that somehow made the world seem bearable again. It would be all right, she told herself. She would make sure of it.

Later that afternoon, they arrived back at Shell Cottage, aching but energized, to be greeted by a delicious smell of baking from the kitchen and a scene of utter chaos in the garden. Robert was struggling manfully with assorted camping equipment strewn across the lawn, while the children were getting underfoot and generally making his life ten times harder. The boys were having sword fights with tent pegs and Libby appeared to be plaiting some of the guy ropes in a particularly unhelpful way.

'What's going on? Are you moving out?' Harriet asked Robert. She was joking – well, pretty much – but her voice clearly didn't sound jokey because both he and Molly turned and looked at her doubtfully.

'Not quite,' Robert replied. 'Freya and Vic are spending tonight away together. I said I'd babysit. Then Dex suggested a camp-out, and the next thing I knew . . .' He spread his hands, pulling a comic expression. 'Here we are. We're going to forage for our dinner out here and everything. That's all right with you lot, isn't it? Nice juicy slug on the barbecue? A few crunchy spiders if you're lucky.'

Libby stopped dead. 'You *are* joking, aren't you, Uncle Rob? I'm not eating a slug.'

'I will!' Teddy said immediately.

'Of course he's joking,' Dexter said, although there was definitely less of his usual bravado on display as he looked at his uncle. 'Aren't you?'

'Oh, am I? We'll see,' Robert said airily, resuming his tent assembly.

'Slug attack!' Teddy yelled, launching himself at his brother with a blood-curdling war cry and a tent peg that went perilously close to Dexter's windpipe. Robert, of course, didn't notice anything as he slotted two silver rods together, peered at them with a frown, then pulled them apart again, and it was left to Harriet to step in as the voice of responsibility.

'Er, guys, be careful, all right?' she warned. 'I don't want your mum and dad coming back in the morning to discover there have been some gruesome tent peg injuries.'

Robert's head popped up at once. 'Oi! Put those down. I told you five minutes ago to leave them alone. Why don't you go and find some sleeping bags? Bring down your pillows too and your teddy collection, Dex.'

Libby giggled and Dexter looked affronted as they vanished. Molly knelt down and examined some of the poles with an authoritative air. 'Robert, you've got the wrong bits here,' she told him. 'When I did Duke of Edinburgh, we had tents just like this so I know exactly how it should all go. Now, where's the main pole?'

Harriet felt like a spare part as her daughter and Robert

bent their heads over the pile of tent components so she slipped away into the kitchen where Olivia was pouring hot water into a teapot. 'Harriet! There you are. I was just making tea, would you like some?'

There was something different about her mother-in-law, Harriet noticed as she sat at the table and accepted a cup of tea, and an elaborately decorated fairy cake with a half a ton of acid-bright sprinkles wedged into buttercream icing. 'Thank you,' she said. 'I hear Freya and Vic have taken off for the night. Have they gone anywhere nice?'

'They're staying at a hotel in Chillington. I think they . . .' She hesitated. 'I think they've had a difficult time recently. Haven't we all?'

Harriet gave a small smile. Hadn't they all indeed? 'We have rather been through the mill this summer,' she agreed. 'How are you feeling now?' She held her breath, unused to asking her mother-in-law directly personal questions. There was a regal air about Olivia that Harriet had always found kind of intimidating; it was like asking the queen how she was doing. But today she seemed willing to talk.

'I'm all right, actually, thank you. I wasn't sure I'd ever hear myself say those words again, but . . .' She shrugged. 'I'm getting there, taking it day by day. And of course, I have plenty left to live for. Having you all around me this summer has helped enormously in reminding me of that.' Her eyes, still so clear and luminous despite her age, became thoughtful. 'It's not an easy business, though, is it, being a wife? As you know yourself. These Tarrant men are wont to giving us nasty surprises now and then.'

Harriet nodded. 'That's one way of putting it.'

'I'm very sorry, my dear. That Robert chose to do such a thing, I mean. To deceive all of us in such an astonishing way must have been particularly hard on you.' She paused, sipping her tea. 'Of course, it's none of my business and I am absolutely not taking sides, but I know he feels very badly about it. A lie that spiralled out of hand.'

'Yes.' And the next lie, and the next lie, and the next. The party and the lunches and the trip to America – so many spirals, she had quite lost count. Still, bitching about a man to his mum was never going to help things, fact.

Neither of them spoke for a moment. 'I went to see Katie today,' Olivia said, out of the blue.

'Wow. Gosh, Olivia. That was brave,' Harriet replied, feeling a new respect for her mother-in-law. 'What did she say? How did it go?'

'I think we were both surprised by how . . . how unremarkable it was,' Olivia replied. 'We were civil, we acknowledged each other as women loved by the same man; we somehow managed not to come to blows over him.' She picked up a fairy cake and turned it upside down, ridding it of at least fifty sprinkles that rained into her tea plate. 'I invited her and Leo here for the barbecue on Friday night.'

Harriet's mouth fell open. 'Wow,' she said again. 'Goodness. How incredibly magnanimous of you.' If Robert had had a secret affair and a love child, she wasn't sure she'd be quite so generous-spirited in the circumstances. Once when Simon's bit on the side had dared call him on the landline, Harriet had hurled abuse into the receiver, screeching like a fishwife on steroids until she was pink in the face. Invite the other woman to a barbecue? She would have been more likely to push her face straight into the hot coals.

Olivia looked pleased by the remark. 'Yes, I thought so too,' she said. 'It's taken me this long to be able to turn the other cheek, though. At the start of the holiday, I was ready to go for her with my claws out.' She stretched out her long elegant fingers and they both studied them for a moment. 'Anyway, the point I'm edging towards is that I hadn't realized until then how good it was going to feel forgiving her. How much lighter I felt afterwards.' She tilted her head, considering her words. 'It's not as if I don't care about what happened. I do. I thought the world had ended for a while. But what good does being angry do, really? It only gives you wrinkles at the end of the day, and goodness knows I've enough of those already.'

'Oh, Olivia, stop right there. You are the most unwrinkled, beautiful, elegant—'

Olivia batted away the compliments. 'I can live with my wrinkles,' she said. 'But I don't want to live the rest of my life with bitterness, looking back and feeling consumed by fury. I want to look forward. What's done is done. She apologized, I accepted, that's that.'

Harriet pursed her lips. She knew what her mother-in-law was hinting at. But Alec was dead, and therefore it was impossible for him to reoffend. Robert, meanwhile, was very much alive, although possibly newly maimed, if the clatter of metal and volley of swearing from the garden was anything to go by. If she did forgive Robert, as she knew Olivia was urging her to do, then what was to stop him going and doing it all over again, some other lie, some other betrayal? Wouldn't it be safer just to cut her ties and walk away?

Chapter Forty-Six

Victor had definitely scored some major brownie points today, Freya thought as she pushed open the door and stepped into their bedroom. Their bedroom, by the way, that just so happened to be in the swankiest and most gorgeous hotel she had ever set foot in. The bed was huge, its frame made from chunky slabs of honey-coloured wood. There was a roll-top bath and a walk-in shower in the bathroom, plus luxury toiletries and thick fluffy dressing gowns. There were French windows that opened onto a small wrought-iron balcony overlooking the sea. In short, she reckoned she could pretty much live in this room quite happily for some considerable time without feeling the need to re-engage with the rest of the world. 'Whoa,' she breathed, dropping her overnight bag to the floor. 'This is gorgeous, Vic. Thank you.'

Victor put his arm around her. 'You deserve it,' he said. 'I'm sorry I haven't been a very good husband lately. This is me trying to make it up to you. This is me opening my eyes and realizing what's been right in front of me the whole time.' He held her tight against him. 'I'm sorry.'

'Oh, Vic.' She felt herself go limp against him, grateful for his solidity. How good it was to lean on someone and let them take your weight. It made her realize just how rigidly she'd been holding herself upright all this time. *Must cope. Must keep going. Must not show weakness.* Well, bugger that for a waste of time. That plan had been about as successful as the square wheel. 'I'm not sure I've been the best wife either,' she said shakily. 'Or the best mum. Or daughter. Or GP.'

He stroked her hair, smoothing it back from her face. 'You're too hard on yourself, love,' he said. 'Did nobody ever tell you that? You're doing fine. Everyone else thinks you're doing an amazing job of all those things.'

She had found herself dreaming of her midnight plunge into the sea on a few occasions lately – her brain flashing up vivid snatches of memory that frightened her every time: the blackness of the water, the seabed vanishing beneath her feet, the weight of her clothes dragging her down. There had been a single terrible moment when she had just wanted to sink below the surface, let the sea take her down, allow the water to pour into her lungs . . . until a second later she'd felt Vic's strong hands beneath her armpits and he'd hauled her unceremoniously onto the sand. It wasn't what she would call 'doing fine', personally.

'Freya? I'm serious. You've had a hard time. Anyone would

have struggled. And if I hadn't had my own head rammed up my arse recently, I would have noticed and been there for you earlier. If you're going to blame anyone, you can blame me, not you. All right?'

Her head was still pressed against his shoulder. 'All right.'

She felt his grip tighten. 'You and the children are what matters most. You are my top priorities, okay? And from now on, I'm going to pay more attention to you all,' he said gruffly. 'That's a promise, Freya. We'll get a decent babysitter sorted so that we can go out together more as a couple. We'll get a cleaner too, so you don't end up doing it all. Hell, let's hire in a full set of staff – chauffeur, butler, the works – while we're at it.'

She laughed. 'Sounds good to me.'

'And Robert's offered to have the kids for a weekend soon – brave, foolish man – so that we can go away somewhere too, just the two of us.' He let go and looked into her eyes. 'I want to make this work, Freya. I want us to get back to where we used to be. Having a laugh. Spending proper time together. Sneaking off to posh hotels like this one . . .'

'Me too,' she said with a watery smile. 'Absolutely.' She thought of all the nights she'd spent curled up on her own in the living room, seeing off a bottle of red wine while she waited for him to come home. All the times she'd put the children to bed alone, feeling resentful, while he was at some gala evening or other being lauded yet again for his heroics.

Being a hero was just as much about putting out the bins and reading the children a bedtime story in Freya's eyes. 'And I'm going to stop bottling things up,' she added. 'It's taken me this long to realize that competitive coping is not remotely noble or impressive – it's actually just a bit tragic and the shortcut to a nervous breakdown.' She tried to laugh to show that she was only joking but it was difficult with the lump in her throat.

'Good call,' he said, squeezing her hand. 'The other thing is, I'm going to knock the drink on the head too. We'll keep the house dry for a while, be teetotallers together. Less temptation for you, less of a beer gut for me.'

'Oh, Vic.' He so didn't have a beer gut. This was all for her benefit and she knew it. The moment they had walked into this room, she'd thought with a pang of how, had things been different, they'd have been popping open champagne and getting sozzled together at this point. She was touched that he was willing to make such a sacrifice. 'That's so lovely of you. Really supportive. Are you sure?'

'One hundred per cent. It's the least I can do. We're a team, aren't we?'

'We are most definitely a team.' God, she loved him for this. She absolutely loved him. It was as if the fog had lifted, and they'd remembered who they were again – Freya and Victor, the very same people who'd fallen in love at a French pizzeria all those years ago. A good team.

'But in the meantime,' he went on, 'here we are, just the two of us, all alone.' He grinned, the dimple flashing in his left cheek, and his hand slid lower down her back, to rest on her bottom. 'I don't suppose you've got any . . . ideas . . . about how we might fill our time away, have you?'

She grinned back, happier than she had been all summer, and tucked a thumb into the back pocket of his jeans. 'It's funny you should ask me that because I do have one or two, now you mention it . . .' She leaned up to kiss him full on the mouth and then their hands were all over each other's bodies and the very posh bedroom was suddenly filled with flying clothes and laughter. They collapsed together onto the enormous bed with a deliciously wanton sense of abandon, reminding Freya of those first heady days back in France.

Mmm-mmm, she thought joyfully, as he tossed her knickers over his shoulder. Now this was *exactly* what holidays were all about . . .

Chapter Forty-Seven

Back at Shell Cottage, there was something of a carnival atmosphere – or a festival, even – with the three tents now standing upright in the garden. Teddy was so excited about camping out that he was capering about in pyjamas already, even though they'd only just had dinner, and usually you had to practically crowbar him up to bed of an evening. He and Libby had stuffed their tent full of blankets and pillows, soft toys and cushions, as well as an elaborate trap to catch any bears that happened to be strolling by. Meanwhile, Dexter was red-faced and exuberant following three energetic badminton matches with Robert, and was demanding more, despite Robert lying on the grass with the racquet on his face, pretending to be dead from exhaustion.

He *was* a good man, Harriet thought, watching through the kitchen window as he lay there, putting up with Libby arranging the shuttlecocks in a pattern on his legs for at least twenty seconds before leaping up and roaring in pretend rage, sending her racing away shrieking. He was a nice, funny, good man. But . . .

She sighed, turning away to distract herself with the washing-up, rather than thinking too hard about the 'but'. Did every man have to have a 'but'? Was that part of the deal when you married someone? To be fair, she probably had a few herself.

Well, I do love Harriet but she's a bloody nightmare first thing in the morning, she imagined Robert saying to a marriage counsellor. True enough.

Harriet's great but she is the messiest woman ever to walk this earth. Well, yeah, okay, he'd have a point. She'd own up to that one too.

Harriet is a loyal wife but she does have a bad habit of flirting with handsome surfers ten years younger than her. She flushed, squirting in washing-up liquid and running the hot tap. All right, all right. Nobody was perfect, were they? Definitely not her. Not Robert either. Maybe everyone had their 'but' points. Maybe that was just part of being human.

She plunged her hands into the water and turned her attention to the lasagne dish from dinner, which had burned-on melted cheese encrusted around the edge. Sometimes it was easier not to think at all, she decided, submerging it beneath the suds and scrubbing with renewed vigour.

*

Robert was keeping his distance, that much was evident, politely waiting for her to decide she wanted to talk. *If* she wanted to talk, that was. In the meantime, Olivia had dabbed on some bright lipstick and gone off to meet Gloria – 'After all my good deeds today, I need a drink,' she had declared cheerfully. 'Don't wait up!' – and Molly had vanished up to the attic for a very intense Skype session with Chloe. (Or so Harriet hoped. It was all she could do not to go and spy through the keyhole in case her daughter had latched on to Inappropriate Man Numero Duo by now. Please, no. There were only so many new grey hairs a woman could acquire in one single summer holiday.)

Harriet sat and read a magazine for a while, then dried and put away all the washing-up, padded back to the living room, switched on the television and flicked through every single channel – rubbish, the lot of them – before switching it off again.

She poured herself a glass of wine and glanced out of the window to see that the children's tents were zipped shut, and that Robert was lying with his head sticking out of his, reading a book. Surely the children hadn't actually gone to sleep already? It was only just past eight o'clock.

She hesitated, her hand on a second wine glass, wondering whether or not to venture outside, whether or not she could face a conversation with him now. He must have sensed her watching, though, because in the next moment, he looked up and saw her at the window.

Busted. She felt she had no choice but to hold up the empty glass and wine bottle with a questioning expression, at which he put his thumb up and grinned, turning the book face down on the grass in a way that suggested he was done with reading for the time being.

Right. So it looked as if they were going to talk now, after all. Dramatic chords boomed in her head and she gave herself a quick pep talk. *Be strong. Be calm. No shouting in front of the children. No weakness in the face of sad-puppy eyes.*

Once outside, it quickly became apparent that the children were definitely not asleep. Harriet smiled to hear the hysterical whoops of mirth exploding from the far tent. 'What's going on in there, then?' she asked, sitting down cross-legged on the grass and passing Robert his wine.

Robert sat up, lifting his glass in mock salute. 'They're having their midnight feast now,' he explained, 'so they can brush their teeth again afterwards. Very sensible really. Dentists everywhere would approve.'

Harriet remembered similarly early 'midnight feasts' that Molly and her friends had had on sleepovers when they just couldn't hold out any longer. 'Sweet,' she said.

'Yeah. I am turning a blind eye to the fact that they sneaked the cake tin in there, by the way. I suspect there will be many rainbow sprinkles and crumbs in sleeping bags tonight, not to mention a few diabolical sugar hangovers in the morning.'

Harriet gave another brief smile, but allowed the conversation to peter out. Now that they were here, she was no longer sure what she wanted to say to him. The air was warm and soft, the golden-blue sky seeming to fold around them in a benevolent, protective way. She found herself wishing they didn't have to have any difficult conversations at all; that they could simply pretend it had never happened and be Harriet and Rob again. But his face had already lost its smile, his mouth was twisting in an awkward grimace and she could tell he was gearing up to apologize all over again.

She was done with apologies, she realized. There were only so many a person could bear to hear before they became downright irritating. 'What are you going to do now, then?' she asked, heading this one off at the pass.

The question took him by surprise. 'What do you mean?'

'I mean, job-wise. Now that the book isn't happening. Will you try again, or . . . ?'

He gave a hollow laugh. 'God, no. Fifty or so rejections is enough to put me straight on that front.'

There was a terrible despair in his face, genuine humiliation. Despite everything, she felt a stab of sympathy for him. 'Don't say that, Rob. I read some of it, remember. I thought it was good!'

'Yeah, well.' He grimaced. 'That's because you're a lot

kinder than all the editors and publishers who turned it down.' He laced his fingers together and cracked his knuckles. 'What I really want to do – don't laugh – is something sporty. Be a personal trainer, do a bit of kids' football coaching. I know it's not exactly highbrow, but—'

'But who gives a shit about highbrow?' she burst out. This, then, was the core of the whole problem – this stupid shame he seemed to feel about his career choices. 'Being a social worker isn't highbrow either but it's a good job. It helps people.' There was a small silence and she felt defensive all of a sudden. 'I mean, the money's not great and there are no fancy parties or glamorous working lunches, but . . .'

He winced. 'Yeah. It is a good job.'

'It's about doing what makes you feel happy, Rob. Doing what satisfies you here.' She banged a fist against her chest. 'It's really *not* about what's going to impress the rest of your family.'

'I know. I get that now.' He ran his fingers through the grass, eyes down. Sad puppy. Apologetic puppy. She wasn't going to let him get away that easily, though.

'Or me! You didn't have to try and impress me either. Because I was already impressed, Rob. Don't you see that? I was already impressed!'

He looked ashen-faced but didn't speak.

'I was impressed when you helped me with the power saw in our woodwork class. I was impressed when you took

448

Molly and her friends to see that awful teenybop band when I was ill. I was impressed when you worked around the clock at that dreadful cycle courier place, Rob, when we were saving up for our wedding!' Her voice had become so loud and high-pitched that the giggling from the children's tent suddenly ceased. 'That's what does it for me,' she said in a quieter tone, hands shaking on her wine glass. 'Kindness and thoughtfulness and hard work. Not you spinning off into some fantasy realm where you think you're famous!'

He recoiled as if she'd slapped him but then nodded with a certain grimness, tacitly acknowledging that he deserved every word. 'I never meant it to get so out of hand,' he mumbled. 'So . . . ridiculous.'

She looked at him. Really looked at him – this man, her husband – as she wondered what was best to do. After Simon, she hadn't been sure she could ever trust another man again, but when she met Robert, it seemed so easy, she was surprised to have doubted herself. So where did they go from here?

Two paths lay ahead of her in this moment. One, where she and Robert split up and she vowed to steer clear of men all over again. A lonely path, but a self-righteous one too. A path where she would never be hurt or lied to or made to feel an idiot again. She would be safe that way.

And then there was a second path, of course. A path where she and Robert started over. A less lonely path but a less certain one for that. She would have doubts, suspicions. It would take her a while before she could continue along the path without sidelong glances at Robert to check what he was up to.

But what good does being angry do, really? It only gives you wrinkles at the end of the day. I don't want to live the rest of my life with bitterness, Olivia had said that afternoon.

Neither did Harriet. 'A sports coach would be cool,' she found herself saying, as if the last part of their conversation hadn't just happened. 'And you'd be a great personal trainer. Think of all those new-year's-resolution-ers in January who'll be desperate to get in shape.'

He looked up, recognizing an olive branch when he saw one. 'I think I'd enjoy it,' he said cautiously.

'I know you'd enjoy it.' She finished her glass of wine and set it down on the grass. Olivia was right, she thought. Forgiveness – even the first tiny step towards forgiveness – left you feeling a whole lot better. They could make this work. She indicated his tent with a tilt of her head. 'So . . . is there room for two in that thing or what?'

His eyes widened, full of hope. 'Are you saying . . . ?'

'I'm saying, you'll have to budge up in there, Bear Grylls. Mrs Grylls here fancies a night under canvas, too. Is that all right?'

The look on his face made it quite clear that yes, this was very much all right.

Chapter Forty-Eight

A few days later, it was the end of the holiday and time for the traditional last-evening party. Bunting and fairy lights were strung around the garden, the barbecue was fired up and the fridge groaned with salads and meat and bottles of champagne. Despite the chatter and the jollity, the spectre of Alec still loomed large, with all of them fondly remembering how he'd loved this end-of-holiday last hurrah. He'd always taken charge, issuing orders from his position at the barbecue, bellowing for more champagne, taking great joy in complaining about whichever music his children or grandchildren had put on ('What a racket!') and then leading the toasts when everyone was sated. 'To the holiday! To my splendid wife! To my magnificent offspring! To *their* marvellous offspring! To the weather! To the wine! To our health! . . .' He would go on all night, given half a chance, thinking up one thing after another for which they should give thanks and celebrate.

And tonight they would have to do it all without him – and

tomorrow night, and the night after that, and all the nights to come, of course.

It wasn't so long ago that this thought had gripped Olivia in a state of fearful paralysis – the sheer terror that came from being left a widow. And yes, of course, there were still moments when she felt his loss most keenly, and looked ahead towards Christmas and the winter, for instance, with a certain amount of trepidation. Yet this summer had proved to her that it was possible not only to survive when the worst happened, but to smile again, laugh again, take your clothes off and cavort in the sea if you felt like it.

It had also reminded her that life went on – and that you could start again. Two days earlier, she and Libby had filled a flowerpot with compost and then carefully pushed in the apple pip. 'Once it's big enough, we'll decide where to plant it out in the garden,' Olivia said, filling the watering can, 'and with a bit of luck, it'll still be producing apples when you're coming here with *your* children.' The flowerpot on the sunny kitchen windowsill was a symbol of that hoped-for longevity. New life to come. Every time she looked at it, she felt optimistic.

The pip-planting wasn't the only positive thing she'd done recently. She had gone out with Gloria a few nights ago, and found herself dancing to a live band in The Hope and Anchor. Dancing like a teenager, no less, as if she didn't have a care in the world! She had even found herself laughingly telling Mitch that she would quite like a tattoo of a scallop shell, just as soon as she plucked up enough courage. 'Good for you, girl!' he'd cried, those blue eyes twinkling.

Girl. It had been a long time since anyone had called her that. It felt wonderful, she thought with a smile. Really wonderful.

Katie and Leo had arrived for the barbecue, both looking slightly anxious as they handed over a Tupperware container of home-grown plump strawberries and a bottle of cava. Olivia couldn't help a catch of breath in her throat as Katie said hello to everyone and introduced Leo, but the awkwardness soon passed, and she saw both Robert and Freya making an extra effort to speak to her and find ways to engage Leo. He was their half-brother, after all. Part of the family. This was how it would be from now on.

'You okay there, love?' said Gloria in Olivia's ear, arriving with a huge Victoria sponge crammed with whipped cream and raspberry jam.

Olivia smiled gratefully. 'I think so,' she replied. 'I can live with it, anyway.'

Now that all the guests were here, the barbecue could get under way, tended lovingly by Robert and Freya, who had stepped into their father's usual position as Guarder of the Meat Tongs and Chief Sizzler of the Sausages. Meanwhile, Harriet and Katie were mixing up cocktails, Molly was teaching Libby and Teddy a series of dance moves, and Victor had set up the telescope to show Dexter and Leo some of the constellations that were just appearing in the sky above.

Yes, thought Olivia, as she clinked a glass of champagne with Gloria, this *was* okay. They had made it through a difficult summer together, and everyone was just about in one piece. What was more, she was planning to stay on a few extra days after everyone had left, to enjoy the peace and beauty all by herself. Well, she corrected herself, not strictly by herself. She and Gloria had already made plans for a return visit to their secret cove and she was going to take the plunge and ask Mitch round for dinner one evening, too. And why not? She was single these days, after all – and didn't everyone say that a bit of what you fancy did you good?

Later on, when everyone had eaten their fill and most of the adults were pleasantly drunk (Freya was managing fine on sparkling water, Olivia noticed, feeling proud of her determined daughter), Robert surprised them all by producing a white paper lantern and some marker pens. 'It's a Chinese lantern,' he said. 'One of those that you set alight and let drift away into the night. I thought we could each write down a few words about Dad, or this summer, or anything at all, then light it together.'

'What a gorgeous idea,' Freya said. 'Kids, did you hear what Uncle Robert said? Think of a nice message to write on the lantern. Maybe about Grandad, or something really lovely we've done together.'

The family leaned around the picnic table, taking it in turns to compose their sentences.

Goodbye Dad. Thanks for all the summers. Robert

Miss you, Dad, wrote Freya. *PS New barbecue chiefs are in town. Hope we did you proud!*

Harriet, after a glance across at her husband, wrote, *All you need is love.*

Gloria looked surprised to be passed the pen but duly scrawled, *I thought your books were cracking – thanks, mate. PS Your wife is awesome.*

Bit by bit, the lantern filled up with messages. Katie – tactfully – just wrote her name and a kiss underneath. Leo drew a picture of the terrier puppy they were planning to bring home in a few weeks. *You so weren't a talamanca, Grandad!* Dexter wrote, much to the puzzlement of everyone except Freya and Victor, who rolled their eyes and laughed. *I likd roling down the hill*, Teddy wrote laboriously, his tongue poking out with the effort.

Libby, of course, couldn't resist one last joke.

Knock, knock, Grandad!

Who's there, Libby?

I map! ('Oh, *Libby*,' Freya said, seeing this. 'Honestly!')

I map who?

REALLY, GRANDAD???!!!!

And then it was Olivia's turn, and all of a sudden she had nothing left to say. She had yelled out her anger and hurt in the first week, she had sobbed out so much sadness and loneliness. Were there any last words still to voice?

Summer wasn't the same without you, Alec, she wrote eventually. *But we've all learned something from it. I hope you're smiling, wherever you are. Your Liv x PS I read the manuscript and I think I understand.*

She turned the lantern over so that nobody else could read her words and smiled brightly at the others. 'Done! Now, how do we light this thing, then, Robert?'

There was something about standing silently in the darkening garden, watching the glowing yellow lantern sail majestically up into the evening sky and out towards the sea, that felt completely magical, thought Freya, slipping her hand into Victor's. Even the children were hushed as the floating ball of fire became smaller and smaller until it was a tiny speck.

Standing there, her husband beside her, surrounded by the whole family, new additions and all, she felt a soft, velvety peace settling on her shoulders. The holiday was almost over. Summer would turn into autumn within a matter of weeks, and they'd be flung straight back into work, as well as the flurry and rush of a new term at school: homework, PE kits, packed lunches. She knew already how quickly the long sunny days on the beach would fade into distant memories. Here at Shell Cottage, life was easier, with fewer pressures to absorb. Once back at work, it might become more difficult to stay on the wagon, when her To-Do list spilled onto several pages, when Christmas shopping became an issue, when she began to panic about juggling homework supervision and carol concerts and nativity play costumes, and the rest of it. But next time, if it all got on top of her again, she would talk to Vic before everything got out of hand. She had learned that it was okay to say, 'I'm not coping very well,' to him or to her mum or even to Harriet, and the world wouldn't come crashing down as a result. Hopefully, this knowledge would make all the difference.

'Mum,' said Libby, sidling up to her just then. 'I've got a joke for you. A really, really good one. Knock, knock!'

And in the meantime, thought Freya, laughing and putting an arm around her daughter, she had Libby and Dex and Teddy to keep her on her toes. That was all anyone needed, really, wasn't it?

Once the Chinese lantern had drifted away into the darkness, Harriet realized that Olivia had vanished as well. Oh dear. Perhaps the lantern had been a step too far. It had made *her* feel like welling up, she could only imagine how emotional Olivia must have felt, after everything else she'd been through lately.

Just as she was about to murmur her concerns to Robert, though, Olivia reappeared out of the back door, clutching what looked like an armful of paper. Harriet nudged Robert and they both watched in surprise as Olivia marched over to the barbecue and heaved the pile of paper onto the smouldering coals.

'Oh!' Robert exclaimed. 'Mum, what are you . . . ?' He gaped, stricken. 'Is that Dad's manuscript?'

The tranquillity of the Chinese lantern's journey was forgotten as everyone whirled around to see Olivia squirting lighter fuel onto the barbecue, causing bright orange flames to flare up with an audible *woof*, licking greedily around the papers. 'Whoa!' Dexter cried. 'Granny's gone pyro on us!'

'I heard that, young man,' Olivia said, but there was a smile of satisfaction on her face. More than that, Harriet observed, she looked positively gleeful, standing there, prodding the burning paper with the barbecue tongs.

'Mum, is this such a good idea?' Freya asked, although it was already way too late to be posing such a question now. The paper was charring around the edges and scraps of ash flew up like soft grey snowflakes into the air, along with twisting plumes of smoke.

'Oh, I think it's a very good idea,' Olivia said, still busily prodding. 'The world doesn't need to read Alec's book about a wife and a mistress, do they? I don't want them to, anyway.'

Katie was standing in the shadows, her hands on Leo's shoulders. 'I don't want them to either,' she said, exchanging a glance of recognition with Olivia.

'There are some things which are best kept within a family,' Olivia said.

And amen to that, Harriet thought. This family had had its fair share of secrets in recent times – some that had festered and caused pain, admittedly – but this kind of secret was one she could endorse. Why create more discomfort when there was no need?

She looked across to where Robert had wandered over to talk to Leo, ruffling his hair and making him laugh about something, and she felt her heart swell. He had already found a couple of sports coach training programmes that he liked the sound of, one of which was based very near Riverdale, the school where Harriet worked. 'We could have sneaky lunch dates,' he had said. 'Catch the Tube home together every night.' She had not entirely forgiven him for the monstrous lies he had told – that would take a while – but she liked the thought of sneaky lunch dates and maybe even cheeky pub stops on the way home together. She was glad, too, that they were giving things another try, rebuilding trust one day at a time. That was all you could ask for in a relationship anyway, wasn't it? Nobody came with a lifetime guarantee that they wouldn't malfunction and go weird on you.

'I think we should have a toast,' she declared, feeling caught up in the moment. 'A toast to us all, and our memorable summer together.'

Olivia bestowed a smile upon her. 'To the Tarrants, and all those we love,' she said, holding up her glass. 'To absent husbands, good and bad – ' her gaze shifted from Katie to Gloria – 'and to a happy future for every one of us.'

'Cheers!' came the chorus, glasses held up in salute. 'To every one of us!'

Harriet looked around the circle. There was Molly, who was now itching to get back to London to see her friends and put her complicated summer love story behind her. There was Katie, so brave in coming tonight, who had maintained her dignity throughout. There was Freya, leaning against Victor and looking happy again, her forehead no longer pinched with a frown. There was Gloria, giving Olivia a hug and shutting the lid on the barbecue now that the manuscript was burned away. And there was Olivia too, of course, still radiant, still determined; a force to be reckoned with and a brilliant role model for all of the other women around her. Why had Harriet ever doubted her own place in the circle? She belonged here – and was proud to be part of this family.

Tomorrow this would all be over, she thought with a pang of sadness; they would put away the buckets and spades and beach paraphernalia for another year, and pack their cars, ready to disentangle their lives from one another again, and head their separate ways home. Together, they'd been great, though, this bunch of women around her. Together, they'd all played a part in a very unusual few weeks, helping and supporting each other, rescuing each other, even, when the going got tough.

She and Freya had already arranged a night out in London together for a few weeks' time. She and Olivia were planning to visit Kew for a day trip one Sunday at the end of the month. And last night, she and Molly had Skyped Simon and arranged for her to go and stay with him, Anne-Marie and the new baby for a couple of days over the October half-term. It was the right thing to do and Molly had seemed lighter and more cheerful ever since. A girl needed her dad sometimes. Even if he was a Pritt Stick, as Dexter would say.

It was left to Teddy, of course, to have the last word. 'Are we *ever* going to have the cake?' he asked pleadingly, and everyone laughed, breaking the spell. And then Freya was bustling around with plates, and Katie was helping, and everyone was congratulating Gloria on her exemplary baking skills.

The nostalgic end-of-holiday moment Harriet had been experiencing was lost – but that was all right, she thought with a grin. Because she knew already that life as one of the Tarrant family meant many more special moments yet to come. Maybe there would be further bumps in the road for her and Robert. Maybe the tyres might come right off at times. But they'd never know without giving it a go. Right now, she felt it was worth a try.

Heavenly Devon

Although Silver Sands and Ennisbridge are fictional (sadly), some of the other places mentioned in this book are real, and well worth a visit if you're planning a trip to Devon.

Bigbury-on-Sea and **Burgh Island**. Set in an area of Outstanding Natural Beauty, the beach at Bigbury-on-Sea has been awarded a Blue Flag and is absolutely lovely – golden sand and shallow water. There are rockpools to explore as well as wind-surfing and kite-surfing hire facilities right on the beach, plus a lovely café if you feel peckish.

At low tide, you can walk across a causeway to Burgh Island where you'll find a beautiful Art Deco hotel favoured by Agatha Christie and Noel Coward back in the day. The afternoon tea is meant to be good (as are the cocktails . . .). If the tide is up, you can ride across there on a lovely old-fashioned sea tractor instead, like the Castledines do in the book.

Coleton Fishacre. This is the house the Castledines go

to, where they all roll down the hill together. It's a National Trust property from the 1920s – a gorgeous Arts and Crafts style house with great views and 24-acre gardens.

Dartmouth Castle (or Darkness Castle as my friend's little girl used to call it). A fab fourteenth-century fortress with stunning views over the Dart estuary from the battlements. You can get a boat over from the town quay (look out for the mermaid statue!) and, as Olivia says, there is a shop selling wooden swords and dirks that any children with you might want to spend pocket money on.

Dartmoor. Put on your walking boots and go for a hike. The landscape is absolutely stunning, there are great pubs to be discovered and the wild ponies are extremely sweet. If you enjoyed *We Bought A Zoo*, the actual zoo is on the edge of Dartmoor, and is a good day out, too. And if you fancy a canoeing trip, like the Tarrants, there are several activity centres where you can canoe or kayak, or build your own raft . . .

I realize I have only scratched the surface here when it comes to great places to explore in Devon. There are hundreds of others! Feel free to alert me to your favourites on my Facebook page:

www.facebook.com/LucyDiamondAuthor.

Happy holidays!

Summer at Shell Cottage
Cocktails

We've teamed up with world-food restaurant giraffe to create an exclusive cocktail recipe especially for *Summer at Shell Cottage* readers.

Cosmo Daisy

25ml lemon juice
25ml triple sec
25ml gin
25ml raspberry syrup
37.5ml cranberry juice
Ice

Place the ingredients in a cocktail shaker. Fill up with ice cubes, and then shake to combine. Once cooled, strain the mixture and pour into a Martini glass.

Alec Tarrant's
Classic Summer Cocktails

Sea Breeze

50ml vodka

50ml cranberry juice

40ml grapefruit juice

Lime wedge

Ice

Fill a glass with ice, then pour over the cranberry juice. Shake together the vodka and grapefruit then layer over the cranberry. Garnish with a lime wedge.

Mojito

1½ limes, cut into wedges
20 fresh mint leaves
2½ tsp granulated sugar
65ml white rum
Splash of soda water to taste
1 fresh mint sprig to garnish
Ice

Mash the limes, mint and sugar together in a highball glass to bruise the mint and release the lime juice. Add the ice and pour over the rum. Add soda water to taste and mix well. Garnish with a mint sprig.

Homemade Elderflower Cordial

30 elderflower heads
3 pints boiling water
900g caster sugar
2 unwaxed lemons
50g citric acid (you can buy this from the chemist)

Rinse the elderflower heads in cold water to remove any bits of dirt (or stray insects!). Pour the boiling water over the sugar in a large mixing bowl. Stir well until the sugar has dissolved. Zest and slice the lemons and add both zest and slices to the water, along with the citric acid, and stir well. Then add the flower heads and leave to infuse in a cool place for 24 hours, stirring occasionally. Strain through some muslin (or a clean tea towel) and decant into sterilized bottles.

Best Barbecue Recipes

Homemade Burgers

500g minced beef
(or pork, turkey, lamb if you prefer)
1 small onion
1 egg
Extra flavourings of your choice –
chilli, herbs, black pepper, etc.

Finely chop the onion, then mix all the ingredients together in a large bowl. Use your hands to divide the mixture into either four or six, depending how large you want the burgers to be. Shape the burgers, ensuring they are all the same thickness. Put on a plate, cover with clingfilm and leave in the fridge to firm up for 30 minutes. Brush the sides with oil before you (carefully) put each burger on the barbecue (or under the grill if the weather is unkind). Cook over a medium heat for approximately 6 minutes each side, although timings will vary according to your barbecue and burger size. Serve in soft sliced buns with salad and relish.

Vegetarian Skewers

Small handful mint, chopped
Zest and juice of 1 lemon
2 tbsp olive oil
1 courgette, cut into 1cm rounds
1 red pepper, cut into approx. 1cm square pieces
225g halloumi cheese, cubed
8 wooden skewers

Mix together half the mint, the lemon zest and juice, the oil, courgette, red pepper and halloumi, then leave to marinate for 30 minutes. Meanwhile soak the skewers in a baking tray full of water for 20 minutes. Thread the vegetables and halloumi onto the skewers then cook on the barbecue (or grill) for 7–8 minutes, turning halfway through to baste with any remaining marinade. Garnish with the remaining mint to serve.

Finger-Lickin' Chicken Drumsticks

8 chicken drumsticks
1 tbsp honey
2 tbsp soy sauce
1 tbsp tomato puree
1 tbsp Dijon mustard
1 tbsp olive oil

Mix together the honey, soy sauce, tomato puree, mustard and oil. Make three slashes on each drumstick then immerse in the sauce, turning until thoroughly coated. Leave to marinate at room temperature for 30 minutes. (If you want to make this in advance you can cover in clingfilm and leave in the fridge overnight.) Cook on medium-hot coals for 20 minutes, brushing with the marinade as each drumstick cooks. If they colour too quickly, move to a cooler area of the barbecue. Ensure they are all cooked right through! (Alternatively, you can cook on a roasting tray in the oven at 200C/fan 180/gas mark 6 for about 40 minutes, turning occasionally and adding more marinade if necessary.)

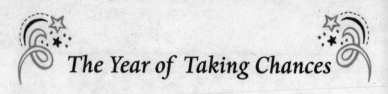

The Year of Taking Chances

It's New Year's Eve, and Gemma and Spencer Bailey are throwing a house party. There's music, dancing, champagne and all their best friends under one roof. It's going to be a night to remember.

Also at the party is Caitlin, who has returned to the village to pack up her much-missed mum's house and to figure out what to do with her life; and Saffron, a PR executive who's keeping a secret which no amount of spin can change. The three women bond over Gemma's dodgy cocktails and fortune cookies, and vow to make this year their best one yet.

But as the following months unfold, Gemma, Saffron and Caitlin find themselves tested to their limits by shocking new developments. Family, love, work, home – all the things they've taken for granted – are thrown into disarray. Under pressure, they are each forced to rethink their lives and start over. But dare they take a chance on something new?

Praise for *The Year of Taking Chances*

'Well-written, full of humour and filled with a reminder about what it means to be kind'   *Closer*